BELLE VUE
C.S. ALLEYNE

Belle Vue

This is a work of fiction. Names, characters, businesses, places, events and incidents are either the products of the authors' imagination or used in a fictitious manner. Any resemblance to actual persons, living or dead, or actual events is purely coincidental.

Copyright 2020 C.S. Alleyne
All Rights Reserved

Edited by: Monique Snyman

Layout: Dorothy Dreyer

Cover Art: Michael J. Canales
www.MJCImageworks

Proofread by: Kat Nava

No part of this publication may be reproduced, stored in a retrieval system, or transmitted in any form or by any means, without the prior permission in writing of the publisher, nor be otherwise circulated in any form of binding or cover than that in which it is published and without a similar condition including this condition being imposed on the subsequent purchaser.

ISBN: 978-1-64669-311-5

Published by Crystal Lake Publishing—Tales from The Darkest Depths
www.crystallakepub.com

WELCOME
TO ANOTHER

CRYSTAL LAKE PUBLISHING
CREATION

Join today at www.crystallakepub.com & www.patreon.com/CLP

Also by C.S. Alleyne:

Power

Other novels by Crystal Lake Publishing:

Doll Crimes by Karen Runge

The Mourner's Cradle: A Widow's Journey by Tommy B. Smith

House of Sighs (with sequel novella) by Aaron Dries

The Third Twin: A Dark Psychological Thriller by Darren Speegle

Aletheia: A Supernatural Thriller by J.S. Breukelaar

Where the Dead Go to Die by Mark Allan Gunnells and Aaron Dries

The Final Cut by Jasper Bark

Blackwater Val by William Gorman

Pretty Little Dead Girls: A Novel of Murder and Whimsy by Mercedes M. Yardley

In memory of my wonderful Mum.

Prologue

Tuesday, 17 August, 1869
BELLE VUE LUNATIC ASYLUM

"Get those frigging troublemakers out of my way. I'll deal with the Grady girl…"

Bill Callahan hung back as the beefy supervisor and one of her assistants pulled the two lunatics covered in vomit to their feet. They propped them up, then dragged them past the remaining knot of inmates huddled on the floor and made slow progress along the corridor toward the infirmary.

He scanned the jumble of limbs and spotted his target moaning and clutching her stomach, her dress covered in a yellow glutinous mess. He bellowed at his men, bludgeons at the ready, to clear the rest of the defectives from the area and restore order. Rolling up his sleeves, he strode over and grabbed the prostrate Ellen by the back of her collar. The girl was barely conscious, but Callahan felt himself harden. He heaved her over his shoulder, placing his left hand on her buttocks and, ignoring the chaos behind him, headed toward the back stairs.

As Callahan descended each step, his mood improved. His urge for some sport beyond a quick fuck had been growing for weeks. Now he'd get what he wanted. Ellen's body, though light, pulled his cotton scarf tighter round his neck and he eased his fingers between skin and material to loosen it.

When he reached the ground floor, he saw his timing had been good. Only a few of the cretins and other drooling idiots, who were too far gone for work duties, populated the hall. As Head Attendant no one would have questioned him anyway, but he didn't want any petty distractions. His anticipation of the pleasures to come was building steadily and he relished the vivid images in his mind. She was badly ill, but that made it more exciting—she wouldn't have any control of her bodily functions and his power over her would be absolute.

Callahan strode across the hall, focused on the large door ahead. With but a few feet to go, a peripheral movement caught his attention. Huddled in the far corner were two useless scraps of humanity. He peered toward them, noting how one shrunk back while the other continued to sup a mug of beer. He recognized them now—old Titus, blind but with a loose mouth, and Chancer who he'd seen on numerous occasions talking to Ellen. The latter stared with wide eyes at her limp body. Both could cause trouble, but he'd deal with them later.

He retrieved a large key from his pocket, opened the door, and stepped through. The heavy slab of iron closed behind him, and he secured it from the inside.

After descending the stairs, he leaned forward and let Ellen slip to the ground. Once, her face had been so lovely, a delicacy to savor. Now, in the low light of the oil lamps, her skin was pulled tight and tinged yellow. Small cracks sullied the once luscious plumpness of her lips. If anything, he wanted her more like this: weak and helpless, in need of his strength.

His arrival caused the worse crazies, chained to their cots in the passageways, to shout and wail like wild banshees. He ignored them and breathed in deeply. The stench reminded him of some of his most pleasurable moments. He lifted Ellen and hoisted her over his shoulder again.

Moving along the north tunnel between the beds and doors to the cells, he reached the end and faced an oak cupboard, six feet high and four feet wide. He seized one of the handles, but rather than pressing down, he twisted it upward and pulled. The door remained closed but the whole cupboard came away from the wall, revealing a passageway behind.

Callahan stepped through with his unconscious prey. As the entrance closed, ignoring the still audible cacophony of the lunatics, he groaned in anticipation. Alone with Ellen, his excitement was all-consuming. A single candle flickered on the tunnel wall, casting shadows that revealed his arousal.

He carried her through an open cell door and laid her on the soiled straw pallet. He retraced his steps and lit one of the lanterns kept near the entrance. Striding back into the cell, he almost tripped over Ellen's body. He hadn't heard her move, but now he could see her gazing up at him in confusion.

"Help me, Bill. Help me."

He smirked. So it was "Bill" now. He liked that.

He reached down and dug his fingers into her arm. She cried out, struggled, and tried to rise, but he wasn't going to allow that. He smacked her chin and Ellen slumped back, her head bumping on the flagstones. After dragging her to the center of the room, he shackled her wrists and ankles to the floor. She was spread-eagled and, he saw, regaining consciousness. Callahan watched her writhe as though spasms were shooting through her. The rattling of chains merged with the sounds of her whimpering.

He stood back, savoring the power of the moment. He felt invincible but her dress spoiled the view. Callahan leaned over, his hands reaching for its round neckline. He undid the first button, but impatience took over. He tore the dress open to reveal a flimsy shift underneath. Ellen moaned again, adding fuel to his hunger. He ripped away the final layer and ogled her exposed body, relishing every lady-like curve. Now she existed for his pleasure alone. Engorged, he could wait no longer. He slung off his braces then cursed as he struggled to unbutton his trousers.

Ellen turned her head and dry retched.

He tore off his shirt and scarf. Naked, his heavy muscular frame loomed above her. A monster in the shadows. He grunted in triumph.

"Let me go, Bill. Please? Don't hurt me. When I'm well again, I'll do what you want. Oh God, anything. I promise."

Her words took him over the edge. He lunged at her, all restraint gone, and made sure she kept her vow.

Hearing her scream his name was worth all the waiting.

Chapter One

Monday, 29 September
Present Day

Catching a sudden movement from the corner of her eye, Claire Ryan slammed her foot on the brake. The screech pierced the chilly night air as her car shuddered to a halt. In the glare of the headlights, a woman stood scowling at her. A rush of heat rose to Claire's face. Surely, she hadn't been that distracted. A cluster of white houses behind the woman, with their jettied upper stories and square-leaded windows, leaned forward like inquisitive crones eager to see how this scene would unfold.

Before Claire could react, the woman touched the car bonnet with her bony hand. Her lips, deep red against the wrinkled pallor of her skin, moved as though reciting something. Transfixed, Claire held her breath. The words streamed out, but strain as she might, she couldn't catch their meaning. With a final withering glance, the woman turned and proceeded along the narrow sidewalk. Claire lost sight of her as it curved round.

She exhaled. From behind, a horn honked its annoyance. She moved off in the same direction as the woman but this time at a slower pace. She glanced left to right, but the path was empty. Relieved, Claire reached the intersection and turned onto the main road.

Ignoring the lengthening line of cars behind her, she replayed the incident in her mind. If she'd gone the usual way to Marianne's place, none of the last few minutes would have happened. It was like those weird things that occurred before, and after, the death of her parents.

But she didn't want to think of that right now. She needed a distraction. Like the woman and her ridiculous wig. A bright red, bouffant helmet—talk about hair with attitude—it certainly seemed to fit her character.

As St. Albans receded to a picture postcard in her rearview mirror and she reached the edges of Detford, her spirits flagged once more. Night's gauze could not soften the town's hard lines, with its glut of concrete and glass boxes, their façades blank or scarred by graffiti. Given the lousy week she'd had so far, she struggled to hold back her rising anxiety. Breathe deeply, clear her mind; she knew the drill but the familiar gnawing had started in the pit of her stomach. She pulled up outside Marianne's flat, her temporary lodgings. An ugly block that matched the bland construction of the area; its only selling point the low rent.

Claire rested her forehead on the steering wheel, eyes shut. What she needed now was coffee, extra strong with a bit of sympathy. She wouldn't get it sitting there, so she pulled out a bunch of keys and quickly negotiated the various locks designed—albeit unsuccessfully—to keep the block secure.

She opened the final door to the usual smell of air-freshener and bleach. Marianne's buxom frame bustled into view from the kitchenette.

"Are you okay?"

Claire nodded. She dropped her bag and jacket on the top of four suitcases piled in the living room, before lowering herself onto the sofa's sagging cushions. Marianne perched on the edge of the solitary armchair. Claire recounted the incident and they laughed at her description of the woman's wig.

Marianne gave her a knowing look and rose to her feet. "Fancy a coffee?"

Claire gazed up at her. "I thought you'd never ask."

Marianne disappeared back into the kitchenette. While she waited, Claire checked her messages, only bothering to read her boyfriend Alex's, asking if she'd arrived home safely. She smiled to herself and replied. As she added some sloppy emojis and kisses, she sensed

Marianne peering over her shoulder.

"Don't you two ever stop?" she asked with an exaggerated sigh.

Marianne placed two mugs on the carefully positioned coasters on the coffee table and pulled out the large envelope tucked under her arm.

"For you," she said. "Looks like property information. You didn't waste any time."

"But I haven't had the chance to do anything yet." Her new state of homelessness was due to her landlord being made an offer he couldn't refuse with the unexpected outcome of her tenancy not being renewed.

Claire glanced at her name printed on the outside, thinking junk mail after a week must be some kind of record. She opened it and removed a glossy brochure with an impressive front cover. She leafed through the pages and smiled.

"Anything interesting?"

"Sounds very grand, and very me."

"And this place isn't?" Marianne asked in mock puzzlement as her eyes swept the room—a dismal throwback to the seventies. "Okay, let's hear it."

Claire cleared her throat and read aloud. "A select development of one, two, and three-bedroom apartments by Charterhouse Properties. Set in thirty acres of parkland, the restoration of the former Belle Vue Manor Estate combines the elegance and exquisite proportion of its Victorian heritage with the convenience and comforts expected in the modern age."

After scanning the rest of the page, Claire added, "I can't believe this. It's fantastic. The price is right. It's close to college. Lots of character and the kitchen is a dream."

After several seconds of silence, she caught Marianne's look of disapproval. "Is something wrong?"

"I wasn't sure you'd want to live somewhere that used to be an asylum. You hate hospitals at the best of times. Imagine living in one."

"A loony bin? They don't say anything about that here." Claire flicked through the brochure and shook her head.

"Well, they wouldn't, would they? 'Flats in ex-mental institution for sale' doesn't have the same ring to it." Marianne said.

"You're probably right, but it sounds perfect. Who cares what it used to be."

Marianne looked like she wanted to say something, but her full lips were now corseted tight. Claire sensed her friend's silence hid more below the surface, but from the moment she saw the photos of Belle Vue, it drew her in. She needed to find a place fast and here was one falling right into her lap.

She glanced at Marianne. "Come with me tomorrow. No lectures, so I'm free first thing. Are you?"

A slight hesitation. "You don't need to rush, Claire. There are loads of flats to choose from."

"Oh, come on, Marianne. We're like sardines in here and we're only going to look at it. Are you coming?"

"Yeah."

Given that she sounded like a volunteer for fingernail pulling, Claire wondered whether Marianne might be jealous. No, not her style. She reached over and jiggled Marianne's knee.

"You never know, some of the old lunatics might still haunt the place." She was about to make a spooky 'ooohing' sound, but then caught sight of her friend's face. "Hey, I was only joking."

Marianne looked as if she'd bitten something unpleasant. Before Claire could say anything further, Marianne collected the mugs and picked up the envelope from the floor.

"I'm knackered. Tomorrow's going to be worse, though. I'm doing an extra night shift at the hospital."

Claire nodded, thankful she didn't need to fit a part-time job into her full diary. She reached for her mobile.

"Thanks, Marianne. Belle Vue may not live up to its name, but it seems like the answer to all my prayers. A permanent place of my own."

Marianne understood as they'd been writing, then emailing each other about it since primary school. Her life once consisted of moving from country to country as she and her mother accompanied her father to each new posting.

Claire twisted a strand of hair into a finger noose and drew in a breath. She willed herself to speak. "Even after my parents…died, I've been shunting back and forth, here and abroad, hotels and rentals."

She pulled her hand down and the noose tightened. Marianne watched her closely as she'd done when Claire had come back from Hong Kong, still in shock, and fearful of things happening she couldn't explain. And when Claire had her breakdown. She couldn't let herself get like that again or expect Marianne to pick up the pieces as she'd done before. This time she had to be the strong one. For herself, and her future. Touch wood, Belle Vue would be a new start. Something twinged in Claire's back. Damn sofa springs. She shifted to the armchair and tapped the speed dial on her mobile.

"G'night, Marianne. I'm going to see what Alex's doing tomorrow then watch the late movie."

Just five minutes more.

Ignoring the music in the other room, Alex Palmer typed the final sentence of his outline and sat back. He should be pleased, but he couldn't hold down the niggling dissatisfaction with what he'd written.

His rear end numb, he stood and moved to the window. Holding onto the ledge, he executed a few tentative leg squats as he gazed out at the clear night sky. He focused on the top of the hill at St. Albans Cathedral in all its floodlit glory. In fact, that place of worship was the source of his discontent. Although he loved anything to do with history, he wasn't convinced his choice of the cathedral in the Victorian years for his final year dissertation was the right one for him. Nothing much happened then, and he wanted a bit of excitement. It was local, though, the right period and so far, nothing else had come close.

Alex picked up his phone and scanned his messages. He tapped three kisses and a smiley in reply to Claire and pressed send. The rest he ignored.

As he joined his flatmates, Paul and Gary, in the lounge, he added his voice to their falsetto wailing that drowned out Bob Marley.

He picked up a can of beer from the coffee table and an unlit spliff. His meeting with Hamish, his dissertation supervisor, wasn't until tomorrow afternoon so he planned to enjoy himself. Lectures—and hard work—began Wednesday.

As the bass throbbed through him, he lowered himself onto one of the armchairs and lit the joint.

"Man, I wanna be back on the beach, not here," Paul said.

Gary, next to him on the couch, burped his agreement.

"Gaz, you remember that Jamaican woman at Earl's Place?"

"Do I? My eyes are still watering."

"She didn't leave my side all night. Couldn't get enough of me."

Alex and Gary grinned. They looked at each other and back at Paul in his bright blue surfing shorts and a yellow T-shirt. Both stretched tight. The sound of hooting filled the room.

Tilting his chin with his finger, Gary simpered. "Don't tell me, Mr. Stud-Muffin, she'd been searching for you all her life. She likes Greek slap heads with hairy butts, hey brudder?"

Catching the instant change in Paul's expression, Alex groaned then stepped in quickly. "More than carrot tops with small willies."

"I think the term is hung-like-a-stallion," Gary said, in his broadest Aussie twang. "Here, let me show you."

He unfolded his lanky frame from the sofa and started to unbutton his fly. In unison, Alex and Paul yelled at him to stop. Gary shrugged and flexed his biceps instead. He grinned and adopted ever more ludicrous poses before announcing, "Gotta take a crap. Back in a mo."

A duet of "ughs" accompanied the music.

They spent the next few hours reminiscing about their summer vacation and seriously dented their supplies of booze, marijuana, and assorted snacks.

During a brief lull in the music, the sound of munching filled the void, but not enough to cover the ringing of Alex's mobile. He jumped up. His head spun and he staggered to his room as though on a rolling boat. He picked up his phone from the desk and gave it a quick glance.

"Hey dere, sweetheart," he said in a very bad West Indian accent, as he half-reggaed, half-tottered back into the lounge. "What choo up to?"

He turned the music down and listened carefully. Gary and Paul pretended to be asleep but kept nudging one another as if he wouldn't notice.

Belle Vue. He'd forgotten about that place. A germ of an idea flitted into his consciousness, then slipped away. His head was doing a great impression of a ball of cotton wool. Belle Vue. Closed because of a scandal, he was sure. He'd love to see what they'd done with it, so he agreed to meet her there tomorrow at nine and mentally crossed his fingers that any hangover wouldn't be too bad.

Before he could stop himself, he added, "Is Matron coming?"

"Of course, but don't call Marianne that."

He smothered a laugh and shook his head as Gary who'd first used the term, suddenly came to life and blew his cheeks out.

Claire continued, "And make sure those two morons keep their mouths shut, too."

"Hey, how come you can insult my friends, but I can't say anything about—?"

"I'm hanging up now, Lexi. Love you."

"Love you, too." He ignored Gary and Paul miming Claire's favorite Titanic scene. When Gary started singing, he decided to call it a night.

Chapter Two

Monday, 10 August, 1868

Ellen Grady loosened the frayed neckline of her Mam's shift and wiped the damp cloth over the hot, mottled skin. Mam twisted in the bed and moaned. In the heat, the stained shift stuck to her gaunt frame. Thin fingers clutched her distended stomach and the twisting grew more agitated. Ellen leaned over as blood began to flow from her Mam's nose. She struggled to hold her still and wipe away the mess. Mam whimpered, and her movements calmed.

"Is Mary here? Mary?"

If only. With little hope, Ellen had sent her neighbor, Mrs. Flanagan's boy out several times to the Green Hog pub by the Docks, but Mary had refused. Her half-sister hadn't come back to Whitechapel when Da died of the same typhoid six months ago and before that hadn't stepped foot in the lane for six years. Ellen's eyelids drooped, her head slumped forward. If she could sleep for just a minute.

Mam bucked again. Ellen snapped awake and dropped the cloth. Blood spattered her face. She wiped it with her palm, but Mam's forearm shot out to push her back. Her heel knocked against the full chamber pot on the floor. She teetered before grabbing the iron bedstead to regain her balance. A cockroach scuttled across the bare boards and she kicked it out of the way.

Mam's body stiffened then sagged. Her unseeing eyes closed. Ellen picked up the cloth and turned to the washstand. She rinsed the bloody cloth in the bowl before cleaning Mam's face as best she could. Her mother didn't stir.

Ellen brushed the damp hair from Mam's forehead. Rapid shallow breathing but her pale face looked peaceful for the moment. She took

Mam's hand, the skin rough, flaky and so very hot. She stroked the space where Mam had so proudly worn her wedding ring, pawned like everything else of value after Da's passing.

Mam opened her eyes and gazed at Ellen. "My dear sweet girl." She half-smiled and Ellen's throat tightened. "Is Patrick coming, too?"

"Yes, I sent for him but an hour ago." Since Mam only called for her when delirious, she didn't mention Mary. Nor did she mention the reason she'd wanted her uncle's attendance so quickly. She didn't want to think about that, the empty pit within her growing larger and more frightening as Mam's illness took its merciless course.

A brisk knock came from downstairs. Ellen hurried down to the small parlor and opened the door. It creaked on its rusty hinges and the sulfurous fog entered with her uncle. Both his hair and face were drenched with sweat. He carried a loosely wrapped paper parcel as well as his leather bag.

"May God be with you, my dearest girl," he said, as he gave her the package.

Ellen pulled the string holding it together and gazed hungrily at the bread, cheese, and bacon. Underneath, she spotted a couple of candles that were also sorely needed. She looked back at her uncle and thanked him. He peered at her in the half-light, pulled a handkerchief from the pocket of his cassock, and wiped her face.

"How is Catherine?" he asked.

All Ellen could do was shake her head. Their eyes met. No more words were needed. Da and six younger siblings now in Heaven made them unnecessary.

Ellen placed the package on the table in front of the open hearth, then quickly followed Father Patrick back up the narrow winding stairs.

He took out the crucifix, a cloth, two candles, and a vial of holy water from his bag and placed them on the top of the dresser.

He lit the candles, but the room with its small window remained dim.

Mam shifted restlessly. She started muttering. Ellen couldn't catch the words, but for the name of her half-sister.

She edged to the other side of the bed. "Mam keeps asking for Mary, saying she's sorry. Why would she do that?"

Even in the gloom, Ellen saw her uncle's face redden. He winced and dropped his gaze as though embarrassed—or guilty—about something. But why would Father Patrick, or Mam, who had only ever done good in this world feel like this?

Her uncle began the first words of the Sacrament.

A scream pierced the air. Mam jerked as though being stabbed and grasped her stomach.

She babbled, her body shook. Ellen couldn't bear to look at the pain in her sunken eyes.

"We didn't know, we didn't know, we didn't…"

Father Patrick made a hasty sign of the cross on Mam's forehead.

"Per istam sanctam unctionem et suam piissimam misericordiam…"

Bloody diarrhea seeped into the mattress. Ellen ignored the smell. Each word brought her closer to a life without Mam. Misery and fear mingled in her mind. Of the loneliness without her mother, of the poverty she would face. She could sew, but so could thousands of others. There'd been no work for months. She looked over at her uncle. Even though he had his own busy life, surely he wouldn't let her end up in the workhouse? But she shouldn't be thinking of such selfish things now. Mam needed her, she might recover, she might…

A deep sigh broke from Mam. She struggled to lift her head as though its weight was too much for her. They looked at each other.

"I love you, Ellen." Mam slumped back against the pallet. Her eyes glazed over. "Tell Mary I'm sorry." The barest whisper.

Then silence.

Ellen's eyes bore into Mam as though by not blinking she could keep her alive. She begged God to ease Mam's suffering, to make her well again.

Father Patrick said the final words of the Sacrament. Mam's eyes closed. Ellen closed hers, too, as the tears rolled down her cheeks. She clutched her crucifix and prayed.

The church bell tolled three. Ellen and Mrs. Flanagan stood on the cobbles under the precarious lean of the shabby building. Her neighbor cocked her head and peered toward the open door.

"I thought I heard them coming. What're they doing in there?"

The old woman pushed back her bonnet and dragged thick fingers across her sweaty brow.

"Oh, lummy, I can't take much more of this heat." She looked at her hand, frowned and then wiped it on her skirt.

Lost in her thoughts, Ellen said nothing. She turned to avoid a cloud of flies attracted by the pools of sewage in the nearby cesspits. Her neighbor closed her eyes but didn't move.

Heavy boots and grunting sounded from inside the house. Mrs. Flanagan gazed at her. "A lot of people are going to miss yer ma, Ellen. A real lady, a good, kind lady."

Ellen nodded, her eyes brimming with tears. Her thoughts turned to Mam's final journey. Mrs. Flanagan's lodgers would carry the coffin for burial tomorrow after Mass to the Church of Our Lady of the Rosary, where her uncle was the priest. Ellen dabbed her eyes with a square of crumpled cotton.

"There, there, darling." Mrs. Flanagan put her arm around her and gave a comforting squeeze. "Oh, my girl, yer getting too thin."

Ellen dropped her gaze. She'd hardly eaten in weeks. She went through the motions when her hunger threatened to overwhelm her, but without Mam…

"And what about Mary? I ain't seen her once." Mrs. Flanagan snorted and glanced toward the door. "You'll excuse me for saying so, Ellen, but she's not a good Catholic girl, not a good Catholic girl at all. She should've been here taking care of your mam, not leaving it all to a slip of a girl like you. What age are you now? Twelve, thirteen?"

"Fifteen."

"And the last one of yer ma's left. I'll wager Mary never showed for the wake either?"

"No, she didn't." Ellen's voice shriveled in the heat. Everyone knew she had not set foot in the lane for years. A mystery to Ellen. After all, Mam had asked Father Patrick to help Mary, just as he had helped Nancy Flanagan, to find good first positions. They'd both been given places at the London home of a couple of French aristocrats, acquaintances of the Bishop of her uncle's diocese but Mary had run off after a few months. Not only that, when she returned, it was as though the Devil himself had gotten ahold of her. She'd used foul language and insulted Mam, even spat in her face before she left. Never to return.

Missing Mary—her best friend not just her half-sister—she'd asked over the years, but no answer had been forthcoming. Mam had said sorry to Mary so many times in her last hours, which left Ellen only more confused.

Mrs. Flanagan's words broke her reverie. "Just like her. Selfish." Her neighbor sniffed. "To think she knows where my Nancy is, but won't tell me, her own mother. Wicked, she is. Wicked and cruel. Mary should…"

The voice grew strident as the bitter words spewed out. Ellen had heard them all before, but this time, her own grief strengthened her understanding of the old woman's anguish. She had lost her only daughter, missing for more than seven years. In all that time Mary, who had been in service with Nancy when she disappeared, had not uttered a single word about her best friend's whereabouts.

Her neighbor's tirade petered out. Mrs. Flanagan wheezed and patted her bulbous chest. "I'm sorry, Ellen. I shouldna done that. Not today."

Ellen nodded, then stiffened as a lined face appeared at the doorway. She clutched at her black skirt, once Mam's, as though it could somehow fortify her.

Mrs. Flanagan bowed her head, and muttered, "About time."

Two men in cloth caps and ragged waistcoats held the flimsy box on either side, with a third man, older and shorter than the others, bearing the narrow end. There not being enough money for a hearse, they would carry the coffin to the church.

The tears streamed down Ellen's cheeks. She touched her hand to the rough elm box, leaned forward and kissed the wood. "Goodbye, Mam. Godspeed."

Through blurred eyes, she watched as the procession made slow but unsteady progress up the lane.

Ellen swallowed and whispered, "Please God, let them get to the church safely."

"Amen to that," said Mrs. Flanagan. "If yer all right, my girl, I'll take my leave now. I'll come by on the morrow and walk with you to the church."

Ellen's eyes remained fixed on the departing group until they reached the end of the alley.

"Thank you, Mrs. Flanagan. "Till tomorrow."

And under her breath, she whispered another prayer that Mary would show, and they might become close again.

Mary Grady strode to the sash window. After a brief struggle, she raised the frame and took a deep breath. The stink and heat outside more than matched the bedroom but she welcomed the slight breeze. It came at a price. The hubbub from the bar of the Green Hog Public House two stories below shattered the relative quiet.

Mary ignored the noise and returned to the padded stool in front of her dressing table. She gazed at her reflection in the mirror. She looked good today, she thought, tilting her chin first left, then right. She felt good, too. Much better than Catherine Grady. The bitch was finally dead and today was Catherine the not-so-Great's funeral. Mary had treated herself and bought a new dress in celebration. She brushed her thick tresses and, lifting one side at a time, fixed each in place with an ornamental comb.

Casting her eyes beyond the looking-glass, Mary admired the new wallpaper. The first of many changes to come. Her room might be the best in the house, but she wasn't satisfied with it yet. Not a problem. She'd soon worm the money out of the Green Hog's owner. She and Jack Callahan had been together for a few months now, and he was eating out of her hand like a hungry puppy.

She'd soon be able to reel him in. As much as she might dislike the thought of being considered her husband's property, a smart marriage was a crucial step toward improving her status and future prosperity. After all, look what marrying 'below her' had done to her once ever-so-lovely and delicate stepmother. Seven babies in ten years, all but one gone, to end up old, poor and now dead before her time. Shame.

Then she remembered what she must do. As her eyes dropped to the drawer in front of her, Mary shivered. She immediately berated herself. This was not the time for weakness or guilt. She pulled herself up straight, but a scintilla of uncertainty remained. Catherine was no more. A fortunate turn. Why not forget?

Because she could never escape the past, however much she tried to erase it from her memory. Someone had to pay for all she and Nancy had gone through.

She opened the drawer and after taking out the item she sought, raised her gaze to the mirror. No evidence of the nerves within showed on her face. With a final satisfied glance, she tucked the small package into her pocket and made her way down to the noisy bar. Her spirit rose to see it so busy. Once they married, Jack's money would be hers for the taking.

She spotted him through the smoky haze and made her way past the long benches filled with drinkers to a small corner table where another man and three pots of beer rested. Bill Callahan, who she'd met last night, didn't stand but acknowledged her with a wary nod. As Jack rose to pull out the chair for her, his wariness changed to obvious astonishment.

"You're becoming a sissy boy, Jack Callahan. You'll be taking up sewing next."

"Get away, Bill. No chance o'that," Jack said, laughing.

Bill shook his head and made a loud hawking noise. He aimed successfully at the full spittoon a few feet away.

Mary scowled at Jack's brother, a lethal combination of physical strength with not much brainpower. His dark hair worn close-shaven emphasized the size and coarseness of his facial features. Although a few years short of thirty, deep lines furrowed the plains of his forehead and cheeks.

"Such an act, Bill, is the sign of a man in love." She cocked an eye at Jack and winked.

Bill leered at her. "Or lust."

She sniffed then regretted her action. The pungent fumes of tobacco smoke, stale liquor, and staler bodies stung her nose.

Jack leaned back in his chair and put his hand on Mary's shoulder. "So, Bill, tell me about this new job. St. Albans is a bit of a way."

"I'm the Head Attendant at Belle Vue."

The name made her start.

"What sort of place is it, this Belle Vue?" she asked, keeping any interest out of her voice.

"A lunatic asylum. Opened a bit more than a year ago and full to overflowing already."

Jack grinned, his gold tooth glistening. "Yeah, but probably more maniacs out here than in there," he said, eyeing his patrons.

"What's it like? Same as the last place?"

Bill took a long draught and wiped his mouth with the back of his hand. "Colney Hatch. More or less, but at Belle Vue, the Matron and Superintendent leave me to my own devices. I have an assistant, too. Name of Brown, Lynton Brown. He likes to play rough with the inmates, which is fine by me."

Jack grinned, "God help 'em. Suppose lunatics don't know what's going on anyway."

They all downed their drinks in thoughtful silence.

Mary put her mug back on the table. Bill's news surprised her. She closed her eyes and kept her focus on the present. The past was not a place she cared to visit without good cause.

She rose to her feet. "I'm going out, but should be back before evening."

Jack gazed at her and winked. "Give your half-sister a kiss of condolence from me."

His eyes glinted at Mary. She stared him down and kept her voice low and icy. "Not even in jest, my love."

"Of course not, Mary. You know you're the only one for me."

She stepped forward and planted her lips onto his in a parting kiss.

He never said a truer word, whatever he might like to think. With the combination of fourteen-hour workdays and her passionate demands, she made sure sleep was his mistress of choice.

The midday heat bore down with exquisite cruelty on Ellen and the dozen or so mourners as they stood, heads bowed, sweating profusely in their heavy, dark clothes. In the small graveyard, the living and the dead jostled uneasily for position.

As her uncle began the words of the interment ceremony, tears trickled down Ellen's cheeks. She prayed Mam had found peace at last and Mary still might show. With Mam gone, surely they could become close again as they had been before Mary had gone up west. Now all she had left were treasured memories of the times she and Mary used to laugh and sing silly songs with Mam. Or when Nancy, Mary's best friend, joined them to learn reading and drawing and the times they visited Father Patrick. They'd play hide-and-seek in the church and later listen to his tales of Ireland and leprechauns and pots of gold.

Ellen couldn't believe Mary would ignore the funeral, but it seemed she was wrong.

Father Patrick, his unprotected face pink and shiny, lifted his head as he sprinkled holy water over the coffin. His brow creased. Ellen followed his gaze to the two gravediggers who had been leaning on the stone boundary wall. Both were now on their feet, one shaking his companion's dusty sleeve and pointing. She and her uncle turned their heads in the direction of the man's jabbing finger. Ellen's heart leaped.

Mary!

Then she flinched, for her half-sister stood not like a humble mourner, but with feet apart and hands on hips. As their eyes locked, Mary's face took on a triumphant expression. Ellen could only stare, her mind a blank as the imposing figure dressed in crimson with a plumed hat atop her fiery red hair, sauntered up the path toward the unwary mourners.

Her uncle stuttered over the next words of the prayer prompting the group to raise their eyes. A synchronized gasp escaped the transfixed figures. Signs of the cross hastily made followed whispered supplications, mostly to the Holy Mother of God. Each mourner shuffled back from the approaching specter as though closeness to such profanity might taint their own carefully nurtured salvation.

Mary stopped at the edge of the burial plot and looked down at the flimsy box. No exhalation of breath disturbed the silent tableau. Ellen prayed under her breath. The venom in Mary's eyes frightened her. Her garish attire seemed designed for one purpose only: to insult Mam's memory. At close range, in the harsh daylight, her heavily rouged cheeks and powdered face made her look hard and unnatural, like a carnival grotesque. Her uncle and other mourners wore expressions of puzzled curiosity. Old Mrs. Flanagan looked as if she wanted to strangle Mary.

If only her half-sister realized how much Mam had loved her.

"Evil will always overcome good," Mary sneered. She glared across the grave as though directing her words to Father Patrick alone. "For those we believe to be good are often the most wicked."

Her uncle's face reddened but Ellen could see the mourners only had eyes for Mary. All stood motionless like unwilling players in a game of statues.

Mary reached into the pocket of her dress. She took out something wrapped in a handkerchief and tied with a piece of frayed ribbon. Necks craned forward for a better view.

Mary held out the object in her hand—about the size of an egg, maybe larger. For an instant, Ellen was certain an expression of vulnerability had crossed her features, but when she blinked, only arrogance remained. Mary glared at her uncle.

"Bury this with your sister, priest, as my memento for her afterlife. Wherever that might be."

She flung the package onto the coffin. "For Nancy," she whispered.

It landed with a single tap and slid to the center of the casket. No one moved. Mary kicked at a mound of earth by her foot, sending clumps of dirt pattering onto the wood. She turned and swept back down the path.

Her departure was followed with indecent haste by all but Ellen and Father Patrick.

"What is that thing? Should we open it?" her uncle asked.

Ellen gazed at the item on the coffin, puzzling over Mary's words.

She didn't know what was in the handkerchief, but instinctively felt whatever it contained was best kept hidden. She voiced her thoughts to him before adding, "That thing seemed to mean a lot to Mary but not in a good way."

Father Patrick nodded. He beckoned the gravediggers. With uncharacteristic speed, both carried their spades to the graveside and scrutinized the package with ill-disguised interest.

"Let's get this burial finished quickly. Leave that rubbish where it is."

The elder stepped forward, his expression of curiosity not yet erased. "Aye, Father. Let's get the job done."

He tipped his head at the other gravedigger and they started shoveling dirt onto the coffin.

Her uncle stepped toward her. "Ellen, go home and rest." He reached out his hand to touch her cheek and said gently, "Mary can't hurt your Mam any more. God be with you, my child."

Ellen remained by the grave as the two men completed their task. She wiped the mixture of sweat and tears from her cheeks. Her mind was in turmoil at Mary's behavior.

What had Mam apologized for? Her uncle would say nothing when she'd asked again. All she knew was that her half-sister had changed after her unexpected return from up west. How she wished she had been able to find out why Mary had run away.

And what had happened to Nancy.

Chapter Three

Tuesday, 30 September
PRESENT DAY

"Hurry up, Claire."

"Coming. Won't be a sec."

Marianne paced the hall and tried to quell the edgy feeling in her stomach. A few minutes later, Claire emerged from the bathroom dressed in a cropped jacket and jeans, long pale hair framing her lightly tanned face. Her lips and eyes united in a smile. One that Marianne ignored as she propelled Claire through the door and double-locked it behind her.

Outside, the gray skies matched the dour surroundings of her rented digs. The red of Claire's car, a twenty-fourth birthday present to herself in June, was the only splash of color. They climbed in and set off for Belle Vue.

Marianne chewed on her lip. Should she tell Claire? The subject had never come up before. She wished her sister Debra was here to back her up, but she had moved to Cardiff to start her university course. Not that Debs would want anything to do with Belle Vue.

Marianne gazed out of the window as they went past increasingly desirable properties. St. Albans wasn't just a popular tourist destination but an area of prime real estate. She wiped her damp palms on the front of her trousers and made her decision.

"It's most likely nothing, but I want to tell you a few things about Belle Vue."

Claire cast a quizzical eye in her direction.

"I've been there before," she said.

"You never mentioned it."

Marianne ignored the pout in her friend's voice and continued. "I went there with Debs about eleven or twelve years ago, long before the developers ever got involved."

As the memories flooded back, she stared unseeing out of the windscreen. "We'd just moved again and on our first day at school, Debs spotted a huge wreck of a building from the top of the bus. For some reason, it fascinated her. She kept bugging me about it and I gave in just to shut her up. I think Belle Vue closed in the fifties and by the time we got there, it was completely derelict."

Claire pulled up as the lights changed to red. "And?"

"We squeezed through a broken gate. Everything was overgrown, but we found a path that took us to the back of the main building, to a half-open door, its lock ripped off. Of course, Debs said it was as though someone was waiting for us."

"Sounds like she was winding you up," Claire said, grinning.

Marianne scowled. "Anyway. We went inside. Two teenagers in an empty old asylum that looked like the set of a horror movie."

Claire's grin remained in place. "So, what happened?"

"Debs kept a running commentary like we were on one of those Murder Mystery tours. You know the type of thing, *'The misery of the lunatics is trapped in these walls forevermore but, on a moonless night, their shadows...'* All the while, I felt like we were being watched. Debra must have felt the same since we stuck to each other like Siamese twins. The place was cold and silent except for our footsteps on the bare floorboards. Every now and then, we'd stop and hold our breaths, straining to catch any sound.

"Then we heard a door slam. Bang! You ought to have seen how high we jumped. We legged it out of there so fast, I got a stitch."

Pause. Marianne looked across at Claire. "But that wasn't what bothered me," she said in a low voice. "Once outside, we followed the path round the main building and saw this chapel. Of course, Debs wanted to go in and, by now, I didn't. While we were arguing, a woman appeared at the door. The chapel was half-side-on to us, so I couldn't see if she'd come from inside or walked around it. Talk about a shock. It sure shut us up quick.

"She stared at both of us. From one to the other, as though sizing us up. Then she smiled, which believe it or not, was worse.

"'*Now, who will I choose?*' she said, in this snide tone. '*You. Or you.*'

"We stood there like two dummies, wondering what on earth she was up to.

"'*What's your name?*' she asked me, and when I told her, she laughed like it was some huge private joke.

"'*I choose you then,*' she said. '*Your fate is now sealed, Mar-i-anne. Poor you, dying slowly is such hell.*'

"She really wanted to scare you two rigid. I bet she's still chuckling about it. Anything else?" Claire asked, moving the car forward as the lights changed to green.

"Isn't that enough?" Marianne felt queasy at the memory. "I'll never forget those words, or the malice in her voice, like some evil old witch. Then the bloody chapel bell tolled. Debs and I looked at each other, turned and ran as if the Devil himself was chasing us. We couldn't get out of there quick enough."

"That's the last thing I'd imagine you doing." Claire's brow furrowed. "Why didn't you stand up to her? She couldn't have been that intimidating, could she?"

Marianne shrugged but didn't answer since Claire sounded as though she wouldn't believe her.

"She was probably making sure you didn't trespass again. One day, you'll laugh about it with your grandkids. After all, no one can really tell the future."

"I hope you're right," Marianne said. "But I think about it sometimes and wonder what made her say such a thing."

She gave a weak grin and peered out of the window at the high stone wall. A large estate agent's sign proclaiming *Belle Vue Manor* came into view. Her smile faded.

Claire slowed the car and turned in through a pair of imposing iron gates.

On their right, a small gabled lodge signposted as the Sales Office for the development. They pulled into the paved parking area behind the building next to a single vehicle. It wasn't Alex's.

Marianne struggled to her feet from the low seat. She glanced over at Claire's blissful expression as she took in the lush tracts of greenery with their few autumnal specks and the line of stately trees arrayed on either side of the driveway as it curved up the hill.

"Hey, this is great."

Marianne's optimism dropped several notches. "Yeah, but don't get too excited, the apartment may be dreadful."

"Miss Grumpy," Claire said, as she rooted about in her handbag. She pulled out a mirror and lipstick. "Since Alex isn't here yet, I might as well put on some more war paint."

Claire puckered her shining lips at Marianne then sashayed toward the sales office laughing.

"Ugh, I think I'm going to be sick," Marianne called out.

She stood motionless for a few seconds. In truth, she did feel nauseous. Reliving the words of that horrible woman brought it all back. The nightmares and the gut-churning worry that what the woman had said might ever come true. The vow never to go near the old asylum again. She felt mean hoping Claire wouldn't like the place, but she couldn't shake the feeling Belle Vue might have something to do with her future though not in a good way.

She only hoped she was wrong.

Alex stepped through the door of the Belle Vue Manor Sales Office. A woman, plastered in makeup was telling Claire in a strident voice, "This might just be your lucky day."

Three sets of eyes, one with a predatory gleam, swiveled in his direction.

Claire introduced him and Angela, the agent, spent a few minutes sounding him out before reverting to the likeliest prospect. "As I was saying, Claire..."

Marianne, in her usual black—this time a baggy jumper and leggings—nodded to him. Her arms were crossed, her face glum.

He briefly wondered if she and Claire had had an argument before tuning in to the agent again.

"One of the best apartments in the main block just came back on the market at the weekend. A bit unexpected. The buyer changed his mind and decided to take one in the new phase. If you're interested, I'll show you that one first?"

Claire agreed, and Angela told them a little of the Manor's history. Alex continued to listen to an airbrushed version of events. No mention of the asylum, only that it had been a hospital.

Despite waking with a head like a bowling ball, he'd done a quick search on the asylum's closure. Scanning a couple of online articles from one of the local papers, the material sparked his interest even more. In the late fifties, a senior nurse at the asylum had gone missing. They never found the woman but, after reading her diaries, her father had made a huge fuss. He accused the asylum of all manner of mismanagement, corruption and worse. It was the straw that broke the camel's back. The asylum closed, and the few remaining patients were transferred.

He asked Angela if she knew anything about it. Her eyes narrowed, and the fake lashes quivered. "I'm sure I don't," she replied, in a sniffy tone. "Probably something the press dreamed up on a quiet day. Most likely, the woman ran off to escape her nosy father and is now living by the sea in retired bliss."

Behind her, Marianne caught his eye and smirked.

Claire, standing on the other side of the agent, pouted. "Angela's right. Anyway, who cares what happened fifty years ago? It's completely irrelevant."

Alex shrugged and raised his hands. "Only curiosity. You know I find this type of stuff fascinating."

Claire didn't look convinced, but at least she gave him half a smile.

Angela gestured toward the wall, "You can see how the old hospital used to look. There's a copy of the blueprints, too."

He took Claire's hand, gave it a squeeze and led her to a large sepia-tinted photograph. They gazed at a group of stern dignitaries in front of a grand Victorian facade. A new label hid most of the original silver plaque. It read, 'Opening of Belle Vue Hospital, 31 March, 1867.'

Marianne peered over Claire's shoulder. "They all look very grim. God help the patients."

She pointed at a dour-faced woman seated at the end of the line. "Now this one looks mean. I wonder who she was. Don't think I'd want someone like her nursing me."

Alex stared at the picture, noting the bars at the windows of the building in the background. Before he had time to comment, Angela's loud voice cut in.

"Let's do the tour now. I'm on my own today, so I'll leave you to mosey around the grounds once I've shown you the apartments."

She shepherded them out of the office and into the weak sunlight. "The best way to get your first impression of Belle Vue is on foot. Let's go."

Angela tramped forward, with the three of them following in her wake. They marched up the drive to the curved apex where the trees gave way to a carpet of green and the main building came fully into view.

Alex took his first look at Belle Vue Manor and came to a sudden halt. Though he'd seen the pictures in the sales office, he wasn't prepared for such a powerful impact. Its past gave it a terrible beauty, stunning yet repugnant at the same time. The Victorian mansion possessed a sense of grandeur and order as though paying architectural homage to the Queen: rigidly regal, but with an undertone of displeasure at being on show.

From either side of its large central section, two gray arms stretched out as though viewed through a wide-angle lens. Three rows of narrow sash windows spanned the breadth of his vision. They looked incongruously like hundreds of clowns' eyes, each topped by an arc of red brick. He'd put money on it, though, there hadn't been much laughter for those looking out.

The place intrigued him so, the germ of an idea that had begun last night blossomed. This could be a far better topic for his final year dissertation. He told the women his plan.

Clearly underwhelmed, Angela muttered something about not leaving the office unoccupied for too long. She set off again at a brisk pace. Claire clutched his hand and beamed at him. "That's brilliant. I'll have to buy this place so you can do all your research first hand."

Marianne, he noted, kept her opinion to herself.

As they strode toward the main building, he half-listened to Angela's sales pitch, but mostly toyed with his new idea.

"What's that?" Claire asked Angela.

Alex looked to where Claire's finger pointed.

With no immediate reply, Claire asked again. Alex glanced at Angela, curious about her newfound reticence. She gave him a lukewarm smile.

"The proper name is a belvedere, but we call it 'the dome'," she said, at last. Her voice held little of its previous enthusiasm.

The four gazed at the circular room perched in the center of the roof above the entrance.

"It's kept open for any resident to use, if they want." Angela's voice trailed off. She fumbled in her pocket and produced a bunch of keys. "Now *this* is what I want you to see."

Alex slowed as he reached the steps of the arched portico to survey the grand entrance. Angela stepped up to the double doors. She opened them with a flourish and stood back to allow them to enter.

Claire stepped through. "It's fabulous."

Alex agreed. He gazed at the expansive foyer with its parquet floors, high ceilings, and magnificent chandelier. Claire, he knew, wanted to invest some of the money left to her by her parents. This looked a winner and nothing like what it had been before. The excitement in her eyes warmed him and he hoped if she did buy here, it would be the base she needed.

Angela's heels clicked on the patterned wood as she crossed to the ornate central staircase. She turned to Claire and pointed downward. "The underground level is now a state-of-the-art leisure facility. Apparently, the extensive rooms and tunnels were built in the late 1700s for the first Belle Vue Manor. But that place burned to the ground. When the Victorians built the hospital, they sealed it off."

They descended the stairs.

Angela led them through to a long windowless corridor with a low ceiling and a row of metal doors. "We converted this smaller side into lockable storage facilities. Only the apartments in the main block, like the one I'm going to show you, have these."

The floor was newly tiled, while the walls had been plastered over and painted a clinical white. How apt, he thought, but about as successful as makeup on a raddled crone.

Marianne looked as if she wished she was elsewhere. "You okay?" he asked.

She grimaced. "I shudder to think about what went on in these rooms. Nothing good springs to mind," she said in a hushed voice.

Although he agreed, he briefly wondered why she was being so negative. Not like her at all. On the other hand, Claire's expression resembled a child unwrapping a coveted toy at Christmas.

Angela started talking about the gym and pool, and his ears pricked up. They crossed the basement foyer to a plush reception area. Marianne's face was now a study in boredom. He smiled to himself, sports definitely weren't her thing. Too much like masochism, she'd once said.

They completed the rest of the tour and Angela continued her spiel as she led them back to the main hall. "I know you'll be impressed, Claire. The apartment I'm about to show you is larger than some of the others that sold for the same price. I thought it would be snapped up. For some reason, people seemed interested but backed off putting in an offer. When I asked them why, they said it didn't feel right for them. Takes all sorts, I suppose."

As Alex reached the first-floor landing, the ceilings were lower, just as the stairs were steeper once out of view of the ground floor. He suspected the reason, but if he did take on this project, he would check it out to make sure.

They spent fifteen minutes looking round the apartment. He and Claire loved it while Marianne—for reasons he couldn't begin to fathom—didn't. She even sniped about the windows saying, "They made the asylum look bleak in that old photo, and it still looks bleak, even with the bars removed."

"Well, I like them. Modern windows would look out of place." Claire cast a conspiratorial glance at Marianne.

Alex thought, not for the first time, he'd never understand women.

They filed out to the hall.

"How long have you been working at Belle Vue?" Claire asked Angela.

"Must be about a year now. I made my first sale the day I arrived to set everything up. Have to admit, though, I didn't need to do much selling."

"Oh?"

"Our first resident came in knowing exactly what she wanted. We hadn't even advertised it but she knew the apartment nearest the main foyer had been finished and wanted to buy it. It was going to be the main show flat, so they did up another instead. Let's just say she's rather forceful."

Angela dropped her voice as though sharing a secret. "Like you,

Claire, she was a cash buyer. It makes me wonder though why she was so keen. She never uses any of the leisure facilities. Bit of a waste. She must be at least sixty or seventy."

When they reached the landing, Claire stopped. "Can we see the dome, please? I bet the view is amazing."

Angela slowed but continued to edge toward the stairs. "There's an awful lot more to see and I *do* have to get back to the office."

"Come on, Angela. I *have* to see it. Otherwise, how will I know if this place is for me?" Claire offered a smile full of mischief.

"It's very dusty. The cleaners keep telling me they've done it, but…"

He glanced at Marianne, her face had lost all its color.

Angela sighed. She crossed the landing and opened an unnumbered door, revealing a small room with steep narrow stairs. They trooped forward, Marianne at the rear.

As Alex emerged into the circular room, he saw Angela was right. A thick layer of dust covered the carpet. The cleaners had definitely been stringing her a line.

Claire raised her nose and sniffed. "How lovely. Lavender."

Marianne did a double-take. "Lavender? Claire, what are you talking about?" Tense voice, a sheen of sweat across her face. "It smells musty. Not nice at all."

Claire rolled her eyes, wearing a faint grin, and said to forget it. Alex joined her at one of the large windows. They gazed out at the hills of St. Albans and the surrounding countryside. An impressive sight and difficult for Claire to find anything to compare to Belle Vue. He picked up her hand and kissed it in the way she liked.

Claire smiled at him, then shifted along a few feet. "Hey, you can see the chapel much better from up here," she said over her shoulder to Marianne.

"Yes, I know. Let's just hope the bell doesn't keep everyone awake," Marianne said.

Claire didn't seem to be paying any attention. She was staring through the trees toward the stone building fringed by a mixture of bushes and flowerbeds.

"What do you think?" Angela asked Claire. "Do you want to see the newly released apartments? There's been a lot of interest already. We sold four over the weekend and a lot of second viewings booked for this week. You'll have to be quick to not miss the boat."

"I think if I buy here, it's got to be 201. I feel I was meant for that place, but..." Claire looked at Marianne. "Let me think about it a bit more."

Alex felt his head start to throb again but was keen to make sure Claire didn't lose out. He asked if Angela would hold the apartment for a day or two.

She agreed. Claire squeezed his hand and whispered her thanks. Her flirtatious look sent shivers to all the right places, but they vanished when he caught Marianne's sullen expression.

He was still figuring out her reaction, when Claire asked, "Is the chapel still used?"

Angela shook her head. "The vicar at the church nearby is responsible for it. No services, of course. For now, it's kept as a quiet place for the residents' use. Reverend Snedley keeps an eye on it, that's all. I think he hoped it would encourage some new residents to join his flock."

Claire turned to look through the glass again. She started, her head jerking closer to the window as though to see better.

"Oh." A single word rife with disappointment.

"Are you okay?" Alex turned to scan the area below where her gaze seemed fixed. Nothing unusual. Marianne and Angela joined them.

Claire's face remained pressed to the glass. "I thought I saw that woman."

"What woman?" Marianne asked as she ran her finger along the ledge. She pulled out a tissue from her jacket pocket and wiped her hand.

"You know, I told you about her yesterday, the one I nearly

knocked down. The one who stared at me and touched my car."

Alex almost laughed at Claire's melodramatic tone but, seeing her face, he caught himself.

"Her? Really?" Marianne said.

They stood in a line looking at the empty space between the chapel and the main entrance. When he slipped his arm round Claire's waist, she looked up at him. The flicker of concern in her eyes disappeared and she relaxed against him.

"I only saw the bright wig," Claire said. "Even if it was her, what does it matter?"

The agent smiled at Claire, the red smudges of lipstick on her teeth creating an unfortunate vampiric effect. "Not a jot. Now, why don't you have a think as you look round the rest of the grounds? Come and see me before you leave."

Claire nodded her agreement. Alex could see the fingers of her left hand were crossed. She gave a contented sigh and said, "I think you were right, Angela. This may be my lucky day after all."

Chapter Four

Monday, 21 December, 1868

Mary sat in the taproom at the Green Hog wearing her winter coat in vivid magenta. Her matching velvet bonnet lay across the chair beside her, and Bill occupied the seat opposite. She yawned, still tired from the night before and closed her eyes. The bar had been busy keeping Jack fully on the go and of course, she'd kept him similarly active when he'd finished work. But now, she'd changed her mind about visiting one of her customers. Those "gentlemen friends" were partially the cause of her feelings of dissatisfaction. She needed to make some decisions about her future.

Jack was a good find. Not excellent, but he'd do for now. The Green Hog took in reasonable money and she, with her occasional clients, made a useful extra. Not enough, though. She wanted more, and damn it, she deserved it. She'd noted long ago though, the harsh fate time and men dealt to whores. If Jack ever found out, she would be out on her rear.

Decision time. Give up the game or continue to keep Jack in the dark. She had enemies at the pub, and elsewhere. Two of them, whose true colors she'd uncovered, the sainted Catherine and Patrick were now out of her hair. Her uncle having met with a fatal accident in his church that, she smiled to herself, Bill Callahan had nothing to do with.

If Jack was to become her sole protector and provide her with the cloak of respectability marriage brought, she would need to think of other ways to increase her income. Preferably quick, easy ideas involving little work.

Jack's voice cut into her reverie. "I didn't bring the drinks, just this pretty little thing."

Mary opened her eyes. How tiresome. Ellen of all people. She looked like a bedraggled mouse. Her tattered coat was sopping and covered with brown splatters, but that didn't stop the men staring as though Cora Pearl had just walked in. She supposed it must be something important for Lady Muck to enter a bar. The cogwheels in Mary's mind turned. She adopted an expression of sisterly concern.

"Ellen, my dear. Are you all right?" She forced herself to pat Ellen's arm.

Mary smirked as she saw her half-sister's face flicker, then light up. She pushed Ellen toward the fireplace, telling her to warm her hands. She gave Jack an order of small beer for the mouse, and he returned to the bar.

Bill, she noted, couldn't take his eyes off the new arrival. The piece of wood he'd been whittling lay untouched on the table as he followed her every move. She'd give it some thought later.

Ellen returned and sat on the edge of the chair. She eagerly took the drink Jack handed her and gulped it as though parched.

Mary leaned forward. "Such a shame about Father Patrick."

Ellen's face crumpled, and the tears flowed. Mary fought her irritation and held her sisterly expression. Ellen wiped her nose with a ragged scrap of cloth. Her voice came out no more than a whisper. "I need your help, please, Mary."

Jack and Bill watched like hawks. Mary sat back and waited.

"I've got no money for next month's rent. I'm looking for work, but everyone is doing the same. Can you help me, please? I'll do anything."

She sighed as though a heavy weight had been placed on her shoulders. "Ellen, I *may* be able to give you some assistance. There might be some work here and space for another lodger, but I need a bit of time to think on it."

Jack opened his mouth. Mary gave him a sharp look and the toe of her boot hard on his shin bone. He closed it again.

Wiping a damp strand of hair out of her eye, Ellen's eyes shone. "Oh, Mary, I am so pleased I came. I was so worried but—"

Mary mustered an enthusiastic smile. She ignored Jack's look of surprise.

"Come when you move from the lane and I'll sort you out."

"Thank you so much. I can't wait."

Mary smirked at Ellen's gullibility, but just as she was thinking how well things were going, her half-sister had to spoil it.

"Mrs. Flanagan died last night. Typhoid, like Mam and Da." Ellen's wan face took on a determined expression.

Mary inwardly groaned. "And?" Her voice held not a smidgen of interest.

"She went to the grave still not knowing what happened to her only daughter. She never got over it. Mrs. Flanagan asked me to find out. Do you know where Nancy is? And what was that thing you threw on Mam's coffin? And why? Mam said—"

"Stop!" Forbidden territory, and her burden. Mary turned to Ellen and in a low tight voice said, "What I know and what I do, Ellen, is no business of yours and let me tell you, dead or alive, old Ma Flanagan is better off not knowing. Understand? Don't ever mention it again, or you and I are done." Mary caught the quiver of Ellen's bottom lip and knew her point had been made. Jack and Bill supped the rest of their ale in thoughtful silence.

Ellen tipped the last drops of her beer into her mouth and dabbed at her lips. She thanked Mary again, nodded at the men and took her leave.

"Such a pretty lass—so lady-like, too. I'll look forward to welcoming her into our abode," Jack spoke in an upper-class tone.

She bristled at his words, teasing or not. They stood, and she moved closer to him as he continued, "and she looks truly an innocent. I didn't think there were any left."

Bill licked his lips and Jack had a wistful look in his eyes. Mary hated Ellen at that moment. "Her ladyship, indeed. She'll be experiencing the real world soon. I'll teach her not to get above her station."

Jack cast a wry glance at Mary. "Well, she takes after her dainty mother, God rest her soul. Luckily, I like a bit of flesh on my women."

He grabbed her rear end with both hands and drew her in.

"Your only woman, dearie." Her mouth was smiling, but she made sure Jack could see her eyes were not.

"Of course, my love." He grinned back as though to humor her. "Let me get you another drink."

She nodded, although her glass was half-full. She sat again and watched as Jack headed for the bar. Bill resumed whittling, his eyes fixed on the knife as it cut into the wood. Mary had reverted to thoughts of how she could ensure Ellen fully repaid Mam's debt.

She surveyed the room before her and imagined other possible ways she could make money from the little mouse.

Three men sat down at the next table. All were dressed in threadbare clothes that must have made the winter weather seem doubly harsh. She noticed the feet of one of them. He wore a pair of ladies' side-laced boots, with the toes cut off. The newspaper stuffed into the top was soggy, caked in sawdust from the floor and almost useless. He spoke to his companions. "Me missus died three months ago, and I wish I'd had some of that insurance. Not to speak ill of the dead, but I could've made a few bob off her at last."

He laughed bitterly as he raised his glass. "Cheers to yer both but I'm an unhappy man. I got two bairns and no woman. I think I'm going to do a runner. Leave 'em with me sister and go to sea."

The other men offered murmurs of sympathy which tailed off as they drank deeply.

Mary considered what had just been said. Insurance?

Maybe she ought to think on that, too.

Bill Callahan sat in the kitchen at the Green Hog listening to Mary's tale of woe as he finished his stewed beef and dumplings.

He pushed his dish away and cast an eye at Mary—a crafty and vicious hellcat. Not such a bad thing to be, but Jack ought to watch out for himself.

He picked up his blade and pared off more shavings to add to his earlier pile. However manly Jack thought he was, Mary always wanted to wear the breeches and get her own way. That wasn't what women were for. To feed and fuck you that—he started as Mary banged the table in front of him. Catching her cross expression, he grunted his attention.

"The nerve of it. Everything is always about Ellen. For my bitch of a stepmother, the world revolved around her pretty, little girl. Never me. Not once. Now Ellen wants my help. She is an albatross round my neck. I certainly don't want her here at the pub, working or not. I need ideas of how to make best use of her. She owes me whatever she might like to think. The insurance business sounds promising but once that pays, it's over. What else, Bill?"

"Insurance is good. Thing is, 'cept for whoring or stealing, there ain't much else a wench can do to make money if she don't have none in the first place. I take it your half-sister ain't the thieving type?"

Mary gave a pained look and shook her head. He put down the wood and set about picking bits of beef from his teeth with his knife. "Of course, Jack's no saint but with your marriage plans and all, I'd be a bit careful there. He don't want the peelers round the pub 'cept as customers," he said.

"What about those rude postcards that are all the rage? I hate the bitch, but she is a looker. That must pay well."

He snorted. "You think she's gonna take her clothes off to fill your coffers?"

"Well, she's not going to sit about here all day, moping for Catherine-bleeding-Grady. We've got to think of something else. Can you help me?"

"I assume you aren't wanting a repeat of the priest? Anyway, what can I do, short of getting her into the asylum?"

Mary's face perked up momentarily before her mouth resumed its downward turn. "That's too difficult. She won't want to go, and we'd have to find a reason for getting her in there. How's it done, anyway?"

He picked up the wood and knife again. After he whittled a few shavings onto the floor, he replied, "You need two doctors and a magistrate to sign the papers. Then twice a week at Belle Vue, we takes deliveries. It ain't too hard to manage. I'm owed a favor or two by one of the doctors at the asylum. He'd oblige me."

Mary said nothing. Bill drank his ale.

She fixed Bill with a piercing stare. "You may be on to something. Just for a bit, mind you. It would get her out of my hair while I decide the best option. I'll tell her it will help her recover from her grief."

He almost smiled. "Right you are." Bill noticed Mary didn't bother to reply, just sat there deep in thought. Gave him something to think about, too. The idea of having a wench like Ellen at close hand was a tempting one. Without a doubt, it would be very good for him.

When he heard Mary's next words, Bill knew life was about to get even better.

"You can look after her in the madhouse. Make it so *anything* is a better option than Belle Vue. How you do it is up to you."

Chapter Five

Saturday, 29 November
PRESENT DAY

Stiff from spending the last three hours hunched over his desk, Alex tilted his chair back and stretched out his arms and legs. He stared out the window. At first glance, the afternoon sun evoked a summery feel. A deception: most of the trees in Verulamium Park that his apartment overlooked were bare. The people walking round the lake were well wrapped in an array of heavy coats, gloves, and scarves.

He rose and went into the kitchen to make a coffee and noticed the shopping list. That reminded him, the housewarming party was tonight. He must get to the supermarket to pick up the stuff Claire wanted, but for now, he had to keep focused, otherwise he wouldn't get his work done.

Alex pulled out his laptop, sat back at his desk and made a space in the center of the pile of books and handwritten notes. The amount of material he found on the history of Victorian asylums had surprised him. He was amazed at the speed at which these institutions had sprung up in almost every town. Not only in Britain but America too, followed by other parts of the empire such as Canada, Australia, and India. Like medical mass hysteria. Nothing prepared him for the tales of how the mentally ill were treated in the eighteenth and nineteenth centuries. Even in the twentieth century, when he'd supposed medicine and the treatment of the insane had evolved well beyond the unacceptable practices of earlier times, the horrific photographs and articles vividly showed this hadn't been the case.

Lost in his reading, the hours flew by. When he completed the preparation he needed for the meeting with Hamish on Monday, Alex straightened the messy piles of notes and cuttings beside his desk. His eye caught the headline of the article where he'd found the information about Belle Vue before it closed. The reference to the nurse reminded him of Marianne and her odd attitude to the place on their first visit. When he'd asked Marianne about her behavior, it hadn't been about the missing nurse. She had filled him in on the details and he had kept a straight face. Imagining Marianne scared and uneasy after all those years from a run-in with some little old lady was difficult to do. He smiled to himself. Matron versus pensioner. He knew who he'd bet on.

Alex typed some keywords into the search box, located two more articles about the closure of the asylum and started reading.

When he'd finished, he sat back and stared unseeing at the pinboard in front of him. He hadn't expected anything like this. He shuddered as he imagined what sort of place Belle Vue must have been for such a thing to happen. Thank God, he didn't have a weak stomach.

Somehow, he didn't think Claire would appreciate him mentioning this at her party.

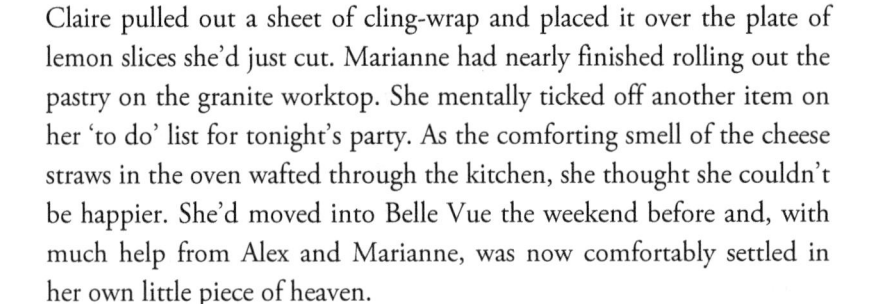

Claire pulled out a sheet of cling-wrap and placed it over the plate of lemon slices she'd just cut. Marianne had nearly finished rolling out the pastry on the granite worktop. She mentally ticked off another item on her 'to do' list for tonight's party. As the comforting smell of the cheese straws in the oven wafted through the kitchen, she thought she couldn't be happier. She'd moved into Belle Vue the weekend before and, with much help from Alex and Marianne, was now comfortably settled in her own little piece of heaven.

She glanced over at Marianne, whose face glowed pink, and smiled. "You look like something out of *Good Housekeeping*."

Marianne looked up, wearing a wry expression. "You know, crisps and peanuts would've been fine."

"Ah, but nowhere near as impressive."

"I assume you've invited the Belle Vue crowd then, not just culinary Neanderthals like Gary and Paul?"

Claire nodded and handed her friend the tin of pastry cutters. "I put a notice up on the board in the foyer earlier in the week and spoke to Sally and Jeff Reichenberg, the Americans who live next door, but they're going to be away."

She checked the clock on the wall and did a double-take. "That's weird. I put a new battery in the other day." Marianne and Claire stared at the clock face. It read 8:00 a.m., though Claire estimated it must be mid-afternoon.

Marianne shrugged. "Forget about it."

"Yes, boss." Claire laughed. "We're nearly done, do you fancy a swim?"

"Ugh. No, thanks."

Expecting that response, Claire said nothing. After collecting her keys, she disappeared downstairs to the basement and crossed the foyer into the health spa.

In the reception area, she stopped by the large window and gazed at the expanse of blue on the other side. In the pool, two heads bobbed up and down. Mr. and Mrs. Eric Beamish swimming laps. She'd met them the day she moved in and they'd been most helpful telling her about life at Belle Vue and all the other residents. Eric was plowing up the water as he swam, followed about thirty feet behind by his wife who, in goggles and a swim cap, struggled with the dog paddle.

Once changed, Claire dived into the deep end and set off with a relaxed breaststroke. She swam about thirty lengths before thinking about going back to get ready. Reaching the far end, Claire flipped over for the final lap. Each time she came up for air, she noticed a po-faced woman watching her from the reception area window. A tall thin woman in a black dress with a white cap. Claire didn't think she'd seen her before, but she didn't look like the party-going type. If she did turn up tonight, it would probably be to complain about the noise.

Clearing the water with her next stroke, Claire looked toward the glass again. Her mouth opened in shock as she felt something grab her ankle. She sucked in the chlorinated water, spluttered, then splashed wildly to stay afloat. Not cramp. More like bony fingers tugging with inhuman strength.

She cried out as she went under, flailing like a woman possessed. Eyes wide open, she struggled to see who was holding her. Still the skeletal grip, but no sign of an assailant. Claire grunted deep in her throat, fought to reach the surface. Still the fingers. Panicking, she gulped more water.

Dear God. Help!

Just as she thought she would pass out, firmer, fleshier fingers grasped her arms and propelled her upward. Her face rose above the waterline. She greedily sucked in a mouthful of air, then another.

Never in her life had she been so glad to see anybody. Eric's bushy eyebrows furrowed with concern as he kept reassuring her, with an almost hypnotic effect, she was safe.

He guided her toward the edge of the pool and a muscular attendant, who leaned over, his arms outstretched.

As he lifted her out of the water, Claire tried to make sense of her jumbled thoughts. The last thing she could tell anyone was someone had pulled her under because nobody was there. Even she could see that.

Eric led her limping to the attendant's empty seat. She'd started shaking and as she sat, she relived in her mind the fright of almost drowning, her teeth chattered uncontrollably. Eric slipped the track top from the back of the chair and placed it about her shoulders.

"Thank you so much. It's nothing. Must be a cramp," she said.

That, or more mind games. The ones the doctors said she must stop. They were making her worse, or so she'd been counselled nearly four years ago. She had to agree to a point. The doctors always came back with a rational explanation for the examples she'd given them and she still did the exercises, both mental and physical, they recommended.

Emma Beamish, whose eyes still bore the outline of her goggles, squeezed her hand. Claire thanked the couple again, but the words came out by rote. Inside, she desperately focused on the pins and needles in her foot. Anything to avoid facing the alternative explanation.

It was almost seven-thirty by the time Alex drove up to the main entrance of Belle Vue. Gary had returned early and talked him into a drink and a few joints before he left the flat. He felt mellow and looked forward to a great party. For now, though, Claire's shopping weighed him down. "Just a few bits so we won't run out of anything," she'd said. Misleading words, to put it mildly. The quickest place to unload all the stuff was through the front entrance.

Balancing half a dozen bags on one arm, he took out the keys Claire had given him and stepped up to the huge oak doors. As he entered, he almost collided with a figure standing directly in his path.

He jerked back. "Sorry. I didn't see you there."

The woman appraised him with cold eyes, one eyebrow raised and a smirk on her lips. She didn't speak. Alex felt she was going to, but perhaps she wasn't sure he wanted to hear what she'd have to say. If she lived here and had read Claire's invitation, she'd probably start complaining about the likely noise. Old and sour, summed up his first impression. Her clothes looked expensive, but they didn't quite work. The brightly patterned scarf of gold and purple around her neck clashed with the red of her jumper and hair.

"Your *girl's* having a party tonight," she stated, in a severe tone.

"Er, that's right. I'm Alex by the way. How did you know Claire was 'my girl'?" he asked.

The smirk dropped, but she said nothing. To fill the void, he continued, "We hope we don't disturb you. It shouldn't end too late."

A faint smile now hovered on her thin lips, as though she had weighed up her approach and decided to be affable. "My name's Moira Bradigan, *Miss* Moira Bradigan. Do you like Belle Vue, Mr. Palmer?"

As Alex wondered again how she knew his identity, he felt like a little boy in short trousers facing a stern teacher. "Yes, Miss Bradigan, I do."

She gave him a calculating look and moved forward. "Hmm. I hope no uninvited guests show up. Today of all days."

Alex caught an earthy scent as she brushed past him, too close for comfort.

As the door closed, he passed half the bags to his other arm and moved toward the stairs. Moira Bradigan hadn't answered his question. Angela the agent had described her as 'forceful'. He'd agree and add 'strange' too. Strange, but oddly compelling.

Marianne let him in. Barefaced, she wore her usual black ensemble, slightly crumpled for effect. He wasn't sure if she was ready for the party, so he maintained a tactful silence. He returned to his car and made another trip upstairs before taking two boxes down to Claire's lockup.

Task completed, he drove round to the main car park and pulled into one of the visitor spots. In contrast to the illuminated front of the property, he got out in near darkness. He remembered Claire telling him the car park lights weren't working.

Relieved of his delivery duties, Alex looked up at the lit windows beckoning from Belle Vue's rear façade and was struck again by its schizophrenic nature as an asylum. The external grandeur hiding its penal underbelly. The dome at the top was half-lit. An outline of someone standing at the window. He waved but the figure didn't move.

The headlights of an approaching car caught Alex in their glare. Its horn beeped loudly. He recognized the number plate. Claire's bitchy friend, Sophie. Everything he disliked in a woman; fake, grasping, and manipulative.

Sophie, dressed to kill, unfolded herself from the car. Her current

BELLE VUE

lapdog, Jay who got out the other side, didn't stand a chance, he thought. She walked over to Alex, her heels clicking on the tarmac. Drawing in a sizeable breath, she said with a loud sigh, "Playing Peeping Tom, are we? You're lucky I didn't run you over."

"Hello to you, too. No, just admiring the architecture. Fabulous place, don't you think?" he said, keen to needle her.

"An old loony bin? Who'd want to live in a nuthouse, however fancy they dress up the name? Not me, that's for sure." Sophie turned to her boyfriend. "Come on. Let's get inside. It's freezing. Jay, quickly. Give me your arm, I can't see where I'm going. Don't the lights work in this crappy place?"

Alex followed Sophie who, clutching Jay with a vice-like grip, tapped her progress toward the building. Bottles clinking in a large bag, carried by her personal attendant, provided her backing track. As they reached the path, the lights came on.

Once inside, Alex took them along the corridor, past the first hall and set of stairs, to the main foyer. Jay gazed around him. "Wow. This is some place." He looked at Alex with something approaching envy. "Your girlfriend must be loaded."

Sophie snorted and headed for the stairs.

As the group reached the first floor, music came from above. By the time they reached the next level, Alex hoped Claire's neighbors were either joining the party, not at home, or deaf. As they walked toward her apartment, Sophie stopped and pointed to a pile of wood shavings on the floor. "I thought professional people lived here, not carpenters and the like. Very down market."

Ignoring the lack of comment, she now wore a smile as he opened the door. Once inside, Sophie gave her coat to Jay and flounced off.

Alex saw Marianne emerge from the guest room, dressed exactly the same as she had when he first came in. Claire, on the other hand, with her hair up and slinky dress, looked stunning. She slid into his arms to greet him.

The hours passed in a blur. More guests, gifts, and bottles arrived, and the party got into its swing. The DJ, a pal of Gary's, had set up in the sitting room. This became the default dance floor with the dining room and kitchen the places for talking and eating. He opened some of the windows to allow the cigarette smoke to escape. More of the Belle Vue residents than expected had turned up, much to Claire's delight. She was thrilled with the party, and his attentiveness. Marianne remarked he was laying it on with a trowel, but he suspected deep down she would love to be in a relationship like theirs. He took a deep drink of whiskey.

Gary nudged him as the opening chords of the next song blared out, and his eyes followed Gary's gaze. Seemingly oblivious to any onlookers, Marianne swung to the music and jigged up and down. From their position by the open window, Gary puffed on his cigarette and composed wisecracks mostly at her expense.

At the end of the song, still smiling, Alex escaped to the dining room where he'd last seen Claire. She stood by one of the tables laden with food, talking to an older couple. They were regarding her with a somewhat protective fondness, and he wondered what that was all about. He picked up a prawn brochette, ate it and then refilled his glass before joining them. She introduced him to Eric and Emma Beamish, who lived on the floor below and, he was surprised to learn, had 'saved' her life a few hours earlier. They rose in his estimation.

Eric, a lean fifty-something with an obvious penchant for bow ties, informed Alex he was the Chairman of the Belle Vue Residents' Association. His wife, Emma, plump, fortyish, with 'mother' written all over her, was the Treasurer. Like matching bookends on either side of Claire, they listened almost as if taking notes to her potted tale of moving into Belle Vue.

"I only know Marianne, the one who greeted you at the door, was thrilled to get her own space back again."

The Beamishes nodded vigorously. Alex murmured a vague sound of agreement then switched the topic. "I met one of the other residents earlier. A Moira Bradigan? She's quite something, isn't she? She seemed to know a lot about us."

Eric and Emma blushed in unison, before Eric admitted. "I told Miss Bradigan who you were. She was very interested about Claire buying this apartment. Normally she's aloof and standoffish. Maybe she's beginning to thaw."

"From my one conversation, I'd say that's a long way off," Alex said, smiling.

"Er, yes. Anyway, she seems to know a lot about the history of Belle Vue. Right back to its days as an asylum, and later a hospital. I think she worked there once or knew someone who worked there. I vaguely remember her mentioning something similar when we were telling her about Claire," Eric said.

Before he could comment, Claire tugged his sleeve. "Alex, I need to check something. Can you help me?"

He took the offered escape route but made a mental note to speak to Miss Bradigan again and see if he could learn anything useful for his research. "Sure. Hey, Eric, why don't you two get on the dance floor? I bet you're a real mover."

Eric beamed again, his spotted bow tie almost spinning with delight. "Oh, I have my moments. Good idea, Alex. Come on, Emma. Let's show them how it's done."

Emma smiled back adoringly. Hand-in-hand, they headed toward the music pulsating from the other room. Alex grinned at Claire and leaned over to kiss her. "Very clever. I thought we'd never be alone. Let's go somewhere dark."

He led her out into the dimly lit hall. The music was blasting out and he could see the temporary dance floor packed with cavorting shadows.

"So, what are we checking? Something for the party, or for me?" He wrapped his arms around her, pulling her close.

"Ha, ha. Do you think Eric's going to check up on us?"

"Having met him, I'd say yes." He kissed her deeply, his passion growing as she responded. Time and the party faded away. It was just him and Claire. Later was definitely going to be great.

"Claire?"

Alex felt her pull away. Jay hovered, a resigned look on display.

"Sorry, but we're going now. Sophie says she's had enough."

Claire flashed him a look that said, 'don't even go there'. "Sure. I'll get your coats."

As she crossed to the guest bedroom, Jay told her how much he liked the apartment. Alex looked across at Claire, who half-faced Jay. She opened the door. In the unlit room, Alex was sure he could see a shape looming behind her. A pungent odor wafted into the hall. Before he could say anything, Claire, her eyebrows now furrowed, turned and reached for the light switch.

A crackle and a flash. The lights and music died instantly, leaving the apartment pitch black. A big cheer went up, followed by an awkward silence. A voice yelled, "Which sex maniac turned off the lights?"

The sound of laughter echoed through the rooms.

"Claire, are you okay?" he asked.

"Shocked more like. Alex, what are we going to do?"

Cutting off his reply, Gary's falsetto pierced the darkness, "Oh, Paul, you're so rough, but I like it."

More laughter. Alex raised his voice before the chatter started again. "Can someone open the blinds in the other rooms?"

He eased past Jay, feeling his way along the wall toward the window at the end of the hall. He pulled up the shade and peered into an inky void. Bugger. A blackout. He blinked. In the instant he opened his eyes, he saw everything outside was lit as it should be. The glow of St. Albans, the lights round the grounds, a car's headlights moving up the drive. Must have been a trick of the eye but the important thing was to get the flat sorted. Most likely, a couple of fuses had tripped. As he breathed in, the dreadful smell hit him again. Stronger this time.

Before he could react, a loud shriek behind him silenced the chatting in the other rooms.

Then another.

He instantly swiveled round, calling Claire's name. He could barely make her out in the gloom. He dashed forward, his hands pulling her to him. He felt her body trembling against his.

"Are you all right? What happened?"

"I think I'm okay. Get the lights on now. Please?"

"It'll soon be sorted. I'm going to check the breaker," he called out with more confidence than he felt.

Gary yelled, "Be quick about it." This elicited a murmur of agreement that ceased as he added, "I'm dying for a slash."

Claire's fingers gripped him like pincers of steel as he shuffled toward the hall cupboard. He opened the door and was just able to distinguish the switches of the fuse box to his left. They had all been tripped. Not good, he thought. Claire would need to watch that. He remembered she'd mentioned Eric Beamish telling her there'd been problems with both the gas and electricity supplies, the car park being a case in point.

He flicked them all back on. The first loud cheers led by Gary and Paul morphed into louder groans as the sounds of cheesy disco music flooded through the apartment. Alex, intending to replace the burned-out lightbulb in the guest room, turned to Claire. She was rubbing her neck. Her frightened eyes met his. "Someone grabbed me."

He breathed out. Was that all? It was pitch black for Christ's sake. He was about to make a joke about it when she removed her hand from her throat. He did a double-take as he took in the red mark around her neck. Alex recalled the shadow behind Claire. The guy, whoever he was, must have taken hold of her in the dark, but he was positive no one had come out of the room. It didn't make sense. With Claire still clutching his arm, they went in and searched. No one. Alex noticed the smell had gone, too, as had the mark around her neck. Like he'd imagined it.

When Jay came in to collect his and Sophie's coats, he left Claire with him. Still wondering about the man, he searched the flat.

The music, like the party buzz, fizzled out. Only a few diehards were still dancing but to a more muted beat. Most people had migrated to the dining room and kitchen where they were chatting quietly in small groups. While he didn't spot anyone remotely resembling the brawny shape he'd seen behind Claire, he did locate the spare light bulbs and another drink. When he'd restored light in the guest room, he found a queue of partygoers in the hall waiting to retrieve their coats.

After another half hour or so, he and Claire closed the door on the last guests, Eric and Emma Beamish. He chuckled. "To think you've found the only other people to leave after Gary and the DJ. Unbelievable."

Claire yawned, her slim fingers quivering as she held them in front of her mouth. She looked tired, he thought, as though her experience tonight—or whatever you'd call it—had sucked some of the liveliness out of her. He wondered if a night of passion was now out of the question.

"Shall we tidy up tomorrow?" he asked, ever hopeful. If he didn't hurry, she'd be sound asleep. Seeing her nod, he put his arms round her and they walked to the bedroom.

"Alex, I'm frightened."

He almost told her not to be silly then checked himself. She was still so fragile. When he and Claire had started going out, Marianne had told him what she'd been through with the horrific deaths of both her parents; murdered at their home in Hong Kong—and after. Not just the grief, but her breakdown and guilt at surviving. He needed to understand her fears not mock them.

He *had* seen a man in the spare room.

Moira Bradigan's comment about unwanted guests and what day it was, came to mind. He also remembered Eric's words about her knowledge of Belle Vue's past. Before those thoughts had a chance to retreat, Alex decided she was definitely worth speaking to again.

Maybe this time he'd get some straight answers.

Chapter Six

Wednesday, 24 March, 1869

The closed cart rattled its way through a set of heavy iron gates. Ellen peered out of the small side window. Her insides quivered as she took in the leafy trees and a sliver of clear blue sky. She whispered its name: Belle Vue. An exotic sound so full of promise. Then came the first view.

She gasped at its beauty, like a magical palace. It was so large, she couldn't see where the two wings of the mansion ended.

"What yer grinning at, missy?" asked the thin, grimy man sitting opposite. He wore workhouse garb, coarse and ill-fitting. "It may look good, but it's still an asylum. A prison fer the likes of us."

Ellen ignored the old fellow shackled hand and foot. For every mile they traveled, she'd felt her spirits rise. London's dense yellow fog and soot-covered structures were replaced by fresh air, stretches of green and buildings still their original color. How wonderful of Mary to arrange this for her. Ellen wondered if she might find work here too, but most of all she hoped Mary would visit her soon.

"Behind those bars is misery," the vagrant said. His tone softened, "I've been 'ere before, miss. Yer'll need to toughen up."

She gazed at his gaunt face. "My name is Ellen. How can you not see the beauty of this place?"

"Percy Chance is me name. Everyone calls me Chancer. How de do de—" He rattled his chains and cackled like a crone, revealing a couple of dark stumps in an otherwise empty mouth. The attendant, seated near him, grunted and leaned down. He poked the old man hard in the ribs with his stick. Chancer coughed and doubled over.

"Don't hurt him." She glared at the guard. The man ignored her and resumed picking at one of the many pustules on his face.

Ellen clutched the brown paper bag with her belongings in it. Apart from Chancer who carried a small sack, none of the others crammed with them in the cart seemed to have any possessions except the rags they wore. For the last few hours, they sat or lay on the floor in silence, presumably lulled by the rocking of the carriage.

"I don't think yer goin' to like what lies behind them fancy bricks. It's the inside's fer the likes of you and me. The outside's fer those who pay fer it. Makes 'em feel good. Charity gets 'em to heaven quicker."

Ellen glanced at Chancer again. He seemed all right. Not like their fellow travelers.

"Why are you here?" she asked.

"I get these halloos things, scary ones. Not all the time mind, but had a bad run of 'em so they brought me back. Worse at night. They tie me to the bed or I wears one of those waistcoats, so I can't attack what I see."

The reason for his warnings, she thought, knowing how much she would loathe such treatment. The horses' hooves slowed, then stopped. Chancer bent toward her. "Gawd 'elp yer, miss, but remember, me and, if he's still inside that is, me mate, old Titus, will look out for yer."

She smiled at his concern, unnecessary as it was, and turned to stare out of the window.

A tall, thin woman in a black dress with a white cap stood surrounded by a group of what must be asylum staff. The men wore brown serge suits. Like prison wardens, their jackets bore stripes and numbers to indicate their rank. The women wore plain dark dresses with pale collars and cuffs. She could see the back of a large brawny man as he walked up to the lady in the center. The others immediately cleared a space for him and when he turned, the bludgeon in his hand was visible for all to see. But that was of no interest to her. She now saw who he was.

Bill Callahan. Jack's brother.

Before she could think about this, she heard the driver dismount, followed by the rattle of the heavy keys as the back door opened.

"All out. Now!" The guard rose and roughly grabbed arms and shoulders, stepping on feet and toes. Loud bangs on the metal sides of the cart. Heavy boots on cobbles. These noises roused the passengers and in a matter of seconds, chaos ensued. Ellen recoiled as the others responded to the yelling and brute force in kind, screaming, kicking, and shoving as they were heaved out of the cart.

One of the guards pushed her toward the exit. Another grabbed Chancer's chains and dragged him across the bolted floor. The old man yelped each time his knees scraped over the metal rivets.

Ellen halted at the open door and surveyed the scene. It looked more like the end of a gang fight than admittance to a hospital. Though trembling inside, she set her face to a blank mask. One of the female attendants clutched her arm and pulled. She stumbled as she landed but received no assistance as the woman was now hauling Chancer from the cart. Hindered by his shackles, he fell awkwardly, cracking his knees and forehead on the cobblestones.

Ellen steadied herself and reached out to help.

"Leave 'em be." One of the male attendants snarled. "Git over there."

She did as she was told. There were a dozen or so women besides Ellen. She tried to catch any eye for a sympathetic connection but, from this group at least, there was none to be had. Chancer, in a smaller group of men, struggled to his feet. His forehead bore torn skin and a bloody mark. One knee of his flimsy trousers was ripped, exposing a red mess below. He shrugged at her. Next to him, a young man constantly twitched and jerked. Every now and then, he'd snicker and put his hands down his trousers.

Ellen looked away and up at the endless rows of windows looming over her. Windows with bars. All shut, though it was a hot day. She could see now they were at the rear of the main building, next to a large middle section that jutted out like the tail of a dragonfly.

The head woman issued more orders, but her words were drowned out by the clamor around her. A burly male attendant led Chancer and his companions toward an iron door. Another orderly, holding a huge padlock and chain, admitted them into the gloom. A babel of noise assaulted her ears until the metal door clanged shut.

Bill Callahan stepped into her line of sight. She wondered why Mary had not told her he worked at Belle Vue. Ellen could do with an ally, especially one on the other side. She crossed her fingers and hoped he would help her make the best of her time at Belle Vue. But as she observed his rock-like face and the bludgeon firmly grasped in his hand, her optimism wavered.

It disappeared completely at his next words. "The first thing that happens when you get inside is *we* hose you stinking lot down. Naked."

His eyes never left hers. She hugged her bag to her chest as though the wrinkled paper could provide some small comfort. It seemed she was wrong about her future brother-in-law. As she struggled to make sense of this new reality, he stepped forward and pushed the end of his bludgeon into her stomach. "Mary's asked me to look after you."

His fingers gripped her arm. He was so close she could smell his sour breath. "And that's just what I'm gonna do."

Ellen stared at his smirking face, at the malice in his eyes. Every shred of hope, that Belle Vue would be a place of solace for her, curled up and shriveled to nothing.

He let go of her arm and pushed her at the other women who were shuffling toward the entrance. She slowed her steps as she joined them, but her mind raced ahead. All she could think of was a nightmare vision of being publicly stripped, not only of her clothes, but of any last dignity. With Callahan, watching, gloating, and leading the mockery—and then, to be hosed down like an animal.

Her stomach churned. She edged forward. The attendant pulled open the iron door and the cacophony of grunts, wails and screeched profanities only added to her anxiety.

Ellen stepped through into the gloom.

Chapter Seven

Thursday, 4 December
Present Day

Alex loped down the steps into the Student's Union coffee bar and immediately spotted his destination: Gary's bright-orange sweatshirt signaled beacon-like through the wisps of smoke and miserly fluorescent lighting. He snaked his way round the chairs and detritus sprawled in his path, before dropping his pile of books on the large rectangular table.

"G'day, mate," Gary drawled.

Alex returned the same and followed up with a jokey "Yiasou" to Paul. Sophie sneered at him and remained silent. She resumed picking at her meal. He thought of anything he'd done to upset her but came up blank. Claire's eyes met his and glinted with amusement. He stroked her arm.

"Oi, Romeo. Are you going to stand there all day or go git some tucker?" Gary asked.

He grinned. "The latter. I'm starving. Anyone for a drink?"

No takers. He quickly returned with the specialty of the day and a beer. The hard, plastic chair squeaked as he sat down opposite Claire. Sophie was in full flight on her favorite subject, something about being spotted as a model.

Glazed expressions. Neutral mumbles. Alex wondered why she ever bothered with college when she wasn't remotely interested in studying. He tucked into his food. Keen to raise a topic of his own, he ate quickly.

Sophie pushed away her half-eaten meal and picked up her

handbag. "Claire, I'll ring you later." She gave Alex a look of unreserved disdain, air-kissed Claire, and flounced off.

"And so, mankind is safe until the next invasion of the killer Gorgon." Gary wiped his brow. "Speaking of saving mankind, Claire, where's Matron?" Not still doing the Monster Mash in front of the mirror?" Gary's face and body twitched. "She dances like she's being electrocuted. No wonder the lights went out at your party."

Alex chuckled as he recalled some of the cracks Gary had made then. Claire flashed him a sour look. She tutted and grabbed Gary's hands. "Stop it. She'll be here soon."

"Okay, okay, but shame she's not one of those sexy little nurses in a skimpy uniform with stockings and—"

Alex sensed Claire's hackles rising. "Enough already," he said, holding down his grin. "Now, Claire, you know Gary can't help it. Desperation does that to a man."

The edges of her lips lifted, and he relaxed. Gary waved a half-eaten chip in front of her. "Ask lover-boy, who is almost wetting his pants, to tell us more about his research on the nuthouse. God, I almost feel like I live there. He never stops going on about it. Now there's a thought. I could do something on 'Sports Injuries in a Straight Jacket'."

Gary was right. Having spent all morning in the library, Alex was itching to tell them what he'd uncovered.

"Well, actually..." he began.

All eyes turned in his direction.

Alex filled them in about another article he'd found regarding the nurse who'd gone missing at Belle Vue before it closed.

"When the police searched the asylum after the complaints from the nurse's father, they found a human heart in one of the patients' belongings. Can you believe it? The inmate told them he'd been ordered to gouge it out from a living donor by, wait for this..." Alex paused for effect, before continuing. "The Devil, no less. They put the man away in Broadmoor, but they never did find the rest of the body."

"Oh, yuck, Alex." All the color had faded from Claire's cheeks.

"What're ya gonna do for an encore? Tell us something more gross so we can all barf in unison?" Gary said with relish.

"I also found this," Alex said. He picked up a musty-smelling book from his pile on the table. He opened it at the page marked with a Post-it note. "If we lived in Victorian times, we'd all have been candidates for the local asylum."

"Yeah, right but I really am Napoleon." Gary wrapped his arms round his body as if in an imaginary constraint.

Alex looked down at the words. "Here's a list of reasons people were sent to an asylum for the year 1862. Masturbation for one."

Everyone laughed.

"But how did they know?" Gary asked, his virtuous expression morphing to a lecherous one.

Alex left the point hanging and continued to read aloud. "'Overexcitement at the Great Exhibition. Sudden loss of several cows. Intemperance of wife. Non-success in business.' Oh, and one thing none of us will ever suffer from; 'over study'. No wonder those places were so full."

"It's surprising there was anybody left on the outside," Claire said.

Reprising his previous imitation of Marianne's unique dance style, Gary asked, "Does it include nurses who wrongly think they can boogie?"

"Referring to me, twinkle toes?"

Judging by Gary's expression, Marianne's voice caught him by surprise.

Gary looked up at her, his face a picture of hurt innocence. "Would I make fun of someone who might be my nurse one day? Who'd want to get back at me?"

Broad smiles all round.

"You better believe it. I can be *very* creative, Gary. A total body shave, an icy bed-bath, a few enemas."

"Oh, I love it when you talk dirty."

Marianne scowled and put her tray on the table. "If that's what turns you on."

Gary raised his eyebrows and panted like an eager puppy. He nudged Paul. "Y'ready, mate?"

Paul nodded, and Alex caught him giving Marianne a hesitant smile. One she returned. Face glowing, Paul rose and followed in Gary's wake. Alex wondered if Paul would ever get together with Marianne. She might not be the hottest ticket in town, but kind and safe was just what his mate needed.

He noticed Marianne eyeing his empty plate. "You'd think the Food and Wine Society would ban its members from coming to a place like this."

"Ah, but you've got to eat the bad to appreciate the great stuff," he said.

"But not at the expense of your taste buds. Wasn't it you who couldn't tell a pickled onion from a lychee at the annual dinner last year?"

Alex dipped his head and put his hand to his chest. "Touché, Marianne. Are you coming to our Christmas party next Saturday?"

Marianne's mouth was full. Claire answered. "She is, but it sure took a lot of convincing. Can you believe she was actually going to do an extra shift at the hospital? Talk about a masochist."

Marianne nodded and continued munching. Claire picked up her glass then put it down again. "Alex, when we left the apartment yesterday, wasn't the heating off?"

"Yep."

"You didn't change the timer or reset the temperature?"

"No. Didn't touch anything."

"Well, that's odd then. When I got home last night, the heating was on full blast. The thermometer read thirty-five degrees. Took me ages to cool the place down."

DIY, not his thing at all. "Why not speak to Eric? He seems to have nominated himself as head of the maintenance committee, along with everything else."

Claire wore a thoughtful expression. "What with the gas going on by itself, the electricity cutting out at the party and a couple of other odd things, I'm going to make a list. There's a Residents' Meeting next week. I'll raise my items then."

His ears had pricked up at her last sentence. "Okay if I join you? I can ask if anyone knows anything about the history of the asylum and is willing to speak to me about it. Maybe Moira Bradigan will be there, too. Now there's someone I want to talk to."

"Sure, Alex," Claire said. She opened her can of soda and stuck in a straw.

Marianne, her plate now empty, collected the trays and took them to the bins. She returned with a Wet Wipe and gave the table a thorough clean. Claire and Alex watched in silence as she went off to dispose of the used tissue.

He kissed her and whispered, "Can you imagine what she does after sex?" This made Claire snort her drink out and start coughing.

"Are you all right? What's he been saying to you?"

"Nothing," Claire said, grinning. "Just a dirty suggestion for later which I'm going to take him up on. If I can stay awake." She blew him a kiss.

"Ugh, you two are so nauseating," Marianne said. "I'm off. I've got a ton of work to do this afternoon. What about you?"

Claire's face dropped. "Dissertation stuff but I could fall asleep right now, I'm so tired. It's got to be done, though, so it's the library for me."

As Marianne departed, Alex collected his books and Claire tucked herself under his arm. They headed for the exit, then walked past the Union and Senate buildings in silence. Claire slowed, and he released his arm.

"Lexi?"

"Yes, my love."

"I've been thinking," Claire said. She took his hand and they ambled through to the next quadrangle. "It's four weeks to Christmas and we haven't made any plans yet. Why don't we have a big get-together at my place? We can start a tradition. Like I used to have with my, my parents. Midnight Mass on Christmas Eve. Christmas morning, I'll wake you up with champagne and lots of pressies, then we can cook lunch for everyone. You, me, Marianne, Debra, and Gary. Paul can come later after his obligatory attendance at his Mum's. I might even ask Sophie. It'll be fabulous."

Shit. Now he was in for it. He chose his next words carefully. "I was going to tell you, Claire. Gary has invited me to stay with him and his Dad."

"Oh...but that's okay. His dad can come, too. Since they won't provide breakfast in bed the way I will, you'll have to let them down gently."

"Er, that's not what I meant. Gary's dad has rented a chalet in Verbier for a fortnight over Christmas and New Year. A couple of his golfing pals from Oz are going to join him, and he asked Gary if he wanted to bring a few mates and make it a 'big boys' bash'. You know I love skiing, and it's all booked." His voice trailed off as Claire pointedly dropped his hand.

"Oh, puh-leaze." she shot back. "You've got to be joking. 'Big boys' bash'? Sounds like a stag night for porn stars. And thanks for not telling me. Didn't you think we could have done something together? It is Christmas."

Alex adopted a hangdog expression. "Sweetheart, it's only just been arranged."

"Don't you 'sweetheart' me. Is Paul going?"

"He is, but not 'til Boxing Day. I think he said they were having Christmas lunch for thirty, all relatives. Can you imagine?" He laughed and hoped she'd see the funny side.

"No, I can't, because *I* shall be sitting alone, in a group of one, solo, all by myself, just little ol' me. To think I come behind two, or rather a whole herd of rampant goats in the pecking order. Not very flattering."

Bloody hell. He was in dangerous territory.

He softened his tone. "Claire, I'm sorry, but you won't be on your own. Marianne said she'd probably be spending Christmas with you and Debra like last year."

"Marianne knew about this and didn't tell me?"

Uncomfortable at the way things were getting twisted, he held up his hands. "Claire, please. I simply asked Marianne what she was doing for Christmas. I never mentioned skiing. If you were offered such a trip, I expect you'd jump at it, too."

She stopped and glared at him, arms akimbo. "Maybe, but I would have discussed it with you first. I'm really vexed. Listen, I've got work to do, and also some thinking, by myself. I might as well get in practice."

"Don't be like that. We've got the rest of the vacation together. I'll only be gone from the twentieth for a fortnight."

"Whatever."

Alex touched her arm. "Come on, Claire, let me walk you to the library."

She brushed his hand away. "Don't bother. Tonight's off by the way. I'm going to catch up on my sleep."

Claire marched off, leaving him to scratch his head in wonder at how quickly it had all gone so wrong.

Claire's library visit was not a success. Each time she tried to concentrate, Alex's words wormed their way back into her thoughts. All her plans were ruined. She'd expect Gary to do something like that, but surely Alex was different. So much for that. After an hour with nothing achieved but a headache, she gave up.

As she drove back to Belle Vue, her mobile rang and when she heard the familiar voice, she welcomed the diversion. The chance for a natter with little mental effort required. She half-listened as Sophie told her about the new dress she'd just bought for the Christmas party next week. Her luck held until Sophie's words, spoken in the same low breathy tone, oozed into sensitive territory. Dark brown molasses spiked with poison.

"I couldn't mention it earlier, but you need to know, and I wouldn't be any sort of friend if I didn't tell you. Last night I saw Alex in the middle of St. Albans with this stunning girl draped all over him. Not even wearing half a dress. They certainly looked very comfortable with each other."

She felt her eyes prickle but covered by telling Sophie she knew all about it. Then she broke the connection. She took a deep breath and thought it out. He said he had family stuff to sort out. Alex certainly wasn't a liar. Sophie could be a bitch, but would she make something up? Who knew? Best to leave it. Unless it happened again.

As she swung into the car park, she spotted Sally Reichenberg heading toward her huge American 4x4. Her neighbor, a petite blond in her late thirties, waved. Claire pulled up beside her and lowered the window.

"Hi, Claire. How ya doing?" Sally said, in her distinctive Texan drawl. When they'd caught up on the local gossip, Claire asked whether she still had any trouble with the gas or electricity.

Sally nodded. "We sure are. Jeff thinks Charterhouse used what was already there and didn't do proper checks. Putting it right will cost the earth, so they'll fight tooth and nail to avoid doing anything."

"The Residents' Meeting is next week, and I want to ask about it there. Are you going?"

"And miss a laugh like that, not on your life, hon. I've been to every single one. Three so far, every six months. Old Beamish produces a lot of hot air, reams of minutes but nothing ever seems to get done. Charterhouse must have put him in as a saboteur."

They arranged to meet for coffee the following week, and Sally breezed off. Claire drove into her bay and dragged herself out of the car, surprised at how physically tired she felt. She traipsed through to the front foyer, checked her mailbox, and climbed the stairs. Claire stopped midway to the first floor and rested her hand on the banister. How wonderful to relish the peace and quiet of Belle Vue's cocooning luxury. At Alex's, if Paul and Gary plus assorted hangers-on were there, it was chaos. Too much noise and no privacy.

She closed her eyes and inhaled deeply. She caught a faint hint of that lovely lavender in the air and not a single sound. Perfect, just perfect. Claire breathed in again.

Without warning, a vile stench, a mixture of decay and overturned earth, hit her. It had a strange familiarity. Her eyes flashed open in surprise.

A hulk of a man—a stranger—was leaning against the wall on the landing above her. As if he was waiting for someone. He hadn't been there a minute ago. She would have smelled him. He didn't move or utter a word. She stood fixed to the spot, unsure what to do. His clothes, a high-necked suit of dark coarse material, looked old-fashioned and uncomfortable. Claire was conscious she'd scarcely dared breathe since she first noticed him. She swallowed. There was something wrong about the way he stood there looking at her. Slowly, her eyes not leaving his, and ready to bolt if he should make any move, Claire inched up the stairs.

She reached the landing, and they faced each other. Unsettled, she said, "hello," then felt herself blush. Still, he didn't respond. Don't act paranoid, she thought. What if he was just an oddball who lived in the building? She'd ask Angela, or Sally if they knew anyone like that. Watching for any movement, Claire inched past him. She then turned and rushed up the next flight of stairs. God, she felt a fool.

She twisted and looked down at the landing. He was still there, same place and position, same sneer, his eyes following her every move. He held her gaze and opened one side of his jacket. Claire saw the glint of metal and watched mesmerized as, inch by inch, he drew out a knife. Trembling, she sucked in a shallow breath, not daring to think what he might use it for. His other hand disappeared into his trouser pocket.

Her heart thudded. He pulled out a piece of wood. Without dropping his fixed stare, he ran the edge of the blade along one side of it.

Claire shivered at the leering malevolence in his eyes and blinked. The spell broken, she scrambled with her keys and escaped into her apartment. Only when she'd double-locked the door and put the chain on the latch, did she dare breathe out.

Short, shaky breaths. How ridiculous. Claire moved away from the door and took her mobile from her bag. She was about to ring Alex when she remembered she was still annoyed with him. She tapped on Marianne's number instead.

As she waited for a reply, she realized her nerves were still stretched tight. Even now in her own apartment. Bloody man. Her eyes swiveled to the chain on the door and the metal bar showing the deadlock in place. He'd unsettled her. Fancy letting him do that.

Marianne's voice message kicked in and she hung up.

Claire switched the heating on. She'd use the time to catch up on a few bits and pieces: non-thinking stuff, the sort she could do in front of the TV.

She couldn't be bothered to take a shower. The flat was still cool, so she changed into a pair of fleecy pajamas, her toweling robe, and some thick bed socks. She half-watched some TV, checked her email and texts, but by eight, she'd had enough. In truth, her thoughts kept returning to Alex and the pig's ear of a Christmas she was going to have.

Indulging in self-pity wasn't like her but she'd had high hopes for a romantic break together: so much for that. And what about this woman draped all over him? She was thoroughly miffed and what with her punishing workload, everything seemed to be getting on top of her. Her one lucky break was the firm she'd worked with during the summer had offered her a job, so at least she didn't have to bother about the milk round nightmare.

Claire padded to her room and turned on the bedside lamp. In the background, she could hear the boiler and radiators working, but noticed they hadn't made much difference so far. The temperature outside must have dropped further than she thought. She took an extra blanket from one of the cupboards. She set the alarm and climbed under the covers. God, it was cold. Was there no happy medium in this place? She tucked the duvet firmly round her. Her fingers reached out and fumbled for the switch. Darkness engulfed the room.

As she waited for her eyes to adjust, she lay on her back and tried a few relaxation techniques. Nothing worked. She couldn't settle. All because of some daft episode on the stairs. Now she could imagine the shadows were shifting. Was the line between the wardrobe door and the frame wider than before? Did the coat on the hook move? Stop being silly, she chided herself. A creak in the hall. She held her breath, straining to hear any sound. Nothing. Oh, good grief, this was stupid. She was so tense, her muscles ached. She wasn't in the mood to read. All she had to do was shut her eyes and loosen up. Free her mind and drift off. No thoughts of what she'd like to do to Alex, or Gary's dad for that matter.

When the alarm went off at seven, Claire struggled to free her arm. The covers were all twisted, and she felt clammy as though she'd been sweating heavily. Ugh. Her body still ached, no doubt from all the stress yesterday. She opened her eyes and reached out to silence the shrill noise. Her head felt like a rubber ball bitten by an overenthusiastic dog.

In the next moment, she noticed the smell. The same one as yesterday, and her mind now remembering with chilling clarity, the same as at her party and, she suddenly realized with alarm, in the 'death house' in Hong Kong. But as the doctors said it was all in her mind.

She groped for the light switch, pulled back the duvet and did a double take. She was naked from the waist down and her top was open. She looked around. Her pajama bottoms lay in a heap over by the wardrobe.

Claire sat on the side of the bed and tried to remember. Her head throbbed. No memory of getting too hot or waking surfaced. A niggle of something, but too elusive to catch. She stood up then stopped. Something cold and wet trickled down her inside leg. Her period wasn't due. She dipped her head to check. No red marks. Maybe she'd had a raunchy dream but nothing she could recollect. She noticed the smell had gone, too, but that didn't stop more old worries snaking their way into her thoughts, releasing their venom. She shook her head, tried to think logically. She was safe. No one had been in her flat. She must be strong. Face her demons. No need to tell Alex and Marianne. Unless...

Claire peered out into the hall. As expected, the chain was still on the front door. She stripped off her top and headed for the en-suite, picking up her pajama bottoms on the way. She dumped the set in the laundry basket, pulled her oversize towel from the rail, and glanced at her reflection in the mirror. On her arm was a row of red blotches. If she was being paranoid like before, she'd say they looked like finger marks. That was even more ridiculous. Not possible. Just her mind playing tricks. Something she'd have to live with. As she stepped into the shower, she reminded herself the awful drugs she'd taken before were not the answer.

Chapter Eight

Wednesday, 24 March, 1869

As Ellen entered the building, she blinked and adjusted her focus to the shadows surrounding her. The woman next to her began to twitch and raised her voice to match the not-so-welcoming din that echoed through the gloom. Bodies jostled her on all sides. She staggered along the hallway to where the corridors intersected. To the right, inmates lined the seemingly endless gallery as though on display. Some were motionless, others swayed to and fro. Manic laughter erupted from scattered figures as though they were sharing a private joke by unnatural means. A man, standing near the corner, scolded an unseen companion.

But it was the humiliation still to come that dominated Ellen's thoughts. She struggled to stay calm. A burly female warder, a few feet ahead, stepped in a puddle then kicked out at the cowering figure at the edge of it. Ellen hesitated, unsure what to do, but a shove from behind propelled her into a room on the left-hand side. The men who arrived with her were already there. Chancer, his trousers torn and bloody, caught her eye. He put his finger to his mouth and shook his head. She nodded, gave him a quick smile and waited. The head woman entered through another door, followed by her troop of uniformed staff. Bill Callahan, with his lethal-looking bludgeon, came in last.

The woman stepped forward and stared with overt displeasure at the group before her. In a jarring voice, she introduced herself as the Matron of Belle Vue. Ellen listened as Mrs. Fishburn droned her way through a long list of rules and regulations. Punishments for disobedience would be rigidly enforced. At this, the Matron cast her eyes toward the selection of manacles and straight waistcoats hanging on the walls. Ellen shivered but noticed most of her fellow travelers were oblivious to the meaning of the Matron's words. Silent beyond a few grunts, eyes rolled, heads nodded, limbs jerked, and mouths dribbled. Chancer kept his eyes fixed on Mrs. Fishburn, and she did the same.

The Matron rubbed the back of her waist as though her corset was causing discomfort. She introduced Bill Callahan. Ellen kept her eyes down but couldn't block the image of him ogling her naked body. A sour taste rose in her throat.

"Before you're taken to your wards, collect your asylum clothes from the orderlies." Mrs. Fishburn nodded at two unsmiling attendants who each held a pile of indeterminate garments. "Your own clothes will be returned when you leave. Change immediately. We like uniformity in looks, as in manner."

No mention of hosing down. Ellen frowned wondering when that would happen. The Matron peered at the sheet of paper she held. Names were called, clothes issued, attendants led their groups of patients away.

"Grady, Ellen."

She edged forward. "Yes, Mrs. Fishburn."

"You are a papist?"

"Yes, ma'am."

Mrs. Fishburn licked her thin lips and her left eyebrow arched its disdain. "We have a number here. There are separate services for the likes of you in the room next door each morning."

The Matron looked down at page again. "Craven, she's yours. In with the epileptic Stubbs. Might as well make at least one of these pauper lunatics useful."

A heavyset woman with the shadowy beginnings of a moustache and several thick hairs sprouting from a large mole on the side of her face lurched toward Ellen. The shelf of her large bosom rose and fell with every step. Her cap had fallen forward over her forehead exposing a dark rim of grime around its fold and the fingers that pushed it back left more grubby marks on the once white fabric.

"Grady, me name's Annie Craven. Mrs. Craven to the likes of you."

Before Ellen could react, the woman snatched her bag. She dropped it on the floor and kicked it into the corner. "Take yer pile of clothes and follow me."

The orderly shoved an untidy bundle into Ellen's arms as the ward supervisor stomped toward the door. Fearing what was coming next, she trailed behind the woman's bulbous backside as it disappeared through the opening.

The corridor was less crowded than before. A woman, leaning awkwardly against the rough brick wall, wore a thick calico shift with one long sleeve at the front so her hands and arms were both hidden and constrained by the material. She flapped the tube uselessly up and down. Her face was sheathed with sweat and her hair stuck out like tufts of dry grass in a neglected garden. An unearthly drone emerged from her drooling mouth. She paid no one any attention and no one paid any attention to her.

Ellen climbed the stairs with Mrs. Craven. Many of those she'd seen in the corridor seemed to have moved to the stairway, though why she couldn't comprehend. Guttural sounds spilled from gaping mouths. Blank staring faces. Several times, Annie Craven shoved a patient aside like an annoying skittle that shouldn't be left standing.

"When are we going to be hosed down?" Ellen asked, her voice shaky and hesitant.

"Wot?" The woman's piggy eyes twisted in her direction. "Hosed down? Don't you know water's scarce here? Yer'll be lucky to get one bath a month, let alone a bleeding 'ose down."

Still wary, Ellen followed the woman and digested this information.

Annie Craven wheezed as she struggled up each step. Although cool, rivulets of sweat meandered down her face. When she reached the second floor, the supervisor stopped and leaned over, catching her breath. Creaking herself upright, she jabbed her finger at the corridors in front of her. "Up 'ere, in my ward, there are four dormitories with about a hundred beds in each. Then there's a few old storerooms made into singles fer private patients, but now they're fer two, some fer three. There's two water closets and one bathroom on this floor fer the lot o'yer."

That didn't sound so bad, thought Ellen. Surely Bill would be too busy to worry about her in such a large and crowded place. If she could avoid him, perhaps everything would be all right after all.

"What do we do during the day?" she asked. "Do they give us any treatment? The Matron didn't make it sound like we saw a doctor much?"

Annie Craven snorted. "That's cos yer won't. There's one main doctor fer men and another fer the women. Ours is Doctor Johnson Nottidge and you'll be lucky to ever see him. Now work, you'll see plenty of. For the likes o'you, it'll be cleaning, washing, or if yer lucky, straw-plaiting. Whatever yer get, you'll need lots of stamina and a pair of hands with tough old leather on them." She sniggered, and added, 'The aim is ter keep yous all occupied and out of mischief. Don't seem to work, though. Another baby due this week."

"How on earth did that happen?" Ellen asked, her anxiety surfacing once more.

Mrs. Craven shrugged. "Who knows and who cares? But you'll keep yer legs closed, if y'know what's good for you. Last new mother here died in childbirth and her baby disappeared two days later."

Annie Craven halted and turned to Ellen. "You'll be sharing with Harriet Stubbs. Nice enough, 'bout yer age. Yer lucky yer not in a dormitory. Some of the things that go on in them after dark, well, keep to yer room. Eyes, mouth, and ears shut. Harriet'll show yer the ropes. Her father pays, but she needs watching. That's why yer been put there." She waddled to an open door and stood outside.

"Harriet!" she bellowed.

Ellen dared not raise her hopes. Someone who could be a new friend would be more than she could wish for. She waited nervously for Harriet to appear.

A slight young woman with light-brown eyes and pale features emerged from the room. Mrs. Craven let out a large burp. Instinctively, Ellen kept her face straight. She glanced at Harriet and saw her doing the same. The hint of a smile they shared buoyed Ellen's cautious longing.

She stole a look at the ward supervisor, but Mrs. Craven was glaring down the corridor, her attention elsewhere. With a sharp instruction for Harriet to sort Ellen out, she lumbered off. Ellen followed Harriet into her new quarters.

Two narrow iron bedsteads were positioned side by side with a small wooden cupboard on the left of each. Nothing else.

Ellen took off her coat and laid it on the bed nearest the door which Harriet said was hers. Ellen changed into the plain gray dress, its material rough and itchy against her skin. It hung loosely on her. She smiled at Harriet and raised her eyebrows. "One size fits all."

She put on the apron and tied the dingy white headscarf over her hair. She squeezed past Harriet's bed and stood at the barred window. The front of the grounds spread out below her. "This place is so big. I hope I can find my way round." She turned back to Harriet, perched on the edge of her bed, and asked, "How long have you been here?"

"Since it opened. Before that, I was at a private asylum. I'm twenty now and I went there just before my twelfth birthday."

Ellen lowered her voice. "The Matron said you have epilepsy. Can't they cure you?"

"No, and my fits are getting worse. I shall probably die here or at some other asylum if I ever move from this one."

"Oh, Harriet. How awful for you. Do you see much of your Ma and—"

Harriet cut in, "My mother died when I was eight and Father couldn't cope when the fits started. Since then, he's paid an asylum to do the coping. I think I'm better off in a place like this. I'm more normal than most here, rather than being a freak to be stared at or spat on in the street."

Ellen took Harriet's hand. "I hope we can be good friends. I'll keep a watch on you and you can help me. It's a bit frightening not knowing anyone in such a strange place."

Harriet clasped Ellen's hand tighter. "I'll teach you the rules here, too. They don't accept not knowing them, you'll still get punished. Mrs. Fishburn's husband runs the asylum, but neither bothers about how we're treated. Some of the warders are very cruel. Others are all right, but Belle Vue is too crowded now. There's no time for the staff to help everyone, even if they wanted to. I'll show you who to steer clear of. Unfortunately, there are a lot."

Ellen picked up the final item given to her by the orderly and tied the dark blue scarf around her neck. As she folded her clothes, she briefly told Harriet about her unfortunate connection to Bill Callahan and what he'd said to her about being hosed down.

Harriet stiffened, and her mouth curved downward. "Whatever you do, keep away from him."

"Why? What's he done? He hasn't hurt you, has he?"

"No, but he's vicious. I saw him take his cosh to a patient who soiled himself. The poor man never walked again. He hasn't noticed me yet, and I hope to God he never does. Patients here have died in odd circumstances or disappeared. Word is Bill Callahan is involved."

Ellen and Harriet shared an unspoken glance. Her fears sidled out of the shadows to taunt her again. She was going to need her new friend more than she expected.

A bell tolled five. Harriet stood and tucked a stray hair under her scarf.

"Dinner."

Ellen, who hadn't eaten all day, relished the prospect of any sort of food. She quickly pushed her clothes into her cupboard and followed Harriet out into the corridor. Mrs. Craven and another attendant herded a group of women, muttering and swaying, three or four abreast toward the top of the stairs. Two women wearing locked canvas dresses, who Ellen hadn't noticed before, were seated on the floor. One stared wide eyed at the dingy wall opposite her. Her elbows were flexed out in front of her and, but for the pill-rolling movement of her thumb and forefinger on each hand, nothing else moved. The other smiled at her companion and seemingly ignored any possible distractions. Such as dinner.

Harriet told Ellen that Fanny and Rose would only be fed if the staff remembered. It depended how busy they were. Ellen wondered out loud whether to take some food back for them just in case, but the expression on Harriet's face put paid to that. They trailed behind the gaggle of women heading down the stairs.

The trencher of dun-colored mush served to them in the main hall was yet another disappointment but as ever, Ellen was ravenous. With a grimace, she picked out a black beetle then grabbed her spoon and ate. Like the rows and rows of the other diners—men on one side, women on the other, all dressed alike—she kept silent.

When the bell sounded the end of dinner, she and Harriet rose. They shuffled forward, carried along by the scrummage of the other patients and attendants. Toward the rear of the dining hall, a familiar voice bellowed Harriet's name and Ellen turned in its direction. Mrs. Craven, her expression surly, beckoned them. She and Harriet joined the rest of the ragbag collection from their ward. As the women shambled at varying speeds along the corridor, the volume of the chattering increased.

Ellen was about to explain to Harriet about Mary arranging for her to come to Belle Vue when an attendant she hadn't seen before, stepped into her path. She and Harriet stopped abruptly. The moving traffic careened around them. The man snickered, a low repellent sound. Ignoring Harriet, he slithered toward Ellen. She leaned back, but his greasy face loomed in, too close for comfort.

"I'm gonna look after yer for Bill, too." He grabbed his crotch.

"Ain't you the lucky one?"

His other hand reached out and pinched her breast. She cringed back. The man slid against her, and then moved on, until only the memory of his repulsive snickering remained.

Ellen shuddered. She caught Harriet's horrified expression.

"Oh, Lord, this isn't good, Ellen. That's Lynton Brown. He's Bill Callahan's Deputy and just as loathsome. His only talent is using those metal tipped boots of his, so keep away from him if you can."

Chapter Nine

Monday, 8 December
PRESENT DAY

Marianne jabbed the doorbell for the fifth time.

"Come on, Claire," she muttered, "It's freezing out here."

She pressed the button again and held it down. When her finger threatened to lose all feeling, she removed it and blew on her hands. It had been warm on the bus, but after her walk up the long drive to Belle Vue's front entrance, she didn't fancy standing in the cold without good reason. She half-jogged to the edge of the step and looked toward the chapel. She'd noticed a flash of blue and white on her way up, but from this direction she had a better view. A stream of tape circling a couple of trees at the back of the small church fluttered in the wind. When she got in the warm and thawed out, she'd ask Claire about it. Marianne trotted back to the door. Another jab, then another.

"Hello?" A groggy voice crackled through the intercom.

"Claire, are you okay?"

"Just woke up. Christ, what time is it?"

"Worry about that later. Let me in before I go numb."

The buzzer sounded. She hurried inside and made her way to the second floor. This time, before she could press the button, the door opened. Claire, ashen-faced and disheveled, stood clutching at her bathrobe. It swamped her frame. Marianne frowned. Normally, her friend could go through a wind tunnel and still come out looking immaculate. Today, she was a mess.

Claire gave a half-hearted smile and stepped back to let her through. "Can you make me some coffee while I get dressed? Really strong, please."

Marianne walked into the sitting room and wrinkled her nose. Before starting on the coffee, she retrieved a can of air freshener from under the sink and liberally sprayed both rooms. As she prepared the drinks, Marianne heard Claire come in behind her.

"That's better. Human once more."

She turned her head and noted Claire's hair and face were almost back in place. She picked up the mugs of coffee and put them on the breakfast bar. "Yep, I recognize you now. You said how tired you'd been the other night, but I never expected you'd sleep this late. Did you take any pills?"

"No. I must have a bug or something. Some nights are better than others."

Marianne raised her eyebrows. "You are planning to pass this year? Sleep is only optional you know." She could see Claire still looked drawn. She ought to keep more of an eye on her, just in case.

"Ha, ha. I actually had a quiet Sunday. Didn't see Alex, but we talked on the phone and I've almost got my head round his Christmas plans. He did a lot of making up on Saturday, but he knows he's got a lot more to do. Hopefully, while he's away, he won't fall for some pole dancer or whatever they get up to over there. Do they have pole dancers in Verbier?" Claire asked, a wan smile on her face.

"Dunno. Never been." Marianne pulled out a stool for Claire. "What's with the tape round the chapel?"

"Sally told me something odd has been dug up. Apparently, Eric knows what it's all about but isn't allowed to say anything yet." Claire tutted and rolled her eyes. "You'd think he was a spy the way he carries on."

"I never did like that chapel. I know my memory has probably exaggerated the whole thing, but I thought it creepier than the derelict asylum." Marianne took a sip of coffee. "Let me know as soon as you hear anything else. I'm intrigued."

"Me too. The Residents' Association meeting is tonight. I'm sure to find out then." She leaned back and yawned. "I'll be so glad when term ends on Friday. Give us both time to catch up and do some girly stuff together. When's Debs arriving?"

Pause. Marianne inhaled and hoped Claire would go along with her news. "Erm, there's a slight change of plan. Debs rang to say she's going to do some work for the cancer charity she's joined at uni. She's wanted to do something ever since Mum died. Every year there's a weeklong Christmas treat for orphans who are in remission so, instead of Debs coming here, I'm going to stay with her for a few days, then help collect the kids for their holiday. Please say you'll come. We'll have a great time."

The last thing she expected from Claire were tears. Alex might have spoiled her plans, but this was different. They'd still be together. "Come on, Claire. Think what these kids have been through. We can make their Christmas special. Some of them might not see another."

Claire wiped her eyes. "I'm sorry, but I can't help my feelings. It's not how I imagined spending Christmas. You always were a big softy. Look how much care you took of your mother."

Marianne's memories of that year painfully surfaced. She breathed in hard, determined not to let her emotions get the better of her. "Mum would have been chuffed Debs and I are doing something like this. I'm looking forward to it. Claire, what do you say?"

"I'm not sure. I'll think about it, but the thought of a long journey and all those kids sounds more than I can cope with at the moment."

"Okay, see how you feel and let me know."

When Alex caught sight of Claire as she made her way down the stairs, he was relieved to see she looked more like her usual fabulous self in a form-hugging T-shirt and long skirt with a low-belt snug around her hips. The twinkle in her eyes made him tingle in all the right places. From the step below hers, he reached out and hugged her to him. She gave him a quick kiss. He lifted her to the floor and they made their way to the basement.

"Let's sit at the back so I can see who says what without straining my neck. Okay?"

"Sure," Claire said. "And it'll be easy to sneak out if it gets too boring."

The first person Alex saw as they entered the exercise-cum-meeting room was Eric Beamish, Belle Vue Residents' Association's volunteer Chairman. He stood at the front, behind a long table, and was speaking to Emma. She appeared to be listening intently, nodding like one of those toy dogs in the back of a car.

A faint residue from the last class remained, the sweaty pong familiar to any gym enthusiast. He hoped Moira Bradigan would be here but, as his eyes swept round the room, he couldn't see her. More people came through the door and he guided Claire to two empty seats against the back wall. He saw Claire wave at a woman who'd just entered, wearing an array of branded clothes and accessories as though she was a mobile advertisement. Claire introduced her neighbor Sally Reichenberg.

"Hi, y'all." Sally air-kissed Claire, then Alex when he'd been introduced. She sat down and leaned forward to speak to Claire. "Still on for coffee tomorrow?"

Before Claire could reply, a loud voice yelling, "Silence!" cut across the general chit-chat. It made no impact. He watched in amusement as Eric raised the hooter in his hand, and a series of loud honks rent the air. All eyes turned to the front and conversation ceased.

Alex laughed and whispered to Claire, "Well, that sure worked."

Eric stood tall like a latter-day Thomas Arnold surveying his boys before he delivered the Sunday sermon. He spent the next twenty minutes grinding through the previous meeting's minutes. Bored, Alex looked round the instant he caught the movement of the door opening. Moira Bradigan stepped into the room. She stood ramrod straight, wearing a haughty expression that bore not the slightest sign of discomfort or apology for her late arrival. Although she'd made no disruptive sounds, it was as though her presence generated the magnetism to propel all eyes in her direction. Eric's voice trailed off and he filled the void with some unnecessary throat clearing.

Miss Bradigan turned her steely gaze to the man seated closest to the entrance. At the barest tip of her head, he got up and offered her his chair. As she took it, almost as one the audience turned back to Eric and he resumed speaking.

Alex had watched the scene with growing fascination. Claire edged forward in her seat. She peered at Miss Bradigan from behind the curtain of her silvery blond hair. He nudged her and keeping his voice low, told her he'd try to catch Miss Bradigan before they left. He heard her sharp intake of breath. She twisted back to face him, a look of disbelief on her face.

"That's her? You're not going to believe this," she uttered softly and then explained. Small world, he thought, followed by the scary image of facing Moira Bradigan after nearly running her down on a dark night. He felt his balls tighten.

Eric thanked his wife profusely for all her hard work and moved to the main item on the agenda. At this point, the meeting livened up since most people, including Claire and Sally, were present solely to complain about their personal snagging issues. Alex was surprised by how many. Emma scribbled away as though on speed, and he was pleased all the problems Claire had experienced were now logged into the system for action.

Finally, Eric moved on to "Other Matters Arising (Not Covered by the Agenda)." Keen to get his business dealt with, Alex stood and waved his arm like a giant windscreen wiper. Eric gave him the floor. He said his piece but, as he sat down again, felt his long shot wasn't likely to produce much of a result. As he'd scanned the audience's faces, none showed anything but polite disinterest. Moira Bradigan never looked in his direction.

"Oh, well. It was worth a try." Claire patted his knee. She gave him a rueful smile which he returned with a shrug. He leaned over and whispered in her ear, "I'm going to need a lot of cheering up." But his timing was off.

"Sshh. Sshh." Claire put her finger to her mouth as Eric spoke again. With the likelihood of the meeting reverting to its earlier tedium, he sat back on the plastic chair and let the words wash over him.

"You may have noticed an area round the chapel has been cordoned off. The vicar's Great Dane dug up a large bone." Eric paused dramatically and puffed out his chest like a preening rooster. "Of course, the reverend brought it straight to me. I thought it looked like a human thigh bone, so we called the police immediately."

An expectant silence engulfed the room. Alex's boredom disappeared.

With the audience's full attention, Eric continued, "I've been liaising with them ever since. They called the coroner in and taped off the area. All very exciting." He paused milking every drop of suspense.

A hush fell over the hall. Alex looked toward Miss Bradigan. Her rigid posture, her frown, her clenched fists, her fixed gaze all exuded an anxiety he did not expect or understand.

Emma nudged her husband. Eric coughed then took a long sip of water. Alex held his breath.

"However, to cut a long story short." Eric's voice reflected his dismay at such a wasted opportunity. "My fifteen minutes of fame never started ticking. After all that, it was only an animal bone." Eric hurried on as audience tension collapsed like a deflating balloon. "You'll be pleased to know though the Reverend Snedley's wound isn't serious and he has vowed never to part his dog Snaffles from a bone again."

The widespread laughter brought a welcome relaxing moment before Eric moved to the next item. He explained with tortuous detail the requirement for everyone to supply him with their emergency contact details. Needing a distraction at this point, Alex leaned forward and turned his head. All he saw was the empty spot where, only minutes ago, Moira Bradigan had been seated. Bugger. After sitting through this whole bloody meeting, he'd missed her.

What to do now? He knew she'd never make the first approach. He wondered if he should knock on her door and ask if she'd speak to him. Did he really want to face the scary version of She Who Must Be Obeyed? Or should he forget about it for now and get cozy with Claire?

Alex couldn't believe he was actually hesitating. Like he was the lead member of Masochists Anonymous. She probably wouldn't be able to help him much, but then again, maybe. Claire put her slender fingers on his knee and stroked his leg. As she gave him a lazy, provocative smile, his body made the decision for him. He caught her eye and nodded toward the door.

They rose from their seats and mouthed their goodbyes to Sally. With Eric still in full flight, they slipped out, quietly shutting the door behind then.

For those of a drinking persuasion, college parties deemed 'great' usually resulted in colossal hangovers. The previous night's Food and Wine Society Christmas bash was no exception. Claire gazed at Alex with little discernible sympathy as he sat at the breakfast bar nursing a strong black coffee.

It wouldn't have been so bad, she thought, if he'd limited his alcohol consumption to the party, but Gary, Paul, Marianne, and a few others had joined them back at her flat with the sole aim of demolishing the booze left over from the housewarming. Now he was paying the price. With her halo intact and the time almost two o'clock, she couldn't resist needling him a bit. Besides, she was hungry.

"I'm going to make some bacon and eggs. Do you fancy any?" She laughed as she caught the queasy expression that crossed his features. "I'll take that as a no then?"

A pained grunt was his sole response.

As she started cooking, Alex did make a move. He groaned, got up, and switched on the cooker hood fan, before muttering he was going back to bed. "I do love you but please keep the kitchen door shut," he said on his way out.

She assembled her breakfast-cum-lunch and polished off the lot. Only the thought of tidying up the mess from last night slowed her down. Since they hadn't gone to bed until nearly six, she was still dog-tired, but joining Alex for a nap now would mean facing it later and, most likely, not being able to sleep tonight.

With a cloth in one hand and a tray in the other, Claire reluctantly made a start in the sitting room.

More than half an hour later, she carried a box of bits and pieces down to the basement storage area. She hovered uncertainly in the corridor. The eerie quietness gave her the jitters. The pool incident and the man on the stairs had left their mark. Best to get moving.

She put the box under her arm and took out her key. As she opened the door, a subtle smell caught her attention. Garlic? How odd. She didn't keep any food down here. She ignored it and switched on the light. The things she treasured most almost filled the space: items belonging to her parents she'd chosen to keep but couldn't fit upstairs. One day, she'd have to decide what to do with them. For now, they were piled up in neat rows with a list of contents taped to the front of each. Courtesy of Marianne.

Claire stepped inside and placed the box on the floor. She was about to push it closer to the others with her foot when she caught a movement from above. Instinctively, she looked up. A flash of black. Something dropped onto her shoulder.

She let out a screech and leaped back, her fingers brushing blindly at her shirt. Looking down at the floor, she screwed up her face in disgust as she saw a huge spider scuttle between the cartons. She peered at the ceiling. A cobweb hung across the gap between the rows of boxes, ready to trap any unwary prey. The spider must have been in one of the crates of her parent's stuff. A few more were probably lurking around.

She'd have to summon her courage and spray the place. Or ask Alex.

Shivering with revulsion, she pressed the toe of her shoe against the box, keen to give it a final shove and get back upstairs. A faint breeze brushed her cheek. Still jumpy, she twisted round. Her view of the corridor quickly narrowed, and the door clicked shut. Damn. The box was fine where it was. She took a first step then halted at a more ominous sound: of a key, the key she'd left in the lock, turning.

"Hey, stop that."

She jolted forward. Bloody joker. The lights suddenly went out, stopping her dead. Claire sucked in her breath. She looked where the gap at the bottom of the door should be but instead of a comforting line of light, total darkness now surrounded her. She fought to stay calm. Bad enough having a power failure in her own flat with loads of people around, but not down here with some moron playing games.

"Let me out," she yelled. A deep brooding silence was the only response. She held her hand out in front of her and took a tiny step. Her stomach lurched as she remembered the spider.

She shuffled forward till her fingers touched a hard surface. It should be the door but it didn't feel right. This felt like rough wood, and the door to her lockup was metal. Heart pounding, she moved her fingers to where the light switch ought to be. She felt a slight dip where the door ended and the wall began, but no sensation of smooth plaster. Only something cold and rough, like stone.

She frantically skimmed her shaking fingers across the alien surface. This was real, this was real, this was real.

A chain rattled behind her.

"Let me out. Let me out!" she shrieked.

The clanging of metal on stone grew more insistent. Now too, not just garlic, but a dreadful stink like something rotting down a sewer. A thousand tiny ice spiders crawled over her flesh. She cringed back against the wall as though, by some miracle, she could force herself through it. Something scurried over her foot and she flinched. Not a spider, heavier, like a rat.

Oh, dear God, no.

She screamed again. Louder this time.

As she slid to the floor, her heaving sobs couldn't cover the pitiful cries for help from the middle of the room.

"Claire, Claire, wake up."

Alex's voice. She felt him shaking her. God, she felt awful. She opened her eyes, then closed them against the glare of the overhead light.

"I can't believe you fell asleep down here? Do you know what time it is?"

He sounded concerned, but when she squinted up at him, his eyes twinkled with amusement. She looked round the room. All the boxes were in place.

"It was so dark. Someone locked the door."

"Well, I found it open. The lights were all on and you, dare I say it, were gently snoring, dead to the world." Alex chuckled.

When he asked what she'd been up to, Claire blamed her red eyes and comatose state on lack of sleep and too much booze the night before.

She kept her rising fear unspoken. Alex and Marianne could not know she was weak, that the mind games were taking over again, that she was falling apart. Belle Vue was supposed to be lucky for her: a secure place and refuge from the past. Now it seemed increasingly to be her nightmares made real. She fixed a smile to her face and took Alex's outstretched hand. As he led her upstairs, she remembered all the advice the psychiatrists had given her and planned how to keep her sanity.

Chapter Ten

Thursday, 22 April, 1869

Mary finished the last of her eel pie. She wiped her lips and took another mouthful of ale. The London & North Western Railway service she'd taken from King's Cross to St. Albans arrived well before noon in good time for lunch. Bill had met her at the station as instructed and they were now seated in the White Hart Inn partaking of a light repast.

She smirked at her future brother-in-law. The blank mask of his expression gave nothing away. Well, neither would she. He didn't intimidate her. She had plans for Bill, just as she had plans for Jack—and Ellen, of course. Her half-sister had been at Belle Vue over two months now. She seemed to spend much of her time composing letters asking her to visit and complaining it wasn't what she expected. No doubt, Lady Muck would expect her to listen to her endless whining. She was curious to see the asylum after all this time, though.

She sat back in her chair and raised her arm to pat her vibrant coiffure. In the crowded pub, Bill's weren't the only eyes feasting on the twin mounds as they strained against the crimson fabric. He licked his lips. She slowly moved her hips from side to side as though seeking a more comfortable position. Her gaze never left Bill's. She could feel the heat coming from him. Good. Brain disengaged, putty for her to mold, so now to business. For the moment, the show was over. She stilled and cast a sardonic eye in his direction.

"So, Bill, how is poor Ellen taking to asylum life? Not too hard for her, I hope?"

Bill showed a few teeth, but the mask remained in place. "I've had

Brown and others make life more difficult than usual for her and the little friend she shares a room with. I keep watch on her, too. She's unsettled now, nervous what might happen. Just like you said. We made a deal. I'll stick with it."

She gulped some more ale and digested Bill's words. "Keep it up. By the time you and I have finished with her, anything I suggest will be the favored choice."

His eyes strayed to her breasts again. "As long as you keep your side of the bargain."

"Of course." She ran her tongue over her lips, mimicking Bill. "We, my friend, are in this together. Body and soul, but if Jack hears a word, or even if he decides he's not the marrying type, you'll find yourself missing a few body parts. The important ones. I'll hack them off while you watch. Understand?"

"Aye, that I do. I like women who put up a fight, makes it more exciting." The teeth appeared again.

"We'll see," she said.

Mary pushed back her chair and rose to full height. She arched her back as though to ease the stiffness of sitting. Well aware of the attention such a movement attracted from those whose brains were firmly lodged in their trousers, she slowly bent forward, pushing her bottom out as she did so. She caressed Bill's lips with her own and snaked her tongue into his mouth. Her audience gasped, then collectively held its breath. She moved back a fraction, her tongue visible and pressed in firmly. As they kissed, she took his free hand and used it to stroke her buttocks.

Mary pulled back suddenly and brushed Bill's hand away, catching him and the fascinated onlookers, unawares. Bill added his voice to the communal groan of frustration. Her lips curled. "I'll see you outside the gate at four and we can finish what we started."

She picked up her drawstring purse from the table and sashayed out of the bar, confident that only when she could be seen no more would any conversation resume.

She hired a carriage to Belle Vue, having parted Jack from most of yesterday's earnings at the Green Hog. From Ellen's letters, the Matron sounded like a snob of the worse sort. Mary knew the type and itched to teach Madam Fishburn a lesson or two.

She spent the journey reflecting on some of the information Bill had passed to her about the asylum. It sounded like a den of depravity and abuse, not a hospital. Oh dear, poor Ellen. Some of the things he and the attendants got up to with the inmates were just as she would have expected. Even one of the doctors had found a novel and lucrative use for them. The Fishburn woman and her husband were nothing more than a pair of clod pates.

So, while at Belle Vue, she would keep a lookout and see if she could find other ways to prosper from Ellen in her new place of residence. Insurance would pay out but once. She'd only set that in motion if she was sure Ellen couldn't be of any more use.

Without bothering to knock, Johnson Nottidge opened the door of Samuel Fishburn's office and strolled in. Two disapproving sets of eyes greeted him.

Nottidge met Adelaide Fishburn's lemon-tinged gaze. He gave her a knowing look in return and a brief nod. If she had feathers they would have bristled. A puzzled expression creased her brow but at least she held her tongue. Her husband, after a pointed glance at the clock on the ornate marble mantelpiece, true to form started to babble.

"Come in, come in, Doctor Nottidge. Most unsavory. Most unsavory. Ha ha. Not you, of course." Nottidge noted the telling pause. "But this most unfortunate turn of events. Who could have done such an unspeakable thing? And on the day I have such important visitors coming." Samuel Fishburn's florid complexion reddened even more. "Of course, we must ensure no word gets out about this. We need more paying lunatics, but if they—or rather their kin—thought that…"

Nottidge didn't bother to stifle his yawn which amusingly made the Matron bristle all the more. He lowered himself onto the leather chair and adjusted his cravat while Fishburn prattled on. He half-listened as the Fishburns pored over the fate of one of the inmates—a violent madman who, by all accounts, repeatedly tore off his clothes, sniffed round the women like a priapic weasel, and caused no end of problems. Now he'd gotten himself torched like a human sacrifice and his body had been found outside the chapel that morning. Nottidge kept his focus on more interesting matters: a party at his club in London tonight. Now there would be a fire display worth watching.

In the end, the Matron departed to visit the dying man and Nottidge was left facing the dyspeptic countenance of the Medical Superintendent. He flicked a speck of dust from his coat and regarded Fishburn with barely suppressed irritation. The man, as ever, refused to meet his eye, and instead shuffled the pile of papers in front of him.

"Now to more pressing matters, Doctor Nottidge. How are things going with Doctor Lush? Have you shown him the ropes? Quick on the uptake, is he?"

Nottidge's eyebrow flicked upward. Months ago, Fishburn had tried to pass on the responsibility of dealing with the new Resident Medical Officer to him. Doctor Sheridan Lush had been at Belle Vue for nearly half a year now and had yet to have a full review.

"To be honest, I wouldn't know, Fishburn." Nottidge took out a silk handkerchief and patted his lips. Fishburn glowered at him.

"*Doctor* Fishburn, if you please. Don't let me remind you again."

Nottidge noted how quickly the man spoke as if fearful he might add the critical "or what?" that would expose the emptiness of his words.

"Could you please clarify your statement, Doctor Nottidge."

"Well, my time has been fully engaged. Women require so much more attention than men, don't you know. I have only spoken to Doctor Lush once or twice, but I think he disagrees with my, nay, *our* philosophy about these defectives."

"You may be correct. This is the man's first posting. He still wears a novice's cloak of goodwill toward those who are, in truth, well beyond the pale."

"He's a taciturn cove, too. I don't like that. If he's not talking then he must be thinking, not necessarily good for us, or for Belle Vue. You and your wife must keep the paymasters content. We don't need any unnecessary boat rocking."

Fishburn nodded.

Nottidge thought for a moment. "The burnt lunatic—is he able to speak?"

"No. Nothing. Only the most terrible screaming." Fishburn paused, then resumed at full pace. "Can you please check on Doctor Lush and make sure he sedates the man so none of the visitors due today can hear any the ruckus. Or hide him in the basement if he lasts that long. We don't want any adverse comments reaching the Asylum Board."

Fishburn cleared his throat and ran his fingers round his high collar. "Doctor Nottidge, you must advise Doctor Lush as much as possible. The board's on about more cost cutting. Now you and I both know restraints are the best way of containing the defectives. They cost half as much as sedatives and you don't need to keep buying more to maintain the same effect. Doctor Lush apparently does not subscribe to this viewpoint."

A mocking smile crossed Nottidge's lips. "I'll bring some of the worst inmates from the basement for him to see. Maybe incite one to attack him. I have my ways, and I'm sure he'll change his tune soon enough."

"Good, good. No details." Fishburn curved his lips upward but his eyes remained fixed over Nottidge's shoulder. "Or broken bones, at least none on Doctor Lush. Just do it, please."

Fishburn rubbed his stomach and his mouth puckered. Nottidge had had enough. If he stayed longer the man would want yet another medical consultation. He got to his feet and made to leave. Then he remembered.

"Tell you what, *Doctor* Fishburn. I'll go see the lunatic and take care of matters for you." He made his way to the door.

Before he exited, he turned and smiled at the Medical Superintendent. "We'll call it a favor, another one."

Mary dismounted the carriage, drew herself up, and eyed the mansion in front of her. Fancy all this for a bunch of dribbling lunatics. If it wasn't for Bill divulging what went on here, she might feel envious of her half-sister. She stepped forward and pointedly gazed into the window at the woman who had been watching her since she'd arrived. Must be the one Ellen told her about. She saw the sour-faced hag start, then move quickly out of sight. One side of the double door was on its latch, so she pushed it open and strode into the hall. The starched string-bean stood on one side, clutching a handful of paper. Mary halted keen to put the Matron in her place. Neither woman moved.

At that moment, one of the carved arched doorways opened and a portly man entered the foyer. He gasped, and Mary watched in amusement as hand outstretched, he tapped a veritable polka across the parquet. Mary caught Adelaide Fishburn's undisguised fury. That must be the crone's husband. Good. Let the fun begin.

"My dear young lady. I am Doctor Samuel Fishburn, the Medical Superintendent of Belle Vue," he said, giving her a flirtatious smile. "How very nice to have so attractive a guest at my hospital." He took Mary's proffered hand and bent forward as though to kiss it.

"Doctor Fishburn!" Adelaide's strident tones rang out across the hall as she charged toward him. "Your time is too important for socializing with a relative of one of our pauper lunatics." Adelaide's raised voice carefully enunciated each word. She smiled at Mary as though trying to muster all her superiority.

Mary grasped Fishburn's hand tighter and breathed deeply so her breasts rose and fell to great effect.

"Doctor Fishburn. A pleasure to make your acquaintance." She flicked a dismissive eye at the glowering Matron. "Your hireling is correct, but I do enjoy meeting important, handsome men."

The man preened like a fat popinjay. She laughed, and he puffed out his chest even more. His dried-up wife looked as though she wanted to spit.

"Do hurry, husband, dear." Snide glance in Mary's direction. "You're needed in the men's section. Doctor Lush said he must see you. Immediately." With a few deft pushes at Fishburn's arm, Adelaide separated the two. Fishburn's mouth gaped like a hooked fish, but before he could do or say anything, she firmly maneuvered him toward the rear doorway.

Her nose quivering like a cranky rat, Adelaide turned back to Mary. "I trust if you visit your relative in future, you'll come by the back entrance. Get her to show you where it is. Charity case visitors are *not* permitted to use the front. Now, follow me and I'll take you to the main dining room where your sister is still waiting."

Before Adelaide could move forward, Mary put out her arm to stop her. "My *half*-sister might be a charity case as you call it, but *I* am not. When I visit again, I will use the front entrance. A friend of mine has the ear of a few members of the Asylum Board. I don't think they'd be impressed at some of the things going on here, do you? I know all about them and not from my relative, either."

The color leached from the Matron's already pasty face. A little stretching of the truth never hurt.

"I could make your life very difficult, *Mrs. Fishburn*."

She almost laughed at the hatred burning in the woman's eyes.

"Miss Grady. You have *my* permission *for the moment*. Follow me." With a face like thunder, Adelaide stuck her nose in the air and hastened toward a paneled door. Mary sauntered behind.

As soon as she stepped through to the dining room, Mary heard her name called. Ellen, wearing a drab outfit, trotted up to her, one half of a matching pair. The twin trailed behind. The rest of the occupants gaped at her as though they were looking at a new and interesting specimen in the London Zoo.

"Oh, Mary, it's so wonderful to see you. This is Harriet, my dearest friend." Ellen's words tumbled out, her eyes glistening with excitement and happiness.

She stepped back as Ellen reached for her and told the other girl to disappear.

Adelaide spoke directly to Ellen. "Take your sister for a walk. Show her the grounds. She looks like she needs some fresh air. I shall watch from the belvedere."

The Matron didn't wait for a reply, but Mary made sure she could hear her laughter as the woman bustled toward the main hall as though late for an urgent appointment.

Better to be outside on a day like this, Mary thought, and get the visit over as quickly as possible. With Ellen beaming, they made their way to the rear exit.

A few clouds dotted the sky as though a blind man had cast indiscriminate splotches of white on a blue canvas. They walked down the path between the lines of majestic oaks and out into the open, the sun pleasantly warm. She turned back to take in the size of the building they'd just left and raised her eyes. Ellen followed suit.

"That's Mrs. Fishburn's favorite place," Ellen said. "Harriet says it's a belvedere. Only visitors the Matron deems worthy are invited there."

"Pah. Who cares? Let's continue our walk. I can't stay long."

Mary half-listened as Ellen babbled on about her new friend before a question brought her up short. Could she leave the asylum? Mary smiled to herself. Good old Bill.

"Mary, I don't like it here. I'd rather be at the Green Hog with you." Ellen said quietly. "And things happen. Things that aren't right."

As they continued along the path, Ellen's words poured out. She wanted to start a new life and felt well enough to do so. She could work at the pub, go into service or do something, anything, so as not to be a burden on her.

Mary now paid no attention to Ellen. Instead, she pulled up sharp and stared in shock at the man seated on one of the cast iron benches at the entrance to the rose garden. She felt as if the air had been sucked out of her.

After all this time.

A book lay open upon the man's lap, and his face was turned upward. His eyes were shut and whether he was asleep or enjoying the warmth of the sunshine, she couldn't tell.

Only that he wouldn't be enjoying it for long.

She felt Ellen tugging at her sleeve, asking in a hushed tone, "Mary, what's wrong?"

Ellen moved into her line of sight. "Mary, are you all right? What's the matter?"

Startled, Mary blinked as though a fairground mesmerist had just brought her out of her trance. She glanced over Ellen's shoulder once more, and then pivoted round so her back was toward the man. She kept her voice low. "Who's that on the bench? Do you know him?"

"That's Doctor Nottidge, Doctor Johnson Nottidge. He's in charge of all the women here. Why? What's wrong?"

"What else do you know about him? Tell me. Quickly."

Mary pushed Ellen toward one of seats under a nearby tree so they would be hidden from view.

"Harriet says he's an aristocrat. She overheard Doctor Fishburn and his wife discussing him."

"Anything else?"

Ellen looked uncomfortable. "Why are you so interested in him? Have you met him before?"

"You could say that." A flicker of pain of that long-held memory passed through her. This was not a time for weakness, she was always strong and now she would draw on that strength to deal with the man in front of her. "Ellen, tell me what else you know. I'm going to speak to this Doctor Nottidge and I want to make sure I'm prepared."

Her half-sister continued, "I only see him occasionally. There are more than a thousand women here, and he's the head doctor for all the females. There's Doctor Lush who is the same as Doctor Nottidge but for the men, and Mr. Fishburn is the—"

"I don't want to know the staffing structure of the asylum, thank you, dearie. Just tell me about Nottidge."

Mary pinched Ellen's thin arm so she couldn't draw away, forcing her to keep talking.

"He's always with Bill Callahan, who scares me, even if he's Jack's brother."

She looked sharply at Ellen—so selfish wanting only to talk about herself—and hissed. "Not now, later, tell me about Nottidge."

"I think Doctor Nottidge is going to be the next Lord Seton."

"I knew it. Seton. That name is carved into my soul." She let go of Ellen's arm. Her hands clenched like sculpted fists of marble.

"Mary, I don't like it here. It's not at all like you said. Will you help me, please?"

She was oblivious to Ellen's plea. She pushed her half-sister's hand away, "Leave me, Ellen. Go back and stay in the hall where we met. I'll come there when I'm finished. Go now."

Ellen hesitated. She opened her mouth but before she could speak, Mary repeated her order. The girl set off slowly toward the main building.

When Mary prayed, it was not to the Catholic God. Instead, she invoked Nemesis, the spirit of vengeful fate personified as a remorseless goddess. Her second demand was finally being answered. For the last seven years, she had buried her memories of Seton, but she had never forgotten a single moment of that night. She knew the measure of the man on the bench, but first, she needed to collect her thoughts and plan her approach.

So as to exact full retribution.

Chapter Eleven

Friday, 19 December
PRESENT DAY

"Hamish? Professor Quigly?" Alex knocked twice. He pushed open the door and peered into the spacious office.

His tutor's round ebony face beamed. Hamish placed the sheaf of papers he held on top of a pile of similar documents. He moved away from the neat rows of books lining the wall.

"Come in, come in," he beckoned Alex, with the merest trace of a Scottish lilt, fluttering his fingers like streamers in a wind tunnel.

Hamish nodded toward the green leather Chesterfield. Alex sat down and took out a wire-bound notebook and pen from his laptop case. Meanwhile, Hamish tidied the journals on the coffee table. Casting a rueful glance at his curious expression, Hamish gingerly seated himself on the matching armchair. "Piles," he said, with a grimace.

"Pardon?"

"Hemorrhoids, man. Bane of my life. Still when you get to over forty-five." Hamish chuckled. "Well, let's say fifty and leave it there." His hand lifted in the direction of his white-flecked afro. "If that's your only problem, you're lucky." He laughed, his dark eyes twinkling. "Now, lad, how are you progressing?"

Alex outlined the results of his efforts on asylums and Belle Vue since their last meeting nearly three weeks ago. Every now and then, his tutor scribbled on his own notepad, interspersed with some "Hmms," a few eyebrow raises, and a couple of frowns. When Alex ran out of steam, Hamish put down his pen and, with great care, sat back against the leather.

"Good. Good. I do like the idea of focusing on the first years of a particular asylum."

"But I'm a bit concerned," Alex said. "There doesn't seem to be much published specifically about Belle Vue for that period. Just one old book from the sixties. Penny Whitbread in the library found it for me. Been out of print for years."

Hamish's eyes took on a wistful expression. "Good old Penny. Nose of a bloodhound for long-lost tomes." He cleared his throat. "I might just have a useful reference for you."

Alex's pen hovered.

"Fellow called Trent published a book about asylums. Photographs mostly. He came here about eight or nine years ago and gave a talk to my students. Given he's local, he might have some information you can use."

As Alex jotted this down, Hamish riffled through a leather box on the table in front of him. He pulled out a card. "Here it is. Jeremy Trent."

He passed it to Alex, who saw there was only a phone number, no email or website. He turned the card over. 'Victorian Asylums: Then and Now. A Pictorial History' was scrawled on the back.

Alex looked up. "Can you remember anything about his presentation? Did he mention Belle Vue?"

Hamish raised his bushy eyebrows and murmured "hmm" again. "Yes."

A hesitant, drawn out yes. Alex wondered if maybe this wasn't such a good lead after all.

"But?"

"Let's just say he's thorough. If you can keep him on track, I'm sure he'll be a mine of information."

"So, it wasn't a great success?" Alex asked, giving a wry smile.

Hamish laughed. "Guaranteed insomnia cure. He could make a fortune. Even when he mentioned murder, no one sat up."

"Murder? At Belle Vue?" This was more like it.

"I think so. Bit hard to tell, and such a long time ago. I remember Trent rattling on about the architecture of the asylums then he veered onto patient treatment and cruelty. I'm sure amongst the various cases he mentioned something about a killing at Belle Vue."

"That's fantastic. I hope it was in my timeframe. It'll give my project an interesting perspective. Everyone likes murder stories, even academics."

Hamish laughed but accentuated his next words with a wagging finger. "Now remember lad, a single crime, if I'm correct about it, is not the whole show. It might not be relevant, so be careful not to get sidetracked."

"Okay, but I'm intrigued already." He wondered if Jeremy Trent referred to the lunatic from the 1950s, the murder he already knew about. There probably wouldn't have been more than one. Might not be worth the bother. Alex closed his notebook and got to his feet. As he put his things back into his case, he noticed Hamish's quizzical expression.

"Sorry. We had finished, hadn't we?"

"Of course, lad." Hamish used both hands on the chair arms to raise himself to his feet. He wiped a couple of beads of perspiration from his forehead. "I'll see you next month, Alex, and you can let me know what you find."

Alex thanked him and as he left his tutor's office, caught Hamish's last words, "My pleasure, lad. Always follow through. You never know where it might lead."

> From: Claire Ryan
> [Claire.ryan@hertscollege.ac.uk]
> Sent: Thurs 25/12 18:34
> To: Marianne Edwards
> Subject: !!!!!MERRY XMAS!!!!!
>
> Hi M. Merry Xmas! Hope you're having a

wicked day! Mine's not so bad tho not what I expected. :-(Just wanted to let u know I'm thinking of you—hope it all went well picking up the kids yesterday—I bet you'll need another rest after having 30 brats screaming at you all week! 😊

Thanx so much for the scarf- I love the color. Did you like your pressie? I hope you didn't open it until today!

Alex phoned from Verbier this morning. Sounded like the monkey compound at London Zoo. God knows what they've been up to, but Paul flies out tomorrow so hopefully he'll keep Alex at least in check. Paul fancies you like mad–you should do something about it!

Alex bought me the beautiful silver and turquoise bracelet I've been dropping hints about for ages (can't believe I didn't open it before today lol). I got him a book on asylums that weighs a ton (he asked for it)—riveting? Not! Still, he's happy.

Haven't done much, I'm so tired all of the time but I can't sleep, either. From the shouting and racket I keep hearing, my neighbors must be doing loads of entertaining—can't be a party-pooper, though—it's only for a week or so.

Just got back from Eric and Emma's for lunch ('nuff said!). Saw that Moira Bradigan on the way back. I waved but she looked at me in a creepy way. Not sure if I ever want to meet her—maybe she's still harboring a grudge or something!

BELLE VUE

Oops, can't believe I wrote so much. Still, I'm comfy here in front of the TV so no hardship, on my part at least.

I'm still stuffed from all that food at lunchtime—luckily the gym and pool are closed today and tomorrow, otherwise I'd be feeling guilty about avoiding it for so long!

Speak soon

Claire xx

P.S. Haven't done any revision or thought about my dissertation (yes, I know I'm the one who picked "ethical marketing" but now I've lost all interest!)—when you get back please get your whip out and be the slave driver you always wanted to be! Your Career Advisor must have got a shock! Lol

From: Alex Palmer
[alex.palmer@hertscollege.ac.uk]
Sent: Sun 28/12 11:58
To: Claire Ryan
Subject: Yesterday's Phone Call

Hi sweetheart.

Having a brilliant time here. Not sure if you'd like it—Gary's dad and his mates are like big kids. Now I know where Gary gets it from!

I know you're bored and said ring or email

every day but it's not always possible. If I can, I will. Okay?

Anyway, everyone says hi, and I am so horny it hurts. Miss you

Lexi 😊 xxx

From: Claire Ryan [Claire.ryan@hertscollege.ac.uk]
Sent: Weds 31/12 15:07
To: Alex Palmer
Subject: !!!!!HAPPY NEW YEAR!!!!!

Hi, lover boy! I am missing u sooooooooooooo much too! And I hope u stay horny—at least until u get back to me! Have to admit I'm green at the thought of u (with the rest of the goat herd) getting invited to that swanky NYE party tonight.

I'm still bored. I should have gone to Wales with Marianne but—though it's for a good cause—I don't think I'd have enough energy to be of any use. Eric and Emma invited me over to celebrate NYE with them but I'm so tired I can't be bothered.

And FYI I don't want to hear one word about how fabulous the party was or what all the beautiful people were wearing or how much champagne you drank—that is an order!

I can't wait until u get back. Come over

straightaway. 2 weeks of celibacy is bad for your health and mine! It's a new year so we should start it as we mean to go on—just like rabbits! I think this year is going to be brilliant for us and I luv you heaps!

Happy New Year!

Claire xxxxxxxxxx

P.S. That bloody old woman is still playing her silly "now-u-see-me-now-u-don't" game—it's doing my head in!

Alex padded back to the bedroom carrying a glass of orange juice and a couple of aspirins. In the gloom, the glowing numbers of the clock read 05:58. Way too early. He didn't need to get up till gone nine. Though term didn't start until next week, he had a meeting booked with Hamish for ten. Might as well relax and, once the painkillers kicked in, get some more sleep.

He sat on his side of the bed, put the tablets on his tongue, and downed the juice in a few gulps. Thoughts of regret at drinking again last night—after the fortnight bingeing in Verbier—surfaced like repentant sinners. He and Claire had soon polished off the two bottles of champagne he'd brought for their reunion.

Alex settled back carefully. He held his breath as his head and stomach groaned in mutual discomfort. He glanced over at Claire's sleeping figure. Dead to the world. When she'd finally opened the door to him yesterday, he'd been shocked by how worn out she looked. So much for her cozy Christmas break filled with rest, relaxation, and culinary treats.

"Are you okay?" He'd blurted out and immediately wanted to take back his tactless words but Claire hadn't taken offence this time. Just raised one side of her mouth in a halfhearted smile as she'd let him in the flat.

"I'm not sleeping too well. I wake aching all over like I've been on the floor all night, not a nice soft bed."

Alex had smiled and leaned in toward her. "We'll get in the tub later and I'll give you a massage. Deluxe version."

She'd chuckled and snuggled up to him. "You have no idea how fabulous that sounds."

He'd opened the champagne and they'd nestled together on the couch as he regaled her with outrageous tales of his holiday—expurgated version, he had to admit—that brought tears of laughter to their eyes. She'd brushed off his questions about her Christmas, saying she didn't want to spoil their reunion with boring talk, she had other things in mind. Consequently, dinner had been a box of handmade Swiss chocolates, courtesy of Gary's dad, a couple of joints for him, and the second bottle of champagne, which they finished in the bath. Claire had lit some candles. The water had been warm and perfumed with fragrant oils.

Several hours later, Alex eased into relaxed consciousness from his deep slumber. The bright rays of the morning sun bathed the room with light through the open blinds, but he was content to keep his eyes closed and enjoy this quiet time. His head felt clear and his stomach ready for a hearty breakfast. He lay on his back with the duvet tucked around him and again, he relished his memories of the previous night—in the bath and after. Alex smiled as he thought of Claire and how great their lovemaking had been. He supposed everybody thought that about themselves. His mates, particularly Gary, often amused one another with ever more fantastic boasts about their prowess with women, but he felt last night had been something special. He and Claire matched each other, knowing by instinct what the other wanted. He couldn't believe how much he loved her, how seriously he felt about her. His right hand left the warmth of the duvet and rubbed his head before ducking back.

Thinking of Claire naked, her silhouette sinuously moving above him in the moonlight, made him feel horny again. He scratched his groin and felt himself hardening as his thoughts became more explicit. Claire shifted restlessly on the other side of the bed but, from her even breathing, she wasn't awake yet. He wanted to move closer, pull her to him and recreate those feelings from last night. He loved the smell of her, especially her hair. It evoked thoughts of freshness and innocence, in contrast to the intense sensuality of their most intimate moments. Sated, he had held her spoon-fashion, burying his face into her silvery mane. He had savored its lingering fragrance, a mixture of perfume, soap and the wonderful private memories they shared. Erotic memories that now stirred Alex to action. Eyes still closed, but with a smile forming on his lips, he moved onto his side and inched toward Claire. He ran a finger down her back.

"Are you awake?" he whispered. He pulled her closer, wrapping his arms tightly around her. She arched her back and curved her body to touch every possible point with his.

She gave a contented sigh. "Mmm. Lexi…"

His excitement almost overwhelmed him. He pressed into her, took a deep breath.

He suddenly frowned as the smell hit him. Alex's body stiffened. As he opened his eyes the pulsating hardness between his legs shriveled to nothing: her hair was filthy, the long greasy strands alive with movement. He leaped away from her, cringing.

"You're crawling with fleas!" he shrieked, frantically slapping at his body. Claire groaned, then rolled onto her back. But it wasn't Claire who stared up at him. A yellow-tinged, black-lipped face fixed him with lifeless eyes.

"What's happened to you?" he screeched.

Frowning, Claire sat up and gazed open-mouthed at the mirror on the opposite wall.

Christ, he was going to puke. He rushed to the bathroom, her words ringing in his ears.

"What the hell are you talking about?"

Alex leaned his hands on the edge of the sink and stared at his wet face in the mirror. What the fuck was going on? The soap and water hadn't helped, neither had brushing his teeth. Thankfully, he hadn't thrown up but every time he thought of that moment when he'd opened his eyes and seen and smelled Claire as that *thing*, his skin crawled. He'd never be able to wash away the sense of contamination, of being tainted by the touch of something long dead.

He pulled the towel from the rail and wiped his face, desperately searching for a rational explanation. That was the problem: it seemed so real. Claire, though, hadn't seen anything wrong. Maybe he'd smoked some bad weed. He wasn't sure he'd noticed anything different, but for now, he needed to explain to Claire. A prickle of guilt pierced his consciousness. He'd left her to it, but to what? He hadn't stopped his yelling like a sissy to find out.

No sound came from the bedroom. He should go straight back in but hesitated, not sure of what he would find and, if nothing out of the ordinary, what reaction he'd get. God, he was confused. He didn't know what to do. Slow down. Be rational. It couldn't have happened the way he imagined. The only explanation was something made him think it was happening. Therefore, he was right. It must have been one of the joints.

With a last glance in the mirror for reassurance, he wrapped the towel round his waist, breathed in, and opened the bathroom door. In front of him, he could see Claire in her thick toweling robe—and it was *his* Claire—sitting on the bed. As he looked at her face, the words 'Cheshire Cat' sprang to mind.

"My hero," she said, laughing.

Relieved, Alex whipped off his towel and shimmied toward her. Claire whooped and held out her arms. He slid into them and held her, gently moving her back and forward.

"It must have been a bad joint, sweets," he murmured. "Made me see things."

The rocking of their bodies grew more insistent, and he stopped thinking. Claire caressed his face with her lips, her tongue. He groaned and tugged the robe from her shoulders. He was back in safer territory. This he knew how to handle. Claire stood up and facing him, let her robe drop. He moaned again as Claire bent toward him. They kissed deeply. She pushed Alex back onto the bed and climbed on him.

In the heat of their passion, neither noticed the large flea caught in the toweling hoops of Claire's robe which lay forgotten on the floor.

Chapter Twelve

Saturday, 11 October, 1862

When Mary discovered what the role of scullion in the Duc de Montalt's London house entailed, she was not greatly impressed. Shocked would be a better description. To think Mam—as she'd called Catherine then—and Father Patrick had put her forward for such a lowly position. Nothing but grinding drudgery in the kitchens from first thing in the morning to gone midnight. It was the only vacancy, they'd said, but for all their poverty, she thought Mam had been preparing her for better work than this. She even slept in a box bed that folded out of a cupboard in the scullery corridor, for God's sake. No privacy at all. Mam had responded by saying if she used her brain and worked hard, she could rise one day to become a cook or housekeeper. Mary noted she hadn't said Lady's Maid, as Catherine had been when her family fell on hard times. As though Mary wasn't cut out for that exalted position. No doubt, the precious Ellen, safe and cosseted by Mam at home, would be. But for Mary, nothing more than a life of backbreaking hard labor had been planned all along. She hated the work just as she hated being at everyone's beck-and-call.

Unfortunately, she soon found she wasn't exactly the other servants' idea of someone they wanted to work with, either. The only person with any time for her was Nancy Flanagan, her best friend from Walsall Lane who Father Patrick and Mam had also helped in finding a place. Already fifteen and now a kitchen maid, Nancy had been working in the London house for nearly a year. They were kindred spirits and both agreed they wanted more excitement and money than their births had entitled them.

And Nancy had discovered a way to achieve it.

When Mary first heard about the parties at the house, she wasn't sure whether to believe her friend. She knew what sex was, had even seen it; figures humping against walls in alleys. But what Nancy described the toffs doing was something else altogether. Mary was still a virgin. Nancy told her she'd get extra pay, so why didn't she speak to Mr. Edgar, the butler, and let him know she was up for more than skivvying?

And so she had performed at her first party. A small one. Only about a dozen bluebloods. She had been plied with drink, and Nancy, who'd kept an eye out for her, said she'd done well, but, oh lummy, it had hurt. Of the Duc de Montalt, there had been no sign. Nancy told her he stayed at his country estate in Hertfordshire. He was ancient and didn't like the uncomfortable journey into town. His brother, Henri, who lived in the London house, had been the first to take her. He'd given her a gold sovereign in payment for her maidenhead. A month's wage for one go! Mary realized then Nancy knew what she was talking about. Later that night as she and Nancy planned their futures in the darkness of the scullery corridor, Mary felt Father Patrick's contact with these rich titled Catholics was a bit of luck after all. She had discovered a way to make a lot of money quickly and easily; if you didn't count the fact, it being her first time, she was sore for the most of the next day.

A few weeks later, word came to her and Nancy of a special celebration, by a group called The Mephisto Club would be taking place the following Saturday. Participation would be at double the normal rate. Mr. Edgar informed them the party would be at Belle Vue Manor, near St. Albans, not the London house. The idea of taking such a journey thrilled Mary, but Nancy didn't want to go. She planned to spend her half-day with the new footman who was taking her to a Penny Gaff. Mary would have none of that and eventually convinced Nancy the excitement and money of such a party would far outweigh anything a lowly footman, or even the Penny Gaff, could offer.

They were the only staff beside Mr. Edgar going to the Manor: he sorted it out for them with Cook.

Once they arrived at Belle Vue, she and Nancy, with about a score of other lads and lasses brought in for the occasion, bathed before being taken to a small room where they were given short shifts of almost transparent material to wear. Mary was proud of her firm, white body, and flaming red hair. Even in this group of beautiful youths, she knew the lion's share of the attention would be on her. Now she would be able to revel in the adoration of those who could turn her life around. She looked forward to the spectacle of a big celebration and the chance to learn more about these men at such close quarters. They had the money, and she intended to use her body to direct some of it her way.

Mr. Edgar instructed them not to speak unless spoken to by the guests and to obey whatever instructions they were given. He led them to the back stairs that took them down to the bowels of the house. Here there were long corridors leading to a set of enormous double doors. Mr. Edgar ushered them through.

Mary gasped as she entered the huge, ornate salon. There were no ladies here tonight, only men and lots of them. The room was luxurious beyond anything she had ever seen before, and very different to the London house. The pictures hanging along the walls depicted every vice Mary had ever thought of, and many she hadn't. Cruelty and abasement dominated. Of images reflecting love and gentleness, there were none.

A strange perfume in the air made her feel heady and light, as though she had been separated from her body and watched the whole scene from afar. She heard the sound of a violin, haunting and beautiful. A raised platform dominated the center of the room. On it were a round dais and a large vertical wheel. Mary saw the leather restraints hanging from the spokes and shivered with unease.

Many of the gentlemen were talking amongst themselves. Dressed in the finest materials, they made no effort to hide their identities. She was nervous but excited at the same time. These were rich men, the only hunger here was for sex and this would give her some power over them. She whispered her thoughts to Nancy, but her friend only shook her head and snorted. "They hold all the cards, Mary. If they like your face you might get extra, but I wouldn't bet on it. They can be right stingy with the likes of us."

The air of expectancy over the throng was growing, the laughter and voices rising and falling, fueled by continuous refills served on silver trays by glistening blackamoors. Mary, naked but for the slip of cream gauze, was led into a space in the center of the room. She saw three other groups dressed in similar garb.

The first, a herd of perhaps a dozen or more figures, awkward and unsure, stood silent watching their highborn audience. Each wore a sheer red shift and was physically deformed. She felt sick looking at their bizarre flaws exposed in the glow of the lamps. A freak show. A priapic dwarf, a pair of obese women joined from neck to hip, a muscular youth with a pin head, a man whose face and body were distorted by huge sack-like swellings. Mary turned away with disgust and growing misgivings. Nancy's expression mirrored hers. A much larger group in blue shifts looked like common streetwalkers who'd been rounded up in the rookeries and brought up here en masse for the night. Hands on hips, parading, showing off their raddled wares. Mary flinched at their dead eyes and the stink of defeat no matter how much they'd been washed. The others, wearing green shifts, looked like they belonged in a lunatic asylum. Some snickered to themselves as though party to their own private joke. Others moaned and dribbled, and several faces bore the identifying distortions of idiocy.

"Oh, dear God," she muttered.

Nancy leaned toward her. "It was so different the other times. I hope I'm not going to have to do anything with some of these, these... I want to leave."

Mary more than agreed, but instinctively knew any moment of escape had passed. She could not believe what these lords and masters, who looked down at the likes of her and Nancy, were going to do.

A voice behind her with cut-glass tones interrupted her thoughts.

She swung around, relieved to see the familiar face of Henri. She smiled, but beyond a slight glint of recognition, he ignored her as he spoke. "Splendid specimens, Seton. Well done. We'll have some good sport tonight."

Mary could only see the back of the tall dark-haired gentleman who answered in a languid drawl. "Would you expect anything less?" He swigged the drink in his hand and placed the empty glass on the proffered silver platter. He waved the servant away. "The games are about to begin. Henri, do the honors."

A blackamoor stepped forward and Henri took a golden horn from the tray and raised it to his lips. A long harsh blare silenced both music and conversation.

Mary, keen to retain every snippet of information about the evening, paid careful attention to the scene unfolding before her. The lights were not as bright now and a shuffling movement opened a path between the eager bluebloods. A fanfare sounded in the background. Her mouth dropped open as eight muscular men, ear-ringed and completely hairless, bore a frightening apparition aloft their shoulders toward the stage.

She held her breath and reached for Nancy's hand. The two stood transfixed. "Is he real?"

Nancy squeezed Mary's fingers. "Sshh."

The men stopped and set the litter down on the marble floor. The figure rose and swaggered toward the platform. With slow deliberation, the towering form climbed the steps. All eyes upon him, the tension stretched ever tighter.

He turned, and Mary felt his eyes rake hers. Trembling, she mentally made a sign of the cross as she gazed at this man dressed as Satan. Tight red leather covered his head from which two curled horns rose at the top and two large pointed ears jutted out on either side. The tip of his beard was sharp, and like his moustache and eyebrows, jet black as though painted for effect. He wore a red costume from which a huge erect leather penis waved obscenely each time he moved.

Mary would never forget this moment. She stared at the unnatural white of his dark eyes and the port-wine birthmark across his left cheek and nose disfiguring the pallor beneath.

"Holy Mother of God," she whispered, tears forming in spite of her best efforts.

"*I am the Hell Master,*" the figure roared at the assembled throng. A howl of approval erupted from every toff in the room.

He spread his arms wide and surveyed the eager crowd.

"Welcome to the celebration of the sixth twenty-four-year period of our glorious brotherhood. Tonight, every one of us renews our contract with Mephistopheles. You must show me you deserve that honor. Do your worst and make Satan proud!"

Another cheering barrage. Mary felt the restlessness of the men and hoped she could keep her wits about her over the next few hours. God knows what she and Nancy were going to face.

"Let the revels begin. Take your pick of the fruits laid out before you. The rooms are ready for your every desire. Eternus vita quod iucunditas. Eternal life and pleasure. Remember. All that comes into being is worthy of destruction. Blood must flow!"

Her nerves taut, Mary watched as the many doors leading off this main room opened. Nancy dropped her hand and, led by the man called Seton, she disappeared through the crush of bodies. As they reached the door, Mary saw him turn when tapped on the shoulder by a half-dressed young man. He threw his head back and laughed at an obviously ribald comment. She committed every inch of his chiseled patrician features to memory. Unsure what to do, she turned back to the figure in red as he bellowed once more to the jostling crowd.

"All you gamblers. The wagers start at ten guineas." He paced the platform, holding a truncheon in his raised hand. "Sir Robert would never imagine what I'm going to do with this! Let's see if one of our beautiful hellcats can take as much as some of the lusus naturae. Place your bets. Ten guineas? Twenty? Bring me the first challenger!"

Raucous laughter, men shuffling, necks craning, heat rising. Mary felt relief when Henri caught her eye and stepped toward her. All around her, club members stripped off their clothes, which the blackamoors discreetly removed. A number of men made selections from the different groups. The Hell Master continued his taunts.

"Can she take the truncheon? Yes or no? Can he?"

At closer quarters, Mary saw Henri's glazed expression. He seemed drugged or drunk. Probably both. Leering at her, he plucked at her flimsy covering.

"My friends are waiting. Let's go."

Roughly grabbing her arm, he pulled her across the floor, past the bronze statues of Mephistopheles, assorted demons and celebrants of Bacchus, and out to a large mirrored hallway. On a velvet sofa, Mary saw three writhing figures clearly enjoying their game; perhaps it wouldn't be so bad after all. They reached the end of the corridor and faced another huge set of doors. Henri waved his hand and two flunkeys pulled open a side each. Stepping beyond the glittering hall, Mary could see it was darker here. The stone walls of a long tunnel stretched before them, littered with hooks on which hung various leather and metal contraptions. Instruments of cruelty Mary prayed would not be part of her evening. Henri caught her worried glance. A snide smile slid across his face. He stopped and placed his thumb and finger on his chin as though about to make a serious decision. He smirked at her then spent several long minutes examining the items on display with great interest.

"Anticipation can be as powerful as the reality, ma chérie. Anything you'd like to try?"

Mary shook her head but said nothing. She thought her voice would reveal her nervousness. As he selected a metal-tipped whip and some sort of mechanical metal tube with a handle, she suspected this night was going to be her worst nightmare and beyond.

Her insides quaked with fear. Henri nodded toward the nearest door and as slowly as she could, she entered the room. Three men were there already; naked, hungry-eyed, drugged, drunk. Henri held his treasures aloft. "Pour ma crotte."

His cronies laughed and surrounded her. What had he said? Before she could react, they pushed her face down onto the bench in the middle of the room. Her arms and legs were spread-eagled and held to the floor with iron shackles.

When Mary came to she was slumped in a corner, free of the restraints. She didn't move, trying to hold down her tears and deaden the pain. Henri and the men were smoking their foul-smelling pipes and drinking. The door opened, and they watched with excited eyes as a blackamoor dragged in two of the street whores. The men rose and reached for their prey but from the sight of her blood on the floor, the shackles and the whip, the women's survival instincts reared up. One slapped Henri's face, the other spat and struggled. This seemed to egg the men on more. Henri roared and grabbed the whip. No one paid Mary any mind. As the group flailed toward the back of the room, she slipped through the door.

Despite the blood oozing from the cuts over her body and from between her legs, Mary felt angrier than she'd ever been. Angry but afraid. Getting caught wasn't an option. She had to find Nancy and try to escape. The long corridor was empty now, but Mary could hear sickening noises from the various rooms leading from it. Down one side, in place of a wall and door for these rooms, red velvet drapes hung from the ceiling. Several were open, exposing the debauched activities within. Biting her lip to stifle her moans, Mary stumbled forward, not sure where she was going but desperate not to draw attention to herself.

A scream rent the air behind her. Mary cocked her head. Another shriek and another, quicker and louder each time as though the torment was gaining momentum. It wasn't Nancy's voice, so Mary tried to ignore the howling pleas, and continued to peer behind each curtain in search of her friend. Then the shrieks were silenced and that, she thought, was worse. God, she must get out of this place. She inhaled slowly, desperate to cope with her pain and rising panic.

"Stop! You're hurting me."

She started at the familiar voice. The curtains in front of her were closed. Edging forward, she slipped quietly behind the velvet and peered round the edge of the wall to the divan in the center of the room.

Nancy was on all fours, side on to Mary. The man called Seton was riding her from behind, pulling with his left hand on her long dark hair as though reining in a bucking horse. With each jolt of his onslaught, Seton's finely muscled body flexed ever tighter like a hunter's bow. He hurled obscenities at Nancy over and over, the same words. Bitch. Bitch. Bitch. Hatred suffused his features. His thrusts quickened. He groaned, his hand moved and then, a flash of silver. Seton jerked Nancy's head up hard and Mary watched in horror as he slit her throat and shuddered as he reached his climax.

Clutching at the swathe of material, Mary couldn't believe what had happened. Instinct kicked in. She dare not make a sound, but tears welled in her eyes as Seton pushed Nancy away with a look of disgust. Ignoring the pain, she slumped onto her knees, never taking her gaze from him. She blinked away her tears, now was not the time for weakness. Oblivious to his audience of one, he stood, still holding the bloody knife, ignoring the girl as though she did not exist. Mary could see for him, Nancy didn't anymore. She willed him to leave so she could help her friend. Turning her scrutiny from Seton, Mary's heart sank, there was no movement from the figure. Seton reached for a towel. He patted his glistening body and taking the single glass of wine from a small table at the end of the divan, swallowed deeply. He dropped the towel on the floor, turned, pulled back the curtain, and strutted out of the room.

Mary exhaled, her breath shaky. After waiting a few long seconds, she crept from her hiding place toward Nancy. She whispered her friend's name and gently shook her. No reaction. As she maneuvered Nancy onto her back, she saw the extent of the gaping wound. No one could help Nancy now. Ignoring her discomfort, she leaned down awkwardly. She brushed a strand of hair away from Nancy's face, her

eyes fixed on the twisted features. Nancy's eternal death mask.
She kissed her best friend's forehead.
Her last act of tenderness.
Ever.

Numb with shock, Mary struggled to focus her thoughts. Nancy was dead. She reached for the towel and, to give her friend some small dignity, covered her with it. Someone would come soon to clean up the blood and, no doubt, get rid of the body. She hated Seton and more than anything, she wanted to avenge Nancy's death. To do that, though, she must stay alive and find a way out, using every ounce of cunning she possessed.

Mary sneaked out through the curtain and hobbled as fast as she could back along the corridor, past a flight of stairs. She tried to remember if she'd seen them before. Mary heard a shout behind her and without waiting, took the steps two at a time. At the top, she faced a closed door. More afraid of what might be behind her than in front, she turned its ornate handle and bolted into a wide opulent hallway. The sound of music, raucous laughter and chattering voices echoed from the rooms on both sides. Their open doors a source of exposure, Mary crossed the corridor and, with the agony of her body screaming for her to stop, hurried up another flight of stairs. On the next floor, she slowed and took her bearings. All was quiet. Unnervingly so. The hallway was darker here, lined with wallpaper of deep red, unlike the bright gold and mirrored walls below. The gas lamps burned low.

She was no safer here than downstairs. Her every sense strained to the limit, she fought to deaden all feeling. Naked with cuts and blood all over her, clothes were her first priority or escape would be impossible. Mary peered along the corridor, only two doors were visible. She crept to the one closest, ignoring the menace in the silence. She grasped the brass handle and slowly pulled it down. It moved, perhaps half an inch, but then stopped. She tried again with the same result. Mary let out her breath and willed the other door to open. She tiptoed across the hall and took hold of the metal lever. This time, it lowered with the smallest resistance. She pushed the paneled wood a few inches and hearing no indignant voice, eased her head through the gap and peered into the room. Seeing it empty, she slid through and shut the door behind her.

A single gas lamp illuminated the room's sumptuousness. An enormous and ornately carved full tester dominated the large space. There were side tables beside the bed and to her right two armchairs with a small table. She tiptoed to the first of two doors on the opposite side of the room and found what she sought. A dressing room: immense and full of clothes. Whoever owned it wouldn't miss a few bits and pieces. Leaving the door ajar so she could use the gas light to see, Mary rifled through the hangers. No dresses, but a pair of old-fashioned embroidered knee breeches and a white ruffled shirt. She quickly put them on.

As Mary stood thinking her next move, she heard a noise. She darted behind the long row of coats, twisted and gasped in shock as her back hit the wood. The shirt stuck to the blood of her wounds, but she bit her lip and remained still. Two men were talking but she couldn't understand their strange words. She waited, the pain and suspense fixing her head and body like an iron maiden. The minutes ticked on, and on. Feeling faint, she cautiously crouched down.

Mary had no idea if she had been asleep, or unconscious, or for how long. Her whole body felt stiff. Struggling to her feet, she forced herself not to cry out. She moved from behind the clothes. With great care, she lifted off the parts of her shirt stuck to her skin and winced as she felt each tear and the blood start to seep through the material again. She tiptoed to the dressing-room entrance, straining to hear any sound in the next room. Silence. They must have gone to sleep or departed. She pushed the door open and peered at the bed. Empty. A candle on the table still burned but no one seemed to be around. She crept across the thick carpet, her eyes focused on the door.

"Who's there?"

Mary spun round in surprise.

BELLE VUE

An old man sat on the heavily padded armchair, its high back having hidden any occupant from view. Wearing a brocade dressing gown and slippers, his exposed skin was chalk-white and papery.

She said nothing. Her mind grasped for a possible excuse for her presence.

"You must be the one who works at my London house." A statement, not a question.

"Yes."

"We like to account for all the bodies that come in and leave the Manor. There is a guard outside this room but whether I call him depends on you."

She said nothing. This must be René, the Duc de Montalt, her employer. She was considering her options when he continued. "What do you think of our little games, ma chérie? I'm too old for them now, but now and then I like young flesh to rejuvenate me."

He let out a phlegm-filled chuckle and clutching at his glass, noisily sucked up a mouthful of its ruby-colored contents. He lifted his hooded eyes toward her and, as he scrutinized her face, savored the liquid before swallowing it with an expression of elation. It unnerved her as she couldn't imagine anything tasting that good.

"Beautiful vintage, chérie."

He took another draught and placed the glass on the table. Sitting back, his eyes roamed over her. She didn't move and watched him carefully in return. Very different to his brother, he looked old enough to be Henri's grandfather, not his sibling. His powdered white hair was pulled back over a pad which emphasized his high forehead and beak-like nose.

"I used to love to take part, you know. I was the supreme Hell Master. Now, my time is coming to a close and new flesh is needed. I want so much to be young again."

Mary, tired and in pain, let the ramblings of a rich madman—obviously near death but who didn't want to die—wash over her. If she had that much money, she wouldn't want to die, either. She thought he'd told her to sit. That was unheard of. A scullion sitting with a duke, French or not.

He waved his hand again toward the chair in front of him, repeating his words, "Sit. Now tell me what you've seen and done. In exquisite detail. Do it well and I'll give you a reward."

Mary lowered herself to the seat, keeping her face blank. So, that was his game. She played along and, holding her voice steady—she would not show any weakness—recounted her experiences of the party. Time and again, he would stop her and ask questions to hear explicit details of each act of depravity. Although feisty and streetwise, unusually for her, Mary realized she was out of her depth with this man. He was part of this, the host of this Mephisto orgy. Still, if she kept her head, maybe she could survive. She finished her answer and waited for the Duc. His hand snaked between the edges of his robe.

"You have much that would excite a man but look, Priapus visits me no more. I have only my memories and these soirées to break the monotony of being old and infirm. Tell me more, what else did you see?"

She knew what he wanted. Bile rose in her throat. "I saw…" Each word raked her soul. "I saw a man kill my friend, Nancy."

"Yes, I know. Seton." He leaned back and sighed. A dreamy look softened his features as though he were remembering some momentous and proud occasion. "How sublime, to expire at the point of ultimate gratification. I hope if I ever leave this life, it will be with such ecstasy. I'm almost envious."

Mary thought the man beyond madness. Lunatics were to be pitied. They couldn't help themselves, but the Duc knew exactly what he was doing. She hated him beyond words. Nancy was dead and for what? Nothing but a party game whose rules allowed murder. Every guest there knew what was going on and had probably done the same. These lords and judges, even a bishop—for she had listened to their careless talk—conspiring with the Devil himself.

The Duc de Montalt appraised her with his rheumy eyes.

"She's gone now and you're still here. You must move on. Choose your direction as we all did. I might allow you to live."

His sneering words chilled her, but she would not be cowed. She had nothing to lose. Although trembling inside, she raised her chin and demanded, "Is that my reward? Our pay for tonight was double rate, not life. Your offer of a bonus extra to that, M'sieur."

The Duc chuckled. "You are right, ma chérie. You have done well to survive and evade capture. No one has done that before." He sat back, as though deep in thought, and swirled the liquid around his glass. He smiled, revealing his yellowing teeth. "Perhaps there is something I can do for you if you are truly strong. In your mind. My life has become so tedious. I shall inject a bit of danger into the mix and see what will happen. Otherwise, all I have is a lot of bother I'd rather not repeat." He sighed. "Therefore, I shall consider your request. All to play for chérie."

Mary licked her lips. Her mouth was parched. He was a strange one. She struggled to understand what he meant and to think how she could gain most from the situation. The Duc held out his glass.

"Are you thirsty? Here take this."

His eyes never left hers as she reached out her hand.

"I shall soon retire. You will stay with me. I can teach you many things."

She took the glass from his taloned fingers and drank deeply. Her face ruckled with disgust. She spat the liquid out, a viscous plume spraying over the floor.

"Ugh. That's foul."

"No, my dear, it's not." The Duc savored his words. "Your Nancy would be hurt. After all, it is *her* blood."

Mary's vomit joined the red stain on the floor and the Duc laughed for the first time that evening.

Chapter Thirteen

Friday, 16 January
PRESENT DAY

Claire gripped the steering wheel, pressed the accelerator, and crossed the junction as the light turned red. She drove back to her apartment by rote, her mind a whirl. The exam this morning had been a disaster: so much for Public Relations being her best subject. On her answers today, she couldn't manage a good turnout for the Pope at a Catholic convention.

What was wrong with her? Okay, she hadn't done as much revision as she'd have liked. She found it so hard to concentrate these days and couldn't remember a thing. Her stomach had rumbled its way through the seemingly endless three hours, despite the cereal, toast, chocolate bar, and banana she'd eaten at breakfast. To top it off, Alex was miffed because she'd told him she was going to stay in and crash this weekend: catch up on her sleep and hopefully get some work done on her own dissertation. Talk about selfish. It was as if he didn't want her to do well. His first class honors was in the bag, the way she was going she wouldn't even pass this year.

Keeping her eyes on the road, she reached for a tissue in her open handbag. She sniffed and wiped her runny nose. As she turned into the drive at Belle Vue, she hoped she'd be able to relax and put the day's bad start behind her. What she could do with now was some girly support. Talk things out. She wished Marianne were here, but her friend had one last paper to get through this afternoon and wouldn't be free until about six. Not Alex in his current mood. He wasn't good at stuff like that, anyway. Whenever she spoke of her innermost feelings,

BELLE VUE

his eyes glazed over, the shutters came down and the fidgeting began.

Claire parked the car. As she got out, her eyes were drawn to the dome. A figure stood there, watching her. She felt a sense of déjà vu. The same white cap, black outfit, grim expression, but, no surprise, the woman hadn't shown at the house-warming party. Part of her thought she ought to go introduce herself, but she couldn't shake the feeling that somehow the dome was out of bounds to her. She hadn't been up there since that first time and she was far too tired now, so she'd give it a miss.

Once in her apartment, she stretched out on the sofa. She stayed that way for a few minutes, relishing the warmth and comfort of her surroundings. Her eyes began to droop when suddenly a cacophony of shrieks and howls shattered the silence. Startled, she sat up, putting her hands over her ears.

The shouting and wailing continued. She got up from the couch and stood in the center of the room trying to get a bearing on the location of the commotion. Hard to tell. It rose and fell as though doors were opening and closing. She had accepted the noise over Christmas and the New Year but, in the last few weeks, it had grown more frequent. Sometimes it wasn't too loud, but today the din was awful. She picked up her mobile and rang the Beamish's number.

She sat on the edge of the couch, scratching at a couple of red spots on her arm. When Eric answered, Claire gave him the details of her complaint, but he didn't know what she was talking about. He even asked her if it was a TV on somewhere. As if she couldn't tell the difference.

"No, Eric," she said, fighting to hold down her irritation. "What about other people complaining? No one? Are you sure? Oh, it's stopped now. You'll look into it?" She leaned back, feeling the beginnings of a headache. A gentle throbbing that would soon grow. She rubbed her forehead with her free hand.

"Thanks, Eric. Let me know if you get any response. Yes, I'll send you a brief description and a list of occasions, as far as I can remember. Can you add it to the Agenda of the next Residents' meeting please?"

The throbbing increased in intensity.

"Yeah, I know it's not for ages yet. I wonder if there's something faulty in my flat for the noise to get through. You will look into it? Okay, Eric, thanks again."

Claire ended the call before remembering she'd forgotten to ask him about the chapel bell pealing at all hours. Damn. She reached for her notebook and grabbed a pen from the coffee table. As she wrote each word about today's noises and Eric's reaction, she had to face they might be all in her mind. What if they were not? She would swear they were real this time. Like being grabbed in the pool, the man on the stairs, the hands round her neck at her party, the chain rattling in her lockup. They had all seemed so real. She couldn't be heading for another breakdown. She wouldn't allow it, she couldn't. Tears of frustration rolled down her cheeks. She chewed on what remained of her nails. As the patter of nerves threatened to become a stampede, she rose to her feet feeling the only thing she could do was fight and get herself through this.

Goaded to action, she wiped her eyes and fetched a glass of water from the kitchen. She took a couple of tablets, her second dose today. As she waited for the painkillers to kick in, she stood at the sitting room window and stared out at the winter scene. To her left, the chapel was more conspicuous without the cloak of leaves and flowers that softened its severe exterior. Now it stood alone, the wide border of earth and skeletal branches isolating the stone house of worship.

The thought of a few minutes of quiet solitude in the small church seemed very appealing. She wasn't religious, but perhaps she could find some comfort in such surroundings and pray for the strength to help deal with her situation. She'd been in once for a quick look round when she first moved in, more out of curiosity about Marianne's tale than anything else. It had been reassuringly safe and bland. She picked up her jacket and keys and made her way downstairs.

The chapel door opened smoothly. She'd expected resistance from its heavy weight. Claire stepped into the gloom and stood for a few minutes, her eyes adjusting from the comparative brightness outside. Although there were several stained-glass windows, albeit high and narrow, the interior seemed impervious to the daylight. It was cold, and the silence absolute. She could see the outlines of two other people seated in the pews, one on each side of the nave. Both had their heads bowed.

Claire tiptoed along the aisle so as not to disturb the other occupants and slid into the wooden bench in the last row. She leaned forward, resting her forearms on the shelf at the back of the pew and her forehead on her clasped hands. She closed her eyes.

A low murmur cut into her thoughts, seemingly from all sides. Menacing. Sinister. Ritualistic. Not right. She opened her eyes, but the sound stopped. Claire bent her head forward again, this time staring at her hands. Peace of mind or any feeling of comfort eluded her. Instead, dark thoughts of betrayal and death dominated, and the pain in her head had started again.

At the click of heels on the stone floor, thankful for the distraction, she looked up. Her neighbor Sally Reichenberg headed toward her. She stopped as she came level with Claire and whispered, "Didn't expect to see you here."

"I thought I needed a quiet place."

"Me too." Sally pulled her coat about her. "It's gotten a lot colder in here. Fancy coming up for a coffee, if you've finished?"

"Sure. There's something I wanted to ask you." Claire cast a glance toward the now empty pew. "Oh," she exclaimed.

"What's wrong?"

"Where's the other person gone?"

Sally shook her head. "No one else here, hon, just us."

"Maybe now, but someone was sitting over there in the front pew." Claire's voice rose, both in volume and pitch. Seeing Sally's puzzled expression, she tried to laugh it off, but deep within the niggle of unease started again. "Come on, let's go."

She slid out of the pew. As she followed Sally through the door, her mind ran through the sequence of her entering the chapel and noticing the two figures.

"Much warmer out here, thank God." Unfettered by the need to whisper, Sally's twang grew more pronounced. She peered at Claire and frowned. "Honey, when did you last sleep?"

"Do I look that bad? No, don't answer. You wouldn't have asked otherwise. It's been a tough three weeks. Had my last exam this morning. It didn't go well."

Sally put her arm through Claire's and together they walked along the path toward the main entrance. "Oh, you have my sympathies, hon. I hated school."

Claire smiled. "But not that much, look who you married. A professor of all things."

"Got me there."

"All the noise going on round here is getting on my nerves. Doesn't it bother you?"

"Not really. I know some of the guys with their flash cars rev 'em up like they're in the Grand Prix, but I only notice it if I've got the window open. Otherwise, very little. One of the reasons we bought this place, in fact. Jeff can only work if it's quiet."

"And he hasn't been bothered by all the shouting and yelling?"

"Nope, and let me tell you hon, if anyone gave so much as a loud cough out in the hall downstairs, he'd be complaining in no time."

Claire said nothing, but her unease continued to grow like an overrunning bath she couldn't turn off. They climbed the main steps and were standing in front of the entrance door when the chapel bell began tolling the hour. She turned to Sally with relief. "That ringing, for instance, is really irritating. Every bloody hour."

"What ringing?"

"Don't you hear it?" Claire moved her head in time with each strike of the bell. "Dong. Dong. Dong. It's doing my head in."

Sally raised her face upward, a slight frown on her features. She lowered her head and looked at Claire as if she were seeing her for the first time. "I can't hear anything, hon. I hate to tell you this, but the realtor said the bell hasn't worked for more than fifty years, maybe longer. It would have been a deal killer for Jeff. It's missing the metal clapper that makes the noise. It can't ring."

At about the same time Claire started her exam this morning, Alex sat at his kitchen table staring queasily into a bowl of cereal. The thought that he should have learned his lesson by now staggered across his mind. But finishing his last exam had provided the perfect excuse for a serious piss up with Gary and Paul. His stomach lurched, and he decided food wasn't such a good idea after all. He pushed back his chair and headed to the bathroom.

After a long, hot shower, he returned to the kitchen. His head had cleared slightly but he needed a shot of caffeine to psych himself up for the rest of the day. Paul and Gary had gone out goodness-knows-where, so the flat was quiet. As he walked past the sideboard, he noticed Claire's Christmas present as yet untouched. That reminded him, he still hadn't heard back from Jeremy Trent despite leaving several messages. He placed his drink on the coffee table, then went back and collected a notebook, pen, and his copy of 'Victorian Asylums: Then and Now. A Pictorial History'.

He leafed through the pages. The pictures of the asylums covered three distinct phases: Victorian architectural glory, closure, and neglect in the mid to late twentieth century, followed by regeneration in the form of other uses, mostly expensive residential apartments. These for upwardly mobile professionals to live in an old madhouse. A hundred years ago they wouldn't be caught dead in it. Crazy.

He was pleased to see a whole chapter on Belle Vue. The first picture comprised a drawing of a huge mansion quite unlike the asylum. The caption identified this as the original Belle Vue Manor belonging to the de Montalt family. He browsed the brief paragraph underneath and, from the sound of it, they were an interesting group.

Unfortunately, no further information. He wondered if Trent had done much research about the places he'd photographed. Over the next few pages, Alex recognized the floor plans of the asylum similar to the one he'd seen on his first visit. He skipped through these but stopped when he saw one detailing the basement level.

Wow, there were more tunnels than he ever imagined from his trips to the storage and pool areas. His finger traced the main passage originating from the central building. It led into others that extended the east-west length of the asylum before veering off into dead ends. He wondered if Moira Bradigan knew anything about them. If he ever got a meeting with her, he'd have to ask.

He also noticed the same photograph from the Belle Vue sale's office of all the dignitaries at the official opening of the asylum. This time accompanied by a smaller picture with the drawn outlines of the figures and a numbered list giving the identities and position of each person. He flicked back and forth, fascinated to learn that, out of fifty or so bigwigs, only three were from the asylum itself. At one end, the sole female—a hatchet-faced woman who looked as though she'd just sat on something unpleasant—identified as a Mrs. Adelaide Fishburn. Behind her, sporting some fine whiskers, heavy jowls, and what looked to be a tight collar, stood Doctor Samuel Fishburn, the Medical Superintendent of Belle Vue.

Of greater interest was the positioning of the other representative from the asylum. He was seated almost at the center next to the head honcho, Doctor Brewer, Chairman of the Metropolitan Asylums Board. Alex noted his number within the outlined head and found the man's name listed below. The Honorable Doctor Johnson Nottidge, Senior Resident Medical Officer. He looked at the picture again. Even in this old photograph, the man exuded patrician breeding and self-confidence. Claire would probably describe him as handsome with his dark hair and chiseled features. To Alex, the man possessed an air of decadence. He looked like a—what was the word?—rake. Not the same century, but the same impression.

BELLE VUE

He closed the book and checked his watch. Half past twelve. His stomach rumbled, so he made himself a sandwich. When he'd finished, he rang Claire. She sounded tired and told him she planned to do nothing, spending what sounded to him like a self-pitying weekend by herself at Belle Vue. He was irritated she hadn't asked how his exams had gone this week, and now she was leaving him high and dry till she felt like seeing him next.

He went to his room and sat at his desk. The picture of Claire on his pin board smiled back at him. With the end of semester exams over, all he'd wanted to do was spend some time with her and get back to how things used to be. So much for that. Looked like curry and another piss-up with the guys was on the cards instead.

Alex wasn't in the mood for work. He'd try Jeremy Trent one last time.

This time luck was on his side or was it, he wondered, as the man prattled on. It turned out "call me Jez" had written a novel, his first. Set at the end of Victoria's reign, he went into tortuous detail about the setting and plot. After several attempts, Alex steered the subject to the murder at Belle Vue, the one Hamish thought Jez had mentioned in his presentation.

Silence.

"Hello?"

"Sorry, Alex, just thinking. Yes, I did a bit of research on the asylums at the turn of the century." Trent chuckled. "A lot of stuff, but I'm a bit sketchy on the details now. Let me think."

The line went silent again.

"Mmmm. Alex, my head's so full of other things at the moment, you'll have to forgive me if I can't remember."

Alex was about to thank the man and hang up when Jez continued speaking.

"I've still got all my notes somewhere. Give me your contact number, and when I get my hands on them, I'll ring you. Okay?"

With his submission date getting ever closer, Alex thought it might be a bit late by then. Nevertheless, he passed his details to Jez and hung up just as Gary poked his head round the door, tapped his watch face and mimed the word, *guzzle*.

Marianne held the letter in her shaking hands. The last thing she needed. What bloody timing. In a huff, she flung it as far away as possible, but the sheet of paper drifted noiselessly to the floor in a cool rebuff at such treatment. She was in two minds what to do. Claire would offer to help, but Marianne didn't like asking things of people. It always made her feel uncomfortable. Now, she had no choice.

She dialed Claire's number and took a deep breath. Keep calm, it would get sorted. She could always try the college accommodation office if Claire didn't have any better ideas.

"Hi, Marianne."

"Oh, hi, Claire." Her voice caught. "Oh, God, I've got to move out of my flat. Like in the next few days."

"How awful. Why? What's happened? Do you need money for the rent?"

"I wish. No, that's not the problem. My crappy landlord says he gotten an offer he couldn't refuse and has sold the place. Now I get this solicitor's letter from the new owner saying they'll pay me if I leave within a week."

"So, what're you going to do?"

"Well, the money will come in handy, but in the meantime, where am I going to live?"

Claire answered immediately. "Move in with me, of course, Marianne. I've got tons of room. It'll be great. What do you say? How do you fancy being an inmate in the asylum?"

A fabulous offer she knew Claire would make. Marianne felt like she was tempting fate. Silly, but what if…

"So, are you moving in with me?"

Claire cheered when she said, "yes."

Chapter Fourteen

Wednesday, 30 June, 1869

*F*anned by the breeze, the warm rays of the afternoon sun caressed Johnson Nottidge's face. He relaxed and indulged himself in a recollection of his numerous sexual encounters over the past month or so. Eyes closed, his memories flitted from his conquests in London to those closer to home. As his mind wandered to his current location—the grounds of Belle Vue—thoughts of Samuel and Adelaide Fishburn turned up like bad pennies to blight his enjoyment.

Dreadful man, with a dreadful wife. Fishburn was nothing but a stooge for his 'lean and hungry' spouse. She was about as trustworthy as Cassius, too. Given the choice though, he still preferred the Matron. Greed, lust, wrath, and vanity were all emotions he understood. He remembered how surprised he'd been when he'd peered through the front window of Bill Callahan's cottage last week and saw her fellating the Head Attendant like some third-rate whore. He had not made a sound and they hadn't noticed him. This information had been stored away for future use. He smiled as he thought of the benefits—to him at least—of life at Belle Vue.

To think he had first wished a pox on his father for threatening to cut him off for bringing the family name into disrepute. If Pater only knew the half of it. After he'd met Henri de Montalt at a brothel in Paris, life had, at last, become interesting. They had returned to London and he'd joined the Mephisto Club. Soon, he became a member of the inner circle, but after the unexpected deaths of René and Henri, he'd had to find new outlets for his cravings. Shame word had gotten back to his father about a few harmless high japes, nothing important—some gambling debts, a duel, and the messy death of one of his mistresses. The old man had exploded and said he must now use his medical degree, or else. So, when he heard Belle Vue had opened as a lunatic asylum, he seized his chance and called in a few favors. It had turned out for the best, after all. He had reassembled the club. A smaller even more select group who knew the cost of a loose tongue. Their celebrations recaptured the best of René's early days. Of course, his father would have apoplexy if he knew. What a wonderful thought.

Nottidge became conscious of something blocking the sunshine from his upturned face. Any intrusion on his precious time was most disagreeable. He adopted a quizzical expression and opened his eyes. A buxom red-haired woman dressed like some doxy plying her trade in the Burlington Arcade stood before him.

"Madame, you are in my light. Kindly remove yourself. I do not wish to be disturbed."

The woman surprised him. Hands on hips, she responded with more venom than a cage of angry snakes. "I see you're calling yourself a doctor these days. How apt, just like Faust, eh? But to me you'll always be one of the Hell Master's little toadies—or don't you go in for those parties anymore? Perhaps your father didn't approve, eh, Seton?"

He placed his bookmark between the open pages and closed the volume. She was no doubt one of the cheap expendable tarts, who had been at a club soirée, and actually lived to tell the tale.

He rose to his feet, straightened his frock coat, and looked down at her. She showed some spirit if nothing else. He decided to see how this game would play out.

"Yes, I am a doctor. Might I enquire who *you* are? A new patient perhaps? Your behavior would suggest it."

The trollop looked like she'd just eaten a rotting toad. My, she did rile easily.

"Not *a* patient. Just patient. Since the 11th of October, 1862, to be exact."

"And your point is?"

"The night of the Mephisto Club's big celebration. I know who and what you are, *Doctor* Nottidge. And I saw what you did."

"Do you have a name?"

"Mary Grady. You would do well to remember that."

He cocked his eyebrow. "I don't think so. Go back to where you belong."

"I'll go when I'm ready. When my purse is, say, ten guineas heavier."

He'd laughed then. She threw him a calculated look.

"Or maybe *more*."

Brushing the front of his jacket, he eyed the woman with pointed disinterest. "Gad, a blackmailer as well as a strumpet. Is there no end to your talents?" He stepped toward her, but she stood her ground. Her cheap perfume and body odor assailed his nose. "I can tell fortunes too, *missy*, and see the end of your street walking days. Your hard face and pox-ridden body only fit for the rookeries of St. Giles with some workhouse drunk. How fitting."

He felt the tension between them and his excitement rose. This was turning into better sport than he ever imagined. Life could be so dull on occasion. He could see the presumptuous harpy working herself up for the next shot, her whole being focused on scoring a bull's eye.

"You can insult me as much as you want if that's the only way you can best a woman. Your usual position for that is from behind, isn't it?" She spat.

But her next words were low and, he could see, heartfelt. A useful weakness.

"My friend Nancy Flanagan wasn't celebrating, though. By then, you'd slit her throat. I won't ever forget, and if you don't pay me, I'll make sure no one else forgets, either. Especially Lord and Lady Seton."

He narrowed his eyes. The gutter classes were getting above themselves. As if he remembered details. There had been so many. He was getting tired of this troublemaker. "And you think they'd believe a piece of baggage like you? Perhaps it is *you* who ought to be in here."

He curled his lip at her. "Oh, you *are* in here. I can arrange it to be permanent. Now, I have better ways to spend my time. Goodbye."

He tucked his book under his arm and turned away when the woman's quiet words stopped him dead.

"I ask your favor, O prince of the East, Beelzebub, monarch of burning Hell, and Demogorgon, that Mephistopheles may appear and rise."

Surely this was trickery. There was no way she could know this incantation. Perhaps she had some actor friends who knew lines about Mephistopheles, the one word she knew of the club. He would not be bled by this harlot who ought never to have left Belle Vue when they'd finished with her. She had shown her hand and now left herself vulnerable. He remembered, too, why her name seemed familiar to him.

"You'll never get a job on the stage, Miss Grady. Not enough projection and if you keep spouting off like a deluded witch, you *will* be locked up in here."

Seeing a flash of hesitation cross her features, his confidence reasserted itself.

The woman stood firm, a look of contempt on her face. "The Duc said he liked you. I can't think why. I shall return to collect my money—*twenty* guineas—at the end of next month. Give it to Bill Callahan. If he asks, tell him it's a medical report about my half-sister, Ellen. I'll collect it from him. Of course, I have taken steps to protect my knowledge and my person."

Her expression smug, she held his gaze. "If you refuse, I will destroy you. Good day."

Mary strode toward the main asylum building. The sun still shone but she was blind to her surroundings and their natural beauty. A surge of exhilaration shot through her. When she'd left Belle Vue almost seven years ago, in her fourteen-year-old mind, she had emerged the winner. She knew she could survive anywhere. Her ruthlessness and cunning against the de Montalts had proved it so. There was no God. The weak would not inherit the earth, there were no rewards for being good, only people who would hurt you, or worse. Liars and hypocrites all.

At that moment, all she could think about were the two who had betrayed her—Catherine and Father Patrick. They had tricked her into believing they had found her a way to make a living and maybe enjoy life if she worked hard and did well. They had lied and were no better than those at the Mephisto party. She had detested her stepmother and the priest for making her and Nancy so vulnerable. She never trusted anyone again and only used people for her own ends before they did the same thing to her. She had learned fast during her time with the Duc. The Devil always won. This time, though, the Devil was on her side, not Nottidge's.

Only he didn't know it yet.

Ellen didn't see Mary again that day. She waited and waited until, at five, Harriet and the rest of the inmates joined her for dinner.

Chapter Fifteen

Friday, 6 February
PRESENT DAY

"Not another workout?" Claire asked, raising her eyebrows in obvious disbelief.

Marianne bustled into the sitting room in her old tracksuit. She stopped by the sofa where Claire reclined with her feet up.

"I know. Weird, huh? It's like a magnet. If you told me a month ago how much I'd be using the health club, I'd have said you were mad." Marianne laughed and wondered aloud, "Maybe there are forces here compelling me to get fit."

"Well, they don't work for me. I feel lousy and can't remember the last time I had the urge to do any exercise." Claire yawned. She ran her hands over her face. "Ugh. Spots, bags, and crusty eyes. I bet I look awful, too."

Marianne gazed at Claire with dismay at how frail and washed out she looked but responded automatically. "No, you don't."

A telling pause as Claire's face seemed to acknowledge her tactful, but untrue words. Marianne continued, "You've lost a bit of your oomph with all this final year stress. Why don't I see if they can fit you in for a massage and facial downstairs? A little pampering never did a girl any harm and it'll make you feel great for tonight's party."

"No, I'm actually going to class this afternoon. With my dismal exam results, there's no escape. Perhaps tomorrow?" Claire said with little enthusiasm. "Alex rang. He's going to pick us up at seven." She gave Marianne a limp smile. "Paul's coming, too."

"Paul, heh? I might have a facial, and maybe they can fit us in for a massage tomorrow."

Claire tilted her head and tapped her ear. "Did I hear that right? You are actually going to spend money on something that isn't a necessity? What's going on?"

Marianne laughed. She was as surprised as Claire. Her outlook had certainly changed since she'd moved in to Belle Vue. After all her worries about the place, everything was working out fine. "Life's too short. Might as well enjoy it while I can."

Claire shook her head with slow deliberation. "I do not believe it."

"I'm ignoring that remark. Will you be here when I get back?"

"Only just. I've got to go to the library as well." Claire looked glum at the prospect. She leaned over and picked up a half-eaten chocolate bar from the coffee table. The one next to an empty muffin case, a banana skin, and a glass containing a thin layer of milk at the bottom.

At least Claire was eating well. Since moving in, Marianne had lost her appetite. Her way, she assumed, of dealing with final year pressure, working every spare hour at the hospital and the initial oddness of finding herself living in the old asylum. She felt more settled now, but her old cravings for anything edible hadn't returned. Just in case, as there'd be tons of food at the party tonight, she intended completing a full workout. She left Claire to her calorific treats and jogged out the door.

On her way back after an intense hour and a half in the gym, Marianne collected the post from the mailbox in the foyer. Nothing for her, but a pile of letters for Claire. She flicked through them, noting with interest one of the branded envelopes.

She entered the flat. Marianne could hear Claire humming to herself in the lounge. She decided against disturbing her and left the mail on the hall table. In the bathroom, she stripped off her sweaty kit and, holding it aloft, grimaced at its worn, sorry state. She needed to buy herself some new gear, and also ditch her usual slob-about-the-house black Lycra ensemble. This afternoon, she might go shopping instead of all this slave labor she'd been so keen on. Claire charged her peanuts for rent and she'd been doing a lot of overtime at the hospital, so why not?

Marianne gazed at her naked body in the mirror. Some toning was definitely in order and a hunger for a sexy new figure overrode her previous contentment with her weight and appearance. She played with her hair for a few minutes, trying different styles. The color looked so drab. Maybe she'd make some changes there, too, and even start wearing makeup. Marianne hesitated and stopped what she'd been doing, letting her hair fall around her face.

She gazed at her reflection again, taking comfort in its familiarity. A bit of exercise and healthy eating was okay, but as for the rest, forget it. She was happy with her looks, and that's what counted.

Marianne showered and dressed. A twinge of uncertainty surfaced. She had some tight assignment deadlines before going on her work placement in a few weeks, so she shouldn't be wasting time shopping. She also shouldn't use her savings unless it was essential.

After running the comb through her damp hair, she grabbed the newspaper article she'd been keeping, collected Claire's mail, and went through to the sitting room. Claire was still on the couch, an empty wrapper clutched in her hand. She seemed tense and Marianne noticed her red nose and eyes. It looked like she'd sat there like a toy with no batteries until Marianne's return.

"Are you okay?" she asked.

"Yeah, I don't seem to have any energy to do anything. I'll have a bath in a bit and see if it livens me up."

Marianne handed the envelopes to Claire and settled herself in the padded chair. "I noticed there's a letter from your solicitor. It made me think."

"About what?"

Marianne placed the article on the table with its headline facing toward Claire: *Government Grab: The Cost of Dying Without a Will.*

"Not a nice thing to raise but—"

Marianne saw Claire's surprised expression, the way her eyes narrowed slightly.

"I can't deal with things like that now. Maybe later." Claire's strained voice trailed off, then she picked up the article. "I will read this, Marianne. My solicitor has been bothering me about it, too." She didn't wait for a reply but disappeared saying she was going to get dressed.

Marianne sat in her chair and wondered if there was something more going on that Claire hadn't told her about. These days her moods seemed limited to either irritable or sleepy. Marianne was growing concerned. This might be a relapse, back to how she'd been after her return from Hong Kong.

But no one could have blamed Claire then for freaking out like that. Finding her parents' bodies: and to know, if she hadn't been late back from seeing friends, she would have been seated with her parents for dinner when the murderers struck.

———

Claire opened the door, wearing an expectant smile. Alex hovered, wondering what to say. Paul stepped forward and gave her a big hug.

"You look wonderful," he said, much to Alex's discomfort.

"Alex?" Claire raised an eyebrow and glared at him as if to say, 'I'm waiting'.

He tried to keep his face neutral and not stare, but her hair looked dreadful. Hadn't she said she was going to wash it when he'd spoken to her on the phone this afternoon? The words *dull* and *lank* came to mind, like the before image in one of those shampoo adverts. He swallowed, feeling awkward, reminded of the night he'd smoked that joint. As he recalled the occasion, his stomach lurched.

"Alex?"

Both Claire and Paul were looking at him with varying degrees of disapproval. He told her how nice her bracelet looked with her outfit.

Then hoping his added *sweetheart* cut the mustard, he pecked her cheek, avoiding what looked like a cold sore at the corner of her mouth. He had tried to be discreet about it, but things seemed a bit tense from then on.

Marianne joined them and though Alex thought she'd made an effort with her appearance, he said nothing. Claire still eyed him like a Eurovision judge who'd decided to award him nul points. When they left the flat, Claire stopped in front of a pile of wood shavings on the landing. Something flickered across her face, though whether it had been puzzlement or fear, Alex couldn't tell. Concerned, he'd put his arm out to guide her on, but she'd flinched away from him.

In the car, Claire had pointedly sat in the back with Marianne and when they arrived at the college, she ignored his proffered hand. It crossed Alex's mind the Food and Wine Society Greek evening might not be a roaring success and he wondered if he could do anything to change that.

They hurried toward the Students' Union building. A light dusting of snow covered the ground. The four of them were bundled up in protective padding against the biting wind. The main paths and buildings were intermittently lit, and similar rotund shapes could be seen flitting between the light and darkness like Michelin men playing hide and seek. Reaching the door first, Alex pulled it open and let his three friends in.

The hall thronged with people unwrapping themselves. Chattering voices and the thud of heavy bass from the main bar along the hall fought against the distinctive tinny plinks of the Greek party below. Coats stowed, they followed the line of people down the stairs.

Alex saw Paul hold out a chair for Marianne and wondered if anything would progress there. He'd told Paul to go for it. Marianne was a safe option for his friend, and from what Claire had said, he was sure she'd say yes.

"What would you like to drink?" Paul asked Marianne.

"A pint of Guinness."

Paul looked at Marianne, then at Alex and Claire. He laughed as if to say, 'Good joke, guys.' Everyone knew Marianne didn't drink. She always stuck with lemonade or Coke.

But Marianne wasn't smiling. A few seconds of uneasy silence passed, before Claire teased, "You've never drunk Guinness in your life. This is a Greek evening so if you want alcohol, at least try Ouzo or something."

Alex, who stood next to Paul, gazed at Marianne's upturned face with interest. Funny, how you thought you knew someone then they do something out of character and you realize perhaps you don't know them that well after all. Paul hesitated, as though not sure if Marianne was making fun of him. Alex nudged him.

"Do you want your Guinness chilled?" Paul asked.

Marianne's voice dripped with irritation. "No, Paul. I don't. Thank you." The last words came several seconds later as though she'd just remembered her manners.

While Paul made his way through the rapidly filling tables, Marianne studied the handwritten menu. The sound of traditional bouzouki music clinked in the background. Claire pushed up the sleeves of her roll-neck jumper. A voice wailed unintelligible lyrics to an instrumental lament.

Alex's mouth watered as the smell of the food from the buffet wafted temptingly across the floor.

Paul returned carrying a tray and set down the pint glass with a flourish. "One Guinness."

Marianne looked up and put her hand on his arm. She ignored the drink and said, "I can't make head or tail of the dishes listed. Come and explain them to me."

Alex raised an eyebrow at Claire as Marianne led Paul across the floor toward the food. She was in a funny mood this evening.

"You think Paul's going to get lucky tonight?" he asked.

"Alex! Don't you think of anything else?" Her voice still held a touch of ice.

Careful now, he thought, as he leaned toward her. "With you, no, but first let's eat and later we'll get lucky, too."

"Christ, who writes your lines? Gary?" Her tone was lighter this time.

Determined to continue the thaw, he took her hand and escorted her toward the buffet.

The rest of the function passed in a boozy haze accompanied by plenty of food, loud music, energetic dancing, and exuberant plate throwing. Alex had been right. He didn't have as much fun as he'd hoped. Throughout the evening, Claire complained the room was too hot, the music too loud, and the jostling of the crowd had given her another headache. As the designated driver, he couldn't blame her grumpiness on the booze either. By midnight, they were both ready to leave.

In the end, she only had to drive him home. Paul and Marianne had taken a taxi to meet Gary and some other friends at one of the late clubs in town. His head woozy, Alex spent the journey devising ways to improve Claire's mood. As they'd walked from the car park and climbed the stairs to her apartment, neither said anything. Once Claire shut the door behind her, he made his move and took her in his arms before she had a chance to take off her coat.

He hugged her and, taking her head in his hands, planted small kisses on her cheeks. She moaned then pulled back. "Oh, Alex. Let's get back to how we used to be."

"I know. God, Claire, I want you so much." As he pulled her closer, she lifted her face to his, but male self-protection, even half-drunk, still functioned. He nuzzled her neck instead before unzipping her jacket. He shucked off his coat, then pulled hers from her shoulders, letting both fall to the floor. They were undressed by the time they reached Claire's room. He picked her up, surprised at how light she felt, and carried her to the bed.

His fingers snaked down and began to explore under the lace of her panties. He kissed her neck again and buried his face into its warmth.

"Ouch!" Claire yelled. "Stop, it hurts." She rolled over and switched on the bedside light.

He groaned in frustration and sat up. "What's the matter?"

"I'm not sure. Let me check." Claire climbed off the bed and disappeared into the en-suite. It wasn't supposed to be like this. He slid under the duvet, wondering if there was some hex over them. All he wanted to do was make love to Claire, but every time there seemed to be a problem, if not with him, then with her. Things had been great between them but since the start of the final year and moving into this apartment, it had all seemed to go downhill.

His eyelids began to droop when Claire came out of the bathroom wrapped in her white toweling robe. "I think I've got a cold sore or something down there."

Alex wanted to lighten the moment, things kept getting too serious. He grinned at her. "I hope you haven't given me anything."

Claire scowled at him, annoyance permeating every syllable. "I think it's the other way round, don't you? I'm not the one with the reputation, you are."

"Hey, only joking, sweetheart." Alex watched as she got into the other side of the bed without bothering to remove the robe. It flashed through his mind that sex wasn't the only thing off the menu. Any physical contact now seemed unlikely. Shit. "Are you okay?"

"I'm a bit uncomfortable. I'll try to get an appointment with the doctor tomorrow and see if she can give me something."

She reached out for the light switch and the darkness enveloped them. In the uneasy silence that followed, Claire turned her back on Alex. She edged as far away as possible, leaving him feeling puzzled and alone. Instinctively, he knew not to mention she should wear more deodorant.

Late next morning, as Alex walked down the stairs to the main foyer, he caught a glimpse of red disappearing along the corridor on his right. He hurried across the parquet floor.

"Miss Bradigan, can I have a word please?"

The figure halted, remaining immobile as though debating whether to acquiesce or ignore the request and continue on her way. She slowly turned. Alex thought she appeared older than when he had last saw her at the Residents' Association meeting. Her ludicrous wig didn't help, as its contrast with the wrinkled face below heightened her pallor.

"Why?" She peered along her lofty nose, disdain and an underlying hint of smugness infusing her features. What's her problem, he thought. She'd been, not exactly friendly that time before Claire's housewarming, but okay. Now she looked at him as if he had terminal body odor. Perhaps she didn't remember him.

"I'm Alex Palmer. We met a few months ago. My girlfriend Claire lives here." He held out a hand but she didn't move.

"Yes, I know who you are and who she is." Pause. "I see she has a new lodger."

"Er, yes. Marianne Edwards." She didn't miss much.

"Good first name, a favorite of mine."

He smiled, but apparently, the limit of Miss Bradigan's bonhomie had been met for her next question was curt. "What do you want?"

"Eric Beamish said he—"

"Mr. Beamish says rather too much for his own good."

"Er, well, yes, but on this occasion, his information really helped. It led me to you. He said you might be able to tell me about Belle Vue before it closed." He adopted his well-practiced killer smile.

Miss Bradigan's ice-cold eyes surveyed his face in silence until even Alex had to admit defeat. The curve of his lips became a straight line once more.

"It is a shame, Mr. Palmer you didn't consider that I might not want to talk to anyone on this subject. If I feel inclined, then it will be my choice, not yours. Age might take away some advantages, but it confers others."

He wondered how he could save the moment. Nothing came to mind. From what Eric had said, Miss Bradigan could tell him a lot about Belle Vue not found in books or articles, and he was reluctant to give up, but she didn't look the type to do anyone any favors. Alex sighed.

"What's your interest in the hospital, anyway? I would have thought a good-looking young man such as you would have other more entertaining pursuits to follow." Her expression, brazen and knowing, disconcerted Alex and he felt the heat rise on his face.

As he briefly outlined his dissertation, the old woman's forceful gaze held his eyes captive. He found her intensity unnerving and the thought she knew already what he was telling her, struck him again. She seemed to weigh his every word like some latter-day Osiris. His words petered out to silence. After several long moments, she turned toward her apartment and spoke over her shoulder. "I will grant you a few minutes of my time. Things may work out better than I had hoped after all."

Unable to fathom what she might mean, he made no comment and followed her down the corridor. She opened the door, stepping aside to allow him entry, and told him to go through to the sitting room. As he crossed the threshold, a musty old-lady smell permeated his nostrils.

The decor of the flat mirrored her appearance. Elements seemed to conflict with each other rather than work together. What Alex could only describe as garish tack jostled for position with more conservative and tasteful touches. While the wallpaper in cream-watered silk was similar to that in his parents' house, the picture of three drunk leprechauns flirting with a young colleen was dreadful. He gazed round noting there were also Oriental knick-knacks displayed on the sideboard and bookshelves, but it was the trashy painting that drew his eyes. Miss Bradigan caught his gaze. "Another favorite of mine."

"It's er…interesting. Strong use of color."

"Lovely girl. Good red Irish hair. I always liked the color." She patted her head. "As you can see."

"And very fine it looks, too." As the words came out, he wished he hadn't attempted the Irish accent.

Giving him a look that could strip paint, she spoke in a low tone. "Be careful, Mr. Palmer, not to make fun at my expense. I might exact a high price in payment."

This was going to be hard work. He'd definitely need a pint by lunchtime.

"What do you want to know?" she asked.

"I'm focusing my research from the time the asylum opened in 1867 to about 1892. The first twenty-five years, but I need to provide some information both before, and after, this period. It would also be great to get one or two viewpoints from people who could talk firsthand about the hospital before it closed."

He saw a spark of interest light up her face before her expression became unreadable once more.

"I'm not promising anything, but I shall give it some thought. It might be cathartic and you could be useful…very useful…" She said, almost to herself.

They'd been standing facing each other and she suddenly seemed to wilt as though her supply of energy had been cut off. He put his hand out to her. "Please, sit down. Can I get you something?"

She allowed herself to be led to the high-backed armchair, where she looked relieved to take the weight off her feet. "Thank you, Mr. Palmer. Being a gentleman requires good deeds, and not just the high opinion of society and one's self. A whiskey would be very welcome."

He noted her physical weakness didn't extend to her mental faculties. She waved her hand toward the heavy oak sideboard where a set of spirit glasses surrounded a bottle of best Irish.

Her eyes followed Alex as he poured the whiskey and offered her the glass.

"May you be in heaven a full half hour before the Devil knows you're dead," she said, in a mocking tone. Noticing his puzzled expression, her lips curled upward. "An old Irish toast."

Miss Bradigan took a mouthful and scrutinized him with such intensity, he started to feel ill at ease.

"As I said, I will think on your request."

"Thank you, Miss Bradigan," Alex said, his finger tracing the dent in his chin. "I noticed you seemed interested at the Residents' meeting when Eric mentioned the bone found near the cha—"

"You are mistaken, Mr. Palmer," she cut in, sharply. Miss Bradigan drew in her breath. In the long pause that followed, Alex sensed the tension.

"Why would I be remotely interested in anything dug up by some old mongrel?"

She arched an eyebrow and smiled at him, but the coldness never left her eyes.

Chapter Sixteen

Saturday, 24 July, 1869

"Who could have done such a terrible thing?" The Reverend Theodore Croft's nose quivered with righteous indignation.

Bill Callahan stifled a yawn. Normally, he and Croft saw eye-to-eye since the vicar took it as one of his functions to strengthen the arm of authority in the asylum. He did this by persuading inmates to accept confinement in this world on the promise of freedom in the next. On this occasion, however, he was on his high horse about a bit of damage in the chapel where they now stood. And, he told Callahan, holding him as Head Attendant responsible.

Croft picked up one of the blood-spattered Bibles. "Such mindless desecration. It only proves my argument that moral turpitude causes insanity." The Chaplain's voice rose. "But how did they get in? I locked the door after evening prayers last night, and I unfastened the padlock this morning."

"Is there another entrance, Vicar?" Bill asked, making no effort to keep the mockery out of his voice.

"You know there's not, Callahan. Now, who else has a key?"

The Chaplain was obviously missing his Christian spirit this morning, thought Bill, deciding to goad him some more. Croft's high ambitions were well known. "Doctor Fishburn holds the masters for all the keys. Do you think I should ask him if he opened the chapel?"

Croft looked horrified. "No. No, of course not, Callahan. You'll say nothing of the matter to him. We can't have any scandal. Anyone else?"

Bill looked the Reverend straight in the eye. "Only you."

"Oh." The Chaplain winced but continued, "That's odd. There must be an explanation, but I can't think of one."

Saying nothing, Bill listened to the man as he gibbered like a novice thief caught with his hand in the cash drawer.

"No one has had my key, and I'm sure Doctor Fishburn would have let me know if his master had gone missing. He'd have needed mine to cut a new one. Callahan, please arrange to have the altar and chancel cleaned. Discreetly please."

"Of course, Vicar," Bill said. The expression in Croft's eyes showed he was well aware of the debt he now owed. After muttering a quick *thank you*, the scowling cleric hurried away.

Before Bill could progress any further toward his destination, he heard Adelaide Fishburn call his name and his mood plummeted. He wasn't the sort of man for regrets, but now, he wished he'd never encouraged Mrs. Fishburn to come into his cottage on that one occasion. It was as though she'd been in heat, which had excited and repelled him at the same time. He let her unbuckle his trousers and pleasure him. Pleasure was the wrong word. He didn't fancy her at all and he'd been shocked when she had actually knelt before him. The jolt of power in having Fishburn's wife service him was irresistible. He couldn't think why she'd done it and didn't care.

"Mr. Callahan, ooh-hoo!"

Bill stopped in his tracks, keeping his face unreadable as the Matron bore down on him.

"Mrs. Fishburn. Can this wait? I'm in a hurry. If you'll excuse me."

Her gaze never wavered from his face as though she were judging his every reaction.

"It's about the other night's incident. You know, Euan Jones?"

He did remember. A troublesome attendant who'd been let go. Bill had found him sleeping at his post in the main male dormitory, unaware one of his charges had managed to escape. Bill knew, though, from the three constables who had spotted the lunatic in his distinctive asylum garb and returned him. Jones had been unrepentant and decided to settle a few scores. At his dismissal meeting with Doctor Fishburn, he'd ranted on about what Bill and Lynton Brown got up to at Belle Vue. Luckily, the Medical Superintendent didn't look or act as though he had listened to a single word.

Mrs. Fishburn continued, "Jones has been dealt with, but Doctor Fishburn is now concerned about the manner of the lunatic's escape. He'd been able to gnaw through the cloth ties that secured him to his bed. In future, the order is that *all* inmates requiring restraint will be shackled with chains. Of course, Doctor Lush has objected but he is no more than a greenhorn who still thinks kindness makes a difference to these drooling idiots. We know his jelly-like firmness with them." The Matron gazed at him. "Quite unlike yours, eh, Bill?"

She blushed, much to his surprise, producing an unfortunate blotched effect on her scraggy features before she seemed to regain her usual formality.

"But don't worry, there will not be any repetition. I don't know what came over me. I desire to stay married, and you, I wager, to stay employed. On the basis of that information, we are even. Of course, there may be a few favors you could do for me should I ever ask."

He might have known, thought Bill. For all her primness, she was as bad as the rest of her sex, always wanting more from a man than he might be prepared to give. They all needed the back of a firm hand or fist to keep them in line.

The chapel bell tolled twelve, the time he was due to meet Doctor Nottidge. So, he kept his thoughts to himself and took his leave.

When Bill reached Nottidge's office door, he knocked and received a curt, *enter*. The doctor sat at his desk lighting a cheroot, the newspaper open in front of him. He looked up at Bill.

"Everything ready for tonight?"

They checked through the arrangements. When complete, Doctor Nottidge picked up his cigar again. Bill reflected that this medic liked to play rough. When he'd first joined the staff of Belle Vue, Nottidge had been looking for someone who would act as his right-hand man. He'd taken Bill's measure quickly, sounding him out before the first lunatic arrived, and after, observing his treatment of the inmates.

Now, helped by a lazy Medical Superintendent and Matron whose chief interest was their own prosperity, and chums who sat on the Metropolitan Asylums Board who would keep Fishburn and his wife continually busy with their demands, Nottidge ran the asylum more or less as he saw fit. With Bill only too pleased to assist. But the doctor liked to invite members of his club over from time to time and partake of practices that would be severely frowned upon should they ever come to light.

Sometimes things got out of hand, like a few weeks ago when the burnt lunatic had been found. That shouldn't have happened. They thought the man dead, but his will to live had surprised them all. He had dealt with the attendant who took care of the wastage that night. The doctor didn't care, the lunatics—especially the pauper ones—were expendable. With such a surfeit and the way things were run here, a few mouths less to feed was no great loss. As Nottidge had told him, if asked, you just marked them cured or deceased, all the same to the powers that be.

But Bill wasn't stupid. More care was needed, especially as Nottidge's demands for entertainment were becoming more frequent. He told of his run-in with Croft.

"Of course, he doesn't know about my key," Bill said. "But he's asking awkward questions. I said I'd ask Fishburn and he twitched like a frightened rabbit."

"I'll tell him I'll put a good word in for him with the bishop," Nottidge said, smiling as he leaned back in his chair. He drew on his cigar. "We'll keep our activities to the hidden tunnels for a while. Leave the crypt and chapel. I'm having too good a time for it to stop now." He smirked at Bill. "And so are you. Though your choice of the Matron is strange. I do like your style."

Bill shrugged, unsurprised by the doctor's knowledge of his activities. The man seemed to know most things going on in the asylum. Not that he showed it. To Bill, he always looked uninterested and not paying any attention to trivial details.

"Actually, Callahan that was a surprisingly smart move on your part."

"Er, yeah." If it pleased Nottidge, maybe it had been worth it after all.

"You never know when such information might be needed, so we'll store it away for now. Such secrets between people are good because it enables us to know where the other's loyalties lie, doesn't it, Bill?" The doctor's eyes glinted as he spoke.

After parting on that note of mutual understanding, Bill collected his post. A solitary letter from Mary. He left the main building by the rear entrance and trudged toward the engineers' department. He opened the envelope and scanned its contents but before he could think of its implications, the sound of loud grunts caught his attention.

He left the path and jogged across the grass. On the left, he saw two figures struggling on the ground. On recognizing them, he stepped behind a low-branched tree for cover. Well, well. Ellen Grady and the epileptic. In mid-fit by the look of it. He watched as the girl's face contorted. Her body jerked like a marionette being played by a madman. Mary's half-sister on her knees trying to help, her hands covered with red as the bubbles sprayed from the girl's mouth. His excitement grew at the sight.

The fit took its course. Harriet groaned and flopped like a discarded rag doll. Bill wondered what they would do now. They were supposed to be straw-plaiting, so on two counts, he could punish them. He was going to enjoy this.

Ellen got to her feet and, after taking Harriet's hands in hers, helped her to stand. She put her arm around her friend and the two staggered toward the engineering and laundry block. Bill followed and saw them disappear into the wash house, probably enlisting aid from

BELLE VUE

Ruth Evans, who ran the laundry.

He waited a few minutes, then stepped through the open door to be greeted by three disappointed and guilty, faces. "Well, what have we here? Phew. What's that stink? Ain't just laundry smells." He raised his voice over the cacophony of the wash house working at full steam. The girl had done more than have a fit, she'd dirtied herself as well. Didn't get much better than that. "You two ought to be working. Who let you out?"

He smirked at Ellen and Harriet. They clutched at the damp bloodstained rags they'd been using to wipe themselves. Tense expressions belied any innocence on their part. "I think you two are in trouble."

Mrs. Evans, a mouse-like woman stepped forward and twitched her nose at him. "Mr. Callahan, Harriet was taken poorly for a bit. She's fine now. The girls came to get a fresh dress for her. They are going straight back to work."

"Right. Just as they are now. Let's see how their workmates like the smell of them."

He sneered at the two glum faces before turning to Ruth. "Give me the clean dress. I'll make sure Harriet gets it later."

He took the thin frock. Ellen and Harriet followed him as he headed toward the workrooms.

Bill paused and swung round to the girls. "I've changed my mind," he said.

His eyes took in Ellen and he felt himself harden. He itched so bad for her but Mary had some other plan for the fair Ellen. Her letter said she would talk to him about it when she came to Belle Vue in the next fortnight. Shame. He would bide his time and, when he did get his hands on the girl, enjoy her all the more. For now, he'd make do with the epileptic.

With regret, he pointed at Ellen. "You, go to the workroom and finish your quota. No meals for you to make up the time you wasted."

Ellen hesitated and moved closer to her friend. "Mr. Callahan, I'll look after Harriet. Please, give me the dress. I'll clean her up, too. We'll both work extra hard."

He gave a contemptuous snort. "I don't think so. *I'll* sort her out. Go. Before I take my stick to you." He stroked the cosh hanging from his belt. The girls exchanged fearful glances and Ellen set off at a snail's pace toward her destination.

"Get!" His voice boomed behind her and she jumped like a startled fawn.

He moved closer to the epileptic and picked her up in his arms. He leaned his mouth to her ear. "Now lets you and me have a bit of fun, eh?"

Back in the workroom and close to tears, Ellen sat on her bench. For every length of straw, she added to her plait, so her trepidation as to what has happening to Harriet grew. The day crawled by. At four o'clock, when they were about to be taken back to their wards and a lead weight of fear lay in the pit of her stomach, Callahan's slimy assistant, Lynton Brown sidled in. He informed the orderly Ellen had to remain. An extra quota to finish as punishment, which made her worry all the more.

Brown spent the rest of the afternoon, snickering at her, and piling ever more straw in front of her. By the time the bell tolled seven, Ellen's fingers were numb and her lips badly chapped from moistening the brittle stalks. At last, she was permitted to leave. Although tired and hungry, her overriding concern was for Harriet. She hurried back to their room, ducking expertly between the figures, moving and still, who had not yet been taken to their beds.

The door ajar, she braced herself and went in. Harriet lay on her bed, facing the window.

"Are you all right?" she asked. Her nerves stretched ever tighter as she waited for the reply.

Harriet rolled over, her eyes puffy and wet.

"What's wrong, what happened?" She rushed to her friend and hugged her.

"Oh, Ellen, I was frightened but so ashamed. I'd dirtied myself." Harriet's words emerged between sobs. "I kept thinking what he might do to me. He'd see me like that." Harriet sniffled and wiped her nose with her sleeve.

Ellen held her friend as Harriet cried herself out. She felt a chill seep through her as she thought of the danger she'd put her friend in—all because of her connection to Bill Callahan.

"What did he do to you?" she asked, dreading Harriet's next words.

"This time, Ellen, I was lucky. Callahan was carrying me toward one of the disused outhouses when Doctor Fishburn appeared with a group of gentlemen. I don't know who looked more surprised, them or Callahan. Doctor Fishburn said he needed some keys to show the board members round these buildings, and could I walk? Of course, I said yes, and Callahan had to put me down to go fetch the keys." Harriet's voice lowered. "I—we—may not be so fortunate next time. Oh, Ellen, what are we to do?"

Ellen looked into her friend's eyes, a little unsure of Harriet's reaction. "I'm going to write to Mrs. Fishburn as well as Mary. I shall tell them how improved I am and ask if I can be discharged. The staff are always complaining how overcrowded it is in here. Surely they want people to be cured and leave."

"I don't think it's that simple."

An uneasy mix of dismay and fear crossed Harriet's features. She quickly continued. "If I can get out, perhaps there's some way you could leave, too? You never see the doctors here and don't take any pills. Why couldn't you be released, too? Your father pays for your care here, so why not do the same but in a place outside? With a nurse to look after you. I could be your companion."

Harriet sat quietly as though thinking this through, then replied.

"I'd never thought of doing something like that before, perhaps because I've never had the desire to be outside on my own, but now, we'd be together. Ellen, I shall write to my father first thing tomorrow. He often asks if there's anything I need. Well, now there is."

Harriet lay back on the bed. Ellen took her hand and watched over her as she fell asleep. Ellen's mind whirled. Would such an idea work? Perhaps they could ask the Assistant Matron, Mrs. Trotter, if such a thing had been done before. Of course, it all depended on Mr. Stubb's response and Mary's. Surely, she wouldn't refuse. Mary disliked Belle Vue. She seemed to despise people like Mrs. Fishburn and Doctor Nottidge. On top of that, the train journeys here were expensive and time consuming. This solution meant her half-sister need never visit Belle Vue again, and Ellen wouldn't be a burden on her any longer. Mary would be thrilled.

Thrilled wasn't the word for it. When Mary opened Ellen's latest letter detailing her plans with this Harriet Stubbs, she was incandescent with rage. How dare the sneaky little bint think she could walk away and expect her blessing after all she had done for her. First Ellen says she's *better* and wants to leave Belle Vue. Then she supposedly has it all arranged. Mary vaguely remembered a girl being introduced to her on her last visit, but she hadn't paid much attention to yet another tiresome lunatic. Mary wished she had now. Still, it wasn't too late. She'd find some way to separate them. She would be visiting Belle Vue next week. In the meantime, she would write again to Bill to make sure he did what they'd agreed.

Mary sat alone at the large kitchen table collecting her thoughts. Trust Ellen to force her hand. Now she'd have to make her move. Leaving the remnants of her half-eaten breakfast, she crushed Ellen's letter and envelope into the pocket of her skirt. Mary pushed the table forward, its heavy wooden legs scraping their resistance against the slate floor. She stomped up the stairs to her room and slammed the door behind her.

Mary dropped onto the stool and pulled Jack's writing box toward her. She took out a sheet of paper, an envelope, and a feather pen. She dipped the quill into the box's small ink well and began to write. Mary scratched out the words quickly and firmly with a large sloping script.

"*Bill,*" it began, "*I shall be at Belle Vue next Wednesday. Nottidge will give you an envelope for me. Ellen is getting restless, but I want to make sure when she leaves Belle Vue, it's for my purposes. She can't be 'cured' yet—make sure of it. Be at the station for midday when my train arrives, we have much to talk about. Mary*"

She blotted the ink dry, folded the sheet of paper and shoved it into the envelope. As she finished sealing it, Jack sauntered into the room whistling her favorite music hall tune. He moved up behind Mary and kissed her neck. She smiled at Jack's reflection in the mirror and, catching his eyes, noticed their hunger for her again. Last night had been good, and she was certain he couldn't hold out much longer. Soon she'd be Mrs. Jack Callahan.

Jack sighed as he took off his jacket and threw it on the bed. The relentless heat had exacted a watery toll. Both his shirt and forehead were drenched. He folded up his sleeves and, for the third time since he'd entered the room, muttered, 'tsk'.

Mary swiveled round to face him. "Is there a problem?"

"Been up to Carters. They weren't going to give me any more credit but I've sorted it now."

Unsurprised by this piece of news, she scoffed. "Jack, you run a great pub, but when it comes to money, you're as good as a pickpocket with no fingers."

"But what's the use of it, if not for spending? We want to enjoy life. I work hard, and the pub's takings are good. I can't fathom why we're always short of the readies."

She kept her face straight. All he needed was a firm hand—hers. She held his eyes and swayed toward him. "You have so much to do, my love, with the place so busy." She snaked her arms around him and pressed her body into his, feeling his instinctive reaction.

"But what's to be done?" he said. "The rent is going up next quarter. How can we marry now? Costs lots of money for a wedding."

"Because you will be getting a wife who can help solve her husband's problems, and make his life easy." She moved her hand down his back and rubbed against him. "And pleasurable."

"I do so want yer to be Mrs. Callahan." Jack's voice came out strangulated as he pushed himself against her hips.

Mary dropped her arms and stepped back. "You leave it all to me, Jack. I'll sort it for you, for us. I have things to do now but later, if you're not too busy, we can come up here and take some more of that pleasure we deserve."

Mary licked the tip of her finger, wiped it along the edge of her lips and watched as Jack's eyes lit up. She collected her purse from the top of the chest of drawers and took the envelope from the dressing table.

"I need to post this letter," she said and reminded herself to pay Solomon Pecker the insurance agent his monthly sub. "I also want to buy some phosphorous. We've got rats again, you know."

She caught Jack's surprised frown as if to say when had she ever bothered about such matters? He knew she had never shown the slightest interest in doing any of the domestic chores fit only, she often said, for the losers of the world.

Well, she had changed her mind. Mary smirked at Jack as she left the room.

Chapter Seventeen

Monday, 9 February
PRESENT DAY

Lost in thought, Claire sat at the dressing table brushing her hair. The dark smudges under her eyes testified to her continued lack of sleep. The sore on her genitals worried her, and the damned noises were still keeping her awake. But now she knew it wasn't only Sally who couldn't hear them. On Saturday afternoon she and Marianne had been in the kitchen chatting over their coffees when the chapel bell tolled. Marianne didn't seem to notice the sound. In the end, she'd asked if the bell bothered her, but Marianne's response, "What bell?" said it all.

She'd pushed it aside by saying, "Just testing." but Marianne had looked at her in an odd way, calculating almost, as though trying to gauge what was going on in her head.

Claire glanced at her watch. Swapping her brush for her mobile, she rang the surgery number. Engaged. As usual, getting through would be a long slog. She shifted on the padded stool and tried to ignore the twinge of discomfort.

After about a dozen tries, she was rewarded by the sound of the connection ringing. She arranged the earliest appointment possible—Wednesday at 11:30—and for this with a female doctor. Her GP was okay, but the thought of a man examining her down there was, to put it in a word, repulsive. Funny, it had never bothered her before.

Placing the phone back on the dressing table, she picked up the brush again. Since she once more had the makings of a bad headache, something else to mention to the doc—she sounded like a rampant hypochondriac—she gently brushed the back of her head and made a mental note to buy some more aspirin. Getting up had also been a chore. She ached all over. Maybe she'd buy some multivitamins, too.

She hadn't seen Alex since he'd crept out yesterday morning before she woke. He'd called in the afternoon but hadn't said anything about when they'd next see each other. Men were so obvious. He probably thought she hadn't noticed him desperately trying to avoid the cold sore on her mouth. Since he was the only one who could have given it to her, that was a bit rich.

Thankfully, good old Marianne was on hand. They'd been sharing now for over three weeks. She enjoyed having the company and, even better, a sounding board for her course work before she committed her ideas to paper. Oh, and a handy shoulder to cry on, should she need it. A couple of times she felt as though Marianne eavesdropped on her and Alex, but she supposed her friend would think the same if she ever brought, say, Paul home and Claire had to make herself scarce. Touch wood, everything would turn out for the best.

She hummed an old Diana Ross song her mother used to sing when she was getting ready for a function. She only knew one line, but who cared? Claire smiled as she remembered the way her mother mimicked the singer's outstretched arms as she launched into full flight. Claire spread her arms and, as she did, focused on her reflection and on the brush full of hair—her hair. She stared, not sure what she was seeing. God, there must be half a head's worth trapped in the bristles. Her hands shaking, she picked out every last strand, throwing them into the wicker basket by her chair.

Watching herself in the beveled mirror, she lifted the brush to the top of her head and as lightly as she could, pulled it through her hair. Once again, the brush was full of her long, fair strands.

She gritted her teeth. Be strong. Be strong. She must be run down. The vitamin tablets would help. Her eyes watered and her image in the mirror blurred. Something moved behind her. She jumped and twisted round.

No one was there.

She plucked the hair from the brush and as she held it in her hand, the only sound that emerged from her lips was a low moan.

Claire unlocked the door to her apartment and shuffled in. Stunned. Numb. She couldn't believe what had just happened. Sophie must have been right about that girl in St. Albans. Goodness knows what Alex had gotten up to in Verbier. Somewhere along the line, he had cheated on her. How else could she have gotten syphilis?

Since they'd started going out, she'd never been with anyone else, and he'd never given her any reason to doubt him. Until Sophie had seen him in town. Bastard.

Claire choked back a sob. She knew she had to hold herself together, but it all seemed like too much effort. At least, the doctor had said it was easily treatable at this stage. The pain of Alex's betrayal, though, she couldn't cure. She needed to talk to someone. Claire went to Marianne's room and knocked.

"Can I come in?"

The door opened, and Marianne appeared, looking irritable.

"Claire, I'm working."

Her guilt kicked in. She'd been so needy over the past month or two. Who could blame Marianne for getting a bit teed off? "Oh, I'm sorry. We'll talk later. I'm too upset now anyway."

Claire sniffled, trying to hold back the tears. She retreated to her room. In the background, Marianne's door banged shut.

An hour later, as she waited in the hall, she heard his key in the door. Ready to talk his way out of a tight spot, no doubt. Alex was good at that, probably rehearsed his lines as he drove to Belle Vue. She had rung and told him to come over immediately then cut the connection before he could argue. She'd switched off her mobile and pulled the plug on the landline. For this, she wanted to face him.

Claire stepped forward. The rat stood there, innocence and puzzlement pasted across his features. His eyes darted straight to the side of her mouth.

As fury surged through her, she landed a hard slap across his face.

Alex's head snapped to the side. He stumbled back across the threshold, into the hall.

"You bastard!" She lashed out at him again, but this time he caught her arm and pulled her toward him. She wriggled and, still yelling, yanked herself free.

"Claire? Sweetheart?" He manhandled her into the flat. "Keep your voice down, for God's sake." Alex's foot reached out and pushed the door shut.

"Why? I want *everyone* to hear you're a lying, cheating bastard who's given me syphilis!"

"What? What the fuck are you on about?"

"I've just been told I've got syphilis. It could only have been you. You're total scum to do that to me. I hate you! You're the *only* one I've ever slept with, Alex."

While she screeched at him, Alex's face morphed through expressions of shock, indignation, confusion.

Claire struggled to catch her breath. The tears streamed down her cheeks. How could he do this to her? Her anger flared again. "To think my friends let me know about your philandering. They'd seen you out with some slag in St. Albans. You told me you'd be sorting out *family business*, and couldn't see me. Fucking liar."

She raised her hand to slap his face again, but he grabbed her arms and shook her. "Stop this right now. That was *my sister*. I had my arms around Nicki. You know, *my sister*, Nicki. She was the family business! She wanted to get away from Mum and Dad and talk things out with me instead. I was with her in St. Albans."

Alex glared at Claire, and she returned the same. Out of the corner of her eye, she saw Marianne's door open a crack.

"Do you want me to give you Nicki's number? Ring her and check?"

"No! You make me sound like some crazy, jealous bitch."

"Aren't you?"

She mentally reeled at the low sucker punch. He'd gone too far now. "You sanctimonious prick. How dare you? I loved you so much, Alex, and what do I get in return? A bloody STD!"

He flinched. "Hold on. Are you sure that's what you've got? Seems a very quick diagnosis. Don't they have to do blood tests to confirm it?"

"Yes, and I gave liters of the stuff but the doctor examined me and said it looked like primary syphilis."

What she didn't tell Alex was her next topic of discussion with the medic. About her hearing things, seeing things. A copy of the referral letter to the psychiatrist sat at the bottom of her bag. She needed to keep that appointment to prove she wasn't mad and find an explanation for all she'd been going through. The doctor had suggested it might be final year stress causing this temporary setback in combination with her at last facing the reality of how her parents had died. She could live with those reasons. Anything else was too frightening to consider.

That whole episode had been one endless nightmare for her. No one had been charged with their deaths. She hadn't been able to bury them until many months later when the police in Hong Kong finally released their bodies, and she flew them back to England. Gazing at their sealed coffins, all she could see was how they'd looked the night she'd found them. A nightmare vision of their mutilated bodies she would take to the grave. For almost four years, she'd locked those images away.

Alex stepped forward and grasped her arm, jolting her back. His fingers pressed into her flesh. "Claire, I did *not* give you an STD, nor VD, syphilis, the clap or anything else you want to call it. I'm going. When you know the test results, call me, and you can say you're sorry then."

She stood before him, fists clenched, face wet and puffy. All she wanted was for him to hold her. To explain, to assure her it was all some dreadful mistake but typical man, he was too wrapped up in himself and turned on her as though it was her fault. He slammed the door on his way out and she despised him in that moment.

A few minutes later, Marianne's door opened. Still slumped on the floor in the hall, her body racked by sobs, she felt her friend's arms go round her.

"Sshh, Claire, it'll be okay."

Claire leaned against Marianne and let herself be led to the sitting room. They sat next to each other on the sofa. Marianne pulled a couple of tissues from her pocket and handed them to her. "Here. Tell me what happened. I heard you two shouting but thought it best to give you some privacy."

Three sodden tissues later, the best Claire thought she could say about her face was that it was dry. Thank God Marianne was here for her. She explained her nightmare situation.

"It's a mess, isn't it? Alex is a total bastard." Claire squeezed what was left of the tissues into a tight ball. "Oh, I don't know what to believe anymore."

"Perhaps Alex caught it before you two got together?" suggested Marianne. "We've covered STDs on the course, but I'm not sure how long the incubation period is. I wonder if he has to have any symptoms. Did the doc say it was stage one or two?"

"She thinks it's stage one, but the tests will confirm it. She's given me penicillin and some cream for the sores, or chancres as she called them. What a repellent word."

"Poor you. No wonder Alex hightailed out of here." Marianne laughed. "Men. I bet he thinks *he* is the victim in all this, with no thought as to what you're going through."

Surprised, Claire gazed at Marianne. "That's a cynical thing to say, not like you at all."

"I call it as I see it, Claire. Nothing more. After all, the only other explanation is Alex has been cheating on you all along."

Alex left Claire's flat in a daze. He was innocent. He hadn't played around, despite plenty of opportunities, but what about Claire? She must have gotten it from someone. Or maybe she didn't have it, which was still a possibility. He didn't know anything about the disease, except that it was sexually transmitted. This meant Claire might have given it to him. He used his finger to feel around his mouth for any signs of tenderness, or a budding cold sore. Nothing yet. He'd make an appointment straightaway with the doctor to get tested. Prove her wrong. He'd need to spend some time on the internet learning more about it. He inwardly groaned, annoyed at another distraction to getting on with his dissertation.

Alex drove to the college. On his way to the library, after numerous attempts, he made an appointment with the doctor for tomorrow afternoon, courtesy of a lucky cancellation.

As he stood in the queue at the main desk, he watched Penny Whitbread, the Head Librarian. The student ahead of him, loaded up with books, moved away. He edged forward to the desk.

Penny's eyes lit up when she saw him. "Hi, Alex. You're in luck. The book you ordered came in and I found another that might surprise you. As you weren't in yesterday, I took it home with me for a browse. Fascinating stuff, absolutely fascinating."

Before he could reply, she ducked under the desk and brought up two books, placing them on the counter in front of him. Penny slid them along and edged away from the terminal. She turned to a bearded colleague sitting behind her and asked him to take over.

The man nodded. She waved Alex to the end of the counter and handed him the top book. From her expression, he presumed he would find the one below it more interesting. "And the other?"

Penny gave an inscrutable smile. "I'm very proud of myself for digging up this one. Of course, the way the library search system works, it can be hard to find something that doesn't have the most obvious words in the title or abstract. This one is called, *The Devil's Disciples: The Rise and Fall of the de Montalt Family*."

She beamed, but it took a few seconds for the significance to register. "They owned the original Belle Vue estate," he said.

"They did indeed."

"That's great. It'll give me some early background material. It's been a bit thin on the ground so far."

Penny still regarded him with raised eyebrows. He got it in the end. "Devil's Disciples? That a bit OTT."

Penny held the book out of his reach.

"You're enjoying this, aren't you?" Alex asked.

"You bet your life—to both. The de Montalts weren't Catholics as everyone thought, they were Devil worshippers. Not that it did the women any good. When the Duc came to England with his brother to escape the guillotine, they left their wives and the rest of the family behind. Every last one lost their head. The Duc bought the land, and when he built Belle Vue he had a whole underground system constructed where they would hold these rituals. Not forgetting a chapel strewn with satanic touches—the antithesis of a holy place of worship."

"You're not joking, are you?"

"No. I couldn't put the book down last night. I know it's a bit off the beaten track as far as material for your dissertation is concerned, but knowing your, let's say, personal connection to the place, I thought you'd be interested."

He nodded and took the proffered book. "You're right there, but first I've got to finish the next section of my dissertation, ready to hand in to Hamish for Monday."

"Go on, take a peek," Penny urged.

So much for not allowing himself to get distracted. He opened the book and scanned the table of contents. "Penny, this is great stuff."

He turned a couple of pages, mesmerized by the plans of the house and a portrait of René de Montalt, the 9th Duc, dated 1787, two years before the family fled to England.

"Glad to be of service. I'll leave you to it as I can see you're hooked. Oh, and check out how it all ended. Pretty ironic as the last Duc, head of these Satanists, Devil worshippers or whatever they called themselves, burned to death."

"Perhaps he wanted a test run of his final destination?"

"Mmmm. With that happy thought, Alex, I'll see you later." Penny moved back behind the counter.

Taking his valuable cargo and bag with him, Alex found a free desk and allowed himself a few extra minutes to browse through the de Montalt book.

In no time, the library surroundings disappeared as he grew more engrossed in the volume in front of him. Using the index for any listing for the later asylum, he turned to the first reference of two. He peered at a diagram of the original tunnel system under the Manor. It looked far more extensive than the plans in Trent's book. Reading the notes underneath, he learned the only part of the estate used for the asylum was a section of the basement under the main building and the chapel. The book also mentioned that prior to any work starting, in the utmost secrecy, an exorcism had been carried out and the church re-consecrated. In addition, blasphemous carvings and other obscene imagery were obliterated and replaced.

He leafed through more of the pages and spotted a familiar name: Doctor Johnson Nottidge. He read the lines with disbelief. Nottidge had supposedly been a member of this Mephisto Club before the Duc's death. Alex wondered if that had any bearing on his choice of occupation or location to practice it. Why would a lord's son bother to work anyway?

Conscious of getting sidetracked, he reluctantly put the book away. Instead of a drink with Paul and Gary in the Union later, perhaps he'd spend the time reading more about Nottidge and the de Montalts.

Alex worked for another hour and completed the section to be submitted tomorrow.

In the end, the liquid attraction was too strong, and he went to the bar. Another freezing night, and it being a Monday, the bar was less than half full. As he entered, he heard his name called and spotted Gary with Paul and Marianne seated in the lounge area.

He waved and walked over, the floor sticky underfoot. "Just a quick one, guys."

Gary pursed his lips and simpered in a high-pitched voice. "Oh, Alex, you always tell me that. Don't you do slow? Like more than five seconds?"

"Ha-ha, you tosser. You know I'm up for the full twenty. Anyone want a top up?"

Three negatives.

As he turned to head for the bar, Marianne got to her feet saying she'd like a word. "You look beat," she said.

"Hmm. Are you going to tell me how I'm feeling, too?" As he said the words, he kept his eyes fixed ahead not sure where this might lead. He'd been hoping for a quiet drink.

"No, but now you mention it, I can imagine confused is a good place to start," Marianne said.

He stopped midway to the brightly lit counter. Hole in one. He turned and saw the look of concern in her eyes. "You could say that, and a lot of other things besides."

"I know Claire blamed you without listening to your side of the story, but it must have come as such a shock to her."

"You're right, but attack isn't always the best defense. At least, not of the person you're supposed to care so much about."

Marianne put her hand out and stroked his arm. "Alex, you have to remember, the summer break was a long one."

"Are you saying Claire cheated on me?" He inhaled slowly.

"Of course not. Did you ask her?"

He snorted. "Huh. I couldn't get a word in edgewise."

Marianne smiled. "Claire sure caught you off balance."

"Well, she didn't need to. The bizarre thing is I'm innocent."

"But is *she*?" She stroked his arm again.

"Claire wouldn't do such a thing," he said, in a low voice. As the words came out, he wondered if he could be certain of that.

"And neither would you—but that leaves us with a rather difficult question. Who gave her syphilis?"

He didn't stay long at the pub and tried to avoid thinking about the answer. Later that night as he lay in bed, Alex returned to Marianne's words, surprised by her not taking sides against him. He appreciated her willingness to consider his view of the situation. Marianne was the only one who knew the situation and as an almost-qualified nurse, maybe she'd be able to advise him on the practical details. Not the sort of thing he could discuss with Gary or Paul.

The telephone rang. He groaned and fumbled first for the light switch, then for the phone.

"Hello?"

Alex listened as Sally Reichenberg told him she and Jeff when returning to their flat, had heard noises and loud wailing from Claire's apartment. They'd knocked for the longest while and rung both her mobile and landline but got no reply. Marianne, they assumed, wasn't home. They'd rung Eric and got Alex's number since Sally thought she remembered Claire saying she'd given him a key. Was that correct?

He agreed it was and assured them he'd get to Belle Vue straightaway.

Chapter Eighteen

Thursday, 12 August, 1869

Of the high temperatures endured during the past few weeks, today seemed to be the hottest yet. Ellen, bored and slightly nauseous, lay on her cot. Her skin, a mass of red marks from her rough shift and continual itching, caused her intense discomfort.

Harriet, on the other bed, lay curled toward the window. A couple of the small panes in each window of the asylum could be opened but by only a few inches. As an unfortunate consequence, the cramped dormitories and rooms were stifling and smellier than rotting fish at Billingsgate.

Hardly any staff had shown up this morning, so straw plaiting had been cancelled for the day. Mrs. Craven, cranky to the extreme, had told them to stay in their room.

Their door was open in the vain hope of some circulating air, but the stench from the crowded halls far from any windows, almost overpowered the instinctive impulse to draw breath. Ellen stared at the ceiling. For what must have been the hundredth time today, she mulled over any possible weakness to their plan. Anticipation rose within her. Mary was expected tomorrow, and this would be her chance to convince her half-sister of its merits.

Ellen heard Mrs. Craven's distinctive approach, the footsteps slow and heavy, the breathing a loud wheeze. Her large figure blocked the doorway.

"You two," she said, before stopping to gulp in the still fetid air.

Ellen prodded Harriet. She sat up and turned toward Mrs. Craven.

"Ellen, take Harriet down to the courtyard. I'll give you an hour."

Ellen didn't need to be told twice. She and Harriet put on their boots and hurried downstairs to the ground floor. They jostled their way to the entrance of the courtyard, avoiding a wild-eyed woman in the corridor whose heavy canvas dress flapped around her thin legs as she tipped side-to-side like an everlasting metronome.

"I wonder who's guarding the door." Harriet sounded worried.

When Ellen saw Maud Trotter, she knew they would be all right. The Assistant Matron was a kindly soul, like Ruth Evans, a rare blessing at Belle Vue. Her face lit up when she saw Ellen and Harriet. Mrs. Trotter pushed the door wider for the two girls and ushered them through.

The fenced quadrangle had a few trees providing shady spots but better still, Ellen could feel a slight breeze. Her dress, which hadn't been changed for over a week, bore numerous wet patches and clung to her skin. Shaking the thin material away from her body had little effect as it only stuck again like fly paper. Maybe an hour out here would dry it. She saw Chancer sitting in the sun with his one-legged mate, Titus Sproat. He beckoned them over with a wave of his hand. They walked across the brown-tipped grass, stepping around the other patients sitting or lying in the sun.

Ellen greeted the two men with a smile. Chancer nodded, but old Titus simply sat there saying nothing, his puckered sockets, and bald pate becoming ever redder in the sun.

"How did Titus lose his leg, Chancer?" She asked in a whisper, settling herself on the wooden bench.

"Eee, I mebbe mad and blind but deaf I ain't. Int game o'cards, pet." Titus chortled as though much pleased with his joke before bursting into, *Rule Britannia* with great gusto. Ellen and Harriet smothered their laughter behind their hands. The old boy sang the first chorus, then stopped. Loud snores followed.

Chancer grinned, revealing his few yellowed stumps. "Same old Titus, he ain't never going to change." He began to recount the oft-heard story of how they'd first met. The sun beat down on them. Sorely in need of some shade, Ellen and Harriet excused themselves and moved to an empty bench under a heavy leafed tree. Heads down, they chatted and giggled about the possible places they could visit together when they left Belle Vue. Ellen regaled Harriet with some of Mary's tales about a place called Cremorne Pleasure Gardens.

She lowered her voice. "Mary also said the whores do a roaring trade there."

Harriet blushed. "Ellen! A lady shouldn't say such things."

A mocking voice interjected. "I don't see any ladies here. Just two mad women cackling like witches. You're not witches, are you?" Bill Callahan leered at them. "You know what I'd have to do to you, don't you, Ellen?"

Ellen mentally cringed at the spite in his eyes. He made a wet sucking noise and spat a wad of phlegm on the ground near her feet. He ignored Harriet as though she wasn't there.

"Answer me, girl."

He bent down, his face too close to hers. She leaned back as far as she dared without falling and spoke with a firmness she didn't feel. "Mr. Callahan, given we are due to become family, why do you torment us so?"

"It's a part of the job I enjoy. A little benefit for my troubles in this unholy place. It's hard graft dealing with all you defectives. You should be grateful you've got a sane man wanting you."

"I wonder whether Mary or Jack would be so pleased to learn you were threatening me."

Callahan's lip twisted into a full-blown sneer. "I don't think so, girl. You say a word and the epileptic might not make it through her next fit. Get my meaning?"

Ellen, glancing at Harriet's frightened face, unfortunately, did. At that moment, she wished with all her heart Bill Callahan didn't exist. He did, though, and she couldn't put her friend in more danger.

"Yes. I won't say anything."

He smirked at her hesitant promise, but Ellen was determined to have the last word, to show he hadn't won. "I pity you, Mr. Callahan. You despise all the good in the world and use your position here to abuse the weak and sickly."

"That's just the way I like it, Ellen. And remember, missy, I've got plans for you."

After their run in with Bill Callahan, both Ellen and Harriet, unsettled by his threats, slept badly that night. The next morning, like manna from heaven, Harriet's long-awaited letter from her father arrived. Eager for news they had made their way to check with Mrs. Trotter who also sorted the post. She sat in the cramped hutch—previously the candle store—that now doubled as a temporary dayroom where main building patients could collect any letters or parcels.

When she gave Harriet the envelope they had excitedly huddled into the corner. Harriet broke the seal and took out a single sheet of vellum. She scanned the florid writing.

Ellen's impatience knew no bounds. "What does he say? Oh, Harriet, is there any chance?" She saw hope and fear dart across Harriet's features like the jerky images in a flick book.

"Well, he hasn't said no." Harriet summarized the letter's contents for Ellen. "Papa asks why, after all this time, I want to live on the outside. He thinks perhaps he could engage a full-time nurse, but first, he questions what I know about you. Are you trustworthy and from a good family?" Harriet snorted. "He ought to have asked that of the people running the asylums."

"What else? What else?"

"He instructs me to provide more information but agrees this may be a way for me to have, what he calls, 'an independent life'. Once he has the answers to his concerns, he will give it his due consideration and make a decision."

Ellen clapped her hands together. "Harriet, that's wonderful news."

"Let's write a reply to my father straight away. The quicker we send the letter, the quicker we'll know his answer."

Harriet folded the paper back into the envelope, her face more serious. "Is Mary coming today?"

"I hope so. I shall ask her again."

"If I have Papa's agreement in writing, that should help convince your sister *and* Doctor Fishburn. You'd be no burden on Mary as you'd have your food and lodging paid for, a respectable job, and a friend to keep you company. Matron and Doctor Fishburn would be able to add more names to their list of patients they have supposedly 'cured'. Two birds with one stone. That will improve the statistics for their masters and make them look good."

Ellen beamed at Harriet. "What more could they ask?"

Bill felt Mary stiffen and could hold back no longer, but before he could relish his final shudder she pushed him away.

"Damn that nosy hag—"

Damn you, too, he thought as he clumsily buttoned his trousers and watched as Mary lifted herself off the kitchen table. She pulled down her crimson skirt and fixed her hair in the cracked mirror propped on top of the sideboard.

"When I saw her glaring at us from that bloody dome, I knew she'd be sniffing around—and sure enough." Mary stared at him, a smirk on her face.

Bill took an old cloth from the sink and wiped the sweat from his hands. He poured himself a beer. "Who are you talking about?"

"The Fishburn harpy. With her mouth gaping and nose pressed against the glass. Not just in the belvedere where she spies on all who enter this godforsaken place, but through your window not two minutes ago." Mary threw back her head and laughed. "You ought to have seen her face. I bet old Fishburn hasn't given her a good rogering for years!"

Bill's irritation with Mary rekindled. That explained why she had suddenly grabbed his crotch then snaked her arms around him and kissed him when they'd walked up the drive. He leaned against the sideboard and drained his mug as he mulled over the situation. Matron's price for keeping quiet? More favors no doubt.

"You have anything for me?" Mary asked.

Bill grunted. He didn't kid himself she'd come here for him. He opened a rickety drawer, pulled out the envelope Nottidge had given him and dropped it on the table. As he turned to refill his mug, Mary snatched it up. "Thank you, Bill. I'll have a beer, too."

She tucked the letter into her purse and pulled the drawstring tight.

"Aren't you going to check it's what you wanted?" he asked.

"No, I'm not. This is my business. No concern of yours."

Before he could respond, Mary continued with a matter she obviously considered was his concern. She outlined her plans for his brother, marriage, and the Green Hog.

"Don't Jack have any say in this?"

Bill saw from Mary's expression that he didn't. As Mary plotted his brother's fate out loud, his mind wandered to what might be going on between her and Nottidge. He didn't think sex came into it. Nottidge clearly despised her and seemed to be playing some sort of game, but Bill didn't know its name or the rules. From what he knew of Nottidge, there probably weren't any. Any mention of the doctor to Mary produced only ice and bile. Still, there looked to be money made on both sides. He'd see what Mary, or Nottidge, would dangle before him.

He liked the exciting sex with her, but he didn't need it. He could get all he wanted at the asylum. Some of the perversions shown to him by Nottidge had satisfied his curiosity, but he lusted after someone like Ellen. A quiet one, who looked like a lady and who he could control totally. Bill knew he had to have her soon. The question merely was when and how. He reached for his work jacket and put it on over his damp shirt.

He turned his attention back to Mary as she gave him a new instruction. Ellen must take a turn for the worse regarding her health or sanity. He'd be more than happy to oblige on that score without any payment. He listened with interest as Mary expanded on her thoughts about Ellen's future and the additional brass soon to come his way.

Mary pushed her chair back and rose to her feet. "I'm going to see Ellen now and make sure she gets no further with her silly plans."

They left his cottage. Mary strode toward the main building and was soon out of sight. Before he could set off, Nottidge appeared from the direction of his grand residence. It dwarfed all the other staff properties including the Fishburns".

The doctor looked pleased with himself. They nodded to each other and Callahan, in case any eyes were watching, saluted as required.

"I gave Mary Grady the envelope," he said, wiping the sweat from his brow. "You don't seem to like her much, so why help her?" Bill rubbed his leg, the heavy uniform making him itch. Although in his frock coat, Nottidge appeared unaffected by the heat.

They walked along the path Mary had taken minutes before. "Who said I was helping her?" Nottidge dropped his smile. "Word has reached me that some of the new Asylum Commission inspectors might take actions that limit, or even stop our activities in the future. A contact of mine, who has read the latest report which Fishburn will be getting..." He pulled an impressive gold watch from his fob and opened it. "...around now, informs me they believe there are places here they haven't been shown. A thorough search will be conducted at the next inspection. That won't be for another six months, but it means we need to think about other venues where we can continue our pleasures, and make sure the hidden tunnels and crypt stay that way. Ever thought of going to America, Bill?"

Bill—who hadn't—shook his head.

Nottidge tucked his watch into his pocket. "The Americans are building more asylums than here. Huge ones. They are new at this and fortunately, most do not subscribe to the namby-pamby principles of the Lushes of this world. Think on it, as will I. You're making good money here from our schemes, but there, you could become rich, very rich indeed."

With that, Bill decided Nottidge's carrot was more to his taste than Mary's. He was about to go his own way when the doctor spoke again. "But before I make any decision, I plan to teach Mary Grady a lesson. Let me explain."

As Mary took her leave from Ellen, she thought the afternoon had gone well. Her half-sister was still full of her airy-fairy idea to live happily-ever-after with the epileptic, but Mary had soon put her to rights. Grief, she'd explained, could take years to recover from. It was far too early for her to imagine she was well again.

Ellen had sat there, head lowered, her lip trembling. "Please, Mary. Harriet's father will pay for me. It won't cost you anything."

"It's not for you but for the doctors to decide." Mary leaned over the table, her chin, and nose close to Ellen's, forcing her to look up.

"No, Mary, but—"

"But nothing. Doctor Fishburn has warned me of the dangers. You might think yourself well but as his experience has shown, most patients suffer worse mental anguish when they leave the care and support provided by the asylum." She stared into Ellen's trusting eyes. "I can't risk that."

Ellen's face crumpled. She pulled a ragged handkerchief and wiped away the tears. Mary didn't know whether to be irritated or amused. "Say no more on the subject. I've made up my mind."

Ellen had nodded and said nothing more on the subject. She did have the cheek, though, to ask if Mary could send her a small food parcel, but Mary had soon set her straight on that whim, too. The girl would bleed her dry if she let her.

She endured Ellen for almost an hour. In the end, she told her half-sister she wasn't looking well and should go and rest. That chore over and the money from Nottidge safely stowed in her purse, she could now head back to London. On the train, she would think of ways to spend it.

Johnson Nottidge first heard then saw Mary Grady, as she click-clacked on the parquet past his open door. He put down the book he'd been browsing and moved to the office entrance.

"Miss Grady!" His voice echoed in the vast entrance hall.

The woman stopped. She turned, head held high, her words dripping with disdain. "Yes? What do *you* want?"

"A few minutes of your time. As long as you don't charge me, of course."

She snorted and sashayed toward him as if she had all the time in the world. The strumpet was such an easy mark. Her face prematurely proclaimed the certainty of victory and he almost laughed aloud at her presumption. She obviously hadn't seen what he'd put in the envelope. Mary Grady was but a mere novice and if she thought he would ever pay blood money for a worthless slut who'd died years ago, she belonged in Belle Vue, not her sister. If she knew he still did the same thing here, and with some of her sister's fellow patients, imagine her shock. What delicious irony. She might be sniffing around but so far her sense of smell had deserted her. Rather fitting for this place where the stink of the inmates fouled every nook and cranny.

He stepped away from the door, adjusted his silk waistcoat, and strolled to his desk. He picked up the book he'd been leafing through and took it to the impressively stocked bookcase, replacing it in a gap on the middle shelf.

The woman stood in the center of the room, hands on hips, belligerence suffusing her features.

"I decided at your last visit that you are as mad as your sister." His gaze slithered over her body until it reached her eyes and held them. "So instead of any payment, I have decided to have you committed."

"You can't do that." She took several paces forward, her face a mask of anger. "What do you mean no payment?" Her fingers scrabbled in her bag for the envelope and once retrieved, she tore it open. The mask darkened as she read his words.

Her eyes flashed at him as she tore the sheet in half. "You think you've set yourself up very well here, don't you, Seton. Knowing your sick tastes, I wouldn't be surprised if you might not be getting up to your old tricks. Using the *poor patients* for your own, and no doubt your friends' purposes, eh?"

He yawned at the bint's tiresome repetition. "*I* can do anything I want. You are of no consequence."

"Oh, but I am. I know what you did at the Mephisto Club celebrations."

"Hurrah! So, you spent a bit of time at a party with a few rowdy young men who liked to enjoy themselves to the full. Who cares?"

"I've heard everything now." Mary spat back at him. "*I* care. Though it seems an odd way to describe old René. He hadn't been young in the last century, much less this one. The elderly tend to have looser tongues."

"Do they?" Nottidge said. René had let this old age lark go too far. Maybe La Grady knew more than she had first revealed. She'd soon squeal if he played her right.

"Yes, and he drank the blood of the girl you killed. Not so innocent were you, dearie? Did you know I spent the night with the Duc and the next day, too? He talked and showed me things. The Book, for example. He even made me an honorary member of your little club after I went through his silly initiation ritual."

Nottidge hid his surprise. A female member? Not possible. René must have lost his mind. The stakes had just risen higher than he could have ever imagined. Not that he'd let the bitch know it. He shrugged and made a small bow. "I congratulate you, Miss Grady. I am rarely caught unawares." As he raised his head, he had to stop himself from laughing. The trollop looked like she wanted to crow.

"Good. I am glad we have that straightened out. I look forward to *triple* payment next time *and* what you owe me from today."

Nottidge said nothing. She might think she had won this round and that was fine with him. Overconfidence led to mistakes.

Swinging her hips, she crossed the floor, then disappeared from view.

He watched her departure with a studied air of disinterest, but his mind raced to plan his next move.

Mary Grady might end up wishing she'd been the one dispatched that night, instead of her friend.

Chapter Nineteen

Friday, 13 February
PRESENT DAY

Gary nudged Alex, who was still half-asleep on the sofa. "Get up, mate. You look like a shagged-out sloth."

Persistent fingers dug into Alex's shoulders. He let out an irritated mumble. "I wish."

He opened his eyes, groaned, and closed them again. The last thing he wanted was the pale gurning face of Gary breathing on him at such close proximity. "Piss off. I'm awake now."

Gary, dressed in a tracksuit, opened his mouth and tipped back his head in a full yawn.

"Just got up myself. Overslept. Again." He grimaced at the leaden sky beyond the window. "No wonder. Still dark out and it's gone eleven. I hate this weather."

"Me too." Alex sat up. He lowered his bare feet to the carpet.

"Fancy a bevie?" Gary asked as he padded toward the kitchen.

Clatters and bangs sounded from the other room. Soon the smell of coffee filtered through to the lounge.

"Looks like Paul's up and gone. Fancy not waking us."

Alex shrugged, thankful for small mercies. He was so tired. Last night had been a long one. When he finally got to Belle Vue, Sally had met him in the hall and they had banged on Claire's door with no result. By this time, he was getting worried, so he'd used his key.

It had taken a lot of shaking and shouting to wake Claire. When she'd finally opened her eyes, she'd looked at him like he was about to murder her. Fear etched her every feature, then suddenly her eyes went blank as though she didn't recognize him. A minute later, she seemed to come to. She had clung to him, crying and begging him over and over not to leave her on her own. Some nightmare, he thought.

At this point, Sally had given him an okay sign and discretely left. Claire was drenched in sweat and shaking. When he'd been able to pry her away, she became limp and unresisting. He pulled off her damp T-shirt. Sober and with no amorous intent, he gazed with shock at her naked body. He could have counted every rib had he been so inclined. She'd always been slim, but the weight seemed to have dropped off her at record speed.

He helped to put on her toweling robe, made difficult as she wouldn't let him go. When he took her hand, it felt rough and dry with hard edges of cracked skin. He remembered his unease as he straightened the bedclothes around her. She looked so dreadful. God, he hoped he hadn't caught it, too.

"Alex, don't worry about the duvet. Just hold me." He lay down on top of the bed and put his arms around her. They had stayed like that for ages until she cried herself out. She then recounted what she could remember of her nightmare.

"It was so good to wake up and not be chained to the floor or feel so sick."

When he got up to switch off the main light, Claire panicked. He left a side lamp on and climbed in beside her. Her arms and body glued themselves to his. The next hours had dragged as Claire fidgeted and twisted in her sleep. Her limbs seemed to locate the most awkward positions like a somnolent game of retribution. It was well past four when, after many attempts, he was finally able to extricate himself without waking her. He had jotted a quick note and left it on the bedside table, before driving back to his flat and succumbing to his sofa's hypnotic appeal.

He and Gary had an unusually quiet coffee, then Alex set off for the college health center.

After all his worrying, his visit to the doctor was uneventful. He

BELLE VUE

wasn't showing any symptoms, but they took blood with the results due early next week.

At barely five, Alex entered the Leather Boot public house, empty except for a lone figure on a stool at the bar. Must be Jez. Yep, the guy had heard the door, spun round, and mouthed Alex's name a couple of times as though he were dealing with a deaf man. When Alex nodded, he waved and beckoned him over.

As he walked between the empty tables, he eyed up the man. Hamish told him Jez Trent was now in his early thirties, but he had that look of going on forty-five about him.

Jez hopped off the stool. "Alex, good to meet you at last."

They shook hands and Alex smiled at the sight before him. Jez wore round metal-framed glasses, black socks, and tan leather shoes which were fine but, between these, a sartorial disaster. Gary wouldn't dress like that, even as a joke. He wore a pair of light-gray tracksuit bottoms pulled up high over his protruding stomach and into which he'd tightly tucked his red polo shirt. Jez appeared to favor the right.

Noticing Jez's near empty glass of what looked like lemonade, he asked, "What can I get you?"

"Thanks, Alex. I'll have a double whiskey." Jez named the most expensive brand stocked by the pub. Once the drinks were served, they moved to a banquette table against the wall. Jez lugged an obviously heavy carryall.

Alex soon found out, in addition to copious amounts of eye-wateringly priced Scotch, the rest of the payment for Jez's notes on Belle Vue took the form of critiquing the man's literary work-in-progress. Jez was keen to share possible plot lines with his captive audience and seek Alex's advice as to the effectiveness of different denouements.

In full flow with accompanying hand movements, Jez darted between characters, locations, and events in rapid succession. After barely ten minutes of this, he started thinking of possible escape routes.

"About my notes."

Alex raised his eyebrows. "Yes?" There is a God, he thought.

"They may not be what you're looking for. My focus was the last ten years of the old queen's reign. From what you told me, that's right at the top end of your timeline."

A dead end? Alex knew these frequently occurred. Frustrated, he couldn't keep the disappointment out of his voice. "So they're not much use to me then?"

"I didn't say that. I found those notes but know I would have made others for the earlier period just in case I needed to use the information with the pictures selected for the book. I can't locate them at the moment, but the ones I'm giving you make interesting reading. Belle Vue definitely had more than its fair share of murder, mayhem and missing patients."

"Really? I'm interested in whatever you've got."

Jez took out three thick files from the bag and handed them to Alex. "I've got to go now, but ring me when you're done. We can have another drink here when you hand them back."

"Thanks, Jez. You're on."

Jez stood and picked up his carryall. He took a step forward then stopped. "That reminds me. The murder at Belle Vue, Hamish said I mentioned? It happened in 1895. Bit of a gruesome tale. An old woman. She'd been the Matron there when her husband had been alive. He died of alcoholism in the late 1870s, and she became a patient at the place she'd once help run. Locked herself in the belvedere and starved to death. That's what the staff said, but since she was found with her heart cut out, they were all lying. No one ever charged, though. Name's on the tip of my tongue. Adeline? No. Adelaide? Yes, that's it. Adelaide Fishburn was her name."

At the sound of her name being called, Claire rolled over and reluctantly opened her eyes. Marianne stood in the doorway of her room, hopping from foot-to-foot. "I'll be back in an hour or so. Are you getting up?"

"What time is it?" she asked, suppressing the flicker of irritation at her friend's pre-gym activity.

"Half eight. My train's at 11:15, so we'll need to leave by 10:45 in case of traffic. What time's your doctor's appointment?"

"Twelve. Oh, Marianne, I'm so nervous. I have a bad feeling." She groaned. Alex had the appointment before her and they'd arranged to meet at the surgery.

Claire sat up, waiting for Marianne's usual words of support as she pulled her robe from the end of the bed.

But Marianne only shrugged, saying she'd better get going, otherwise, they'd be late. As she heard the front door slam, Claire shook off the feeling that maybe sharing with Marianne hadn't been such a brilliant idea. At first, it had been great to have the company, but now she and Marianne seemed to be out of kilter with each other, in a way that Claire couldn't understand.

She yawned as she got out of bed and wrapped her dressing gown around her. Claire put on her slippers and padded to the kitchen. God, she felt lousy. Like someone had sucked all the energy out of her. Her muscles and joints ached with this wretched syphilis and her reaction to the antibiotics. The only thing not suffering was her appetite. Famished, though she'd had a late supper last night, she poured a large bowl of muesli and turned the radio on.

Seated at the breakfast bar, she ate a few mouthfuls concentrating on the enjoyable taste. The radio crackled with static. The music died and an indistinct whooshing sound replaced it.

She got up and switched off the radio. Back on the stool, she took another spoonful of cereal. As her teeth crunched down, she registered an unexpected movement and foul taste. She looked down at her bowl to see black beetles and maggots wriggling in the muesli.

Her stomach heaved, and she spewed the contents of her mouth across the breakfast bar. But nothing moved on the granite top or in the bowl. Only the usual suspects were evident: raisins, oats and the like.

Claire jumped up, frantic for an explanation. She wasn't

imagining everything, the syphilis, for instance, so she couldn't be going mad. She'd also made an appointment with the psychiatrist, so she *was* behaving like a normal person, but oh dear God why was this happening? Had she done something to bring it on? Search as she might, no answer—or none she could face—appeared.

She went to the bathroom and brushed her teeth. For almost ten minutes. She gargled with copious amounts of mouthwash, but nothing could erase the disgusting sensation of splitting the cockroach's outer skeleton then tasting the bitter softness of its insides. Ugh. It had seemed so real, it made her nauseous thinking about it. It was only a hallucination, though. Like before. By realizing that, surely this time she was part of the way to overcoming her fears. If the doctors could find the rest of the cure.

Her mind desperately focused on 'safe' topics. Claire returned to the kitchen and cleared away the mess. Her thoughts turned to spending the next four weeks alone in the flat while Marianne was away on placement in Bath. She didn't want to be by herself. With all this confusion. Not knowing if Alex had cheated on her or not. He'd been there for her last night and she'd clung to him, but in her head, she hadn't wanted to. Just in case. It hurt too much to face the reality. If only they could get back to their old closeness. Or maybe that had been an illusion, too. After all, they'd never had to face such a test of their trust in each other before.

As she stepped out of the shower, she heard Marianne coming back into the flat. When dressed and ready, Claire went through to the hall. Marianne fiddled with her bags.

"You know, I'm going to miss you."

"It's not for long, you wuss," Marianne said. "It's funny, but I feel as if I've always lived here, not barely a month. To think I was nervous that I wouldn't feel comfortable here. Seems I take to luxury very well."

Claire took one of the cases and opened the door. "Have you got everything?"

"Think so. I can always buy anything I forgot. Last night, when Paul and I saw Alex—"

"Oh? You didn't tell me about that." Claire said, surprised Alex hadn't mentioned it when she'd phoned about the doctor's appointment.

"Last-minute thing. I've hardly seen you this morning."

They left the apartment in silence. When they were in the car and driving out of the gate, Claire raised the point needling her. "Marianne, why wasn't I invited last night?"

"I told you. It was a last-minute thing."

"Yeah, but in the past, we've always rung each other. To say we're here if you want to join us."

Marianne stared at the windscreen, letting the time hang before answering. "Look, I wasn't going to mention it. It's nothing really, Claire. You shouldn't worry."

"What do you mean, I shouldn't worry? Tell me." She knew she sounded whiney but she couldn't care less. Not knowing was worse.

"Well, I am your best friend and I don't want to see you hurt, especially after all you've been through."

Claire tried to concentrate on her driving but instead succumbed to her curiosity. What, she asked, was going on? It must be something about Alex. All week she'd been racked by the belief he'd given her VD. No other way she could have gotten it.

"Well, the last few times I've seen Alex, he was with Sophie. She came with us last night."

"Sophie? Are you sure? He can't stand her." She clutched at the steering wheel as though it could absorb her hurt.

"I don't think so. They were laughing and joking."

Silence.

"Marianne, I can't deal with this now. All I can think about is this damn result. I'm also a bit nervous about being on my own over the weekend and the next month. *On my own,* though that might be something I have to get used to." Claire knew she was babbling but she couldn't help it. All she wanted was some reassurance.

"Claire, are you all right? I don't like to say it, but you look awful. Did you have a late night, too?"

"I'm still not sleeping well. You know what I'm going through but now everyone else must know it, too, since I'm sure Alex blabbed about it. My nightmares, etcetera etcetera."

"He didn't say a thing, Claire. In fact, your name wasn't mentioned."

"Well, that's even better then."

"Something wrong, Claire?"

"No. Another change of subject, please. You and Paul seem to be getting closer."

"For now. He's a bit of fun but nothing serious. I've got bigger fish to fry."

Claire checked to see if Marianne was joking, but no teasing gleam shone in her friend's eyes nor shared smiles to be had at this unlikely scenario. Claire frowned as she pulled into the train station. When she switched off the ignition, she turned toward Marianne. "Bigger fish to fry? What on earth does that mean?"

Marianne said nothing and avoided her quizzical gaze. They got out of the car. Claire stood and watched as her friend lifted her cases from the boot. Marianne had dropped a few pounds and all those workouts were giving her body real definition. She was able to note this, Claire realized because Marianne wore a new outfit which wasn't black or baggy. A double first, she smiled to herself.

"Listen, Claire, why don't you come up for a weekend and we'll have a girly break with lots of food, gossip, and pampering?"

Claire looked at Marianne's guileless face. At the familiar safe twinkle in her eyes.

"You've had a hard time, and you know the results may make it even tougher for you. Why not get away and have a think about things."

"That sounds wonderful. I might just do that. Oh, Marianne, I wish you weren't going."

"I know. Promise you'll call when you get the results."

"I will. Bye, Marianne."

They hugged, Claire, noticing how much slimmer and firmer

Marianne felt. As Marianne departed, she fished for a tissue from her pocket and blew her nose.

She reached the doctors' waiting room just before twelve. Alex wasn't around, so she assumed he'd already gone in. She sat on the hard wooden chair clutching the numbered card. Her mouth was dry. For the last few days, she'd convinced herself the doctor had made a mistake.

The long minutes ticked by. Claire fidgeted, picked at the dry skin round her nails, scratched the spots on her arm and tried not to think.

The door opened, and Alex appeared. She stood. He moved forward, his face blank, his eyes avoiding hers. She put out her hand toward him but he drew back out of reach.

"Alex. Is it bad news?"

He'd stared at her then with a horrible coldness.

"For you, not me. I don't have it. I'm going to have to think about this. I'll call you when I've decided what to do."

Then he'd walked past her, leaving her there alone and wishing she were dead.

The nightmare continued. Her tests had come back positive. It was clear the doctor did not believe her when she said she'd only ever slept with Alex. The woman kept repeating her words: to protect the man who infected her was taking a risk with another woman's life.

Claire left the surgery on autopilot and couldn't remember the drive home. Only the thoughts uppermost in her mind: Alex believed she had cheated on him and would never trust her again. Drained by the time she got out of her car, she made her way to her apartment. The last person she wanted to meet was that horrid Moira Bradigan, the one who kept staring at her. She ought to stare back. God knows, that wig was definitely worth a second look. The heat rose on Claire's face when the hatchet-faced crone strutted toward her in the foyer and asked her if she was well. All the things she wanted to say went out of her head. Instead, Claire lowered her head and said she'd been better.

The Bradigan woman asked in a snide voice, "Nothing catching I hope?"

Chapter Twenty

Tuesday, 17 August, 1869

After Mary's visit and the letter of refusal from Doctor Fishburn she'd received this morning, Ellen felt increasingly despondent. Not just about the failure of their escape plan, but because of an ominous worsening in their treatment. Attendants, who she had never worried about, now seemed to target her. She first noticed it a few days ago at comb out.

Fifty or so women, two attendants, and four combs. There were no mirrors for the patients in the asylum. They were not allowed any hairpins or combs, and the rules prescribed one style for all, a single plait, covered by a headscarf. Ellen had sat on the bench waiting her turn, thankful she had no sores on her head like some who'd scream as the comb raked over the scabs. Her own hair was still matted and damp from the previous night, but nothing prepared her for the rough jerking and pulling through her tangled locks. She bit her lip and endured the pain. Back in their room, she had asked Harriet to check her head. Her friend had been horrified to find patches of her scalp raw and bloody.

Worse, Callahan had taken to appearing out of nowhere. He would leer at her like a hungry wolf preparing to strike. Ellen made sure neither she nor Harriet went anywhere alone. There was an increasing tension building inexplicably around them and it frightened her. Every morning, she prayed good news would arrive from Harriet's father but each day, they returned empty handed from the post room.

A little over a week later, Ellen and Harriet went to check the mail. They entered the post room to see Mrs. Fishburn standing with a loosely wrapped parcel in her hands, the string untied and hanging down. The Matron seemed flustered and her face reddened upon catching sight of them.

Mrs. Fishburn cleared her throat. "Ellen, this delivery is for you. I've just finished checking it."

Ellen glanced at Harriet in surprise. Mary's refusal to send any food meant she wasn't expecting anything. Perhaps she'd changed her mind? How wonderful to receive a package. Thanking Mrs. Fishburn, she took the box. Harriet tugged her sleeve and she followed her out of the room. Ellen was desperate to take a peek but since Harriet moved quickly through the sea of shuffling bodies, she kept close behind so as to avoid any damage to her treasured package.

She flitted from one guess to the next as to what could be inside. It was so difficult to be patient when she held the answer in her hands. She hoped for something she could share with Harriet. She gently shook the parcel. One item, she thought, not heavy but with some weight to it. Harriet opened the door for Ellen and let her through, shutting it behind them.

Harriet clapped her hands. "Open it, Ellen. Aren't you excited? I wonder what it is."

Ellen placed the package on her bed. Her hands were shaking, and it took her several attempts to pull away the string and crumpled paper. She maneuvered the lid from the box and peered in.

"It's a cake. Oh, Harriet, I love cake!"

"So do I." Harriet laughed, then asked, "Who sent it?"

Ellen couldn't see anything resembling a note or card. She carefully lifted the confection to check underneath. Nothing. She put the cake back and shook her head.

"How odd. Did the sender put their name on the wrapping?" Harriet asked.

Ellen reached for the brown paper. She held it up. It bore two penny stamps and a Wapping postmark, but no details of who might have sent it. She looked at her name and address. "I asked Mary to send me something to eat when she last visited, but she said she would do no such thing. I'm not sure if it's her hand as she doesn't write back to me."

"Worry about that later, Ellen. Aren't you going to try some?"

"Of course." Ellen rubbed her stomach in anticipation of the feast to come. She sat on one side of the bed, with Harriet perched on the other. They gazed into the box between them, at the vibrant yellow cake.

"You first. Take a hu-u-u-uge piece." Harriet spread her hands apart to show how large a portion she should take.

Ellen tore almost a third of the cake and held it up laughing. "It's as bright as gold in the middle and it looks so soft." She took a first big bite, savored its texture and swallowed. Another mouthful disappeared as quickly as the first.

"Does it taste good?" Harriet asked. She pulled off a small piece.

Ellen hesitated. "I like the taste, it's unusual, but I'm not sure what sort of cake it is. A lemon cake is sweet and sour like this, but I don't think it's lemon. Do you like it?"

Harriet took a little more. "Yes, but it's very rich. I don't think I can eat much of this, so more for you."

"I'll see if Fanny and Rose want any," Ellen said as she finished a few more mouthfuls. With a lick of her fingers, she tore off two smaller portions and took them out to the two women.

Rose's eyes immediately fixed on the offering and she reached out her hand. Ellen gave her the larger piece then knelt beside the other woman.

"Would you like some, Fanny?" she whispered, anxious not to alert any of the other patients wandering up and down the corridor. Jesus might have performed miracles with the loaves and the fishes, but she could not. Taking a small amount from the remaining portion, she touched it to Fanny's lips. The woman's mouth opened, and Ellen pushed the cake in a bit at a time, hoping Fanny wouldn't choke. She watched as the woman worked her jaw then grimaced before spitting out the bright-yellow glob. Fanny grunted and shook her head. Disappointed, Ellen took the end of Fanny's skirt and wiped her mouth with it. She looked across at Rose, pleased to see she had finished her last morsel without incident and gave her the rest of Fanny's portion.

As Ellen stood, she felt a twinge in her stomach. Her back ached, too, but as it was nearly her time of month, she expected no less. She left the two women and returned to her room.

"Aren't you eating any more?" she said to Harriet still seated on her bed.

"No, thanks, Ellen. I ate some, but I'm not sure if I like the taste after all."

"More for me then," she said and split the final piece in two. "I'll eat this bit now and the rest tomorrow …" She smiled, "or maybe this afternoon."

Harriet laughed, putting her hands on her hips. "And you plan to eat lunch as well?"

"Of course. I'm a growing girl."

She and Harriet sat in silence for a few minutes before reverting to their favorite topic of conversation: the escape plan. They followed this by imagining all the places they dreamed of visiting when they left Belle Vue. Harriet had chosen the Lake District and was telling her about a poet called Wordsworth when Ellen thought she heard something odd. She cocked her head to one side. "What's that noise?"

They listened, first in puzzlement, then with alarm. The sound of violent retching and shrieking outside the door increased in volume. As Ellen rose from the side of the bed, Harriet rubbed her middle and groaned. At the same time, a wave of nausea flooded through her, followed by searing pain. She bent double as the cramping intensified. Harriet spewed a glutinous yellow mess over the floor. Ellen's stomach heaved at the sight, and a torrent of sour vomit gushed from her mouth.

Dear God, help. This was torture. Harriet grabbed her arm, her eyes filled with fear. "What's happening?"

Ellen couldn't answer. She didn't know. Only that she'd never felt such agony in her whole life. She stumbled out to the corridor, ignoring the vomit smeared across the floor. Harriet followed. Rose's wailing pierced her ears. The other inmates, no doubt drawn by the new noises, thronged toward them. They knocked blindly into each other like nine pins as they slid on the mess. The screeching and howling built to a crescendo.

Ellen retched again.

A piercing whistle, orders barked out, and the tread of heavy boots added to the chaos. The attendants charged in. She flinched as they pushed her aside and rained bludgeons down in all directions. Harriet took a blow and fell to the floor. Claire could do nothing to help. The excruciating spasms overwhelmed her, and she passed out.

Callahan barked the instructions to his men: get order restored quickly and the uninjured lunatics moved back to their beds. Then he would be able to find out what, or rather who had caused the ruckus and punish them. He stepped over the inmates still sprawled across the corridor and spotted the epileptic leaning against Annie's legs, vomit covering her clothes. Bloody troublemaker getting her just desserts.

"Well? Who caused this, Mrs. Craven?"

Annie lowered her voice so he had to lean toward her to catch her words. "Harriet 'ere and Rose over there. Real sick, they are."

Harriet struggled to her knees. "Help me. Oh God, it hurts. I'm burning inside."

"Take them straight to the infirmary, Mrs. Craven. Anyone else ill?" he asked.

She shook her head. "Don't think so, Mr. Callahan." Harriet pulled at her skirt. She and Callahan looked down. "Ellen. She ate most of the cake. Help her please."

Callahan's eyes widened at this unexpected opportunity. He issued his orders again and surveyed the chaotic scene in the dull light.

"Get those frigging troublemakers out of my way. I'll deal with the Grady girl…"

Chapter Twenty-One

Monday, 23 February
PRESENT DAY

Home alone, Alex switched on his laptop and congratulated himself on getting his dissertation framework and a chapter on the background of asylums handed in to Hamish on time. The Prof had been pleased with his speedy progress and, after a quick scan of the text, with the quality as well. They'd spent a useful half hour discussing the next stages of his work, the timing to submit his Masters' application then caught up with the details of his meeting with Jez Trent. Hamish had observed Alex seemed a bit tense and warned him not to overdo it.

"Easy to get too engrossed in your subject to the detriment of all else," he'd said, reverting to lecturer mode.

If only Hamish knew how difficult he found it to keep focused. All he could think about was Claire and dismissed any notion he was getting obsessed with the whole asylum business. Until last night. He'd returned to the flat and briefly mentioned Belle Vue to Gary and Paul. Admittedly, they were watching the football match, but Gaz had opened his mouth and waved his hand back and forth in front of it.

"Alex shut the fuck up about those bloody nuthouses. We don't want to hear any more."

Paul had squirmed in his chair but, as he hadn't disagreed with Gary, Alex realized he probably felt the same way. Since he didn't want to cause a rift in their happy household, he promised himself he wouldn't say any more on the subject unless they brought it up. A difficult task. Not only was his fascination with the subject growing, but it provided a welcome diversion from 'the other business'.

He picked up *The Devil's Disciples* and opened it to the section on the origins of the estate. He'd already written his introduction to the Belle Vue case study. So now he composed a brief history of the two-hundred-fifty-acre estate before the construction of the asylum. He included its purchase by the Duc de Montalt after his escape from the revolutionaries and the mansion's problematic build. Apparently, not one workman stayed for the project's duration and the accidents were many.

In 1862, fire destroyed the manor house, leaving only the chapel untouched. As an end piece, the authors noted for the reconstruction of Belle Vue, the Metropolitan Asylum's Board concerned above all with cost, ordered the architect and builders to use the original foundations and concrete over what they didn't need. For the chapel, the only change involved removing the blasphemous inverted crosses and obscene statues to replace them with artefacts more in keeping to a place of worship, or rather, Christian worship.

His task completed, Alex turned to some of the more salacious chapters he'd noted when Penny had first given him the book. He discovered the Mephisto Club were a veritable coven of pseudo-warlocks, sadists, and perverts who indulged in black magic at its darkest and brought misogyny to new heights. Membership exclusively male, women were only admitted to whatever part of the proceedings chosen for them—usually abuse and torture, often death. Fortunately, for the Club, but rather less so for the women concerned, the grinding poverty of London provided endless ready meat to be toyed with and consumed at will.

He sat back, dazed by the information. The stuff here sounded like hardcore porn. Even Gary would open this book. He continued reading.

Membership of the group was small and select, limited to the cream of society, predominantly aristocrats and those at the pinnacle of their fields. About the inner circle who led the club, Alex could only find sketchy information. The Club supposedly began with a de

Montalt in Paris in the early 1700s and ended with René de Montalt's death in the fire that burned Belle Vue Manor to the ground. It was rumored the Club had reformed some years after its fiery demise and might, said the authors, still exist to this day. If so, its approach to secrecy appeared to be more effective since the authors didn't give a single detail to support the claim. The majority of members populated various outer circles. Movement toward the core was achieved by the successful completion of initiation tasks, reportedly more depraved than the group's usual activities. The ultimate position in the group was that of Hell Master. Alex almost snorted in disbelief when he read this. What a bunch of whackos.

Turning to the chart he'd noticed earlier, he checked through the names of those the authors identified as being members. Yes, there it was. Doctor Johnson Nottidge. He found the page with the man's entry, but the information appeared to be incomplete. Only his date of birth was given—1835—with no information as to his activities after 1870. Nottidge was listed as a member of the inner circle and his position at Belle Vue Asylum was included. It crossed Alex's mind if the man *had* been a member of this club, then it didn't bode well for the patients. Many of those institutions were bad enough without a sadist and Devil-worshipper being in charge.

Alex flipped to the paragraph about the fire and René de Montalt's death, then back to the portrait of the Duc painted in 1787. Something about the picture bothered him. Okay, the man with his beaked nose, ivory skin, high forehead, and powdered hair resembled a movie version of Dracula, but that wasn't it. No doubt it would come to him later but for now, he couldn't stop his thoughts drifting onto sensitive territory: Claire.

He stared unseeing at the page in front of him and sighed. He had a mountain of work to do this week but too many distractions. His messy love life being the prime culprit. Much of last week had been spent struggling to keep his emotions at bay. It had been hard, too hard. He was hurt, angry, and confused. She'd cheated on him, for

God's sake. Another part of him couldn't believe it. It wasn't her style. If she'd met someone else, she'd have told him and they'd have parted. None of these lies. Well, that's what he'd like to think. Maybe he didn't know her as well as he'd thought, and he wasn't going to be treated like a prize idiot. She'd been trying to contact him, but he couldn't hack speaking to her at the moment. Let him get through the week and then they could talk it out. She could tell him the truth about who she was protecting, and he'd tell her they were through. Decision made, he reached for his mobile and texted her he'd come over on Saturday afternoon. If it wasn't okay, could she let him know?

With a sense of relief for the extra time, he focused back on the book again. He smiled as he read the next paragraph. All along he'd felt that a lot of *The Devil's Disciples* was nothing more than Gothic hype, but not this far-fetched:

'The Mephisto Club was rumored to possess a book of secrets that gave them supernatural powers. Amongst other things, it supposedly enabled the Hell Master and members of the inner circle to cheat death. Of course, there is no proof of this, but we would bring to your attention that while René de Montalt, the 9th Duc escaped to England during the French Revolution in 1789, the René de Montalt who died in the fire of 1862 was also reported to be the 9th Duc. A comprehensive search of the local records failed to identify any issue from the Duc, but they revealed that a René de Montalt lived at the Manor during the whole period. A mystery, unfortunately, that will never be solved.'

At the same time, Alex was delving into the dark history of Belle Vue Manor and planning his week, he was also at the back of Claire's mind. She'd woken late after a rough night. Thoughts of Alex and what was happening to her had given her no peace. He hadn't been in touch and wasn't answering her calls, texts, emails. She'd never felt so low, physically as well as mentally.

Her robe and pajamas hung off her even though she was eating like a sumo wrestler. She scratched her arm then lifted the sleeve. More of those red spots. Since the pills for the syphilis ought to be working by now, she hoped this wasn't something else for her to worry about.

Claire wandered from the kitchen to the nearest window in the sitting room and looked out over the grounds. Last night's frost had all but disappeared. The flat was warm, though. Too warm, Claire thought, and stuffy. She undid the latch and tried to push it open.

The window didn't budge. Not to worry, she'd leave it. She couldn't be bothered.

She flopped down at her desk and started to organize her assignment's rough notes while mulling over the state of her relationship with Alex. After a few minutes, feeling too warm for comfort, she tried the other window. That was also stuck tight.

Apprehension wormed its way to her thoughts. Even if her mind was playing tricks, did that mean she wasn't actually experiencing all these horrible things? Would she ever be able to tell the difference? Curious, she tried the others in the apartment to see which would open. The answer was none. Now that she couldn't get any fresh air, her need had become so much greater.

The flat felt closer and hotter than before. Her head ached. Should she go for a walk or get out of here in case something was about to happen? If she called someone, no doubt they'd come over and every window would open as if by magic. She was torn. She so wanted to be strong and she still had her assignment to do. Was she being lazy and using the hallucinations as an excuse? She couldn't put her work off any longer. The flat might be on the tropical side but changing into something cooler should solve the problem.

She dropped her robe and pajamas onto the bed swapping them for a loose T-shirt and shorts. Deep breaths. Relax. Focus. She couldn't waste this chance to get her assignment finished. Luckily, it was so quiet she might have been the only one in the whole building.

She returned to her desk and switched on her laptop. In seconds, she got up again, to pour a large glass of iced water.

No matter what she did, Claire couldn't concentrate. Thoughts of Alex encroached where they weren't wanted as did her worries about what might be about to happen. Her good intentions were receding fast. A fine sheen of perspiration covered her body. She wiped away the damp hair sticking to her forehead and tucked it behind her ear.

Claire placed her hand on the radiator then pulled it back in shock. The metal was burning hot. She hadn't changed the settings, so it shouldn't be on. She went into the kitchen and checked the boiler. The flame was yellow. Claire vaguely recalled an advert on the TV showing blue and yellow flames saying one color was fine but the other was potentially dangerous. Since she couldn't remember which was which, she decided to go next door and check if Sally was also having any problems with the central heating, and with the windows, too. She started to feel light-headed.

Irritation and worry surfaced. Uneasy bedfellows. She needed to get on with her work, not waste time bothering the neighbors. But what if...?

She put on her slippers and padded to the front door. She pulled down the handle. Nothing happened. For God's sake, don't say that was broken, too.

She jerked it up and down. The door wouldn't open. She tugged again and again, then in frustration, kicked at the unyielding wood.

"Shit!"

The soft moccasins she wore offered little protection. Her big toe throbbed with pain. Frustration and fear joined the mix. Tears rolled down her cheeks and her mind froze as though she was trapped on an icy lake and any thoughts would lead her to fall through.

She limped back into the kitchen. The smell was so much stronger now. She still wasn't sure what it was. Natural gas didn't smell, did it? This was far more pungent and raw, but she wasn't going to take any chances. Claire switched off the boiler. The flame stayed alight.

Oh, Christ. Oh, Christ. Oh, Christ.

All this weirdness, it couldn't be happening. She wouldn't allow it. None of this was real. She must—

Her head pounded and as nausea suddenly swept through her, she staggered to the sink and vomited.

Claire swayed back wiping her mouth, ignoring the dizziness. She seized the house phone from the kitchen wall and put it to her ear. A voice murmured words she couldn't understand. Low and sinister, over and over like some sort of chant.

"Help! This is an emergency. Please get help. Are you there? Hello? Hello?"

No response. Only silence as though someone were holding their breath, waiting. The handset slipped from her fingers. "Oh, God."

She grabbed her mobile from the breakfast bar and opened it. No light. No signal. This was ridiculous. Her phone should be on. She stabbed at the buttons. Nothing. She flung it at the window. It clinked against the glass and dropped onto the floor.

Adrenalin kicked in. She stumbled to the cupboard below the built-in oven, opened the door, and grabbed whatever came to hand. Saucepans and lids clattered onto the tiles until at last, she pulled out the heavy cast-iron frying pan.

Struggling with its weight, Claire lurched toward her bedroom. She felt drowsy and disoriented. She was sweating like a pig in the sweltering heat and, for fuck's sake, everything couldn't suddenly go wrong. She had to do something drastic and fast. After trying to open the window one last time, Claire gazed blindly at the cloudless blue sky. She lifted the pan with both hands and swung it as hard as she could at the glass.

The reverberation shuddered through her. Not even a crack to show for her effort. She swung again and again, winding herself each time. Her arms ached and the dizziness was worse, but she couldn't stop now. Ever more determined, she kept slamming the pan onto the window, but it was as though the pane had no intention of breaking whatever she threw at it. She let the pan fall.

Using her damp T-shirt, she wiped the tears and sweat from her face. With hardly any air, what small breaths she could take burned her nose and throat like razors flaying her skin. Her strength fading fast, she picked up the pan once more. As she heaved it against the glass, she heard the chapel bell toll.

The skin on her hands was raw. The blood and sweat made it difficult to get a grip on the handle.

"Oh, God, oh, God, oh, God..."

Exhausted, she raised the skillet again. One last go. She must have weakened the pane enough. Claire swung again and as she did, she looked down. Her eyes caught those of Moira Bradigan staring up at her. Her arms shook as the pan hit the glass, but no breaking sound rewarded her efforts.

Wheezing, she let go of the heavy weight. It thudded onto the carpet.

She pounded on the window with her fists, waved her arms, and howled her frustration.

The damn woman just stood there. Smiling at her. Claire could hardly breathe now. She clutched at the curtain and gasped wildly.

All her strength had deserted her.

She slid to the floor.

Chapter Twenty-Two

Friday, 20 August, 1869

Harriet stayed in the infirmary for three days. Rose, in the next bed, was discharged after two. During that time, Harriet asked anyone who would listen if they had seen Ellen. The answer was always 'no'. She hadn't seen a doctor or the Matron at all, but when Mrs. Trotter came in to her ward on the third morning, Harriet begged her to check Ellen wasn't in the mortuary.

When the Assistant Matron returned saying the only death in the past day had been an old soldier who'd fallen down the stairs and broken his neck, she was at first relieved.

"That weasel Lynton Brown brought him in." Mrs. Trotter's round face shone with indignation. "Do you know, he wheeled Titus Sproat in on a barrow and tipped him out on the floor like a sack of potatoes? When I told Brown to have more respect for the dead, he said, 'He's beyond any pain now, ain't he, Miss Fusspot,' snickering in that foul way he has. The nerve of the man."

Harriet swallowed. "You don't mean old Titus, do you?"

Mrs. Trotter confirmed it was he.

Upset by the poor man's death, Harriet worried more about Ellen.

On her discharge from the infirmary, Harriet struggled to climb the stairs. Her head felt heavy and her stomach tender. When she reached the second floor, she bent over, hands on knees trying to catch her breath. A minute later as she pulled herself upright, she caught a glimpse of Annie Craven waddling away from her.

"Mrs. Craven!" Harriet hurried as best she could, dodging around the usual inmates milling about the corridor. The ward supervisor slowed. Annie Craven's chest swung round before the rest of her, and Harriet, her heart pounding, halted.

"Mrs. Craven, have you seen Ellen?" Her voice emerged as weak and shaky as a newborn chick's.

"No. In't she in the infirmary?" Mrs. Craven frowned.

Harriet shook her head. Near the end of her tether, tears rolled down her cheeks.

The ward supervisor pulled a frayed handkerchief from her pocket and held it out. "Blow yer nose, girl."

Harriet did as instructed, then wiped her eyes.

"Feeling better, Harriet?" Mrs. Craven's lips pulled back in a macabre imitation of a smile.

"Not really. I'm so worried about Ellen. I even checked the morgue, but I can't find her anywhere." Harriet's voice continued to rise, sounding ever closer to outright panic, but she couldn't stop herself. "Where is she?"

Mrs. Craven patted her arm. "Calm down. Come, lemme take you back. You better have a lie down."

The Ward Supervisor led her along the corridor and pushed opened the door to their room. Harriet felt Mrs. Craven's thick hands at her waist guiding her toward her bed.

"Here girl, you stay put and rest."

The room and mattresses had been wiped down and everything reeked of carbolic. She ignored Mrs. Craven and opened Ellen's cupboard. Empty. She asked the supervisor about Ellen's belongings. Put away for safekeeping was the reply, but Harriet wasn't sure she believed her. Another thought came to mind. "Mrs. Craven, what happened to the cake?"

"When I came back from taking you and Rose to the sick bay, I tol' the attendant cleaning the mess in here to chuck it all away. Weren't much left any'ow."

She gazed at Mrs. Craven in dismay. "Oh no. I'm sure that's what made us ill."

"So? This is a big place, lots of food goes bad, ain't nutting going to stop that."

Over the past three days, Harriet had done a lot of thinking. To help Ellen she must give voice to those thoughts. "Bill Callahan has been threatening Ellen and me. Maybe he did something to give us a scare."

Annie Craven's fingers clenched into a fist and she moved threateningly toward her. "Here my girl, don' you be saying such things. He and the Matron'd skin yer alive."

Harriet, with no more space to retreat, felt the metal of her bed frame press into the back of her legs. She raised her hands to protect herself from the onslaught if it should come and forced herself to speak up. "But Mrs. Craven, we've got to find Ellen. Mr. Callahan was there when we all got sick. Do you think he has taken her somewhere?"

The supervisor said nothing. Harriet waited, wondering what was going through Mrs. Craven's mind. The woman tutted. "No, Harriet, he must've gone off to attend to something else. I ain't seen much of him these past few days, he's been so busy."

Mrs. Craven turned, and clumped out the door, adding as she left, "Let it go no further, girl. Nothing we can do."

Feeling dizzy, Harriet lay down on her bed. Unconvinced, she intended to go out and search again for Ellen, but her eyelids were so heavy she couldn't keep them open.

"Oh, dear God."

The stench hit her first, then the pain. Ellen whimpered and struggled to open her eyes. The sticky crust split to reveal an impenetrable darkness. She squirmed, but short heavy chains chafing her ankles and wrists held her spread-eagled on the stone floor.

A rough piece of cloth covered her but despite the intense heat, she couldn't stop shivering. She tried to swallow but her throat was too parched and swollen. Panic rising, Ellen gasped for air.

Without warning, violent cramps ripped at her insides. She dry-retched, splitting her lips further. Another wave of agony pounded through her. Exhausted and knowing she couldn't take much more, she prayed and prayed.

New sounds cut into her consciousness. The rattle of metal on metal, a key turning in a lock, the creaking hinge of a reluctant door.

She blinked and twisted her head away from the flickering light. Her blistered tongue gave a tentative lick at the blood on her lips. Ellen welcomed the soothing dampness but craved more. A sliver of hope won out and she turned her face toward the new arrival. Through narrowed eyes, she could just make out a shadow.

"Help me."

The shadow became a man lunging toward her. Two steps to the center of the room. One quick motion and a gush of cold water slapped into her face. She spluttered, shaking her head.

"Today's water." The man sneered. "No more 'til tomorrow, if yer lucky."

The voice sounded familiar, but she couldn't think who it might be. A sharp kick in the side from a metal-tipped boot; then another added to her indescribable pain. The man's eyes glittered with malice as he increased the onslaught. She cried out and struggled uselessly against her chains. The pail clattered onto the flagstones.

"No food either." The boot went in again. "You. Only. Waste it."

With every kick and grunt, his sweat sprinkled over her like a perverted holy rite.

But now, beyond her flesh yielding to the repeated blows, she didn't move.

Chapter Twenty-Three

Saturday, 7 March
PRESENT DAY

Alex drove through the gates of Belle Vue for his showdown with Claire. Though sure he had made the right decision, a part of him still hoped for a rational explanation. One that would turn back time to before it all turned sour.

He also hoped she wouldn't cry and shout. All he wanted was the truth. He didn't want to hear her protest her innocence, tell him lies—though they wouldn't be lies if the doctor had made a mistake. The papers were full of such cases. Maybe she'd had another test done and waited for the results. Maybe. Maybe not.

And, though angry and hurt, he still loved her.

He parked his car then sat motionless, hands still clutching the steering wheel. He listened as one of his favorite songs played on the radio. Delaying tactics. Anything to avoid setting off a chain of events that might be difficult—impossible—to stop.

He leaned back against the headrest ignoring the temptation to start the car and drive away.

The sound of a door closing, voices, footsteps on gravel, triggered him to action. Through the windscreen, he saw two men walking toward the car park. One, he vaguely recognized from Claire's party. From the look of them, they were going to play golf. He wished he could join them.

Alex took his key from the ignition and got out of the car. He exchanged nods and passed the two men. It took him longer than usual to reach the back entrance. The door, sturdy and resolute, barred the way. He rang the bell and glanced at the sky. A nothing sort of a day. No sun, no rain, not warm, not cold. Just there. He was just here, but he didn't want to be.

He pressed the buzzer again and waited. Perhaps she'd gone out. He hadn't said exactly when he'd be over, so he couldn't expect her to be sitting on the sofa, hands clasped, waiting patiently like some Stepford wife. If that were the case, knowing her, she'd have left him a message. Although he hadn't replied to any of her texts and emails, he'd read them all. She'd given up after Monday. He now looked back at the car park. Her red Mini was parked in its space.

Not sure what to do, he considered another option lurking unwanted at the back of his mind. Claire hadn't been well. She might have collapsed or had an accident. At the very least, he should check in the flat. Marianne was away and, unless one of the neighbors noticed something wrong, as when Sally and Jeff had heard her the other week, she could be in there and need help. He took the spare key she'd given him from his pocket and let himself in.

He made his way through to the entrance hall and caught the back of a familiar figure standing in front of the rows of post boxes. He stepped onto the parquet and walked toward her, his trainers making only a slight squeak. Moira Bradigan took a newspaper from one of the slots. She unrolled it and was scanning the front page when she suddenly flinched and stepped back as though she would lose her footing. He rushed forward, putting his hand to her elbow. She started a second time and bristled like a cornered hedgehog.

"Miss Bradigan, are you all right?" he asked.

She folded the newspaper, the New York Times, and inspected him with her piercing gaze.

"Thank you, Mr. Palmer, I am fine. A name from the past caught me unawares. Now remove your hand, I'm not going to fall and break."

Too right, he thought, as he withdrew the offending body part. There was steel under those wrinkles and beneath that, heaven only knew. She unsettled Alex but, for the life of him, given she was only a grumpy old woman, he couldn't think why.

He nodded to her and it was then her lips curled upwards and an expression of triumph crossed her features. "I'll let you get on," she said and he could feel her watching him as he headed for the stairs.

The second-floor landing was as quiet as the rest of the building. He noted the wood shavings were still there, spread along the skirting board. Claire was definitely no Marianne when it came to cleaning. He was getting sidetracked again. Focus on what he was going to say or do.

At Claire's door, he knocked loudly, called out her name. No response. He knocked again. After waiting a minute or so, he put the key in the lock and opened the door.

The smell hit him at once, as did the wave of dread.

Oh, Christ. The apartment was stifling, as though the central heating had been left on full blast. He took out an old tissue from his jacket pocket and clamped it over his nose.

Something was seriously wrong. He shouted Claire's name. Nothing. Holding his breath, Alex darted from the hall to the sitting room. Nothing. Dining room. Nothing. Kitchen. An opened cupboard with a pile of saucepans on the floor. As he moved into the room, he noticed the handset hanging off the wall, then dried vomit in the sink. His stomach lurched. He raced back to the hall, repeating her name like a mantra. Bathroom. Nothing. Claire's bedroom.

He pushed the door open and entered. Even with the tissue pressed to his nose, the stench was worse than in the kitchen, but a different smell, as of burnt flesh.

"Claire?" It came out as a choked whisper.

He tried not to gag and blinked to clear his eyes. The bed was made, her bag open upon it. One side of the curtain rail had been pulled from the wall. The brass rings and material they held had slid down against the finial. He dared not think what this might mean.

Alex edged forward to the space between the bed and window. He stared at the sight before him.

Kneeling on the floor, her head and body pressed against the radiator was Claire.

Bloated. Discolored. Seeping.

Dead.

Alex reeled. His foot knocked into a large frying pan. What the fuck was that doing there? He wanted to look away, but her body exerted a magnetic pull. For the flies, too. A bitter taste flooded his mouth. That couldn't be his Claire. It wasn't. It couldn't be.

Oh, dear God.

Chapter Twenty-Four

Saturday, 21 August, 1869

When Harriet woke the next morning, her mouth was parched and her tongue still slightly swollen. But with her first priority clear in her mind, she was ready for the new day. Breakfast passed without incident. She sat silently through the meal and once again played through the events of the day of the cake delivery. Her memory was a jumble. All she could remember was the confusion around them when she and Ellen had staggered out of their room. That, and the fact that before she was taken to the infirmary by Mrs. Craven, Bill Callahan had been there.

Should she report Ellen's disappearance to Mrs. Fishburn? The Matron would first ask what she had done to find Ellen, so she would wait until she had exhausted all other possibilities.

Excused from straw plaiting until Monday, she decided to speak to Mrs. Trotter again. Ask her if she had seen Bill Callahan or heard any information that might connect to Ellen's whereabouts. Harriet made her way toward the infirmary where Mrs. Craven told her she'd find the Assistant Matron.

Harriet opened the door and stepped through. The fetid smell, familiar from her recent stay, seemed stronger than before. A warder pointed out Mrs. Trotter's plump figure at the end of the long ward, but as she walked past the small iron bedsteads, so close they were almost slotted together, she became conscious of only one sound. An inhuman guttural moaning. Full of unspeakable suffering. In all her time in asylums, she had never heard such a chilling noise.

Her steps slowed. Mrs. Trotter was leaning over the last bed. The one pushed against the wall, separate from the others. The one where the sound came from. Then it changed to short breathy whines, rising in volume, then to a long-drawn-out scream. Of fear and pain. Bare legs kicked out, a body encased in a strait waistcoat twisting, rocking, a head shaking from side-to-side. The other lunatics seemed cowed by such torment. Harriet prayed under her breath. Mrs. Trotter, who had pressed herself over the patient as though the physical contact might pacify him, kept up her litany of soothing words. The man stilled until only his low mewls remained.

Harriet hovered, wondering whether to return later or wait. Mrs. Trotter straightened herself and stood back. Harriet's gaze was drawn to the wizened man on the bed, his mouth and face half covered with a blood-soaked bandage, and uttered a cry of her own.

The Assistant Matron turned toward her. Harriet's stomach knotted at the expression of misery on her face. Chancer. Oh, dear God. She glanced at him again and caught his eye. Not a trace of recognition. He whimpered but lay helpless and unmoving on the canvas-covered pallet.

Mrs. Trotter led her away and spoke in a low tight voice. "Someone cut out his tongue last night. It's sent him over the edge. Chancer wasn't really mad before, but now he is completely insane. Pray for him, Harriet, that's all you can do."

"Oh, that poor, poor man." Her eyes filled with tears. At the same time, she realized she would have to wait to ask about Bill Callahan. Mrs. Trotter returned to Chancer and stroked his forehead. Harriet bid farewell and retraced her steps, praying as she went.

Back in the main building, she made slow progress through the heaving bodies. She moved like a sleepwalker but while her eyes were vacant, her mind was as busy as the corridor itself. Ellen had arrived at Belle Vue with Chancer and was very fond of him. She would be devastated by this news. Chancer and old Titus were close friends, too. A prickle of fear edged into her thoughts. She hoped none of these events were connected. She couldn't see how, though, and she mustn't

BELLE VUE

let her imagination run away with her. That wouldn't do Ellen any good. She needed to keep her wits about her, especially if Bill Callahan was part of this.

She spent the rest of the day wandering around the asylum, asking both attendants and patients if anyone had seen her. By cruel fate, a letter from her father arrived saying he had found a suitable nurse and would pay a visit in the next fortnight—his first for a year—to see Doctor Fishburn and make the arrangements. Harriet was torn between excitement at the news but without Ellen, knowing she would never leave Belle Vue.

By the time darkness fell, Harriet had to admit defeat. Drained by her exertions and the relentless heat, she returned to her room. Deep down she felt something dreadful had happened to Ellen. Would she ever see her again? She knelt on the floor by her bed and prayed. When she finished, she rested her head onto her clasped hands and wept. Since her mother's death, she had been so lonely and Ellen was her first true friend. One who had been through so much and Harriet couldn't bear to think anything worse might have happened to her.

She wiped her eyes and made up her mind to go directly to Mrs. Fishburn in the morning and take the consequences. If Ellen was then found, it would be worth it. She was desperate to tell her the good news. Tomorrow was also the Lord's Day and there were numerous chapel services to attend. Perhaps she could seek the advice of the chaplain as well. For now, though, she felt completely drained and of no help to anybody.

As Harriet got to her feet, she heard some whispering outside her room. A few seconds later, Mrs. Craven peered round the edge of the door. The woman pushed it open and shuffled in, holding a mug in her hand.

"You been through a lot, Harriet. Drink this. Make yer sleep better."

"Er, thank you, Mrs. Craven. I've still got this terrible thirst."

She took the mug and peered into it. "Milk?"

Mrs. Craven nodded. "Now let me see yer drink it all, so I don't need to leave the cup."

Harriet drank it in several large gulps.

"Gimme yer frock, too, and I'll take it to the store."

She handed her the mug and pulled off her dress. She gave it to Mrs. Craven who slung it over her arm.

Harriet bid her goodnight and Mrs. Craven left the room. The door closed but did not click shut.

She fell asleep as soon as she lay down.

In the morning, Harriet heard the chapel bell sound seven but kept her eyes closed. All she wanted to do was stay in bed until the pain in her head went away.

Minutes later, she forced her eyes open and looked toward the window. The weather seemed to have turned. Instead of an expanse of blue, the sky was smudged gray. It seemed cooler than the previous day. Maybe the heatwave had finally broken. She stretched out her arms, yawned, and rolled over.

For several moments, Harriet stared without comprehension at the figure in the next bed, at the back of Ellen's head.

She stifled a sob of elation. At last! As logical thought took hold, so too did the first inklings of unease. Ellen would have woken her.

She cried out her name, but Ellen didn't move. She leaped out of bed and shook her friend.

"Ellen? Wake up!"

Why wasn't she answering? Dear God, let her be all right. Harriet darted round the narrow iron bed frame and crouched in front of her friend.

The thin sheet was pulled up high, and she lifted it away to reveal Ellen's face.

A black-lipped, yellow-tinged face, whose sightless eyes stared back at her.

Chapter Twenty-Five

Monday, 23 March
PRESENT DAY

Alex shuffled out of Hamish's office and checked his watch. Eleven fifty-five. Paul was meeting him here at twelve. He scratched at the stubble on his chin and sat down on the hard plastic chair.

He distracted himself by contemplating the woman at the cluttered desk opposite him. Hamish's new secretary. Zena Theodorou. A female version of Paul without the bald patch. His mind flicked to Paul hugging Claire before the Greek Food and Wine party, while he'd stood back and found fault with her hair and face. His stomach churned. Christ, he'd been a smug shit. And now it was too late to—

"Hi, Alex. Sorry I'm late."

The clock above Zena's head read 12:03. Alex stood so he was level with Paul's eyes and the concern in them.

"You okay?" Paul asked. "I heard you moving around early this morning but by the time I was up, you'd gone."

"I'm still not sleeping much."

"Let's go somewhere quiet, get a drink and some lunch." Paul glanced at Zena. She gave a hesitant smile that he returned.

Alex nodded. Paul put his hand on Alex's arm and they trundled like two old-timers along the corridor. He felt like he was moving through glue: fixed into an alternative reality that operated at a different speed. Nothing seemed real. He appreciated Paul's instinctive understanding. Just as he'd found comfort in the support he'd received from Gary and his other mates. Most days, Marianne rang him, too, and more and more, he relied on her calls. To hear her soothing voice.

Still early by college lunching standards, the cafe was quiet. Relieved, Alex sat and waited as Paul collected two cappuccinos and a couple of BLTs.

They ate in silence, both evading the subject on their minds. Keeping his attention fixed on a colorful picture on the wall in front of him, Alex spoke first.

"The funeral is on Friday, Paul. At St. Nicholas Church. That's where her parents are buried, and I think..." His voice cracked and he stopped to clear his throat.

"We'll go together. You, me, and Gaz," Paul said, his voice low.

Alex's eyes searched Paul's. "Marianne rang me last night, so she also knows the arrangements. Her placement finished on Sunday, so she was coming back tomorrow anyway."

He wasn't sure he'd be able to move back to the place where Claire died, but Marianne had assured him, it would help her stay close to her best friend. And of course, Marianne hadn't actually been in the flat and seen what happened to Claire.

At first, the police had cordoned off the apartment while they carried out their investigations. Once the postmortem had established Claire's primary cause of death was carbon monoxide poisoning, the gas company had also taken over the flat to ensure everything was functioning properly. Now, a cleaning firm eradicated all traces of Claire's fate.

"What's happening with you two?" Alex asked. "Neither of you have said anything, and I've been..."

His voice trailed off as Paul shrugged. "Precisely nothing. Seems it was only a fling." The smile was light-hearted but, knowing his mate, it had been much more than that. "We're back to that well-known 'just friends' state. You know the one when you've been given the push by someone who doesn't want you bad mouthing them to your mutual pals. I kept ringing, but all I ever got was her voicemail, and last week, the 'Dear John', or rather, 'Dear Paul' email popped into my inbox. At least my Mum will be pleased. After all, the only candidate she'd ever consider is a nice Greek girl from a nice Greek family with her nice Greek hymen still intact."

Alex laughed, then stopped abruptly.

Leaning forward, Paul said in a quiet but firm voice, "Claire would have laughed, too. Don't beat yourself up. It won't bring her back."

Someone had finally walked on those eggshells. He was glad it was Paul.

The coffee forgotten, his friend's words opened feelings he'd been blocking for the past three weeks. "I know, but I am *so* mixed up about it all. Mostly with guilt and regrets. I should have done something."

"Alex…"

"Of course, no one else knows the full story." He thought for a few seconds. "Except Marianne, I suppose."

"Oh, I didn't know that." Paul paused. He frowned and shook his head. "It doesn't seem real, does it? Claire not being around. I suppose it won't really hit home 'til the funeral."

Alex nodded.

"I admire the way you've dealt with everything. Add the grilling you got from the police. I think I would have cracked."

He winced. If Paul only knew. "That was one experience I wouldn't wish on my worst enemy. Or maybe I would since it was so bad. I suppose being Claire's boyfriend and finding her body made me a prime suspect, but I hadn't realized how intimidating that could be."

Thinking back to his run-in with the surly Chief Inspector Martin Pugh, who led the investigation, brought him out in a cold sweat.

First, there were all the questions as to why he hadn't been in contact with Claire over that last week. Had they argued? Were there problems in the relationship? The police seemed determined not to believe his account.

Second, when the postmortem revealed Claire's syphilis and she was also suffering from malnutrition, the police had dragged him in again as though they'd been right all along.

Pugh seemed to relish in his discomfort and repeated most of the same questions about his and Claire's relationship. Even to Alex, his answers made him appear slippery and self-serving. Never dropping his look of disbelief, Pugh had then cut to the chase. "And do you have syphilis, sir? Were you the one to give it to her?"

"No, I don't and no, I wasn't." Before Pugh could shout 'Bingo!' as it seemed he was itching to do, Alex had continued. "When Claire told me she had it, I got myself tested and the result was negative. That was the real reason we didn't see each other for the week. A bit of thinking space. I told her I'd come round on that Saturday and we would talk about it then. Mostly, I suppose, to tell her I wanted to split."

Throaty chuckle, raised eyebrows, building to the denouement of a third-rate detective film, Pugh pressed on regardless. "Sure you weren't full of rage? You were a right patsy, weren't you? She'd been cheating on you all along."

Back and forth, back and forth. Alex fought to stay calm and not lose his cool at Pugh's goading. When it seemed Pugh had gotten enough mileage out of their fragile relationship, the Chief Inspector moved on to his amazement at Claire's malnutrition.

Alex had told him she ate enormous portions and lots of them. Luckily, everyone the police interviewed backed him up, and eventually, his alibi for the day Claire died was substantiated.

The evening before that interview with the police, Marianne had called and, echoing his own guilty thoughts, wondered if Claire might have committed suicide.

"You certainly weren't to blame, Alex. She was unhappy and confused. How could you ever trust her again? What about the bastard she was protecting? She never told me his name. Well, whoever he was, he gave her the clap and got away with it. You were the innocent party in all this."

He'd felt a closer bond with Marianne after all her support. She understood his viewpoint and for that he was grateful. The police finally confirmed they did not regard suicide as likely: there was no note or any relevant preparation.

BELLE VUE

After the postmortem, the inquest opened but was then adjourned so further investigations could be carried out. Since there were still some questions about the state of Claire's body, the coroner did not release it for burial.

When it was revealed, apart from a few small bequests, that Marianne had inherited Claire's entire estate, the police had gone to Bath to interview her, but since she had been at work during the relevant period, she was hardly under suspicion. Alex appeared to be their only suspect. No other possibilities of who could have given her syphilis were identified. Two weeks later, the inquest reconvened. Despite the best efforts of the investigation, the jury found it was not possible to determine whether Claire's death was suicide or an accident since there was no fault to explain the gas leak. An open verdict was passed. For Alex, a weak and unsatisfactory finding.

As he recounted all of this to Paul, only omitting the syphilitic elements, he ended with his doubts. "It all sounded so pat. It was reported as if everything Claire went through had a rational explanation. A logical progression from one state to the next. Like going to sleep, but that's bullshit. I saw her face and body and hands. Christ, Paul, I will have nightmares for the rest of my life. To me, it seems all wrong. Don't ask me why, because I don't know. So many questions still haven't been answered."

The next day, Alex received a letter from Moira Bradigan in response to his now-forgotten note asking her to meet him again. It said little, merely instructing him in a hand reminiscent of a different age, to visit on Wednesday at four o'clock. No phone call or email for that lady. Nor any doubt he would show.

He made his way to Miss Bradigan's apartment, curious as to why he was bothering. Her contribution to his project was hardly critical, but he felt drawn to her and curious as to how she fitted into the jigsaw.

Given what Claire had said about Miss Bradigan, he'd even wondered if she had anything to do with the strange occurrences. That was crazy, though. They'd be locking him up next. She was only an old woman for God's sake. Perhaps that was why he felt uneasy about her. Likeable she wasn't.

Marianne had also called. When he told her about his imminent visit to Belle Vue, she immediately invited him up when he'd finished with Miss Bradigan. Once he'd got through that ordeal, he felt a dose of Marianne would be the medicine he needed. Nothing beat a laugh with a pal. Well, almost nothing, remembering his self-imposed celibacy.

He stood at Miss Bradigan's door, nervous like a little boy about to meet a fierce great-aunt.

When she answered his knock, she looked healthier than he remembered as though she'd been taking some curative tonic that actually worked. Her face seemed to have filled out and lost much of its papery texture.

"Come in. Don't tarry. This won't take long."

Her words were still as sharp. She stepped back for him to enter.

"Thank you, Miss Bradigan." As Alex moved into the hall, he caught her distinctive smell again, same as the letter. Earthy with a slight touch of mint. Not unpleasant, but definitely an acquired taste.

On the console table, he glanced at a dog-eared copy of the New York Times. Heavily underlined in red, the words of one of the headlines—'Reclusive billionaire Nathan de Vere...' but before he could read the rest, a prod in his back pushed him forward. He didn't think he'd heard that name before, but it was obviously one Moira Bradigan was interested in.

Alex turned and watched Miss Bradigan follow him into the sitting room. Her movements seemed more agile than before.

"Now what do you want this time, Mr. Palmer?"

"My dissertation is due soon. If you can tell me anything about the asylum, I'd be most grateful."

"Would you, Mr. Palmer? I wonder."

"Please call me Alex."

"No, thank you. I like to retain a certain distance with people."

Alex was careful to keep a straight face. "So, will you talk to me?"

"Yes, Mr. Palmer, I will."

Hallelujah. He might as well start by finding out what her actual connection was with the asylum. "Eric Beamish thought you worked there before it closed."

"No, that is not so. I made donations to the asylum, and before those stupid politicians shut Belle Vue, for a time, I rented one of the large detached properties on the edge of the estate. Johnson Nottidge one of the earliest 'doctors' at the asylum used to own it, but it didn't serve its purpose. Then they knocked it down for flats when some of the land was sold off."

"Oh," he said, digesting this information.

Miss Bradigan walked to the ornate Victorian sideboard and picked up a framed photograph from amongst the jade ornaments. Alex didn't remember it from his previous visit. When she turned back to him, he looked as though she was enjoying a private joke.

Holding out the frame to him, she pointed to one of the figures. "The woman was one of my contacts at Belle Vue when it still operated as a hospital. They stopped calling it an asylum early in the last century if I remember correctly."

"Was she a friend?"

"No, she was not, Mr. Palmer. One can't be friends with lunatics or those who look after them."

"Oh." Twice now. He sounded like a tongue-tied idiot.

Alex took the picture and sat opposite Miss Bradigan. She perched on the edge of the high back armchair like a vulture expecting a good meal. He examined the black and white photograph. A formidable-looking woman, middle-aged or perhaps older, wearing a coat with a fur collar, hat, and gloves, stood beside a young uniformed female. The photograph had been taken in the grounds at the front of Belle Vue.

The edge of the chapel was visible at the side of the frame. He peered closer but, as the figures were slightly out of focus and at a distance, it was hard to make out the features. His impression was that they bore some resemblance to the lady watching him now.

"Are they relatives of yours?"

Miss Bradigan conjured her unsettling smile. He felt as if he was about to be led down a path, most probably of the garden variety. "In a manner of speaking."

Miss Bradigan's eyes never left his face.

"What was their connection to Belle Vue?"

"The older also liked to visit and she made donations to the asylum, too. Her name was Maureen Grady." A pause. "The other was a nurse there."

Miss Bradigan spoke the words as though she expected a reaction and was relieved when one was not forthcoming. Alex thought he'd never fathom her out.

"Another Irish name. Is that how you knew her?"

"Why do you say that, Mr. Palmer? Do you know much about genealogy? It's long been an interest of mine."

"Not really, but the two names struck me as Irish. A bit like I'd know someone called Epstein was Jewish or a McDonald had Scottish roots. What year was this taken?"

"1957. I remember it clearly."

Miss Bradigan didn't elaborate, so Alex asked a number of questions around what she knew about life at Belle Vue. Nothing earth shattering was revealed, though, given the lady in question, he'd hoped there'd be some exciting stuff, too. Some deep dark secrets perhaps. Like the lunatic with the human heart? When he said as much, she simply brushed him off. Instead, he got a greater amount of information than expected, but of a more mundane variety. As she spoke, he sensed an underlying tension in her, but couldn't imagine its cause. Probably nothing to do with him. She kept fiddling with her scarf and rubbing her finger between the silky material and her neck as though scratching at an annoying itch.

He was about to ask what had become of Maureen Grady when, without warning, Miss Bradigan veered onto a new topic. She cast a steely gaze at him. "Mr. Palmer. I'm getting old and it'll be time to move to the next stage of my life soon."

He said nothing, wondering where it was going to lead.

"I have many things still left to do."

"I'd say, Miss Bradigan, with all due respect, that at your time of life, you can choose to do only what you really want. I look forward to that freedom."

"Ah, but 'that freedom' is an illusion. There is no such thing as choice or free will, Mr. Palmer. Most people are mere puppets to be manipulated while others, to a greater or lesser degree, pull the strings."

"Surely, we make our own choices? Right or wrong. Of course, many things like our upbringing, education, and how much money we have or want, influence these, but at the end of the day, we are the ones in control of our destiny."

"Naiveté. How quaint," she said it as though it were on par with finding a slug under her shoe. "Your youth and immaturity are showing. I thought you knew more of the world, traveling and studying history as you do. No, it is the dark forces that shape our behavior, Mr. Palmer. Or do you not follow the newspapers? Wars. Massacres. Corruption. Slavery. Lying politicians. As always, Satan's side has the upper hand and there is no end to the increasing scale of human misery."

Miss Bradigan sat back as though mulling over her thoughts. "Religion was once described to me as 'smugness for the inadequate.' Are you inadequate, Mr. Palmer?"

He almost laughed. "I hope not, but surely others should be the judge of that. Otherwise wouldn't we all say we weren't?"

"Correct. Human nature never changes. Ego is all."

While Alex thought of a suitable response, her fingers grasped the arms of the chair and she raised herself to her feet.

"That is all for now, Mr. Palmer. I will be in touch again. You've given me something to consider."

She guided him firmly out the door. As it snapped shut behind him, he stood in the hall and collected his thoughts. Alex realized Miss Bradigan hadn't mentioned Claire once.

He now faced two conflicting emotions. On one hand, he was keen to see Marianne, but on the other, he wasn't sure how he would feel going into the apartment again. Everyone told him how important it was to move on: returning to the flat would be a first step. With a good friend there as support.

Alex made his way up to the second floor and knocked at the door. Heels clicked on the wood parquet of the hall.

Taking a deep breath, he looked up as the door opened.

Marianne.

Sultry kohl-rimmed eyes, shiny pouting lips, breasts spilling over a low-cut bodice.

"Christ!"

"Don't sound so shocked."

He hesitated, unsure what to do. Marianne reached out and pulled him to her. As their bodies touched, then melded together, he could feel her curves, her heat, smell her perfume.

She stepped back, eyes glittering.

"Pleased to see me then, Alex?"

He was beyond speech, beyond thought. He pushed her back against the wall, crushing her with his body. His mouth found hers. Ravenous. Devouring. Intense deep kisses. Her fingers raked his hair, then down his back. They moved to the front.

His hands stroked her legs, pushed up her skirt. Only skin.

She snaked her tongue round his lips, touching, teasing. Her hips ground into his.

He moaned, his senses aflame. Marianne whispered, her hot breath brushing his neck.

"Fuck me, Alex. Fuck me now."

Chapter Twenty-Six

Sunday, 22 August, 1869

Having completed a morning constitutional of unparalleled boredom, Nottidge stepped into the main foyer with Sheridan Lush. Almost immediately a red-eyed barefooted figure rushed toward them, arms outstretched.

Lush raised his whistle to alert the attendants when she called out, "No! Please don't do that. I must speak with you. It's *very* important. Please." The last word came out as a pitiful sob. Lush's hand paused in front of his mouth.

Nottidge eyed the girl's thin shift, unkempt hair, and tears with irritation. Could no one keep these lunatics in check? He would get Callahan to sort out the culprits. He looked again at the girl—quite attractive and prone to a bit of drama—so then maybe he wouldn't. Here was an unexpected chance to amuse himself: and perhaps trifle with the sanctimonious Lush.

"What's your problem?" Nottidge asked.

"Ellen's dead, oh God, Ellen's dead," she cried. "Poor Ellen, poor Ellen, all our plans."

Nottidge held back keen to see the other doctor's reactions. Lush lowered the whistle, a wrinkle of concern appearing on his forehead.

"Er, yes, but life goes on. While I am sure you are sad about this, it is no excuse to drop standards, is it? Please return to your ward and get dressed. Are you aware you shouldn't be in this area?"

The girl shook her head. "No, no, Doctor you don't understand. She's dead upstairs. Here in the asylum, in our room. I think she was murdered."

Lush's face registered his shock. Nottidge raised an eyebrow. He could imagine what the greenhorn doctor was now thinking. In fact, he'd been talking on that very subject during their walk this morning. There were so *many* deaths at Belle Vue he'd pontificated. Too many. More than the asylums he had visited during his training. He wanted to do something to prevent such occurrences. Nottidge had tried to put him straight but Lush remained wholly focused on the need to kowtow to lunatics and pander to their every whim. Egad, he was actually guiding the girl to a seat by the wall. The man was supposed to be a doctor, not a bleeding heart.

"First tell me your name."

Nottidge almost burst out laughing at the soft tone in Lush's voice. Like some lovesick pup.

"Harriet Stubbs, sir."

Lush pulled out a handkerchief and passed it to her. She blew her nose. The girl was quick to say she was an epileptic. Smart. She'd be paid more attention than if she had been committed for a different type of mental deficiency. From Lush at least. She recounted her story through intermittent sniffles. Her voice trailed off and she sat in her worn linen petticoat, eyes downcast, shoulders slumped as though bearing an intolerable weight. A pretty sight.

Lush reached forward to help the girl to her feet. "Come, Harriet. Take me up to see Ellen."

"Thank you, Doctor Lush. The women are *my* responsibility. You can go now." Nottidge prodded the girl to move forward and they headed toward the stairs. Lush walked alongside. One of the doors to the patient corridors opened, followed by the distinctive click of the Matron's precise footsteps on the parquet. Her stiff frame came into view.

"Doctor Nottidge!" Her voice boomed across the cavernous room. The Matron glared at them, no doubt, angered by the girl's state of undress in an area reserved for only the most important guests. Face set to stern disapproval, Mrs. Fishburn crossed the entrance hall. She nodded at him but directed her question to Lush. "Doctor, what is the meaning of this?"

Lush gave him a quick look then to his annoyance blurted out. "Matron, this young lady has just reported an unusual death. Of someone who apparently had been missing for the past few days. I…we…were on our way to investigate further before calling in Doctor Fishburn. However, now you are here, we can verify this unfortunate occurrence together."

Nottidge held back. Lush was a surprise. Perhaps he wasn't such a chump after all, but this was none of Lush's business, so once more he tried to dismiss the man. This time it was Mrs. Fishburn who poked her long nose where it wasn't wanted.

"Oh, let Doctor Lush attend. One day he might take over the female wards. He needs to learn." As she waved a dismissive hand, Nottidge took the measure of the two fools in front of him. He would leave them be—for now.

The Matron continued. "But I am *very* busy, so let us be quick. I'm sure this is nothing out of the ordinary."

Some ten minutes later as he, Doctor Lush and Mrs. Fishburn studied the face and shoulders of the girl's body, Nottidge knew she was wrong. He could see in their eyes, they knew it, too. Serious damage had been inflicted on the girl before death. Interesting.

At first, listening to the epileptic's description of the symptoms as they'd climbed the stairs, the Matron suggested she might be another victim of the current outbreak of typhoid. Once he looked beyond her savage injuries though and saw the yellow skin and black lips, he suspected the true cause.

As did Lush. The man aired his suspicions and remarked a postmortem was essential.

The Matron bristled. "That is not for me to say. Doctor Nottidge and you will have to speak to Doctor Fishburn and carry out the proper procedures." She leaned over. "The face looks familiar. Who was she?" She gazed round at the girl sniffling in the corner.

"Ellen Grady, Mrs. Fishburn."

"Good God," she muttered.

As did he. Under his breath. So this was what had been diverting Callahan's attention. The Grady whore's sister. He mulled this over. There could be sport to be had here.

Lush reached out toward the marks on the corpse's neck, but Nottidge brushed the man aside and pulled the sheet over the dead girl's face. He caught the Matron's eye and tipped his head. She nodded and bustled the girl toward the door.

"We have much work to do. Harriet, find Mrs. Craven and tell her I want to see her. Immediately. Then get your day dress on and go down to breakfast. We'll find a replacement to share with you, though it may take a few days to sort out."

Lush, he could see, was still keen to meddle. The man added his piece. "I suggest you go to the church service after your meal, as will Mrs. Fishburn and I when we can. We'll pray for Ellen's soul. Did she have any relatives, Harriet?"

Nottidge saw the glance that passed between Mrs. Fishburn and the girl. As he listened to the sorry tale of a wasted life and a family, who according to the epileptic would not be interested in Ellen's fate unless money was involved and heading in that direction, he kept his face straight, and was gratified to hear of the cake sent to the girl from where her half-sister lived.

Mary Grady had just fallen into his lap.

Mrs. Fishburn's nose quivered. "I will leave Doctor Nottidge to inform Doctor Fishburn and ensure that all the necessary arrangements are made. I suggest we proceed without delay. Doctor Lush, I'm sure my husband will speak to you later, but for now, we all have our duties to attend to."

Lush opened his mouth, no doubt to keep in the thick of things, thought Nottidge, and that he now felt was a good idea.

The door opened, and a large ungainly attendant plodded into view. As the Matron rattled off a stream of orders and questions, he took Lush to one side.

"We both need to convince Doctor Fishburn a postmortem is advisable. I know he might resist, but this case is most worrying. The poisoning for instance."

Nottidge looked Lush in the eye. "This really *is* a police matter."

Lush puffed himself up and informed a delighted Nottidge he would visit his friend, Superintendent John Gostick this evening. A word in his ear for a visit to be paid to Doctor Fishburn, and a few questions asked.

Next morning, Nottidge made sure he met with Fishburn as early as possible. He had primed the Matron to fill her husband in on the events of the previous day, but he wanted to ensure the Medical Superintendent was under no illusions about the importance of such an investigation to Belle Vue—and himself, of course.

Superintendent Gostick of the St. Alban's Constabulary was, as Lush had indicated, a punctual man. He arrived on the dot of eight.

Nottidge and Fishburn watched as Gostick placed his stiffened top hat on the chair beside him. The police officer scratched his bulbous nose and looked about to speak, but Fishburn got there first. "Your visit, Superintendent, is most fortuitous."

The Medical Superintendent outlined the situation and his suspicion of poisoning as the cause of Ellen Grady's death. He repeated both Nottidge's and the Matron's concerns about the actions of the girl's sister. What was her name? Yes, that was it. *Mary* Grady.

Gostick's face wore a thoughtful expression. "Murder is a most serious charge, sir. As you must surely know, we, in Hertfordshire, have not had such an occurrence for nigh on thirty years. You indicate this Mary Grady is the most likely suspect? Good, good, that makes our job much easier. I'm most grateful for your information, most grateful indeed."

Fishburn beamed.

The Superintendent rose to his feet. He strode to the door, barked out a couple of names and stepped back. Two constables, sprouting lines of wispy hair around chins, trooped into the room and saluted. In the summer warmth, their blue serge coats and matching trousers, white buttons, and stiff collars, made them look uncomfortable. Nottidge noted the array of law enforcement paraphernalia—handcuffs, rattle, wooden truncheon, and cutlass—hanging from their heavy leather belts. Most reassuring.

"Constables Grubbe and Cruikshank, Doctor Fishburn."

Gostick ordered them to search the asylum and they duly departed. The Superintendent hovered uncertainly. "I think I ought to view the body, Doctor Fishburn."

"Oh, do you?"

Nottidge smiled to himself as he saw Fishburn fighting to hold down his irritation, no doubt at being diverted from more liquid pursuits. As Gostick went out the door, he stepped forward and spoke sotto voce. "Just think *Doctor* Fishburn, you'll have pride of place in the courtroom. You could tell everyone about how you suspected all along it was Mary Grady. I can see the newspaper headlines now and no doubt you'd be photographed." The buffoon lapped it up like a cotton-mouthed sot.

So, it was that he and Fishburn met with Superintendent Gostick several times over the next few weeks as the case was built against Mary Grady. Nottidge was most interested to learn that when they arrested her—as the two metropolitan police constables would later testify during her trial—she appeared saddened by the death of her half-sister.

While the first words of grief might have worked in her favor, her second enquiring whether she would still get the insurance money, did not.

Chapter Twenty-Seven

Friday, 27 March
PRESENT DAY

To Alex, the brightness of the sunshine for Claire's funeral seemed inappropriate. He felt numb with uncertainty, guilt, and confusion. Was he really so shallow? Claire wasn't even buried yet and he had slept with her best friend. Was this his way of getting his own back? If so, he felt like a heel but Marianne had been so hot, and he more than ready for it. The sex had been awesome. For Christ's sake, he shouldn't be thinking of such a thing now. He stood before Claire's open grave and refocused his mind.

The glare of the sun grew increasingly uncomfortable. He closed his eyes and listened as the vicar read the dismissal, then repeated "Amen" with the rest of the mourners.

He opened his eyes and gazed across the churchyard. Moira Bradigan stood on an incline staring at them. She wore darkish clothes accompanied by a bright hat and scarf.

The vicar cast a handful of earth onto the coffin. Alex did the same before several others close by repeated the traditional act.

The ceremony over, some of the mourners started to chat or move away. Alex looked around and spotted Marianne, who had been missing from the church ceremony. He made his way toward her. Guilt fought the excitement of seeing Marianne, the suggestive gleam in her eye, the promise of what later might bring, and lost.

She looked fabulous. Not quite funeral fare, her top low and skirt tight, but as she stretched out her arm toward him and the sleeve pulled back, he saw she was wearing Claire's bracelet. His gift to her at

Christmas. Shit. He hesitated, conscious once more of the occasion, but she moved in, wrapped her arms around his neck and kissed him. Open mouthed with her tongue snaking between his teeth.

Oh God, she felt so good.

But all he could think of was Claire.

Marianne finished kissing Alex and stepped back. She put her arm through his and tried to make eye contact, but he seemed unusually nervous, babbling about some of the mourners. Although she kept her face neutral, she felt unsettled.

First, the woman who stood apart and watched the funeral from the hill. Marianne couldn't see her features clearly, but she was convinced it was the same woman she'd met on her visit to the derelict Belle Vue. The memory of her rigid upright stance and the superior attitude that emanated from her had never left Marianne. If that didn't give her a shock, Alex now told her it was Moira Bradigan. The same person Claire thought was playing some odd stalking game with her, all because she had nearly run her over. This weird connection and what it might mean unnerved her. The memories of being 'chosen' by the woman, but not knowing for what. It was as if things were happening over which she had no control.

Another part of her was exhilarated by this new ride she was on. Life was so much more exciting these days, opening up a wealth of possibilities she'd never considered before.

Other mourners now approached them, cutting off her thoughts. Hamish and some woman who looked vaguely familiar, on one side. Paul and a dark-haired woman who could pass for his sister, on the other. Gary with Sophie, the latter casting daggers at her. She stifled a yawn.

A sea of faces surrounded them. Marianne stayed a few more minutes but found it all far too boring. The only highlight was the spinsterish pucker of disapproval on Paul's face when she said hello to him. Gary, true to form, seemed to be mentally undressing her as he tried to tackle acceptable flirting at a funeral. As if she'd be interested in him.

Marianne leaned into Alex, "I'll meet you at the flat."

She sauntered back to the mini, mulling over her future. Claire already seemed so far away now. She needed to move on and, while not forget her friend, put her to one side. Alex had been as good in bed as she'd expected. Better, in fact. That first time had been fast and furious, but the next more than made up for the speed and one-sidedness of their initial encounter. Life was certainly looking up. Belle Vue hadn't been unlucky for her after all.

Driving home, she recalled how spooked she and Debs had been by their experience in the derelict asylum. The only fly in the ointment was Debra's refusal to come and visit her.

"Marianne, there's no way I'm going into that building, renovated or not. Sorry, but why not come across and see me here?" Debs had said.

With the fun, she was now having? No way. Odd that, after so long, the place still had such an effect on her sister. She would ask her about it next time Debra rang. Or maybe not. Life was too short.

Reaching her destination, she swung the car into the drive and through the magnificent gates. Her whole frame suffused with pride at owning a place here. She might not have done any work to get it, but the important thing was that the apartment and the rest of her inheritance—assuming she didn't fritter it away—made her financially secure for life. A comforting thought. Once, that would have been all she'd wanted, but now an exciting world of men and money awaited her. A career was the last thing she needed.

As she rounded the crest of the driveway, Marianne glanced at the long rows of windows catching flickers of the reflected sun. Belle Vue lay before her in all its glory. A movement distracted her, and she caught sight of a figure heading toward the chapel. The Bradigan woman. She'd taken off the extravagant hat she'd worn at the funeral. Even if it was her from all those years ago, there was nothing for her to worry about. The batty crone looked like she'd be keeping Claire company soon. For now, all she had was the empty church. What a boring way to spend an afternoon. She supposed when you got to that age, past sex, past having fun, then the hand of religion was probably the best you could get.

Marianne pulled into the car park. Sally Reichenberg and her husband stood next to their 4X4, facing each other. Marianne shut off the engine, grabbed her bag, and swung her legs out of the car. As she admired her new black stilettos, a few words of a heated discussion drifted across to her. Sounded like man trouble for old Sal. A door slammed. The Professor remained on the tarmac. The vehicle revved up and screeched out of the parking lot.

Marianne pressed the remote control and the central locking clicked on. Red-faced, Jeff Reichenberg rotated on his heel to face her. She smiled, adopting what she hoped was a look of concern, and said in a low voice, "Hi, Jeff. You okay?"

"Yeah, thanks, Marianne. You won't believe it, but we were actually arguing about you."

"Me? I hope I haven't done anything wrong?"

He shook his head, then walked toward her. When he was almost level, she reached out and placed her hand on his arm. "Jeff, can you steady me, please? I've got a cramp."

She leaned forward, lifted her leg slightly and rubbed her left calf. After returning her foot to the ground, she dropped her hand and tentatively paced a few steps. She turned, licked her lips, and smiled at him.

"Thank you, Jeff. You are a gentleman. I'm really thirsty. Fancy coming in for a coffee?"

"Don't mind if I do."

Out of the corner of her eye, Marianne could see him ogling her. She moved forward with obvious difficulty toward the path.

"Those heels are pretty high, Marianne. Would you like to take my arm?"

"Thank you again, kind sir. Are you sure you're not a Southerner?" She put her arm through his, and they progressed at a leisurely pace toward the entrance and up to the second floor. During that time, Jeff revealed although he had lived in Boston for most of his life, he was in fact born in Virginia and gave a potted history of southern manners. All without her yawning. A Herculean feat. Reaching their destination, Marianne let go of her rescuer. She caught his hungry eyes and held them. Fanning herself, she waved her long fake nails in front of her face.

"It's hot in here after all that climbing and in these clothes. Before I make us coffee, Jeff, you must let me take them off. You know, change into something more comfortable."

Hook, line, and sinker—but at that moment, the Professor's mobile trilled the Star Spangled Banner. Cursing, he lifted the side of his jacket and fumbled for the offending item in what Marianne could see was his burgeoning trouser pocket. He pulled out the phone and checked the caller ID.

"I better go." He pressed a button cutting off the music and put it to his ear. "Hi, Sally. No. Just left it in another room." Jeff patted Marianne's arm, mouthed "next time," before moving with deliberate quietness toward his apartment.

She nodded. As Marianne closed her own door behind her, she smiled broadly.

"Definitely next time."

Chapter Twenty-Eight

Selected Extracts from Coroner's Inquest

BELLE VUE INSANE ASYLUM
Before Robert Gribble Esquire,
Her Majesty's Coroner for the County of Hertfordshire.
Re: Ellen Catherine Grady, Deceased
REGINA v MARY GRADY
Depositions of Witnesses taken at the Coroner's Inquest
13th September 1869 – 20th September 1869

Witnesses for the Coroner
RE: Ellen Catherine Grady deceased
REGINA v MARY GRADY

Information of witnesses severally taken and acknowledged on behalf of our Sovereign Lady the Queen touching the death of Ellen Catherine Grady at the Belle Vue Lunatic Asylum in the Parish of Saint Nicholas Church, the 13th day of Sept 1869 before Robert Gribble Esquire one of Her Majesty's Coroners for the said county on view of the Body of the said Person laying dead in Belle Vue Lunatic Asylum, St. Albans in this County.

Document dated: 20 September 1869

1. SAMUEL STOTT FISHBURN—Belle Vue, Medical Superintendent

I reside at the Belle Vue Lunatic Asylum. I am the Medical Superintendent in charge of the institution. On Sunday morning of the 22nd August around 9AM, I was informed by my wife Mrs. Adelaide

Fishburn who is Matron of the asylum, Ellen Grady had been found dead in her bed by Harriet Stubbs, another patient. Mrs. Fishburn, Doctor Johnson Nottidge—the Resident Medical Officer in charge of the women and Doctor Sheridan Lush the other Resident Medical Officer who is responsible for the male patients—had briefly examined the body.

On Monday 23rd August at about 7 AM, I met with Doctor Nottidge who described to me the state of Ellen Grady's body and I immediately suspected she had not died of natural causes. It sounded like some sort of irritant poisoning. I did not see the body at this time but decided a postmortem ought to be carried out.

At precisely 8AM that same morning, I received a visit from Superintendent Gostick. I provided him with the details of the previous day's events and took him to see the body of the deceased. He agreed a postmortem should be carried out and asked to be informed when I received a reply from the deceased's family concerning the matter.

I duly instructed Mrs. Fishburn—who undertakes many of the administrative tasks—to write a letter in my name informing Ellen Grady's family of her death.

A postmortem was carried out on the deceased on Thursday 26th August by Doctor Nottidge.

Specimens were sent from the asylum to Doctor Snooks, the Home Office Pathologist, on the same day as the postmortem and it was confirmed by him to me in a letter of the 2nd September that Ellen Grady had died of phosphorus poisoning.

2. JOHNSON NATHAN COURTHOPE DE VERE NOTTIDGE—Belle Vue, Doctor of Medicine

I reside at the Belle Vue Lunatic Asylum. I am the Senior Resident Medical officer responsible for the females in the asylum. The deceased was one of the patients under my care.

On Sunday morning of the 22nd August, I had just taken a morning walk with Doctor Lush, and we had returned to the main hall of the asylum when a distraught girl informed us of Ellen Grady's death.

On Thursday, 26th August I carried out the postmortem on the body of Ellen Grady.

The body was covered with numerous skin eruptions in the form of sores and red rashes. The face showed yellowish discoloration of the skin, whites of the eyes, and mucous membranes. The lips were badly split and almost black in color. Her glands were swollen.

There were several bruises on her left arm, left hip and leg and waist. Most of these appeared likely to have been caused by the deceased falling against furniture and the floor when she was first taken ill. The facial skin and eyes appeared inflamed and scratch marks, mostly healed, were evident. Deep scratch marks were also found on the scalp. There was evidence of considerable hair loss. There were also marks around her wrists. I am of the opinion these were made by cloth restraints used to protect the patient from self-harm. In an asylum—as much as we might not want to use such a method—tying a patient's hands to their bed is sometimes the only way to stop them from causing self-inflicted injuries.

There was no clothing for analysis. Rigor mortis had passed, and I would estimate the deceased had been dead for more than a couple of days.

The mouth, tongue, esophagus, larynx, and trachea appeared swollen and irritated. I found a number of chancres in her mouth and also on her vulva and anus. These indicated she was in the first stages of syphilis. The liver was enlarged, yellow and fatty. The kidney was swollen, reddish and soft. The liver, heart, and kidneys all showed evidence of necrosis and there were hemorrhages in the intestinal tract. The stomach was empty. These organs possessed an odor of garlic. When I uncovered the body in darkness it glowed.

My opinion at the time was that Ellen Grady died of acute phosphorus poisoning and this would also explain her desire to scratch. I prepared four jars containing the deceased's organs and a letter detailing the findings of the autopsy. These were sent to Doctor Snooks of Guy's Hospital London for analysis. I presented my findings to Superintendent Gostick on the afternoon of Thursday 26th August.

I met Mary Grady once when she visited the asylum. I do not remember the exact date, but it must have been late June or early July. She asked about her sister's health and was most insistent Ellen should stay at Belle Vue. At the time, I did not enquire as to her reasons.

Cross-examined (X Ex'd) by Mary Grady. No, that is not true. The only time we ever met was on the occasion of your visit to the deceased in the summer. You stopped me as I have said and told me your sister must not leave the asylum.

X Ex'd by prisoner. Yes, of course, there is a supply of phosphorus at the asylum. None to my knowledge is missing.

3. ADELAIDE FISHBURN—Belle Vue, Matron

I live at the Belle Vue Lunatic Asylum. I am the Matron there.

Ellen Grady, the deceased, was admitted to Belle Vue on 8 May 1869 after the deaths of her mother and uncle, suffering from melancholia. She appeared to be responding well to our care. Ellen shared a room on the second floor in the main building with Harriet Stubbs, the girl who found her.

On the morning of Sunday 22nd August, I was on my way to my office at about 8 AM when I was stopped by Doctors Nottidge and Lush who were with Harriet Stubbs in the main entrance hall.

I have met Mary Grady on several occasions. During our last meeting, at the end of July, she gave instructions. I must not let Ellen leave the asylum. She said she wanted her where she could find her.

X Ex'd by prisoner. No. I do not bake cakes.

X Ex'd by prisoner. We mostly use traps, but phosphorus is kept at the asylum.

4. SHERIDAN BABBINGTON LUSH—Belle Vue, Doctor of Medicine

I live at Belle Vue Lunatic Asylum. I am the Resident Medical officer responsible for the male patients in the asylum. I did not know the deceased, Ellen Grady.

On Sunday morning last, the 22nd August, instant I awoke at six in the morning and after dressing went for an early morning constitutional with Doctor Nottidge. This was at my request.

When I first saw the deceased in the room she shared with Harriet Stubbs, she was lying on her back under a sheet on the bed. I watched as Doctor Nottidge examined the body of the deceased for no longer than a few minutes, but we could see—as Miss Stubbs had told us—there were suspicious circumstances to the girl's death. The skin was tinged yellow and the lips of the deceased were black. The deceased had been dead for at least thirty-six hours since rigor had passed, and the body was relaxed. There was extensive bruising, torn skin, and scratch marks all over the poor girl. I also noticed the skin around her wrists and ankles was broken. In my opinion, it looked as though she had been both restrained and badly beaten.

As well as the expected bodily odors, there was a smell of garlic about the deceased. On the basis of our examination of the body and Miss Stubbs' version of events, I reached the conclusion that the death of Ellen Grady required further investigation. I suspected irritant poisoning might be the cause of death.

I did not take part in the eventual postmortem of the deceased and did not examine the body again.

X Ex'd by Mary Grady. I was not able to examine the body for long enough to form an opinion as to whether the injuries caused by the bruises and other marks might have led to Miss Grady's death.

5. WILLIAM CALLAHAN—Belle Vue, Head Attendant

I live at the Belle Vue Lunatic Asylum in St. Albans. I am the Head Attendant there for both the male and female wards.

On Monday 16 August at around five in the afternoon, I was with Mrs. Annie Craven on the ground floor of the central building when we heard a disturbance upstairs. I instructed the strongest attendants to come with me. On the second floor, many patients had become

BELLE VUE

agitated. I also saw three patients who were vomiting and complaining of becoming ill after eating some cake. At first Mrs. Craven wanted to take all three to the infirmary but Ellen Grady became more upset and begged not to be taken there. These lunatics all have their strange ways and we decided it was easier to keep her calm if she stayed on the ward.

Mrs. Craven and I cleared out a small side room on the same floor. Mrs. Craven looked after her there. When I visited Ellen on the Thursday evening, she said she felt much better and thanked me for visiting her when I was so busy. I suggested to her that since she had been so ill and was frightened someone was trying to do her harm, it might be best if she stayed hidden for a few more days. I said I would attempt to find out who had supplied the cake that made her and her friends ill. On Saturday morning, Mrs. Craven came to see me to say Ellen had been taken bad in the night. By the time I got to her, she was in a very poor condition and she died later that day. Mrs. Craven said we must do right by Ellen and so I carried her back to her room when those in the dormitory had gone to sleep for the night.

I know Mary Grady well as she was planning to marry my brother, Jack. She lives with him at his pub, The Green Hog. She never lost a chance to insult her stepmother who was Ellen's natural mother. Mary Grady told me several times she hated Catherine Grady—now deceased—and wanted to make her half-sister pay for all the woman had put her through. I don't know what that was. She hated Ellen, too.

On one occasion, before the deceased had been admitted to Belle Vue, I was with Mary Grady when we overheard a couple of customers in the pub speaking about relatives being worth more dead than alive. Mary told me it gave her an idea for making more money so she and Jack could marry.

Mary told me another time, she planned to keep an eye on Ellen as she had plans for her. She wanted me to make sure Ellen stayed at Belle Vue. She said it didn't matter how I did it. I asked her why it was so important, and she said it would be better if I knew nothing about her intentions. As part of that conversation, she told me "a death, or two can set us free." I asked what she meant but she wouldn't answer.

X Ex'd by Mary Grady. No. I did not agree to help you. My position at Belle Vue is too valuable to me to risk losing it. As I said to you then, that was a wicked way of thinking and not right. I went to two services that Sunday.

6. ANNIE CRAVEN

I live at the Belle Vue Lunatic Asylum. I supervise the patients and staff in the C1-Ward. I report to Mrs. Adelaide Fishburn. I have worked for the asylum since it first opened in 1867.

On Monday 16 August at about 5 PM, there was an incident involving Ellen Grady, the deceased, Miss Harriet Stubbs, and another patient, Rose Garvey.

When I arrived at my dormitory on the second floor with Mr. Callahan, Harriet and Rose were vomiting and I took them to the infirmary. Ellen Grady was also vomiting but told me she did not want to go to the infirmary as she was in danger. She said someone was trying to kill her and they would find her there. She pleaded with me to hide her.

Mr. Callahan and I cleared out a small room used for linen storage on the same floor. We secretly cared for her there. In the first two days when she was really sick, I overheard her talking to herself in the room where we hid her. She was moaning in pain and kept saying "What have you done Mary? What have you done?"

After a few days, she seemed to get better and thanked Mr. Callahan and myself for looking after her so well. Ellen thought the cake she had eaten was poisoned. Mr. Callahan told her she still might be in danger, so she should stay where she was for a few more days to recover from her ordeal.

On the next day, she took worse again and Doctor Nottidge was away, so we couldn't call him, and it happened so quickly and she died that evening before we could get help. Mr. Callahan and I carried her back to her room after bedtime. We returned Ellen to her room so she could 'sleep' a last night in her bed with her friend nearby. Mr. Callahan and me were planning to alert the Matron the same morning.

The deceased always bruised easily. Sometimes even a gentle knock would make her skin look as though she'd been beaten. We used a soft cloth to bind her hands because she was complaining she itched everywhere and making herself bleed with her scratching.

I told Mrs. Fishburn the whole story on the morning of the 23rd August when she and Doctor Lush found Ellen's body.

X" d by Grady. No. No one has paid me anything for my testimony.

7. SOLOMON PECKER—London, Insurance Agent

I live in Tolpuddle Lane, Stepney. I am an Insurance Agent for the East London Friendly Society.

On Wednesday 20 January, Mary Grady came to see me and asked about taking out an insurance policy on her half-sister, Ellen's life. She said it was so she could give her a good funeral. She then asked about the terms of the policy. I told her if her half-sister died in the first four months of the policy, she would only get half the £100 she had taken the policy out for. The policy would become void if the assured, in this case, Ellen Grady, died by her own hand, by dueling, by the hands of justice, or if the premium was not paid monthly within the thirty days of grace which are allowed from the date it became due.

Since Ellen Grady died on the 16th August and the policy was taken out on the 20th January with all due premiums paid, Mary Grady will receive the full amount.

She had also told me Ellen Grady was employed at the asylum, not that she was a patient there.

8. JACK CALLAHAN—London, Publican

I live at the Green Hog Public House in Great Hermitage Street near the London Docks. I own and run the pub. Mary Grady lived with me until her arrest.

She and I were planning to get married, but I told her we could not do it the way she wanted as the pub had money problems. We'd have to wait.

On Wednesday 21st July at nearly 11:30 AM, Mary told me she was going out to buy rat poison. This surprised me as she'd never involved herself in that side of running the pub.

I did not see Mary use phosphorus for the rats and we are still overrun with them.

X'd Ex'd by Mary Grady. Yes, we did have a bad problem with rats, but mostly we used traps to catch them.

9. JOHN ALFRED GOSTICK—St. Albans, Superintendent of Police

I reside at Redbourn.

I am the Superintendent of the "F" Division of the Hertfordshire Constabulary. St. Albans is comprised within my Division. I am the officer in charge of the investigation into Ellen Grady's death.

On Monday 23 August 1869, from information I received the previous evening from Doctor Lush, I proceeded with Constables Cruikshank and Grubbe to Belle Vue Lunatic Asylum arriving there shortly before 8 am. I met with Doctor Fishburn who gave me the details about Ellen Grady's death and took me to the mortuary to view her body. The body of the deceased was tinged yellow and had been badly scratched. I agreed with Drs. Fishburn and Lush, the circumstances appeared suspicious.

I ordered the two constables to search the asylum and gather all evidence available. I also gave specific instructions, after receiving information from Mrs. Fishburn, to search the asylum rubbish tip for the packaging in which the cake arrived.

On Tuesday 24th August, I spoke to the coroner to confirm my suspicions and obtained authorization for a postmortem to be undertaken.

On the third day of the investigation, Wednesday 25th August, Constable Grubbe found the discarded brown paper cake wrapper and handed it to me. It bore two penny stamps and was postmarked from Wapping, the district where Mary Grady lives. No cake remained except a few crumbs, which we threw away. No other items which could be connected to the deceased's death were found.

When Doctor Fishburn and I viewed the writing on the brown paper against that on the letter from Mary Grady, we agreed the handwriting looked similar. I asked an expert we have used on occasion, Mr. Thomas Bennett, to analyze the two samples. It was his opinion Mary Grady had written both items, though some attempt had been made to disguise her distinctive lettering.

During the course of our investigations and when interviewing members of staff, the name of the accused was mentioned a number of times in relation to unusual behavior regarding the welfare of her half-sister.

On Thursday 26th August, the postmortem took place at Belle Vue Asylum and late that afternoon I discussed the findings with Doctor Nottidge.

On Friday 27th August, I wrote another letter to Superintendent Riddle at Wapping Police Station detailing our case and asking them to arrest Mary Grady and search her premises.

Sergeant Nott delivered Mary Grady to the lockup at St. Albans on Monday 30th August. He also brought with him a couple of items taken from the search of Mary Grady's room at the Green Hog, and which I now produce. One was a bottle of rat poison containing phosphorus. The other is a copy of the insurance policy dated the 21st January on the life of Ellen Grady for £100.

10. ABRAHAM NOTT

I am a Police Sergeant of the Metropolitan Police, Thames Division and stationed at Wapping.

On the Saturday 28th August, having received instructions from Superintendent Wilbert Riddle, I went with Constable Hacker to the Green Hog public house to arrest Mary Grady at about two o'clock.

She was wearing a red dress, which I thought odd, not right. But then she said, "I am most sad my dear sister, for she was fully that, not a half-sister, is dead. We were so close. I do miss her."

In reply to questions put to Grady by myself, she stated she had not sent any packages to Belle Vue Lunatic Asylum for her sister. The accused stated, "I am not in the habit of wasting money providing food when the asylum is supposed to do so".

I said to her she was under arrest and I cautioned her as to what she should say. She then said, "You're playing a trick on me. Why would I want to hurt Ellen?"

I said, "If you are innocent you can prove it in court." And Mary Grady said to me, "If I go to court, does that mean they won't pay out on the life assurance policy?"

I replied I didn't know, but perhaps not. This appeared to upset Mary Grady more than her half-sister's death.

Constable Hacker and I went back the next day to search the Green Hog public house and Jack Callahan showed us around the premises. In the room used by Mary Grady, I found a bottle labelled Phosphor Paste with a poison mark on it. It was in the bottom drawer under some clothing. Constable Hacker searched her writing desk and found the insurance policy documents. We took these items back to the station.

On Sunday, 29th August, using information given to us by Mr. Callahan, Constable Hacker and myself, visited Porters the Chemist in Wapping High Street. We spoke to the shop assistant, Miss Violet Tiptree. She confirmed she had sold two penny bottles of phosphor paste to Mary Grady on Wednesday 21st July.

I took Mary Grady to the lockup at St. Albans on Monday, 30th August.

11. LEONARD EUGENE SNOOKS

I live at Harcourt Lodge, Gresham Road in the Parish of Lambeth Surrey. I am a Doctor of Medicine, a Fellow and Examiner of the Royal College of Physicians of London, Lecturer on Chemistry & Medical Jurisprudence at Guys Hospital, and Official Analyst to the Home Office. On Saturday, 28th August, I received a letter and certain articles

BELLE VUE

from the Belle Vue Lunatic Asylum. Viz four jars of organs from the body of Miss Ellen Grady and a bottle labelled as containing phosphor paste. The jars and bottle produced are the ones I examined.

The first jar of organs contained the liver which was enlarged and showed fatty degeneration and acute yellow atrophy.

The second, containing the stomach and bowel, revealed both inflammation and hemorrhage.

The kidneys in the third jar were enlarged, greasy, and of a yellow color. They showed evidence of necrosis, as did the heart in the fourth jar.

The organs, when viewed in a dark room, glowed as is found with elemental phosphorus.

It is my opinion Miss Ellen Grady died of acute phosphorus poisoning.

The bottle produced is the bottle I examined. It did contain what it said on the label, namely, phosphor paste.

There was enough phosphorus in this bottle to kill three people.

All the above testimonies have been signed and dated as taken upon oath by each witness.

Before me. (signed: ROBERT GRIBBLE) Coroner.

Document dated: 20 September 1869

Chapter Twenty-Nine

Monday, 27 April
PRESENT DAY

The month after Claire's funeral, Alex focused on completing his dissertation, applying for his Masters and starting the prep for next term's exams. Usually, he would spend the spring break at more leisurely pursuits, such as clubbing, drinking, playing and watching sport, with only the occasional session devoted to study. This year, with his finals looming and the desire for a first, serious attention was required. Or that was the theory. In truth, recompense for his previous abstinence took a disproportionate amount of his time and energy. The other afternoon for instance, after a particularly frenetic round of sexual gymnastics, he'd moaned at Marianne for leading him astray when he ought to be working. She had curtly informed him, "Why? Where's the fun in that?"

Not bothering to open his eyes, he'd murmured, "I'm too tired to argue, but life isn't just about fun."

The bed moved as Marianne sat up. She pinched his arm. "Well, it should be. What else is there?"

He'd been hoping for a quick nap before he went back to the library for the rest of the day. No such luck, as Marianne, clearly with other things in mind, pressed closer and licked his navel. Matron was still taking him by surprise. So different from anything he imagined she'd be like. Where had kind, fun, reliable Marianne gone? He didn't know, but God, the fox in her place was so exciting—and demanding.

For the moment, he would lay back and enjoy the ride.

For Marianne, the last four weeks made her realize life was too short to waste. All her scrimping and saving, working every hour God gave, putting other people first. Now she knew better. 'Good girls' were simply slave fodder. Having lost the extra weight and being able to afford to treat herself, she'd seen what life could really be like. There would be no stopping her now. Out with the old, in with the new—and that meant making the apartment her own.

Claire's stuff and that of her parents' in the lockup were a fascinating and lucrative treasure trove. Private photos and letters she binned. She selected a few bits and pieces to keep and handed the rest over to a local dealer, as she couldn't be bothered with the hassle. Decorating was the next task. With money no object, she discovered a penchant for bold colors. Claire's neutral look, previously admired and aspired to, was but a distant memory.

Relaxing against the plump pillows of her king-sized bed, she surveyed the room with satisfaction. Because it had been Claire's, she'd had it redecorated first. Now the deep red walls, with touches of black and gold looked sexy, not prim. The curtains and bedding cost a fortune but, what the hell, you only live once. When Alex had first walked in, he'd been shocked. Then relieved.

"Well, this certainly doesn't bring any memories back."

He'd said it more to himself than to her, and she hadn't been sure if it was the drink talking. In fact, sometimes at night lying alone in the dark, she wanted to pinch herself. How had she ended up with pots of money, a sexy new figure, and someone like Alex Palmer?

An unexpected worm of guilt would wriggle into her mind. Her dreams seemed to have come true on the death of her best friend. Much too high a price, but in the morning, she would regard such feelings as a sign of weakness and wipe them aside. Each redecorated room consumed another morsel of Claire's memory.

In the cold light of day, too, any remaining self-doubt disappeared. Alex Palmer was the lucky one to be screwing her, not the other way around. He was a good catch for now, but she was keen to play the field a bit and enjoy all the male attention coming her way. Might as well see what she could reel in. Alex might not be the end result she wanted after all. He could be a bit conservative in his tastes and, although black suited him, its continual reminder of Claire was getting a bit tiresome.

Anyway, Alex had toddled off to hand in his beloved project on nuthouses. Thankfully his endless carping about "Belle Vue this" and "Belle Vue that" would finally be over. Having given up the hospital job, she had the afternoon free. Revision could wait. She knew enough to wing the exams, even if she didn't read another word.

Now Gary definitely thought more on her wavelength. Maybe she should give him a try, too. Marianne mentally shook her head as she flopped on the sofa, reminding herself she still had some sanity left. She had to admit, though, sometimes she cringed at the things she'd said and done recently. Amazing how money, pampering, and a bit of masculine appreciation increased one's confidence. No more Miss Invisible or Goody-Two-Shoes.

She rooted amongst the magazines and cushions for several minutes before finding her mobile down the back of the settee. A treat for Alex was taking shape. He'd been so tense recently, working every hour to get his project handed in on time. She would give him a surprise to help him relax. Well, not at first, but after. She listened as the number dialed and rang. Alex answered.

"Hi, handsome. Tired?"

He laughed. "You could say that. I had no idea you were so insatiable."

"Making up for lost time. How shall we celebrate tonight?"

"And what are we supposed to be celebrating?"

"Handing your dissertation in. It being Friday night. The fact I'm feeling horny. Who needs a reason?"

"And I thought Gary was our party animal. You leave him standing."

"Who said anything about a party? I was thinking just you and me staying in this time. You bring some champers and I'll sort out the nibbles. What about it?"

The line crackled but silence was the only response.

"Alex?"

"Sorry Marianne, what you said threw me off guard. Claire and I had shared champagne and snacks when I got back from Verbier and it brought the memories back."

She rolled her eyes. He could be so anal. "That's not very tactful, Alex. You certainly know how to spoil the moment." She was sure she heard him sigh.

"I said I was sorry swee...Marianne. I didn't mean to. I'd love to celebrate handing in my dissertation—which I'm just about to do—and spend the evening together. Any preference on champers?"

She named her new favorite brand, and they agreed on a time.

As Marianne cut the connection, she frowned at his disregard for her feelings. What she needed now was to make sure he forgot any feelings he still might have for Claire. She had a few tricks up her sleeve. They required a little retail therapy, but she didn't want to go alone. Sophie would give her a run for her money. Should be amusing. When they finished, she could leave Soph to her own devices and deal with a couple of little matters she needed to take care of. She flipped open her phone and waited for an answer.

"Hi, Sophie. Fancy going shopping?"

Ten minutes later, she closed the mobile before disappearing into the bathroom to put on her war paint.

Alex placed his phone in his jacket pocket and stood in the corridor to the history department admin office, trying to sort out his thoughts.

Jostled by a few fellow students and one irate lecturer who'd muttered "excuse me" in an indignant tone, he edged toward the side of the hall. His brain, having returned home from its southerly vacation, was now torn as to what to do about Marianne.

The first few times had been fabulous. Mindless sex had been his medicine of choice and he was ashamed to admit at the time that was all he'd wanted. After all he and Claire had been through, it was too early, the memories too raw for him to be part of a steady twosome again.

As he reached the door to the office, he decided he would discuss it with Marianne, if not tonight, then definitely tomorrow. It had been fun, but for now, he needed some thinking time. Exams were coming up, so maybe they could take a step back for a few weeks or more and see how things panned out then.

"Are you handing in your dissertation?" The school administrator peered at Alex through her bifocals, repeating the question twice before he responded.

Later that evening as he drove to Belle Vue, he recognized the wisdom of his decision. Coming out of the department building earlier, he'd felt an overwhelming sense of relief. Having refined his first thoughts over a pint of beer with Gary, he planned to enjoy this "celebration" with Marianne. In the morning, he'd raise the idea of taking a short breather over the exam period. He parked and grabbed the bottle of chilled champagne.

By the time Alex reached the apartment, he realized he was more than a little excited about what the evening might bring.

He pressed the buzzer and stood back as the click of heels on wood grew louder. The door swept open and Marianne, in leather and black lace, stepped forward as though she were making a Broadway entrance.

"Ta-da!"

His mouth dropped open. "Christ! What have you done?"

"I've dyed my hair, you moron. What's the matter? Don't you like red?"

Chapter Thirty

Tuesday, 19 October, 1869

> "Madhouse Murder trial starts today!"
> "Read All About It."
> "Murderess Faces Judge and Jury."

The whey-faced paper sellers ran to and fro doing a brisk trade. Johnson Nottidge stepped down from his carriage into the bustling Hertford Street as the downpour started. The coachman hurried forward and held an umbrella over him. Using the end of his walking stick, Nottidge prodded a ragamuffin out of his path and made his way into the courthouse. Behind him others followed suit, seeking shelter and, even better, a few hours' entertainment in the warm. He removed his doeskin gloves and looked around the main courtroom. The public gallery and reporters' box were already fit to burst—standing room only—and now the jumble of rainproof trappings, discarded willy-nilly, added to the chaotic atmosphere. In the enclosed surroundings, the air was pungent with the mix of sodden clothes and unwashed bodies.

He breathed in deeply and relished his anticipation. He was eager for the proceedings to begin and hasten the Grady whore to her rightful end. From listening to the excited chatter around him, he judged the courtroom rabble agreed. Since the inquest and its finding of 'willful murder' against Mary Grady, he'd noted with growing satisfaction how the newspapers and gossip-mongers had worked overtime to incite a frenzy of interest but little if any, sympathy for her. Only by showing some remorse might she be able to sway the jury and spectators in her favor, but as he had remarked to Callahan yesterday, "Hell would freeze over first."

Nottidge moved across to the witness seats. He nodded at Callahan and the Fishburns and sat down in the front row.

Callahan leaned toward him, but before he could say anything, the usher's shout pierced the surrounding hubbub.

"Silence in the court!"

Nottidge focused his gaze on his old friend George Pinchbeck QC, the bewigged barrister for the prosecution and then on Isaiah Codd, the third-rate chump acting as counsel for the Defense. Pinchbeck halted in the midst of conferring with his junior while Codd continued to hold his head in his hands. As he well might with such a client, thought Nottidge, his enjoyment increasing by the minute.

The clerk gave the order to stand. Nottidge rose and looked round, as did most of those in the public gallery. All eyes fixed on the huge frame of Mister Justice Henry Walmesley as he made his entrance. With a record to match that of 'Hanging' Judge Jeffreys, his friend's hawk-like countenance complemented his severe reputation. 'Old Harry' settled himself at the bench and, after some gruff coughing and rubbing of his chin, signed with his hand for the case to begin.

Silence descended. Necks craned forward, while eager faces strained for a better view. Nottidge tensed. He had to force himself not to move to the edge of his seat. He couldn't help but stare as two burly gaolers brought Mary Grady in and put her to the bar.

The courtroom's first sight of her did not disappoint. It wasn't her fiery red hair or Amazonian physique that would later be the topic of so much fervent discussion: it was, he acknowledged, the sheer force of her presence. The trollop swaggered through the court like a triumphant prize-fighter. As she stood in the dock and surveyed the mass of curious onlookers, it was as though she was judging them—judging and finding them all wanting. The only moment of uncertainty, so fleeting it might not have happened at all, was when she looked into the face of Justice Walmesley.

At that, the sensation of triumph that shot through him was as addictive as the most potent drug.

Old Harry and Mary locked eyes.

He and the rest of the courtroom watched with bated breath. The judge's clerk cleared his throat, distracting Walmesley. Nottidge laid odds that the next edition of the local rag would deem Mary Grady to have 'scored' first.

Not that it would help one jot as she had obviously ignored any advice her counsel might have given her. It seemed of no concern she was on trial for her life and, like it or not, her appearance, her demeanor, her attitude should all reflect the feminine deference the jury would expect. No. As she turned her gaze to the men who held her life in their hands, she was the antithesis of a grief-stricken sister. She looked hard, she acted hard and, Nottidge smiled to himself, if he stuck her with a pin, not one drop of blood would emerge.

Hearing Old Harry begin, he turned his attention back to the proceedings.

"Mary Ann Grady, you are charged this day that on Monday, the sixteenth day of August, one-thousand-eight-hundred and sixty-nine at Belle Vue Lunatic Asylum in the Parish of Saint Nicholas Church in the County of Hertfordshire, did feloniously and willfully and with malice aforethought murder one Ellen Catherine Grady against the peace of our Lady the Queen. How do you plead?"

Mary's scornful voice echoed loudly through the full chamber.

"Not guilty."

The judge peered over his spectacles and snapped. "You will address me as Your Honor."

She scowled at the man opposite as if weighing up her next action. A hush, an anticipatory silence descended over the courtroom. It was as though no one dared breathe, the expectations of witnessing a sensational drama were so high. Nottidge smirked.

The seconds ticked on.

Mary Grady's words rang out, each one coated in venom. "Not

Hell Master?"

A collective gasp of shock broke the momentary lull, but not from Nottidge. He was only surprised it had taken so long. Old Harry's fist slammed down on the polished wood. Isaiah Codd covered his face once more. The poor man's client was like a tiger waiting to pounce but the spite etched into her features was entirely human. An emotion, Nottidge was pleased to note, the jurors would infer as guilt.

"You look more like a Hell Master to me." Her lips curled with disdain. "Your Honor."

At first, low whispering, then voices rising in astonished exclamations at such disrespect. Yet again, she was serving his purpose. He could imagine the collective viewpoint. Mary Grady *must* be guilty to have so little shame. She was surely the work of the Devil himself. Old Harry's face flushed crimson to match the port-wine birthmark on his nose and cheek. Papers rustled, journalists scribbled, the prosecution barristers shared knowing glances.

Codd took out a handkerchief and dabbed at his sweating brow. Nottidge surmised the man would give anything to get rid of this case. Judge Walmesley came from one of the finest families in the land. He had a long and distinguished record in the courtroom, however harsh his sentencing. A murdering harlot from the gutter of Whitechapel could not be allowed to disparage her superior with impunity. Nottidge mused they ought to bring in the gibbet now and get the business over with.

Keeping her head held high, and her nerves buried deep, Mary stood rigid in the dock. Her mind grasped this new reality: her fate was sealed. Judge Henry Walmesley. Whoever would have thought it? She would have known him anywhere the moment she saw the blood-red stain splayed across his face.

For Mary, the whole procedure was nothing more than a tedious repetition of the betrayal that passed for justice at the Coroner's Inquest. A few more questions asked of the witnesses, but any answers, even by those she thought held no malice, seemed destined to incriminate her. She scrutinized the reactions of each member of the jury, holding their gaze until they dropped their eyes. She'd got their measure. Most believed her guilty before the first witness took the stand.

Her counsel, the pompous flabby Isaiah Codd, acted as if he assumed her guilty, and his every utterance seemed to display his dislike of defending her. She told him she had been set up. Why use phosphorous when it was easily traced to her? Did he think she was so stupid? Any number of people could have sent the cake or put the phosphorus in her room or paid the police to plant it but she saw the disbelief in his eyes.

"Why would eminent doctors and a lord's son bother incriminating someone of such little standing?" he had spluttered at her.

Codd thought only of his own future. If he went around making insupportable accusations, it would ruin him and so, he told her, "Miss Grady, unless you have twenty nuns and lords of the realm swearing they saw this or that person buy a bottle labelled 'Poison', put it in the cake, and post it to your half-sister, you cannot go around rashly accusing pillars of the community. I need not tell you, a background involving public houses and other shady activities does not work in your favor."

Now she sat stone-faced as forces outside her control shaped a new future for her. Unless she could outwit them. Mary wondered whether de Montalt's words and his silly book were true after all. Little enough of the things he'd promised had come her way so far. He'd said he could make her a puppeteer so *she* could pull the strings, manipulate the destiny of those who so mistakenly believed in the premise of free will. Religion's confidence trick, he'd said. As she fought to hold back the first tendrils of fear, she had to believe she could be the master of not only her own fate but also of those who sought to destroy her.

Given she was not rich and in court on a murder charge, she realized the chances of success were slim. Nancy would be betrayed again.

So, she would fight by any means possible. With the verdict and punishment, a foregone conclusion, she had nothing more to lose. There were no witnesses for the defense, no one of any standing to provide an alibi or character witness. It looked bad for her, but the few people she'd thought would be on her side were testifying for the prosecution. Codd had told her, once he'd heard the long list of those appearing against her that she seemed to have gone through life alienating everyone she met.

Jack had disowned her. He had packed up the rest of her belongings and sent them to the prison. Her letters to him were returned unopened. Of her few friends, tarts or thieves all, Codd had warned her no jury would favor their word over those of the exemplary prosecution witnesses. The lunatic who shared a room with Ellen had also been interviewed by Codd, but for some reason, this woman had nothing good to say about her. Since Nottidge and his toady, Fishburn certified she was not fit to testify, it didn't matter anyway.

Unfortunately, even she had to admit, Nottidge's performance on the stand was mesmerizing and devastating to her. Codd had told her about the press reports in anticipation of today's case. So many gushing words about the aristocratic doctor working for the benefit of mankind who was appalled at the taking of an innocent life, one he had tried so gallantly to heal. Pah. Unlike many of the witnesses, the bastard didn't exhibit the slightest discomfort. He was in his element. His every word conjured a vision of her as the guilty party. Needless to say, Codd did nothing to change that image.

As Nottidge weaved his tale from the witness stand, he congratulated himself again on the fast thinking which led to the situation he now stage managed. The superb tactics of an expert player against a novice.

Stupid bitch. When this charade was over, his life could continue unencumbered by blackmail or the pretensions of the incompetent Fishburns. The Matron had easily been persuaded to perjure herself and convince her husband to do the same. All he'd had to do was mention her tryst with Callahan, and usefully she seemed to hold an intense grudge against the accused. Following his advice, she embroidered an overheard remark—not mentioned at the inquest—of Mary Grady cursing her half-sister and wishing her dead.

Callahan was with him for the long haul. He, too, provided a deadly testimony and had ensured his brother did likewise. Lush was the only one left to his own devices in the knowledge that whatever he said would be overwhelmed by the volume of evidence against the Grady whore. A few favors were called in with Georgy Pinchbeck and Old Harry. The rest, such as Craven and Pecker, had been paid off as required. Easy.

He had watched Mary Grady throughout the proceedings. She was good, he had to give her that. Didn't bat an eyelid. Luckily, she wasn't able to testify. Although if she were, her far-fetched version would only send her to the gallows even faster. Who would believe her? Innocence was relative. She was guilty as sin. His sole aim was to make sure the murdering harlot couldn't escape her rightful punishment.

Codd's voice droned on and on. Dear God, even if the jury didn't believe she was guilty, they would convict on the grounds they'd had to suffer the long, tedious speeches of her counsel. Nottidge didn't bother to stifle his yawn and neither did half the jury. He cast his gaze round the courtroom and stopped when it reached Mary Grady. The adrenalin surged through him. The hatred that blazed in her eyes was reward enough for the time being and soon she would know—if she didn't already—the power he wielded over her fate.

Codd stopped speaking.

Nottidge watched as the bint fixed her steely gaze on Old Harry as he began summing up the case. In one direction.

When Walmesley's words ceased and the jury shuffled out to consider their verdict, much whispering and nibs feverishly scratching across paper could be heard. Nottidge's confidence soared. For the press and public alike, La Grady's cold arrogance gave them little difficulty in choosing sides. The general assessment would be a watertight prosecution case against a defendant who was vindictive, deceitful, and a sinner. Whereas before the trial there was little sympathy for her, now he was certain there was none.

The clock ticked on.

While the jury made their deliberations, there was no sign from her she cared a fig for the outcome. The insolent gaze remained. No trembling fingers gave her away, no continuous licking of the lips gave lie to her icy hauteur, no tell-tale stains of sweat revealed her true distress. She kept her sneer in place and stood, her face unreadable as to what she thought of the proceedings, witnesses, galleries, except contempt. He ignored Callahan and the rest so he could savor these moments and what he knew was coming.

And how she would react.

It took the jury eleven minutes to decide her fate.

Nottidge stood as the earlier entrance procedure was duly repeated. All in place. The clerk called out each juror's name to which they responded, followed by: "Gentlemen of the Jury, have you agreed upon your verdict?"

The foreman, a bulldog of a man, answered, "Yes."

"Do you find the prisoner at the bar guilty or not guilty?"

A momentary hush, a general intake of breath.

"Guilty." The man actually smiled as did Nottidge.

Mister Justice Walmesley nodded to his clerk, who rose from his desk bearing a square piece of black cloth.

Nottidge noted Old Harry did not ask the defendant whether she had anything to say regarding why sentence should not be passed. As if it would make any difference.

The clerk, who with elongated limbs and matching face could easily have passed for an undertaker, ceremoniously placed the black cap on the Judge's wig.

Then to his delight, Mary Grady laughed, her dismissive tone cutting across the crowd of riveted onlookers.

"More fancy dress eh, Hell Master?"

Walmesley banged his hand on the wooden bench.

"Silence!"

Once again, the remainder of the judge's face turned as red as his port-wine mark. Fury infused his every word.

"Mary Ann Grady you are sentenced to be taken hence to the prison in which you were last confined and from there to a place where you will be hanged from the neck until dead and thereafter your body buried within the precincts of the prison and may…"

Her livid gaze swung first to him then back to Walmesley's smug countenance. It was as though she would explode such was her fury. A delicious sight. She was obviously going to make sure she drowned out Old Harry's last words.

"Damn you all to Hell!"

Chaos erupted. Even Callahan and the Fishburns uttered their shock. Journalists scurried out to get their story published first: this was newspaper gold. Four warders descended upon her. Excitement and fear sizzled through the courtroom. Even as they dragged her away, she continued cursing with a malevolence of frightening intensity. "Betrayers! Murderers! I shall get every last one of you and your kin. However long it takes. Beelzebub and Demogorgon I call on you!"

Mary Grady's outburst would be reported word for word in the newspapers and local rags with snide remarks about such boasting words that had no chance of ever being achieved. Thank the Lord, this was a civilized Christian country to deal with evil killers who reveled in their lack of godliness. The drivel would be endless.

But he should have remembered to tell Old Harry a few more details about her experiences with René.

The judge was now being helped out of the room by the usher and one of the clerks who had also administered the smelling salts when Old Harry collapsed.

Chapter Thirty-One

Saturday, 2 May
PRESENT DAY

The morning after his celebration with Marianne, Alex left her sleeping as he crept out of the apartment. Before they'd finally dozed off, Marianne had mentioned meeting him in the Union bar at about one. Nothing had been confirmed. He needed to take a pile of books back to the library first, then he'd contact her and decide how to play the 'take a breather' conversation.

Jeff Reichenberg was in the hall. To judge from the dampness of his hair and sports gear, he'd just finished a strenuous workout. After a few words of greeting, Alex made his way down the stairs to the main foyer. The man had given him a strange look. It made him feel awkward as though he was somehow letting Claire down by being seen leaving Marianne's. Last night had been as wild as ever. After that first shock and her reaction, it could have all gone horribly wrong, but she'd taken the champagne from him and clad in that outfit, led him willingly to the bedroom. She then did things to him, if the discussions of the gym changing room were anything to go by, most guys only dreamed about.

That, and seeing Jeff's reaction, made him feel sleazy. As soon as he got home, he'd take a shower. Wash himself clean outside, if not in. Best not to think of the reasons.

Descending the stairs, Belle Vue's grand entrance hall came fully into view as did the familiar figure of Moira Bradigan.

When he was level with her, she stepped forward as though to block his path. "Have you completed your opus? Found any of those dark secrets, Mr. Palmer?" Said the spider to the fly, thought Alex, almost expecting her to lick her lips.

He was about to reply when her eyes shifted as if she saw something over his shoulder. Alex could have sworn her face took on an expression of smug superiority. Her head gave a slight shake.

He turned, curious since he hadn't heard anyone approach. The foyer was empty.

"Is something the matter?" she asked.

"No, Miss Bradigan. I thought you were looking at something."

"I didn't take you for being so fanciful, Mr. Palmer. Are you going to answer my question?"

"I handed in my dissertation yesterday."

"Good."

He wouldn't let her death's head smile faze him and watched closely for her reaction to his next words. "I did some more digging and found quite a bit of interesting material. About the manor house that existed before the asylum was built. Does the name René de Montalt mean anything to you?"

Her hands, the ones he'd thought so wizened before but now appeared plumper, clapped together a few times then stopped.

He frowned in puzzlement at her calculating expression.

"Bravo, Mr. Palmer."

"You know about this Duc?"

"Only what I've been told, of course. Useful to keep connections with the past. I like continuity, a little foible of mine."

"Did you know he was the leader of something called the 'Mephisto Club'?"

"I had heard. The evil carried out in that crypt all in the name of the Devil and the monstrous egos of men."

So she did know more than she had ever let on. Of course, such information was useless for his dissertation. It was only hearsay and not about the asylum. She probably didn't think he'd want to hear about that.

"Or women, come to that," she added, almost as an afterthought.

Something she'd said struck him as odd, but the more he tried to hone in on what it was, the more elusive it became.

Moira Bradigan tucked the newspaper under her arm. "I've said enough for now, young man, and you've taken up too much of my time. Goodbye."

She tapped her way across the hall. Conscious of the time, he strode briskly toward the nearest rear corridor.

He opened the door and as he hurried toward the car park, realization dawned. What crypt? All the way home, he wondered why, of all the things you could say about the Duc and Belle Vue Manor, she'd mentioned that. He didn't remember reading about any crypt, either. The basement and tunnels yes, but nothing else. Maybe the de Montalt book would give him the answer. When he had the time to look at it again, he'd check.

After a long, hot shower, Alex collected his books and drove to the college. Now the countdown to the exams had begun, both the car park and library were busier than a normal Saturday when the power of Hypnos usually triumphed in the student world.

At the main desk, he asked the woman who checked in his book returns whether Penny was working today.

She glanced at his library card before handing it back. "You're in luck, Alex. She's in the basement sorting out the dissertations and theses. New lot in soon."

He thanked the woman and made his way down to the lower level. Rows and rows of castored shelves surrounded a number of large rectangular tables and chairs. Today, most of the shelves were fully open and Alex walked along the edges looking for Penny.

A dozen or so rows along, he found her.

"Hi, Alex. How are you doing?" she asked, her face mirroring the sympathy in her voice.

"Okay. I've had my head down for the last month, what with one thing and another. I got my dissertation handed in on time, but er, you know..." He cleared his throat, tried not to think beyond saying the words. "We didn't get a chance to speak properly at the funeral and I wanted to thank you for coming. It meant a lot."

Penny placed the volume she was holding onto the shelf and stood. She moved toward Alex. "You're welcome. I liked Claire and wanted to pay my last respects."

He stepped out of her path. "It was good to see so many familiar faces from the college. To know people cared enough to come."

Penny patted his arm. "I'm sure it was. It must have been hard having to get straight back into your dissertation. I don't envy you that."

By tacit consent, they strolled past the shelves and sat down at the corner of the nearest table.

"Well, it's done now, and exams are coming up. No time to dwell on anything else."

"But you'll have to face it one day, Alex."

"I know. Not just that, but I also need to decide where do I go from here. Things have changed and I'm not sure what I want now."

"Most don't give that question enough thought without all you've been through. I know it's a cliché but try to take it one day at a time. That's all any of us can do."

He nodded, and Penny continued, "Speaking of your dissertation, were you pleased with the final effort?"

"Yeah, it all came together. One of Claire's neighbors gave me some help." He lifted his chin and gave a puzzled frown before smiling. "Maybe help is not the word for it. At first, it was like getting blood from a stone, but the old Palmer charm seemed to kick in and Moira Bradigan told me quite a bit about the place before it closed. I used some of it for a section in the appendices. You might have seen her at the funeral?"

"Not sure. What does she look like?"

"All I need say is she was wearing a red wig and a large bright hat."

Penny's eyes widened. "Oh, her. Intriguing character. I noticed she stood apart from the rest of us. Is she as mean as she looks?"

"Worse! But every now and then a spark of humanity flickers only to die out almost immediately. I wouldn't say I like her, but one thing's for sure, she's never boring."

"Did you find anything else interesting about the old Devil clan?"

"They sure worked their spell on me," he said. "Every time I should have been writing my dissertation, I kept thinking about the whole weird Mephisto set-up. I sure underestimated those Victorians."

"And that's only one group. Mention the Victorians to people and they immediately think of prudishness and covered table legs. If they only knew."

"Between revising, I'm now going to read the book from cover-to-cover and see what else I can learn."

"Well, Alex, if you find any more fascinating details, let me know."

"I cert—"

"Very cozy."

He turned in surprise to see Marianne standing there, hands on hips.

From the look in her eyes, she was definitely spoiling for a fight. What was it with these female hormones? Was no one safe? He sighed, thinking he didn't need this.

Penny smiled up at the painted face staring daggers at her. "Hi. Haven't I seen you around? I'm Penny, the head librarian."

"How nice for you." With that dismissal, Marianne turned her attention to Alex as though Penny didn't exist. She put her right hand on the table and leaned toward him. The edge of her bracelet knocked on the wood, catching his attention. Claire's Christmas present. Again, he wished she wouldn't wear it but now was not the time. Stopping her rudeness was. "Don't speak to Pen—"

"I've been waiting in the Union bar. Do you realize what time it is?"

His eyes flicked to the clock on the wall. Almost half past one.

"We hadn't agreed anything, Marianne. I think you owe Penny an apology."

"Excuse me? You're late, but I'm the one who's supposed to say sorry? I don't think so."

Penny pushed back her chair and caught his eye. "I'm intruding here. I have work to get on with. Bye, Alex. Marianne."

"Yes, you are. Goodbye."

After a fleeting nod and half smile at him, Penny walked away with a dignity he could only admire. He was furious with Marianne, but before he could say anything, she cut in. "I'm hungry, Alex. Let's get something to eat." She stood with her arms crossed, belligerent and demanding.

He was in no mood for the inevitable argument. "No. You go. We need to talk about this, but not here, and not now. I still have a lot more work to do this afternoon. I'll come round this evening about seven. Okay?"

"Fine, but I'm not sure if I'll be in. Ring first," she retorted, before stamping out.

He watched her leave, wondering what to make of it all. She'd pissed him off. Tonight, he'd definitely tell her they should call it a day. At least until after the exams and then see what happened. Somehow, he thought they'd never resurrect their earlier friendship which would be a shame.

After returning to his flat at about five, he went for a long run by himself. Gary was away rock climbing and Paul had gone home for the weekend. He then took another shower. During all of this, he spent the time pondering his decision and came to the same result. They, or rather he, needed some space. Marianne had turned into a Jekyll and Hyde character with the latter growing ever more dominant. Now, if she could combine the kind, safe Marianne of old with the wild, sexy one, he'd be a happy man. He would mention this to her. After all, she kept harping on about fun, but the sad thing was, she wasn't fun for him anymore. She'd lost her sense of humor and her old personality.

Being hot and sexy was fine, but if there was to be any chance of a relationship, she needed to find them again.

With this thought in mind, Alex set off to Belle Vue. Unfortunately, in his calculation as to how the evening would progress, he had neglected to consider Marianne might not see things from his point of view. From the outset, before he could broach the matters he wanted to discuss, she was in a defensive mood. When he saw the state of the apartment, he couldn't help but grimace at the mess. She'd started on him then. Things went downhill fast from there.

During a temporary lull, as she fixed herself a drink, she told him about her new career plans. Looking after the sick and the dying, she had concluded, was not for her.

"But I thought you wanted to do nursing to help people like your mother so they could spend their last days with their dignity intact. I always admired that about you. It wasn't about the money, but for the good you could do."

Her nose flared. "You pompous windbag. Don't you dare lecture me."

"I wasn't. I thought we were having a discussion."

"You're a hypocrite. I don't see you planning to save the world or work for a pittance, so don't expect me to, either. Why do you keep picking at me about it?"

"I'm not."

"You are, Alex. No wonder Claire got sick and tired of you."

The metaphoric slap hit home. "That's not true. You're twisting things."

"Am I? She did the cheating, not me. You don't get something like that gardening or peeling spuds, eh, Alex. I'm the one with you now, yet all you do is criticize me." As Marianne's irritation grew, so did the volume and stridency of her voice. "Everyone's against me. Debra's ruining any fun I might get from my good fortune. You're still treating Claire as though she was a saint, not a syphilitic tart and—"

"Stop!" Alex yelled. "Now you've gone too far."

"Oh. Blame me again."

"No! No. No. Marianne, we were friends, and that was great. Then suddenly you're a man-eater and, before Claire's in her grave, you leap on me. I should have stopped you. We weren't thinking. Let's cool off for a bit because I don't want to say anything I might regret, but let me tell you, never insult Claire's memory."

They were both standing, squared off like matador and bull. As Alex picked up his jacket, Marianne stamped her foot down hard, the heel making a dent in the wooden floor.

"I call the shots here, not you."

"No, you don't, and I don't know what's got into you, Marianne. I don't like it and I hate your red hair."

"Don't you turn your back on me."

But there was no reply, only the slam of the front door.

"Bastard!"

Her wig the only distinctive splash of color within the chapel, Moira Bradigan sat stiff and upright in the pew nearest the exit. Though it was warm and sunny outside, in the gloom, a coldness pervaded the air. As usual, she paid no attention to any aesthetic appreciation of the chapel's interior. Instead, Moira stared with unseeing eyes at the cross above the altar. Her inner excitement gave lie to the rigidity of her pose. She was about to make a new beginning and there was still much to be done. So she sat unmoving as the minutes ticked by. Watching, waiting, and thinking.

Watching, because she was not alone. In a pew toward the front of the chapel, a solitary figure prayed.

Waiting, because for what Moira wanted to do, she required no audience. An observer could thwart her best-laid plans.

Thinking, because often those best-laid plans could be caught off balance. As had been proved by that single, newspaper article, revealing that her eternal enemy still lived.

She always knew she would reach her goal, but on many occasions in the past, she'd had to bide her time and be patient. At that thought, irritation rose within her. Wrong choice of word. Too passive. She was tireless, determined and persistent, not patient. Actions tempered by experience and maturity. No critical mistakes for the sake of a few transient pleasures. Not like some she could name.

In all her years, she had remained focused. She never wavered, never lost sight of her goal. That was why she had been so successful. With the help of The Book, of course. What a fool de Montalt had been to show it to her and answer all of her questions. When she decided to get its earliest sections translated all those months ago, she'd been astounded at the new opportunities open to her. Of course, now she knew Nottidge had done the same. She should have known. With this priceless information, she could also complete her final task and truly enjoy life.

Things had certainly livened up recently and she intended that trend to continue. The cat-and-mouse game, for instance. One down, the second lined up in her sights, and the third—one Alex Palmer—being nicely primed like a Christmas turkey. She smiled to herself at the thought of the next stage of her plan, and visiting pastures new, once today's work was over. She loved to travel. Each journey was like a wonderful new adventure, especially if it had enabled her to tick off another name on her list. Just over four years ago since she'd last been abroad. Hong Kong held such satisfying memories.

Another adventure was about to begin. Although she hoped this trip would be a pleasurable distraction, it would be combined with business of an overriding seriousness. Success required careful planning and focus. But for now, she sat here waiting for the unwelcome visitor to depart. Moira's thoughts strayed and turned to other unwelcome visitors who had taken to showing up with increasing frequency. Of course, she was too powerful for them and had soon tricked them at their own game. You'd think they'd have learned their lesson by now.

Opening the gates of Hell allowed egress for all.

Enough of tiresome intruders, let her think on the future and Mr. Palmer. What a find. He was handsome, that one, and a gentleman. Not too many of those today. Not in the sense she meant. Someone with a bit of honor, trustworthy, not just well-bred. Shame he wasn't around when she was his age, or younger. Her life might have taken a different direction, but it was too late to worry about that. The future was her concern. He needed a few choice scraps of information to push him in the right direction. The one she wanted him to take. Given his ability to surprise her, she hoped he'd rise to the challenge and do so again. Keep things interesting. And of course, her prey wouldn't be expecting a man.

She winced as the hard wood of the seat pressed against her hip bones. It had been like this before, not wise to let her aches and pains get to this stage, but the remedy itself was fraught with its own risks making it worthwhile only as a last resort. Yes, a change would be good. Perhaps this time she would go further than before. After all, the challenge was going to be that much greater.

To help take the weight from her sore limbs, she leaned forward and rested her forehead on the fingers and thumb of her right hand. With her left, she steadied herself and slightly lifted her haunches off the seat. Some small relief.

Movement. The sound of a zipper, the jangle of keys. Moira tensed but didn't look up. The woman's footsteps grew louder as they passed within a few feet of her then fade 'til, after the knock as of a door closing, she couldn't hear them. From experience, she waited another five minutes. Who knew what the dozy mare might have left behind.

At last, with slow deliberation, Moira rose. After picking up the folded sheets of paper on the bench next to her, she moved back toward the narthex to check the door was shut. She halted, listening for any sounds of possible intruders. Nothing.

Taking a deep breath, she turned and walked up the central aisle toward the chancel and altar. The usual mixture of trepidation and exhilaration spreading from her throat to her groin was so potent, it was almost sexual.

As she reached the front pew, she veered left toward the arched door that led to the bell tower. She passed the end of the altar rail and the pillar, then turned again, this time to the right, and made her way to the only tomb in the chapel.

The stone effigy lay in the corner on a low marble plinth. About two feet above the top of the tomb and connected by a bronze plate, a large mural monument dominated this section of the wall. Two shields, one on the monument and one at the foot of the recumbent figure contained matching coat of arms. She scanned the chapel interior to check she was still alone. Resting her left hand on the wall for support, she pressed the toe of her shoe into the center of the raised coronet at the top of the shield near floor level and pushed. It moved forward until flush with the shield. Hearing the metallic click, followed by a scraping noise as the bronze plate rose up and under the monument, Moira removed her foot.

The marble base on which the effigy lay slowly slid forward, exposing the dark chasm beneath.

Chapter Thirty-Two

Monday, 15 November, 1869

The weather was dank and overcast. A suitable morning for a hanging.

Johnson Nottidge stood next to the Governor of St. Alban's Gaol as the man took out his fob watch and looked at it for the third time in as many minutes. Frederick Butt held it out for him to see and tutted. The man's nerves were obviously getting the better of him. 7:45 a.m. Still, a quarter hour to go. Nottidge's excitement rose. The thrill of watching Mary Grady die would be an experience hard to equal.

The gibbet dominated the small prison yard. They stared at it, Nottidge with fascination while Butt wrinkled his nose with distaste. There being another hanging at Maidstone that day, William Calcraft, the General Executioner of Great Britain, was unavailable, but one of his assistants had stepped in. By all accounts, Ernest Ruggles was efficient at his job. So far, Nottidge had to agree, the man, in addition to his fee, had negotiated with Butt to keep the clothes and personal effects of the condemned prisoner plus the rope. Only to be expected, he supposed. Mary Grady's case had been highly publicized with feelings running high. All of these things could be sold for good money, especially if Madame Tussaud's were interested for dressing the latest waxwork in the Chamber of Horrors.

Butt peered at his watch again, then back at the gibbet. He frowned and gently rubbed his stomach.

"Are you well, Mr. Butt?" Nottidge couldn't resist a smile.

"Yes, Doctor Nottidge, very well, thank you. I was just remembering some past horrors I've had to witness at the gallows in other prisons. Let's hope this one goes off smoothly. No frantic tugging to finish a shoddy job."

"She would only be getting her just desserts," muttered a voice from behind.

Nottidge wholeheartedly agreed with the prison guard but said nothing, imagining instead that preferred scenario. Perhaps he should have dealt with Ruggles, too.

He glanced around. Everyone seemed to be in place. The Under Sheriff of Hertfordshire looked green about the gills. Since the last execution in the county was in 1839, this was apparently a first for him, too. All the other observers and participants were gaol officials, Butt having refused all applications from members of the press.

The governor turned to him. "I must say again, sir, I am most grateful to you, most grateful indeed. Whatever would we have done?"

Much to Nottidge's amusement the man actually shuddered. As if he would have left such a momentous occasion to chance. The gaol's doctor was a small price to pay. So Nottidge, already there to observe the execution, had stepped in when the man didn't show and offered his services as the certifying doctor.

The prison chaplain led Mary Grady, flanked by two warders, up the steps to the platform. She twisted her head and stared straight at him. A triumphant look. Bold as brass. Well, he thought, she won't be looking so pleased with herself in a minute or two.

Then she turned and smiled at the governor.

Sweat broke out on Butt's forehead though the November morning was cool. As Nottidge watched her performance, he wondered how much was bravura, and how much confidence in what René had supposedly taught her. He had been unsettled to learn from Butt earlier she'd been active in ways that swung in favor of the latter. The governor had railed at him about the damn woman being no end of trouble since she'd arrived back at the gaol after being sentenced. As usual, they were overcrowded with the scum of the lower orders, so she had been put with a dozen others in one of the cells. All night there'd been the usual shouting and fighting from these hellcats but only eleven came out alive. One woman had been horribly mutilated. None of the other prisoners would say they saw anything, but one of the guards had reported to Butt the fear in their eyes suggested otherwise. Only Mary Grady appeared unperturbed. The governor said he suspected she had something to do with the butchery, but no weapon was found and what was he to do? You couldn't hang someone twice. So, they'd buried the body posthaste and no one was any the wiser.

But although he was almost certain she didn't have The Book and she'd never be able to remember all the steps even if René had told them to her, it had made him wonder.

This time it was Nottidge who took out his watch and glanced at it. Eight minutes to go.

The executioner fastened a leather strap around her ankles and over her prison skirt to preserve her modesty.

The chaplain started to read the burial service.

"Stop that noise, priest. I don't need your prayers. I shall watch you all burn in Hell!"

The cleric let out a low gasp. He stopped in mid-sentence. Silence fell over the yard and only the background hum of voices from the huge crowd outside the prison walls could be heard.

Mary Grady smirked as the white hood was held aloft over her head.

What a shame he wouldn't be able to look into her eyes at the moment of her death. Then her fear would really show. But she still knew he was watching and gloating at his triumph over her. A fitting end.

Butt's watch reappeared. Nottidge looked down and saw it was four minutes to eight.

Marianne stirred from her restless slumber thinking she could hear someone talking. Had she left the TV on and fallen asleep on the sofa? It felt cold and hard, not like—

"Is that you, Alex?"

Eyes still closed, and not yet fully awake, Marianne's thoughts drifted. She hoped he'd come back and hadn't meant what he'd said. With any luck, he wouldn't notice what she'd done. She'd fix that later. He still had Claire's key, so perhaps he was coming in to surprise her. She almost purred in anticipation.

"Alex?"

No response, just that damned murmuring. She'd be really pissed off if he were playing silly games. She wasn't in the mood. Cool air had replaced the cocooning warmth. She shivered.

The chaplain stood about three feet from Mary Grady as the executioner pulled the white hood down and covered her face. He started to recite the burial service again. The woman muttered something. The priest stopped again and leaned his head closer to her. Presumably, ordering him to be quiet. The bint would definitely be a match for Beelzebub when she arrived at the gates of Hell. He noticed the chaplain was still praying, probably for his own soul this time since La Grady's already belonged to another.

Marianne frowned as conscious thought sensed impending danger. She was standing. When did she do that? Was she still dreaming?

Puzzled, Marianne opened her eyes, but she could only see white as though she was covered by a dust sheet like a piece of old furniture. Her eyelashes scraped against the rough material enshrouding her face and head. A thick band tethered her elbows to her body and her hands were tied at the front. Her legs were strapped together over a swathe of heavy material and these too were held tight.

Claustrophobia, confusion, and panic surfaced as one overwhelming emotion. She screamed but, if she stopped moving her head from side-to-side, the hood was sucked into her mouth, muffling her cries. Her legs buckled, and Marianne felt strong arms grab her from behind. She squirmed but the arms tightened their grip, keeping her upright. A voice, *louder now, from the front, seemed directed at her.*

"Mary, keep still. Repent. Make your peace with God, and Heaven will be yours."

Nottidge noticed the chaplain made no attempt to sound sincere. Mary Grady had that effect on people, even the clergy. He smiled to himself. Not long now.

Who was Mary? Did these people think she was someone else? Had she been kidnapped by mistake? What the fuck was going on? Where was Alex? Wild thoughts jumbled together. Nothing made sense.

The warder, trying to keep the agitated Mary Grady still, leaned his mouth in close to her right ear, "Not so tough now, eh, bitch?"

High on adrenaline, Marianne's body shook with fear. What a bloody awful nightmare. Wake up. Wake up, for God's sake!

But the firm hands still pinioned her, and she could now feel something else being put over her head. Was that a rope? A dead weight of foreboding dropped into the pit of her stomach. Her mouth opened...

A low continuous groan from beneath the hood was heard by all in the small prison yard. On and on it stretched as though seeking to mark every man there. So, Nottidge acknowledged, the Grady trollop was a sham after all.

The bell began to toll. Butt waved his hand at the Under Sheriff and as the last chime struck, the man spoke.

"Mary Ann Grady, may the Lord have mercy on your soul."

With unspeakable clarity, Marianne grasped what was about to happen to her. This wasn't a nightmare, it was real. She heard a sound like a bolt being pulled back. Dear God, let it be quick...

As her head exploded with pain, she felt her bladder and bowels provide a final humiliation.

Nottidge watched in rapt silence as Mary Grady danced on the rope for almost ten minutes before her body finally hung still. He also noted the crowd of thousands outside the prison had given a loud cheer when they saw the black flag being raised.

When the body ceased to move, Butt turned to Nottidge. "I'm glad that's over. Though I wish…" The governor took out his handkerchief and wiped his brow before returning it to his pocket. "I think some refreshment is in order. You will join me, Doctor?"

Nottidge had no such intention and fobbed Butt off. He stood instead with Ernest Ruggles and Jimmy Penrose, the gaol's newest recruit, for the full hour required by law—and himself—to make sure there was no chance of resuscitation. As Nottidge stared at the body suspended from the short rope that would soon belong to the hangman, he decided she had been nothing but bluster after all.

Ruggles idly picked at his teeth with the end of his finger and leaned against the side of the platform. "Odd old hanging, this one."

Jimmy nodded. "I didn't like when she smiled at me, gave me the creeps."

The body gently swung in the breeze. Nottidge half listened as his two companions concurred, the woman had held her ground much longer than expected. Ruggles said hard men who started out with a swagger gave themselves away with sweat on their brow or shaking hands when they saw the gallows. Some even wept.

But not Mary Grady.

Ruggles noted it was only when the hood had gone over her head and been tied, she seemed to change and lose her nerve. The reality must have suddenly hit her. She'd started to shake and twist, then her dreadful moaning. Penrose's expression turned queasy.

BELLE VUE

As the hour wore on, Nottidge took out his watch several times so keen was he to deal with the next stage of the proceedings.

The bell tolled nine. Ruggles and Penrose cut down the body. The latter would take the corpse to the dead room and get everything ready for Nottidge as certifying doctor to check the body and authorize the interment within the prison walls in an unmarked grave. The inquest would be held at eleven o'clock, after which his business with the Grady slattern would almost be over. He had one last amusement planned at her expense.

Ruggles and the assistant warder manhandled the still-hooded and bound body onto a rough wooden trolley. Nottidge walked with Penrose as he trundled his heavy load from the empty courtyard to the small room off the infirmary where bodies were laid out prior to burial. Ruggles went off for a cup of tea.

The rest of the prison seemed unnaturally quiet, and outside the heavy stone walls, no sound could now be heard. The boy swallowed and prattled nervously about his dislike of this part of his job: the sight when the prisoner had died hard, the grotesque bulging face, eyes that had popped and tongue hanging out as if on display at a butcher's shop.

Penrose began to whistle a well-known music hall tune and wheeled the trolley to the end of the infirmary block. He let it down on the cobbles and opened the dead room door.

Nottidge waited while Penrose maneuvered his passenger inside the empty chamber. The lad then nipped out to the storage room next door. He returned with one of the rough deal boxes produced in abundance by the prisoners and took it inside. Nottidge could hear the lid and bottom of the coffin being propped against the wall.

Then silence.

Nottidge was about to enter when an almighty shriek came from the dead room. Penrose staggered out and ran straight into him gasping frantically. "Mary Grady is the Devil. She's not dead. Someone else is under the hood!"

The boy raised the white material he was holding toward his brow before dropping it to the ground as though it had seared his skin.

Could it be? A chill ran through him. It wasn't possible. The bitch couldn't have done it. Nottidge grabbed the boy. "Are you sure it's not her?"

"God help us, I saw her get hung, but it isn't her, oh lummy, it's not her." Penrose wrung his hands.

Nottidge pushed him out of the way and stepped inside.

The stink of Mary Grady's final sneer had spread like mold through the room. He walked over to the body and stared down. Relief then anger overtook any anxiety.

"You stupid clod. That's the bloody woman. No one else."

The boy peered at the body. At *Mary Grady*'s body. "I knows what I saw, sir. It was someone else. Not her, but it's her now."

He looked at Penrose. Hard. Searched his eyes. "No one paid you to play tricks, did they, boy? Mary Grady, for instance. I can just see her doing such a thing."

"No!" Penrose continued to wring his hands. "No, Doctor Nottidge. You're not going to report me, are you?"

Nottidge didn't bother to reply but concentrated his attention on the woman in front of him. Given how long it took her to die—more than ten minutes—and the tugging done by Ruggles, the mark of the noose around her neck was deep. He examined her thoroughly but there was no real further need. Mary Grady was no more. Imagine him being worried. Still, she had been an added fillip for his search of ever more exciting amusements.

"Let's bury her quick, I say, Doctor Nottidge," Penrose said in a voice barely above a whisper.

"Is the grave dug?"

"Almost."

Nottidge instructed the boy to find another warder, complete the digging, and return for the body. They left the room. Penrose fumbled with the keys and locked the door.

"I've decided not to inform the governor of your behavior, but you do know you are now in my debt."

"Thank you, sir. I'll do anything you want." Penrose's face lit up before he hurried off.

Nottidge headed to Butt's office to complete the paperwork before leaving posthaste for Belle Vue to plan the next Mephisto celebration.

Nottidge was unaware that barely half an hour after his departure, Penrose stood in front of the governor to report when he returned to the dead room, Mary Grady's body was nowhere to be found.

Later that evening, at his rooms in Lambeth, Ernest Ruggles opened the trunk containing Mary Grady's belongings. He was pleased with the booty. She'd been quite extravagant with gee-gaws and fancy clothes. What his fianceé, Mabel, did not want, he'd be able to sell for a good price. Picking through the garments one by one, he lifted out a woolen shawl when he felt from its weight something was wrapped inside. His fingers were quick to uncover a tin box.

He held it toward the candle for a better look. From its battered exterior, Ruggles didn't anticipate it would contain anything of value. There was something inside, but although he gave it a tentative shake, he couldn't make out what the contents might be. There wasn't any lock. After a brief struggle, he opened the hinged lid and peered in. A crumpled piece of dirty cloth hid something underneath. Ruggles took hold of the frayed material and pulled it back to reveal his prize.

Time seemed to stand still. As Ruggles grasped exactly what the box contained, he remembered one of the warders telling him Mary Grady had been known as Satan's whore. Closing the lid, any excitement about his find drained away completely. He felt sick. Holding the box with only the fingertips of his left hand as though it was contaminated, he collected his key from the mantle and let himself out of the front door.

The cold air hit him sharply, but he ignored the need for more than his thin jacket. His only thought now was to get to the river as quickly as possible and cast Mary Grady's tainted legacy into the water. To be lost. Forever. His only hope was his brief ownership would have no adverse effect on him. Tomorrow, he'd take the trunk and all its contents and have them burnt. Tussauds be damned.

For now, he had to get rid of the mummified heart.

The dried shriveled organ that against all of God's laws was still beating.

Chapter Thirty-Three

Sunday, 10 May
PRESENT DAY

Alex stood in the kitchen waiting for the kettle to boil. His mobile rang, breaking his scrutiny of the St. Alban's skyline at night through the distortion of a rain-spattered window. He slid the phone from the pocket of his sweatpants and checked the number before answering. No name listed.

"Hello?"

"Is that Alex Palmer?"

"Speaking."

"Hi, Alex. It's Debra Edwards."

The kettle switched itself off, but he ignored it.

"Thanks for returning my call. Is Marianne with you?" he asked.

"No. Why?"

"I haven't heard from her for over a week. When did you last speak to her?"

"Must be two or three weeks ago. She was still in a strop because I didn't want to come and see the apartment. And given her moods these days, Alex, I hate to say this, but she's probably avoiding you. Had you thought of that?"

He laughed. "It did cross my mind, but I've emailed her, left phone and text messages asking her to let me know she's okay." Alex paused and swallowed. "After Claire, I guess I'm a bit on edge about not hearing from someone, er, close."

"I understand and so should she. I hope she's not doing this on purpose. It was never her style to be mean. Now, I'm not so sure. Tell you what. I'll contact her and call you when I know she's all right."

"Thanks, Debra."

"It's weird, after all this time, the place still gives me the creeps. If I live to be a hundred, I don't ever want to set foot in there again. When I told Marianne, it really set her off, but I'll find out what she's been up to, Alex, and let you know. Okay?"

Alex thanked her and hung up. He ambled into the lounge. Gary dragged his eyes away from the sports round-up. "You gonna join us? The football's on next."

"Not this time. I'm knackered."

"Worn you out already, has she?" Gary grinned at Alex. "And to think Mr. Studmuffin got a date with this sex goddess." Gary turned to Paul. "I can't believe you let her get away!"

Paul, his eyes remaining firmly on the screen, said, "Yeah, but you didn't think so before. You're the one who first called her Matron and decided she wasn't your type. Or have you forgotten?"

"Bad mistake, I admit it." Gary put his hands together as if in prayer. "Oh, Lord, turn back the clock. Let me have my chance again."

Alex lingered, half-listening to their banter and half-watching the TV. He waited for an advert and broke in. "Listen, you guys. I've just spoken to Marianne's sister. You know what I said earlier? Well, Debra hasn't seen or heard anything from her, either."

Gary shrugged. "Wait a bit longer, mate. So she gives you the brush-off for a bit. She's probably gone off for a break before she gets stuck in for her exams. You know how women are. She's gonna let you stew."

He held up his hand. "Okay. Point taken but let me know if you hear from her, all right?"

Eyes now glued to the football, Paul and Gary nodded in agreement.

Alex retreated to his room. He grabbed a book and climbed into bed. Sitting back against the pillows, he opened *The Devil's Disciples* and turned to the index for any references to a crypt. Only two. The first was the layout of Belle Vue Manor he had glanced at when he originally got the book from Penny. He studied the plan, noting there were several larger spaces as well as the complex tunnel system with its prison-like cells. One of these, he saw as he cross-checked the small print of the numbered footnotes, was identified as a possible crypt. This led on to the second reference, a paragraph detailing the rumors about the crypt, said to be the place where the Mephisto Club carried out their most depraved activities. Because it was never found, the authors assumed it either didn't exist or had, at some stage, been sealed off from any access. From what he could remember, there had been no mention of any crypt in the plans of the Victorian builders who constructed the asylum.

A dead end. As Alex read more of the speculation and gossip surrounding the de Montalts, Belle Vue and the Mephisto Club, he wondered if the Duc and his brother had simply been having fun at the expense of the gullible locals. The more outlandish and frightening the tales, the less likely curious eyes would bother them. He read the paragraph he'd seen before about their supposed supernatural powers and wondered what these rumors referred to—ghosts or flesh-and-blood people brought back to life like something out of Frankenstein?

But the book was too vague, and since the whole thing went up in smoke almost one-hundred-fifty years ago, it was hardly something he could check. Anyway, as far as he knew, every Victorian medium, psychic, producer of ectoplasm, or seer of fairies, had been proved a fake.

He read for another half hour then lay open-eyed in the darkness. Sleep eluded him. He couldn't get Marianne out of his mind. Déjà vu. He'd argued with Claire and she'd died. He'd done the same with Marianne and now she was missing. Too soon to call the police, but he had a gut feeling something was wrong. Of all the times to pick, too. Not to be selfish, but first, it was his dissertation, then his exams. If he got the degree he wanted, it'd be a bloody miracle. As he drifted off to sleep, he decided he'd take the key Claire had given him and go over first thing tomorrow and check on Marianne. No other way to stop worrying.

During the drive to Belle Vue, Alex's memories of the sight, and smell, of Claire's body resurfaced. The fear of what he might find made his mouth dry. God, he hoped Gary was right: Marianne had simply gone off somewhere for a break and was letting him stew. The worry of it being more sinister than that remained.

Alex let himself into the main building and went up to the second floor. All was quiet. He knocked on her door but, as expected, there was no answer and no sound from within. He reached into his pocket, pulled out the key, and took a deep breath before pushing it into the lock. It turned smoothly, and the door opened. His insides felt like stone.

"Marianne?"

He detected a faint smell. Like burning. He peered in, anxious to see if there was any damage. Oh Christ, please don't let this be like it had been with Claire. Nothing looked out of order. He swallowed as possible explanations flitted through his mind. If it had been serious, the fire alarm would have gone off alerting all and sundry. Eric was sure to have called him.

Alex went through to the lounge first. The place was a tip. Designer labelled shopping bags, clothes, magazines and brochures strewn over the sofa and floor. The room smelled stale. Claire would be shocked. Marianne's days as the self-named 'clean freak' were certainly over.

After checking the kitchen, he walked to the nearest front window and debated whether to open it for some fresh air.

He decided there wasn't time and was about to continue his search when, out of the corner of his eye, he caught a movement on the grass below. He looked down to see Moira Bradigan walking along the path with an almost eager tension to her progress. As she disappeared into the chapel, he wondered what she was up to, but then let the thought slip. He didn't want to stay any longer than necessary.

He quickly checked the other rooms. Though messy, everything seemed all right. As he came to Claire's bedroom, now Marianne's, he hesitated. Bracing himself, Alex opened the door and stood at the edge of the darkness. The smell of burning was definitively stronger here. The blinds were closed. He switched on the light. Almost at once, he saw where the smell was coming from. A few feet away, in the space between the rumpled bed and the row of drawer units, the metal bin contained some partly burned material. He peered closer and noted with dismay the sacrificial items appeared to be his. At least the room was empty.

Deep in thought, most of it of the negative variety, Alex walked back into the lounge, intending to leave the key on the sideboard. As he placed it down in one of the few clear spaces, he noticed an envelope on a pile of sheets marked 'Last Will and Testament'. He moved it aside to see what was underneath—an open bank statement. He leaned over and scanned the long list of transactions. The most noticeable was a huge deposit, which must have been the cash part of Claire's bequest. Wow, no wonder Marianne's head had turned. He raised the top sheet, feeling a fine sheen of dust on his fingertips, and scanned the latest entries. A number of large cash withdrawals, payments to retailers and, he noticed, a travel agent. The final transaction was especially interesting. A check made out to a Marilyn Gradwell accounted for almost all the remaining amount. He had no idea who she was, but it looked like Gary was right after all. Claire had told him Marianne had never been abroad so perhaps that was the answer. She had gone off somewhere exotic and, still in a strop after burning his stuff, decided to keep him in the dark.

He felt a flicker of disappointment that things had turned out like this. Her cruelty, knowing what he went through with Claire, was all the more difficult to take. He'd been a mug after all and so wrong about her, but wouldn't it be more logical to wait until the exams were over? To him maybe. Alex accepted he would never figure out women, even if he lived to be a hundred.

The envelope was too tempting to resist. He picked it up, relieved it was unsealed. He peeked inside. It was Marianne's will, not Claire's as he'd expected. He took the papers out and scanned the contents. He frowned. For some reason, nearly everything of Marianne's would also go to this Marilyn Gradwell. Debra got a paltry amount as did a cancer charity, which didn't make sense. From what he knew about Marianne's relationship with Debra, they were very close. A spat or two wouldn't change that. He'd never heard Marianne, or Claire, mention the other woman's name. To find out more he'd have to approach the matter carefully, assuming Marianne ever spoke to him again. In her new persona, she certainly seemed to hold a grudge.

Drained by the conflicting—and unwelcome—tugs on his emotions, Alex left the apartment and made his way down to the foyer. He decided to go to the chapel and ask Miss Bradigan if she had seen or spoken to Marianne in the last week. If not, he might ring Eric and Sally to see if they knew any more about her movements. Why was he still bothering? After all, they'd had a big row, so what better reason to get away from the source of all the friction. She might even have taken some revision with her.

As he walked toward the chapel, it struck him again how impressive the building was for what had started as one family's place of worship. The heavy arched oak door was firmly closed, and it took several attempts to pull it open.

He stepped inside. As the door shut behind him, the sun's bright rays vanished, and the cool shadows reasserted their dominance. Alex expected to see Miss Bradigan seated in one of the pews, but from his sightline, no one was visible. He moved to the center aisle and advanced a few paces for a better look. There was no sign of Moira Bradigan or her wig.

"Miss Bradigan?" Nothing stirred at his half-whispered call.

He turned and walked back down the aisle, deciding she must have left after all. A short visit seemed more in keeping as he hadn't taken her for the churchgoing type.

Back in his car, Alex drove around the main building and along the front driveway. He glanced over to the chapel only to see Moira Bradigan stepping out from the porch. Where the hell did she come from?

He groaned in frustration. All this emotion stuff was playing with his mind. Guilt. Grief. Missing Claire. Confusion over Marianne. The strain of the final year. The puzzle that was Miss Bradigan and now, the unknown Marilyn Gradwell.

Where was it all going to end?

Driving into the rapidly filling car park of the Leather Boot a few days later, Alex hoped he could get through his meeting with Jez Trent in quick time and without too much damage to his wallet. It had been a busy week and he was shattered.

As he walked into the main bar, a disembodied voice boomed across the room. "Alex, Alex! Over here."

He spotted a waving hand above the crowd of heads. Weaving his way through the chattering groups, where Jez had bagged a small table. Alex noticed he still seemed to be wearing the same outfit as last time, but now a purple cravat was tucked into the neck of his polo shirt as though "going on forty-five" was a bit on the low side.

Smiling, Jez held out his hand. "Good to see you, Alex. How's life?"

How long have you got, he thought and gave a noncommittal response before drawing attention to Trent's empty glass. He named the brand Jez ordered last time and tacked on a question mark.

"Thanks, old boy. A double, if you don't mind." Jez lowered his bulk onto one of the chairs and Alex, after first handing the man his notes with a word of thanks, went to the bar.

When he returned, Alex was a little disconcerted to notice a box of A4 paper in front of Jez who was gazing at it with an expression bordering on rapture. Must be the novel. The box seemed heavy.

Trent took a mouthful of his drink and beamed at Alex. "I've finished my book at long last. I was hoping you could take a look at it and give me some feedback. Sort of quid pro quo if you like. I printed a couple of copies, so you can take it with you. Mark it in red pen so easier for me to add in what I want and avoid having to decipher the 'track changes' muddle."

He lifted the lid from the box and pushed it forward. Alex's heart sank as he quickly scanned the first page of single-lined size ten text. To say Jez's style was opaque would have been generous praise indeed. Noting the optimism in Trent's eyes, he tried to be diplomatic.

"Jez, it looks really interesting, but I've got exams coming up and straight after they finish, I'll be away. Normally I'd have been happy to do it but, of course, you won't want to wait six months, maybe longer."

A disappointed Jez concurred with this, saying he might contact Hamish and ask him to read it instead. Continuing his earlier bout of tact, Alex said nothing and drank his beer.

But as Alex admitted a few minutes later, he'd been unfair to his drinking partner. Jez hadn't been content simply to lend Alex his research notes, as he now explained. "When we last met you stirred up my interest in asylums again, so when I had a spare moment, I looked up the earlier period. It seems as well as the murder in 1895—though that was never brought to trial—there was one at Belle Vue during the period you were researching. It caused a sensation at the time."

His ears pricked up. "How come I never came across it?"

"Most likely you didn't look in the right places. You probably used historical or medical texts, instead of those on criminology. My book makes no mention of it, or of Adelaide Fishburn's horrible death for that matter, simply because it wasn't relevant to its focus."

Alex nodded. "Well, I've finished the dissertation now, so it's too late for that." His curiosity was sparked, though, and he couldn't help himself. "What year was it?"

"1869. A young girl called Ellen Grady. Poisoned by her sister Mary."

"Oh, very nice."

Jez finished his Scotch. "They hung her, you know."

"Who?"

"This Mary Grady."

"Gruesome. At least she did something to deserve it. In earlier days, they used to execute people for things that wouldn't get you a telling off today and in public, too."

"Yeah." Jez chuckled. "I think we've progressed some on our idea of a 'good day out.'"

"Ah, but it would still have included a stiff drink." Alex took their empty glasses and returned to the bar, only continuing when both had a refill in front of them.

"So, what moved it from your bog standard murder to being a sensation?"

Jez filled Alex in on what he'd read. He leaned back and smiled. "And to cap all that off, the assistant warder at the time of Mary Grady's hanging wrote an account of the event after he retired. Jimmy Penrose was his name. In it, he claimed the woman was never buried because her body disappeared. There's no mention of that in the official records."

"Sounds intriguing, but they're all dead and gone so we'll never know how much was fact, and how much fiction. If you ask me it was probably very little of the first, and a whole lot of the second."

Trent glanced at his watch. "You're probably right. While there seemed to be a lot of evidence she was indeed guilty and wished her sister dead for some insurance money, so she could marry her lover, there were also a lot of questions apparently never answered. Or for that matter never asked. Who made the marks on the body which Mary Grady couldn't have anything to do with? Why didn't the timing fit properly? Rumor was her sister's body disappeared, too, before it was found in bed by her unfortunate roommate. Was Mary Grady set up? Her counsel was incompetent, and the way people like Doctor Johnson Nottidge testified against her, she had no chance. Absolutely fascinated me."

Trent's animation as he spoke reflected the veracity of his last statement. Alex decided not to mention Nottidge's connection with Devil worshippers, or Jez would start writing his next novel as they spoke.

Checking his watch again, Jez downed the rest of the Scotch. Alex was wondering if an offer to buy the next round was on its way when Jez stood and carefully picked up his notes and prized novel.

"Listen, Alex, I've got to rush. I'm going to meet someone who knows someone who knows a publisher and I'm late already. I'll see you round, okay?"

"Fine and thanks, Jez. Thanks very much."

Trent disappeared into the throng of Friday night drinkers, leaving Alex to finish his beer and ponder if there was anything in the fridge for dinner.

He picked up his glass, but his recall of Marianne's behavior pushed aside any thoughts of food.

"Hi, Alex."

Turning in the direction of the familiar voice, he saw Penny Whitbread closing in on him.

He greeted her and pulled out a chair when she told him her friends hadn't arrived yet. Alex took her order and set off through the scrum to the bar once more. On his return, he sat down.

"I'm sorry about what happened in the library last week, Penny. I don't know what got into Marianne."

Penny smiled, a hint of sympathy in her eyes. "It's forgotten, Alex. We all have our off days."

Relieved, he filled her in about Mary Grady's murder of her sister in Belle Vue, revealing the unknown mixture of fact, rumor, and the mysterious ending to the case.

"Last week when we were talking, you mentioned the old woman who lives at Belle Vue. Did I get her name right? Moira, Moira Bradigan?" Penny asked.

"Yes, that's right," he replied.

She didn't say anything more as her group of friends arrived and he took his leave.

As he made his way out of the bar, he wondered why she'd asked that question.

It wasn't until he called her the next day in response to an email she'd sent, he found out.

"When you mentioned the name of the woman who murdered her sister, something rang a bell, Alex, and knowing your interest, I wanted to run this by you."

He was curious now and completely in the dark. He said as much.

"It may be nothing, but since my Dad retired, he spends almost every waking hour researching our family tree and he's always getting me to find things out for him. The names kept niggling me, so I asked him and then did a quick check on the internet."

"And?"

"Well, Alex, next time you see your Miss Bradigan, there's something you could ask her. Why are the words 'Moira' and 'Bradigan', nothing more than a spelling variation of the name "Mary Grady"?"

"What do you mean? I'm not sure I understand."

"Alex, over time, people changed the way they spelled their names. There must be thousands of these sites now for researching your family or name and they list all the possible variations. I looked up 'Grady' first, and as I suspected 'Bradigan' is one of them, along with O'Grady, O'Brady, McBrady, Grada, Gradwell, and so on. Also, the end can be spelled with an 'ay' or 'ai'" or 'ie'."

"How confusing. No wonder you can spend years searching for long-lost relatives."

"I tried 'Mary' next and Moira is derived from that, as is Manon, Marilyn, Molly, Miriam, Polly. There are loads. Even Marianne is one of them."

"Marianne?"

"Yes, Marianne, but surely that's just a coincidence?"

Chapter Thirty-Four

Monday, 29 November, 1869

Johnson Nottidge felt good this morning. Having slept soundly last night, he woke refreshed at nine, with an all-too-rare sense of anticipation of what the day might bring. He leaned back against the leather of his wingback chair, closed his eyes, and contemplated some of the activities he had planned for the evening. It was arrivals day, too, so he was keen to learn if the latest delivery threw up any interesting specimens. Cocooned in his luxurious office, away from the cacophony of madness, the crackling of the fire was the only accompaniment to his contemplation.

Little in this world bothered him: losing at cards, Fortnum's running out of his favorite port, being present when Samuel Fishburn moaned about another Asylum Board inspection, even his father threatening to disown him. These were mere pin-pricks of irritation, but nothing that might interrupt his lifelong pursuit of satiating his every whim. When the local newspapers reported the rumors Mary Grady's body had disappeared from the prison and she possessed magical powers, he had laughed. If her powers had been so great, she would never have hung, but how sloppy of the prison services. Disgraceful.

Even when Old Harry had dropped dead in his chambers a week after the Grady whore had swung and the Funeral Contractors' premises had burned down with him in it, he'd only felt amusement. Another Hell Master caught so short? Walmesley should have learned from de Montalt's mistake. *He* would never make that error. Age bore too many risks for their kind, even a gambler like himself.

But he, on occasion, could be prey to the games played by fate. And so the day that had started so well and promised to get much better, took a series of downward turns. The first occurred while he was still musing about the evening's entertainment. A knock at the door interrupted his reverie.

"Enter."

Lynton Brown sidled in. He dipped his head and then pushed his cap back over his greasy locks. "Yer post, sir."

Nottidge regarded the fawning figure before him with distaste. "On the desk."

Brown edged forward. Nottidge ignored the man who dared to befoul his office with his presence. The book open in front of him, a new erotic tale, was of far more interest.

Brown reached out with his scabbed hand and dropped a jumble of letters onto a clear space on the desk, but he didn't back away. He lingered, almost touching the polished mahogany. "Your lordship, sir?"

Nottidge took out a perfumed handkerchief and raised it to his nose, waving his other hand dismissively at Brown. "Stand back, man. What do you want?"

Lynton Brown stayed where he was and tapped the stripes on the arm of his uniform as though this might mean something to Nottidge. Egad, he wasn't a mind reader.

Brown's whiny voice cut in. "I dug up the body like Bill said, sir, and buried it where no one can find it."

"Tell Callahan, not me."

"I ain't seen him today. He went off yesterday morning and he ain't come back."

Nottidge raised an eyebrow. He was confident of his man. Callahan would be here for the big celebration tonight. In honor of the Grady trollop getting her just desserts. With a re-enactment to liven up the proceedings. Of course, they wouldn't lose the body like the blockhouse boobies. They would defile, mutilate, and burn it in homage to his powers and those of Mephisto. The bitch could, at last, be of useful service, providing them with a different theme to spice up their debauchery and do the club proud.

Callahan was making the arrangements and had sorted out a body. Shame it wasn't Mary Grady herself, but one of the pauper lunatics from the tunnels would have to suffice. Strange, though, Callahan having gone without a word. Nottidge grimaced at the man still soiling his office.

"That will be all. Tell Callahan on his return."

Brown lingered and, in a wheedling tone, said his piece. "I've got ambitions, sir. If Mr. Callahan don't come back, I'd like to take his place. Not just his job here at Belle Vue, but what he does for you. That's what I really want. Money and pleasure. Yours and mine, if yer know what I mean. You can trust me."

Nottidge's hackles rose. As soon as Brown uttered those final words, he marked the man as a liar and trickster. Not bad things in themselves, admirable qualities in some, but not for a right-hand man. The deputy's ambition and loose tongue made him a risk. He'd already overstepped the mark, killing Ellen Grady before Callahan had decided what to do with her. When Brown had come boasting to his boss, Callahan had wanted to deal with the man there and then, but with the police crawling round the place, he'd told him to wait. Brown was trouble. When Callahan came back, he'd tell him to deal with his traitor. Brown could be used as one of the amusements, and then disposed of. With that happy thought, he toyed with the deputy for a few minutes before sending him on his way. He'd enjoy watching Callahan remove the backstabber's smug smile.

Putting the man from his mind, he flicked through the pile of letters. Several were from friends including a chum now resident in the United States, one from his father, one from his tailor in Savile Row, and the last bore the return address of Isaiah Codd. What could Mary Grady's counsel want to say to him? He opened a side drawer, took out a silver paper knife and slit the envelope. There was a single sheet of vellum inside and another envelope, which bore his name only.

He unfolded the latter and read Codd's tortuous explanation for contacting him. From her prison cell, his client, Mary Grady had dictated a number of letters to his clerk and given instructions for their delivery on confirmation of her death. The barrister ended requesting Nottidge not to attach any blame to the messenger for the nature of their content, adding, "I am, kind sir, as part of my professional remit, discharging my duty to my client."

Nottidge turned this new development over in his mind. First, he'd read what the bitch had to say, then he would throw it on her substitute's pyre. Irritated, he sliced open the other envelope and removed a lone sheet. It was written in a small crabbed hand so typical of the pen-pushing sort. He began reading the letter as though it were a bit of a joke.

When he finished, he read it again, this time concentrating on every word.

He slumped back in his chair, wondering how many of those boastful words he could believe. Her tale of the time she'd spent in Belle Vue Manor. De Montalt must have lost his mind. What a monstrous ego to think he could reveal the club's innermost secrets with no consequence. Had the Grady bint really cut René and Henri's throats as they slept, then set fire to Belle Vue? He'd always believed their book had perished in the flames, but now he wasn't so sure. She said she'd taken it and would use its lessons to cheat the gallows.

A dark shadow passed over him as he thought this through. Everything Mary Grady said she'd done fitted with what he knew, and just as she'd said, her body was reported missing.

He pounded the desk with his fist. Damn her to the vilest tortures in Hell! Was this the ultimate revenge? He would not know whether she had cheated death, or truly swung from the rope until, until, she made her move. He would be looking over his shoulder forever.

He sat for several minutes considering the implications of this new reality, then threw back his head and roared with laughter.

The impudent hussy! Now the game was really beginning. A rush of exhilaration shot through him. This was more like it. Tonight's frolics would be especially pleasurable. The hint of fear always raised the stakes. De Montalt was a fool. Wanting to try everything once, he'd allowed himself to age beyond that possible for a man, as though that in itself was an exciting risk. He'd grown too old and too blasé and had crossed over from activity to passivity. That boredom had cost him an eternal life of endless satisfaction.

But as much as he enjoyed this frisson of danger, Nottidge wasn't about to needlessly risk losing the powers he'd spent years fine tuning. Perhaps it was time to move on? If he stayed here and La Grady really had delayed her final judgement, then he was too easy a mark. Life would become a never-ending battle to remain alert. Tedious and a blight on his amusement. She might still be a novice, but one lucky shot was all she'd need.

He reached for his snuff box and took a large pinch. The day's arrivals must be here by now. Give him something else to consider. He could not stop imagining the possible ways she might take her revenge, though. Pushing back his chair, he rose and brushed a few flecks of tobacco from his trousers. The coals burning in the fireplace provided welcome warmth to the chill of the day. He stepped closer and stood admiring his reflection in the mantel mirror.

Several loud knocks distracted him once more. Nottidge turned in irritation as Bill Callahan burst into his office. The door left partially open, the new arrival strode toward the doctor, breathing heavy, uniform askew, chalky skinned with dark, haunted eyes. Such an expression he never expected to see on Callahan's usually impassive face.

"What is it that causes you to lose your manners?"

Callahan halted in the middle of the room, his thick hands clenching and unclenching.

"Sorry, Doctor Nottidge, but I've had a letter. You won't believe—" Callahan swallowed, "From beyond the grave. My brother got one, too."

Nottidge's left eyebrow went up.

"So did a couple of others from the pub, the ones who testified against Mary. The rumors are true. She really was – is a witch."

"Do you have the letter with you?"

Callahan reached into his jacket pocket and drew out an envelope.

"Is that it? Nothing more?"

Callahan shook his head. "They're all the same. I went to see Jack as soon as I got mine. He says it's not her hand, but the words surely are."

He saw Bill Callahan's name and the Belle Vue address written in the clerk's hand on the envelope and pulled out its only enclosure, a sheet covered with matching penmanship. The lawyer appeared not to have bothered to enclose any cover letter to Callahan and his ilk, only his client's bitter threats.

He half listened as Bill recounted ever-more fantastical stories of Mary Grady's rumored posthumous powers, wondering if the Matron had received one as well. She would probably be too stupid and lazy to realize its true threat. The Grady baggage had certainly been productive in her outpouring of bile. Seemed she'd set herself a busy schedule of retribution, too, with Belle Vue a major target.

This changed everything. Definitely time for pastures new. His mind worked furiously. He would visit his father and sort out a deal with him. Pater's attempt to bribe him into toeing the family line by threatening his inheritance had been rescinded after, to quote his father's words, 'the sterling work you have done in convicting a murderess and at the same time, caring for the insane. The latter is not a direction I myself would have chosen, but it has revealed your resolve and strength of character. Well done, Johnson.'"

Not that it would make his father feel anything but his usual bewilderment at siring an heir who showed no interest whatsoever in following the family's political footsteps. His lordship's abiding wish, of which he made no secret, was for his younger son and ambitious politician, Edwin, to inherit the Seton estates and title. Nottidge decided, assuming he got what he asked for, he was about to make the old man very happy.

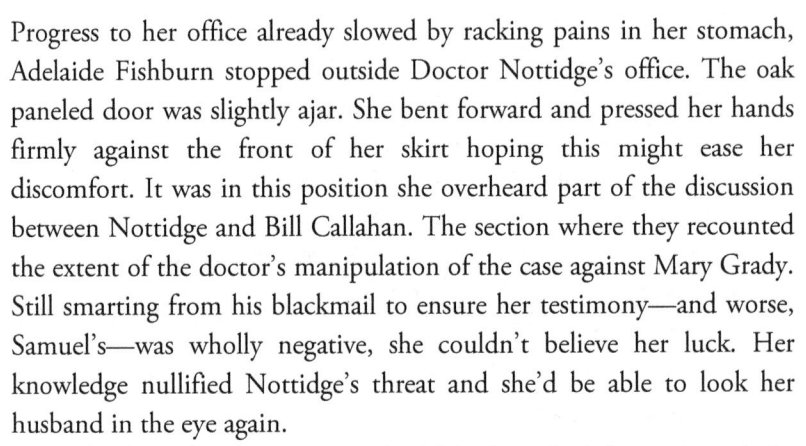

Progress to her office already slowed by racking pains in her stomach, Adelaide Fishburn stopped outside Doctor Nottidge's office. The oak paneled door was slightly ajar. She bent forward and pressed her hands firmly against the front of her skirt hoping this might ease her discomfort. It was in this position she overheard part of the discussion between Nottidge and Bill Callahan. The section where they recounted the extent of the doctor's manipulation of the case against Mary Grady. Still smarting from his blackmail to ensure her testimony—and worse, Samuel's—was wholly negative, she couldn't believe her luck. Her knowledge nullified Nottidge's threat and she'd be able to look her husband in the eye again.

Clutching her lower stomach, Adelaide inched forward until she reached the sanctuary of her office. Once there, she took a draught of laudanum to both ease the pains in her body and, as she had found to her great satisfaction, the pains in her mind.

Not wanting to be disturbed, she closed her door and turned the key in the lock. Adelaide sat back on the newly purchased Morris & Co. adjustable chair and closed her eyes to wait for the treatment to work. Later, she'd think carefully as to how she could make best use of her secret knowledge.

Nottidge was a rich man and she and Samuel could benefit from a nest egg for a comfortable old age. She could also...her thoughts of serious matters faded as the pleasing thrill crept upon her.

She opened her eyes and stared up at the ceiling rose. Mesmerized, she shivered in delight as the tips of its leaves grew and began to curl forward like living breathing entities 'til they swallowed the brass gasolier whole. But instead of erasing the light, the petals opened and shining golden cherubs burst forth on beautiful rays of shimmering color.

BELLE VUE

In Nottidge's office, no such transformation had occurred, more a shift toward begrudging acceptance of a changed reality.

He had, with the minimum of possible information, explained what the letters meant to his and Callahan's future wellbeing.

"The problem, Bill, is that one day Mary Grady's threat to you or I may come to pass. From now on, we must be on the alert, which is not the way I want to spend the rest of my days."

He saw the uncertainty in the head attendant's eyes. Nottidge surmised Callahan's belief in the power of the fist was struggling to override his newfound belief in Mary Grady's witchcraft. To convince him, Nottidge asked how the woman could have known before death her body would disappear. Callahan couldn't answer, but a worried expression crossed his features. Nottidge outlined his plan for them to find new excitement and continue the diversions they had enjoyed to date. Without having to look over their shoulder. Well away from where Mary Grady could reach them. Assuming she had actually survived, which they wouldn't know until it was too late.

He even promised Bill to show him how she had achieved such a feat. For now, he knew Callahan's appetites were growing, and there was the chance they would be caught one day—a leak by one of those who had enjoyed Nottidge's parties or someone like Lush, overhearing loose talk from one of the staff or lunatics.

"It will be better on the other side of the Atlantic. The asylums there can provide us with many possibilities for much more excitement."

"But not for the inmates, eh, Doctor Nottidge?"

"Only for those who enjoy depravity and torture, Bill. That reminds me, Lynton Brown came to see me this morning."

Chapter Thirty-Five

Sunday, 17 May
PRESENT DAY

After a full day of revision and numerous rounds of beer in the Union bar, Alex and Paul sat at a corner table in the Bengal Tiger restaurant, waiting for their order to arrive. A contented hum from the many diners mingled with the low, but distinctive tones of the background sitar music. Two waiters drew up with a laden trolley and began placing numerous dishes in front of them.

"I've got to say this, Alex," Paul said. "When you started seeing Marianne, it was like I was pushed out of the picture."

Uh oh, this didn't sound good, Alex thought, wondering what had triggered this topic. Conscious the delivery rate had slowed somewhat, Alex used eyebrow semaphore to signal Paul to hold until the waiters had finished. His mate, however, seemed oblivious of the additional audience and continued.

"I'm friends with lots of girls, but to get a special spark is rare for me. You can sleep with someone, but you know something's missing, and it's that spark." Three sets of eyes glued to Paul as he plowed on. "Well, Marianne and I didn't have it. We weren't really going anywhere. But Alex, I think I've found it now with Zena. She's sexy, funny, gorgeous, smart and Greek. I think she may be a virgin, too. What more could my mother ask for?"

The king prawn balti and keema naan hovered in mid-air as all pretense of disinterest from the servers ceased. Alex tugged the sleeve of the one closest to him. "Excuse me, but the food's getting cold."

He leaned over to Paul. "Let's have our meal first, then talk."

The remaining dishes made their way speedily to the table, and the waiters departed. He and Paul made short work of the food and beer. Pleased for his friend, he asked a couple of questions about Zena. She had, he learned, invited them and a few others for a Greek meal at her place the following weekend. They sat for a few minutes in silence contemplating the likely menu, broken only when Paul asked whether he had seen or heard anything from Marianne. He shook his head.

"I called Debra again, but although she's tried the works—phone, email, text—there's been no word back. Most likely she has taken off on holiday. Debra's really annoyed Marianne would behave like this." Alex paused, as his uncertainty about Marianne's disappearance resurfaced. "What would you do, Paul? I'm totally confused. One minute, I think she's set this up to annoy me and the next I worry that something's happened to her, just like Claire. Should I call the police or not?"

"So far, nothing actually seems wrong. You had an argument with her, and now she's gone off to sulk somewhere. Maybe she splashed out on a fancy hotel and is studying like mad for her exams, which is what you ought to be doing. I know you're going through the motions, but your mind is elsewhere. That means Marianne's plan, *if* that's what it was, is working. What are you going to tell the cops? You had a fight with your girlfriend and she's vanished? The way they treated you before? Yeah, right. What's that going to do to your revision if you're down the nick being treated like Public Enemy Number One?"

Remembering how aggressively the accusations had been directed at him, he accepted Paul's point immediately.

"I'd leave it for now," Paul said.

"Maybe, but I'm still torn. On one hand, everything looked fine in her flat, apart from it being messy. Nothing to indicate anything bad had happened. But, after Claire, I want to be sure Marianne's all right, even if she does hate me for it. I think I'll wait a couple more days, then if she hasn't shown, I'll report her missing."

The waiters cleared the table at speed since both he and Paul limited their conversation to ordering coffee.

Alex decided to change the subject. He told Paul about his meeting with Jez Trent and Ellen Grady's murder at Belle Vue, ending with the details of what Penny had told him about Moira Bradigan's name.

"Weird, huh? At first, I thought it odd, but it's probably a coincidence, nothing more. Then I wonder…"

Paul remained silent, then looked Alex in the eye. "You know what they say, there's no such thing as a coincidence."

"Yeah, and that's the point. On its own it's nothing, but when you think of everything that's happened."

Alex's voice tailed off.

The waiters served the coffee. Paul heaped a couple of spoons of sugar into his cup and stirred vigorously. "I suppose the first thing to ask is, was Penny correct? If not, then it's a non-issue."

"She was right. I checked it all out on the web."

"So, what do you think it means?"

"I haven't a clue. Moira Bradigan isn't your regular joker, so who knows. When I think about what's happened in the last eight, nine months, the more it seems like I'm in an episode of the *Twilight Zone* with no control over what's happening. Not a feeling I like at all. For instance, before Claire died, things got very strange. She even thought Miss Bradigan was always watching her. I told her she was imagining it, or it must have been because Claire nearly knocked her down in the car."

Paul raised his hand. "Hold on, hold on. You've lost me. First, we're talking about a murderess from a hundred odd years ago, having a similar name to someone who now lives in Belle Vue. Next, the poor old woman is a stalker and, are you also saying she caused strange things to happen to Claire?"

Alex rubbed his forehead. "Oh God put like that, it sounds ridiculous." He looked at Paul. "Let me lay out all the different bits and pieces and see if we can make any sense of them. Maybe the stress of the exams is getting to me and my grip on reality is slipping."

His friend nodded. "Fire away."

Alex filled Paul in on most of the details about Claire, his experiences and what she'd told him. As he worked his way through the pool incident, the mark round Claire's neck at the party, the fleas in her hair and the hideous face he'd seen, her losing so much weight, though she was eating large amounts, he felt his guilt grow. All she had been through without much support from him. Alex couldn't bring himself to mention anything about the syphilis to Paul, but that, too, he noted, added more weight to the mystery. Claire's parents' deaths were strange as well.

"Then for my dissertation, Penny found this book about the guy who first owned Belle Vue. He and this Mephisto Club of his were into Devil worship and other weird things. They supposedly had supernatural powers. One of the doctors at Belle Vue, when Mary Grady killed her sister, was a member of this group. Her body disappeared after she'd been hung. Who knows if there was any connection or not? Maybe she and this Nottidge were lovers and he helped her somehow?"

Paul listened, his face pensive. Their coffees grew cold.

"So, what do you think? Am *I* going mad?"

Paul unwrapped a chocolate mint and shrugged. "To be honest, Alex, if I didn't know you, I would wonder, but there's something else, too. Marianne."

Alex sat back, pleased he and Paul were on the same wavelength. "I think I know what you're going to say."

"Good. We all really liked Marianne. Past tense as in before she changed. She was our nice, safe friend who was happy being chubby and liked a laugh. Sexy? No. Man-eater? No. Nasty and short tempered? No. I still fancied her whatever she looked like, but couldn't believe my luck when she lost all that weight and suddenly oozed sex. At first, it was great, but then she started to act like a diva with PMT. Didn't you find that, too, Alex?"

"I suppose. It was easier not to analyze it."

"Did something happen to make her change?"

Alex put his head in his hands. "This conversation is getting too heavy for me." He hadn't thought about it from that angle. Too close, he supposed. He wondered how much of the drink was talking.

Paul ate another mint. The waiter placed a black leather folder on the table. Paul ignored it and spoke again. "But that's just it. It all might seem weird on the surface, but actually, everything can be explained. Think about it. Marianne loses weight. Despite what she'd said in the past about being big, she now finds she has more confidence and male attention. This makes her act sexier, and also reveal what she is really like. Maybe she was only being nice because she thought no one would like her, being overweight and all, if she spoke her mind and upset people. Now Marianne also doesn't have to worry about money, so she does what everyone does when let off the leash. She runs wild. End of mystery. If we go through everything you've said, it doesn't mean there's a connection, it doesn't mean anything supernatural is going on."

"Okay. It sounds convincing, but something tells me it's not true."

He could see Paul had gotten onto his soapbox and wasn't to be pulled off by anyone. "Another thing, Alex. You're a twenty-five-year old, soon-to-be history graduate. Why should you suddenly figure it all out? If there was anything in all of this supernatural stuff, don't you think it would have been proven already? Instead, it's all a bit of a joke, no one will ever admit to more than the odd palm reading at a fair, going in the haunted house at a theme park or watching the occasional scary movie. All of which we know are fake."

"So, what you're saying is, if anything's going on, and a big if, then why pick Alessandro Salvatore Palmer to be the ace-detective, solver of all supernatural puzzles. What can he do when the greatest minds through the ages got nowhere? I agree Paul. Now let's pay the bill and change the subject."

"What's the damage?"

Alex opened the leather folder and looked at the bill. His mobile rang. He picked it up from the table and answered.

"Hello, Alex. Eric Beamish here."

He half-listened, expecting the usual long-winded recital of life with the Beamishes. Alex pushed the bill over to Paul and felt in his back pocket for his wallet. He yawned, but midway his mouth snapped shut. "Pardon? Eric, say that again?"

"Moira Bradigan's dead. I found her. Dreadful, just dreadful it was."

"What happened?"

Body tense, he sat up in his chair and concentrated on Eric's words. Paul executed a quick mime and disappeared to the men's room.

"I went down to her apartment as she'd sent me a note saying she wanted to see me about something. I was going to ring the bell, but I could see the door wasn't latched, so I called out her name and went in. I wish I hadn't now, but I did."

"How did she die?" Alex was surprised by the news and keen to hear the details. She had seemed fine when he last saw her. He fidgeted to a more comfortable position.

Eric continued as though he hadn't spoken. "As I got to the lounge, I saw her straightaway. Believe it or not, she was still sitting upright in her chair and, do you know what, Alex?"

"What Eric?" He sighed.

"When I got a bit closer, about ten feet away, I could see her skin was as dry as parchment. It was like she had been dead for years, not hours or days. Creepy. The worse thing was, she was smiling. A big rictus grin that stopped me dead in my tracks. She didn't ever crack her face much when she was alive, so goodness knows what she was smiling about at her own demise. I know she used the surgery Emma and I go to, so I rang and informed them. Her doctor came and looked as sick as I felt when he first saw her sitting there like a Halloween dummy."

Clutching the scissors in his hand, Alex stood by his desk deciding on the best way to open the large package in front of him. The one addressed to him in Moira Bradigan's distinctive hand.

Last night Eric's continuing tale of her death had contained a surprise for him: "While I was waiting for the doctor, I had a look around to make sure everything was in order and she hadn't been burgled or anything. On the table was a package, addressed to you. I remembered she was helping you with your project and this is probably some related stuff she wanted you to have. Now I know once all the legal paperwork starts, you can be looking at months of waiting before probate is granted. That's on a straightforward basis and goodness knows how complicated old Moira's estate might be. The package is in my apartment if you'd like to have it?"

Alex said he would. He'd come to Belle Vue and collect the parcel the next day.

Now back in his own room with the mystery parcel, he cut through the string and the layers of tape before pulling away several sheets of brown paper. Inside was a lidded cardboard box. He pulled off the cover and peered at the items within. A plain white envelope with his name on it lay on top of a larger manila one, thick with unknown contents, and a loose-leaf folder underneath.

Eager to see what Miss Bradigan had up her sleeve, Alex picked up the envelope and opened it. He took out two sheets of cream-colored paper. The writing matched that on the front of the package. He read her words with his full attention:

Mr. Palmer,

This you must know: what began with René de Montalt continues. He is no more because he thought he was invincible and shrewder than a fourteen-year-old girl. Mary Grady learned some of his secrets and used her knowledge against him so he couldn't cheat the Grim Reaper any longer.

As you have recently discovered, death is rarely noble or dignified. Your Claire was given warnings, but against the dark powers of Johnson

BELLE VUE

Nottidge—one Johnson Nathan Courthope de Vere Nottidge—they were too weak to have any impact on your girlfriend's fate. Surely, you must want vengeance for her suffering?

To this end, I leave you the story of Mary Grady. Your research has completed part of the jigsaw and I am giving you more of the missing pieces. Whether you will like the image it reveals is another matter. Don't rebuke yourself. The one thing you must accept is you were powerless to change any of it—but the future is yours to control.

Mary thought the tricks of Satan could help her win against Nottidge, but the Devil is a wily Master and should never be underestimated. I have recently learned Johnson Nottidge lives on, as does the Mephisto Club. It is he and his wretched group who were responsible for Claire's death.

So, don't judge Mary Grady, Mr. Palmer, for what you think she may or may not have done. She didn't make the rules, only played to stay in the game. She was but a novice and lost out to one who had made evil his immortal life's work. You are young and smart, but a man such as Nottidge is not easily defeated. Time and geography do not restrict him, as Claire found out to her cost.

To help your quest, I suggest you see for yourself the work of de Montalt's successor. You will find the instructions to the crypt on the next page.

Niccolo Machiavelli wrote: "If an injury has to be done to a man, it should be so severe his vengeance need not be feared." Wise words. Digest them well. Mary Grady at fourteen knew them by instinct and so was able to eliminate de Montalt. You must defeat Nottidge the same way. Remember, those who made their pact with the Devil can only be destroyed by fire.

I leave you the name he uses now: Nathan de Vere. My time is nearly over. It is now in your hands. To avenge your girlfriend's death and put an end to this monster.

Moira Bradigan

Typical. More riddles than he knew what to do with. He recognized the name she'd underlined from the *New York Times*. She seemed to have created her own reality with a fixation on the past and seeing historical figures, or rather one historical figure, as the enemy. Wasn't there some sort of illness like that? Psychosis? Schizophrenia? He knew little of psychiatry but to him, Miss Bradigan hadn't ever seemed delusional or mad.

Alex put the letter on one side of his desk and took out the sealed manila envelope. Lifting one edge of the flap where the glue had failed in its duty, he pulled up the strip. He took out the thick bundle of papers and photographs clipped together. From their color and condition, they appeared to include many sources and time periods.

The first sheet with a large black '79 scrawled in the right-hand corner was, when he checked, out of sequence. The heading at the top of the sheet pulled him up short. CLAIRE RYAN—MATERNAL LINKS. Below her name was a family tree. For some reason, the old woman had been interested in Claire's background. Curious, and not what he'd been expecting.

The first name at the top of the tree was a Judge Harry Walmesley (1811 - 1869) whoever he was. Alex scanned the other names until he reached Claire's parents with their daughter listed below. Each name had been crossed out. Claire's parents had been killed in Hong Kong. He wondered if there was some connection.

He wasn't sure what was going on here. Was this something to do with Nottidge supposedly brought back from the grave and carrying out his evil? He must be mad to think such a thing. He turned to the next page in the pile, marked as 1 in black ink. This sheet appeared much older: faded and worn round the edges. It contained a list of names, a long one. It looked as though further additions had been made over time. Under each one, there were cross-references to what he assumed were other pages in the collection.

The name on top was one he immediately recognized: Johnson Nottidge. He turned to the first page number listed. Although the same name was written in large black capitals and underscored with several deep lines, the sheet was empty except for a single notation, Nathan de

Vere NYT, and a date. Strange, given what Miss Bradigan had said about this guy, there ought to be loads more information.

Alex flicked back to the first page and looked at the next name, but it meant nothing to him. One Bill Callahan. This had a question mark in what he hoped was red ink. What did that mean? The next name he did recognize. Adelaide Fishburn. Marked by a similar cross to the others and dated 15 November 1895. He vaguely thought that was the year, Trent said she was murdered.

What an odd list. He scanned the rest of the names, but apart from Samuel Fishburn, who he knew was Adelaide's husband and the medico in charge at Belle Vue, they meant nothing to him. Patrick O'Leary, Jack Callahan, Lynton Brown, Annie Craven, Isaiah Codd. The list went on, and all but Johnson Nottidge were marked by a cross. He was still no wiser and hoped the handwritten volume would enlighten him.

Alex wondered if this was a tally of something achieved perhaps by Mary Grady or Johnson Nottidge. Or someone else for all he knew. He frowned, trying to understand how Moira Bradigan fitted into this? She could have changed her name or was some distant relative of Mary Grady. These papers might have been passed down through the generations as they tracked these people, searching for some link to Johnson Nottidge and his fate. The other pages were a mixture of family trees, addresses, and a proliferation of asterisks with attached notes, some scratched out. Feeling he'd gone as far as he could, for now, Alex shuffled the papers together and pushed them back in the envelope.

The loose-leaf binder was next. Untying the cord holding the front and back covers together, he opened the faded cover to the first sheet, also tattered round the edges and yellow with age. The title, handwritten in black ink, simply read 'Mary Grady'. Alex turned to the next page. With conflicting emotions of uncertainty and curiosity, he started to read.

"The happiest day of my life was when they buried my stepmother,

Catherine Grady. It was one less person to hate for the wrongs done to me in my first twenty years. She and her brother, the priest, hypocrites both, were my sworn enemies. I trusted them, and it was that trust which led to my best friend Nancy Flanagan's death more than six years ago. We both worked for the de Montalts, sent there by Catherine and Father Patrick O'Leary who betrayed us by making false promises. Instead, they delivered us into Satan's den.

Standing at the edge of her grave, I gave the bitch a memento of her wickedness. Dear Nancy's mummified heart. Given to me by Catherine's friend, René, the Duc de Montalt as a reminder of his power and depravity. No eternal life for her. Nancy was thought to be worthless. By Seton, by the de Montalts, by Catherine, and the priest. Now Catherine's journey to heaven would be halted by the evidence of her villainy on earth, and her unwillingness to repent this mortal sin.

How did I get to this and how did my quest for justice fare? To start, I was born of Brenna in 1848 and named Mary. My mother did not last the day. My father, Frank, found her replacement with indecent haste—so Catherine O'Leary came into our lives and ruined them."

It took Alex over three hours, but his eyes never left the pages. The story they weaved, up to Mary's death sentence for Ellen's murder and Nottidge's role in the whole process, was mesmerizing, horrific and bizarre all in one. But the following pages were the most worrying of all. They must have been recently written by Miss Bradigan and told how Claire was stalked, then murdered by Nottidge. His character as described by Mary Grady and Miss Bradigan was frightening. Alex knew the doctor was into Devil worship from the de Montalt book but was he immortal and still plying his evil trade? Did he somehow kill Claire, or die of old age in his bed? Only a crackpot could think the first one possible. Alex knew he couldn't take this to the police. They'd laugh him out of the station.

So where did that leave him, beside with a headache? Was Moira Bradigan mad, deluded, or neither? He was more confused than ever.

How had she come by Mary Grady's firsthand account anyway, if that's what it was? Didn't Mary say she hid the Mephisto Club's book and her notes in Father O'Leary's church? Had Nottidge, or perhaps Moira Bradigan, found it? Who knew?

According to the tale he had just read, Mary Grady was unjustly accused and found guilty. She paid the ultimate price. End of story—but that left the later tale and only led to more questions about Miss Bradigan. Remembering how Claire had thought the old woman was watching her, he wondered if Miss Bradigan had been trying to keep an eye out and help her.

Bloody hell, what a mess. He got up and stretched. When he sat back at his desk, he gazed at the photo of him and Claire on the pin board. He'd never taken it down, even when he'd had his fling with Marianne. Mainly because she never came to his flat after they'd got together. Because of Paul, he supposed. Claire's smiling face gave no clue to her horrible fate. A lump rose in his throat. He had loved her, even after the test results, but then he'd left her to handle it on her own. If all this was to be believed, she hadn't cheated on him. His feelings of guilt stirred. Christ, he had some serious thinking to do when the exams were over. Go away and sort his head out. Get in control of his life again.

He glanced at his watch. Almost three. From the thoughts whirling round his mind about Claire, Miss Bradigan and the rest, he wasn't going to get any revision done today. For now, he'd check whether some of the things Miss Bradigan said were true and then put this all away. Tomorrow, back to exam prep. Decision made, Alex piled the rest of the bits and pieces of Miss Bradigan's package onto the one side of the desk and pulled his laptop in front of him. He powered it up and when the default search engine appeared, he typed in the words 'Nottidge' and 'Seton'.

After half an hour of fruitless browsing, Alex understood the reason for the blank page. The only information about Nottidge after 1869 was, at the end of that year, he had apparently disappeared off the face of the Earth. Never to be heard of again. His brother, Edwin became the next Lord Seton when Nottidge's father died, and the family carried on as though Johnson had never existed.

Frustrated, he switched off his computer and set about putting Plan B into action. If what Moira Bradigan had written was correct, the chapel, or more accurately its crypt, contained some interesting examples of Nottidge's handiwork.

Alex picked up his car keys and headed to the utility drawer in the kitchen for a few things he was going to need.

Chapter Thirty-Six

Monday, 13 December, 1869

Adelaide pulled her cape tightly round her shoulders and began the short walk from her residence to the main asylum building. The darkness and fog made it almost impossible to see. The gas lantern she carried was of little use. Like a blind woman, she edged forward relying on habit to find her way. If anything, her nerves rather than lack of sight slowed her progress. Every few feet she would stop to check nothing was following her. As she shuffled forward again, Adelaide turned her head one way then the other for the same reason.

Mary Grady's letter had chilled her to the bone. It arrived the day after she'd overheard Nottidge and Callahan talking. That night she'd gone to bed worrying so much Samuel had commented on her distraction. He'd complained she had barely said a word to him all evening and hadn't given him so much as a goodnight kiss. Let him sulk, she thought. She had curled into a tight ball at the edge of the bed and thought this new problem through.

Adelaide accepted she would have embroidered her testimony without Nottidge's blackmail. She despised the woman and wanted to see her punished. From her attendance at the inquest and trial, she had also believed Mary Grady guilty. After overhearing how much of the case had been twisted by Nottidge though, she wondered if the Grady woman might have been innocent after all. You couldn't go round getting people hung just because you didn't like them.

When she'd heard a couple of the infirmary nurses gossiping and been told the outrageous claim not only had Mary Grady's body disappeared, but she was a witch, a sorceress, a devil worshipper, who had supernatural powers and was now seeking revenge on those who had betrayed her, she'd almost fainted. She had tried praying and spoken in vague terms to Reverend Croft, seeking some ministration and comfort. The man had little to offer beyond the same rote words he used for every occasion. She devoured the newspapers searching for any mention of the discovery of Mary Grady's corpse, but there was none. Nothing but wild rumors that grew ever more outlandish until about two weeks after the hanging, the tales ceased as new headline stories hit the front pages.

The letter had almost pushed her over the edge. When she grasped the meaning of the ugly, threatening words, she felt sick with fear. She had checked Samuel's pile of mail and finding a similar envelope and writing, had removed it at once. Back in her office, she'd opened that one, too, and although not as personally insulting as her own letter, it had also threatened her husband.

It was at that stage, Adelaide regained some of her spirit. The woman was dead and, no doubt, at this very moment, being judged for her many sins. As a God-fearing woman, she had no reason to be frightened of Mary Grady, deceased. But even after a fortnight of convincing herself Mary Grady had gone for good, her nervousness had not diminished one jot.

Lost in her thoughts, Adelaide slowed.

A hand tapped her on the shoulder.

She shot forward, letting out a squawk before twisting round. Priming the lamp for use as a makeshift weapon, the light revealed only Johnson Nottidge's sardonic features looming out of the dark mist.

"Did I frighten you?"

She staggered back, holding her hand to her heart as she tried to recover her composure. "Doctor Nottidge! You surprised me. That was all."

Adelaide was grateful for the power she now had over him. She'd once thought him admirable amongst other things, but no longer.

"I do not want to be the one to scare you, Matron." He smiled at her, insincerity lathered across his face. "But I thought a letter from Mary Grady might? I've been told you received one."

Feeling a hot flush coming on, she had had enough. The doctor's obsidian eyes were full of disdain, his face smug. Damn him. She drew herself up. "Doctor Nottidge, any correspondence I may or may not have received from that murderess would be small beer compared to what she might have sent you, or Callahan. Or perhaps I shouldn't have referred to her as a murderess after all, given the *criminal* way certain people manipulated her trial and its outcome. What uproar there would be if that came out!"

"Is that a threat?"

"No, Doctor Nottidge, it is not. I overheard you and Bill talking, and just as you used your knowledge of something I had done to your advantage, I would be remiss not to do the same."

Nottidge tipped his head back and peered down his nose at her. "Do continue."

Trying to calm herself, Adelaide sucked in her lip as she mentally formed her words. She was about to respond when the door they were standing in front of opened and Sheridan Lush barged out, nearly knocking into them. He halted mid-step. "Ah, Matron I've been looking for you. We were due to meet at seven forty-five and it is almost the hour."

Adelaide wasn't sure if she were glad or annoyed at the interruption. It would give her more time to think and plan how best to profit from the situation. "My apologies, Doctor Lush. I am sure Doctor Nottidge and I can continue our discussion at a later time?"

"Of course," Nottidge replied. "I do so want to hear what else you have to say."

Ten days later, Adelaide sat at her desk waiting to see the sole applicant for the position of Deputy Matron. Maud Trotter had resigned a week ago. Her daughter in Kent had died and it fell to Maud, long a widow, to move in and care for the six children under eight and her good-for-nothing son-in-law. So now she was without another important member of staff.

For Adelaide, it was getting all too much. The endless toils and worries weighed heavily on her shoulders. Samuel was wrapped up appeasing yet more inspectors sent to check everything with a fine tooth comb. The bleeding-heart Lush was in seventh heaven and flapping about looking out for some other expensive and quite useless 'aid' for treating the lunatics. Queen Victoria herself probably didn't get as much care and attention lavished on her as these degenerates. What a topsy-turvy world they lived in. Society itself must be mad.

To add to her worries, Samuel's drinking was becoming more difficult to control. Before he had kept it to a moderate tipple at home every night, but now there were empty bottles in his office, the glazed expression by noon, and whole days when he reeked of liquor. How utterly selfish of him to risk everything they had built up for themselves. Life here at Belle Vue had been very comfortable and it was in danger of unravelling before her eyes. At the very time when she had devised a way of securing their future prosperity.

Maud Trotter's resignation was the first of many. Bill Callahan, another. Apparently, he had come into some money and was setting off for pastures new. All very mysterious, and the last thing she needed. With Samuel so distracted and no new doctors permitted, Adelaide had to admit Bill and Doctor Nottidge virtually ran the asylum. As she put her head in her hands and massaged her forehead, she felt a migraine coming on. There was no replacement yet for Callahan, but his own deputy, before the news was out, had started harassing her for his job. She'd been willing to consider him, but then he too had left them in the lurch. Bill told her he'd gone to some mental institution up north. As a head attendant, no less. Well, the nerve of it, if Lynton Brown thought her husband would give him a character, he was mistaken.

With Bill's departure next week—so soon after Maud and

Brown's—they would be desperate. The past month had also seen a flurry of resignations from the general workers. Finding replacements was ever more difficult. The rumor going round the town that Mary Grady had cursed Belle Vue meant no one wanted to work at the asylum any more.

To add to her problems, gawkers fueled by the newspaper reports of the Mary Grady case, visited Belle Vue in droves to see where Ellen Grady died. Ghouls all. As a pauper lunatic, the girl had been buried in the usual sack cloth in the cemetery. These intruders had stamped around looking for her grave. In the end, she had asked Bill to dig up the body and bury her in an unmarked spot elsewhere. She thought she would burst under all the strain and doubly cursed Mary Grady.

Adelaide glanced at the clock on the mantelpiece. Tucking a stray strand of hair under her cap, she tried to forget her throbbing head. How she wished for the peace and quiet of the belvedere.

A little more than two hours later, Adelaide returned to her office with a rare feeling of satisfaction. She had just shown Miss Bradie out of the main front entrance and secured herself a new Deputy Matron. What a find. The woman was everything she could possibly want. Polite, willing to learn, and in complete agreement with her and Samuel's views on how lunatics should be treated. Some of her cost-saving ideas were inspired. Her letters of character sounded exemplary from her five years' service in nursing. Adelaide had been appalled, however, to discover a thief had stolen Miss Bradie's bag which also contained her references when she visited the ladies' room at the train station. She'd been only too happy to give poor Miriam money for her return ticket. Adelaide also agreed to refurbish the newly vacated Deputy Matron's cottage to Miriam's requirements and her veritable savior would start in a fortnight's time.

Adelaide sighed with relief. At first, she had hoped Mary Grady's threats were merely the last gasp of a bitter loser, but when her luck took such a downward swing, she began to fear they might be real. Now with Miriam as her new deputy, Adelaide thanked God for sending her such a fine woman. Even her migraine had gone. Maybe it would be a festive Christmas after all with a better new year to come.

The day was not over yet and Adelaide had one more trial to face. As she closed her office door on her way to find Samuel and tell him the good news, she saw Doctor Nottidge advancing toward her. It was the first time she had seen him since Doctor Lush interrupted them. Samuel said he'd gone away for a few days to see his father. She was ready for him now. A good omen for her to prevail against the doctor. Lifting her head and straightening herself to full height, she waited as he approached.

"Doctor Nottidge. You are looking pleased with yourself," she said, her tone arch.

He stopped, and she inwardly shivered as his cold eyes seemed to examine every flaw on her face. To her shame, she felt herself blush.

"Mrs. Fishburn, we didn't finish our conversation, but it is redundant now. I have just informed your husband I am leaving Belle Vue."

Her chin dropped. That was the last thing she expected. It changed everything. She could see the money and favors slipping from her grasp. Her mind whirled. The next thing she felt was relief. Good riddance. With both Nottidge and Callahan out of the way, the threat of exposure to her husband had disappeared. They were even. Better than nothing she supposed.

But Nottidge hadn't finished. "Doctor Fishburn asked me why I would want to leave such an excellent position. I, of course, have my own reasons that are none of your, or your husband's, business. He also asked if I knew why Callahan was leaving. So, I told him. I think he'll be asking you some questions, too, Mrs. Fishburn, if you get my drift. You do, don't you?"

The reptilian smile attached to those words sent a spurt of unease down Adelaide's spine. The nerve of the man.

"You, you bastard!" She raised her arm then gasped as his hand shot out. He gripped her wrist and squeezed.

BELLE VUE

"Madam, you are playing a dangerous game. Let me warn you now. Your life is about to take a much darker turn. When Mary Grady comes to Belle Vue and finds only you and your sniveling excuse for a husband as fodder for her vengeance, she will be very angry."

Holding her terrified gaze as he spoke, Nottidge had been twisting and twisting her wrist until she thought she would pass out. Then his other hand took hold, too, and he wrenched it with such force, she heard the snapping sound above her shocked screech. As Nottidge's footsteps and cane tapped out his leisurely departure on the polished parquet, Adelaide crumpled to the ground, thinking she had never known such pain in her life.

As she was to find out time and time again, that statement did not hold true for long.

Over twenty-five years later, Adelaide Fishburn would be more than relieved when the end finally came.

Chapter Thirty-Seven

Monday, 18 May
PRESENT DAY

Alex collected a torch, pen knife, and a box of matches to take with him to Belle Vue. Thoughts of Claire, and how she'd faced her death alone, darkened his mood. As did his uncertainty about giving Miss Bradigan's words any credence.

His journey to the chapel was uneventful. A few nods in the car park to a couple of residents he knew by sight, but no one he needed to speak to. The brightness of the afternoon sun lingered though it was past four. As he opened the heavy oak door, the gloom of the interior pushed its way out to the porch. He stepped inside, registering the drop in temperature. The chill made the hairs on his arms stand to attention. He moved farther into the chapel. Surrounded by silence, he stood alone at the back of the pews. His awareness of this solitude stretched his nerves further.

Alex took out the scrap of paper on which he'd jotted Miss Bradigan's instructions and scanned his notes. He walked along the central aisle, turning left, then right until he faced a single monument on the far wall and below it, the soles of an effigy. So far, so good. He scrunched the paper back into his pocket. Now to see if he were on a wild goose chase or Miss Bradigan knew more about Belle Vue than she had let on.

As he moved closer to the sculptured figure, he looked around at the other walls. There seemed to be only one tomb. Yet the de Montalts had lived in the manor for almost eighty years before it burned down. He wondered where the rest were buried.

He stopped a few feet from the effigy and read the inscription on the raised marble plaque. 'Near this place lie the mortal parts of René Xavier, Duc de Montalt, a devout worshipper of the true Master. Manet insontem gravis exitus.' There was no date. He recalled Miss Bradigan's translation with a shudder. 'A grim end awaits the innocent.'

How had she described the engraving? The Duc's idea of a joke? In Mary Grady's story, it was already there when she visited the chapel with de Montalt, the day after the infamous celebration. Weird sense of humor, those French. He walked to the head of the effigy and looked down at its face. The eyes weren't shut as he expected, but open and staring straight at him. A superior expression, a sneer almost and not dissimilar to that often found on Miss Bradigan's features.

Conscious of the time, he returned to the lower end of the statue. He lifted his left foot and pressed the toe firmly into the shield between the Duc's stone feet.

As the tomb moved forward, a rush of dismay swept through him. He'd hoped the story would prove false. Round one to Miss Bradigan. He peered into the dark opening but could see nothing below. He didn't want to go down there. He wasn't a coward, either.

He switched on his torch. The stone stairway was deeper than expected. All the while, he tried not to think of his likely fate if this were a horror movie. On reaching the last step, he saw two lamps, a couple of empty matchboxes, some half-burned matchsticks and a branded lighter scattered on the floor. Had Miss Bradigan used these, or someone else? He'd noticed the increasing coldness of the place during his descent, but now as he inhaled, he also caught its repellent smell. An earthy mustiness tinged with something else. Something that evoked images too macabre for the current state of his nerves. He concentrated on breathing through his mouth.

Alex fanned the beam of light back and forth, illuminating the dust motes he'd disturbed as they drifted downward. He stood in what looked like an anteroom. A row of large sconces lined the stone walls. Most contained at least an inch or so of thick candle with many layers of wax solidified over the holders. Although he assured himself there was no reason to be jumpy, the act of lighting the oil lamps and the candles gave him more confidence. He'd just have a quick look round. His imagination was already working overtime, and he didn't want it to be getting dark up at ground level, too.

The wall opposite the stairs was dominated by an arched doorway. He tucked his torch into his waistband jeans and carried the two lamps to this entrance.

One he placed on the ground. With his other hand, he retrieved the flashlight and switched it on again. The dim glow from the lamps and the stronger beam from the torch revealed an astounding tableau.

His chest tightened.

This reaction wasn't caused by the cavernous space before him with its many circular columns of carved obscenities.

Nor by the vaulted roof with its principal intersections covered in gargoyle-like heads leering at the scenes of murder and debauchery painted on the spaces between.

Neither was it the back of the enormous statue, horned and naked, that stood in the center of the room. He shone the flashlight for almost a minute at the red figure on its high plinth to check it wasn't real, nothing more than a sculpted nightmare.

Dear God, no. His senses, already on high alert, reeled from the shock of the rows of bodies positioned upright against the walls. Dressed as if this were a grotesque lesson in historical costumes, there must have been a hundred figures, maybe more.

He edged forward, the torch spotlighting the cobwebs and dark leathery skin of each withered form. Above and between them, bracketed on the walls were various weapons and instruments of torture that made his balls shrink. His eyes were drawn unwillingly back to the corpses. Just as Miss Bradigan's note had warned him, there was something else about them. Each body had been defiled. The shirt or bodice ripped open, the ribcage protruding to reveal a dreadful cavity where their heart should be.

He took a couple of hesitant steps, shining his torch on each figure. One still wore a wig awry on his head. Another's jaw had sunk, leaving the hardened strip of tongue hanging down. A woman drooped against a wooden bar that supported her, her lips pulled back in a toothsome grimace.

A bitter taste rose in his mouth. He tried to reassure himself this was like being in a museum. These mummified figures had been dead for more than a hundred years. Nothing to worry about. He peered at their tattered clothing, noting the changing styles.

He aimed the shaft of light at the next body, stared at the cadaver, and then angled the lamp toward the figure beside it. Jesus Christ. *These* bodies weren't from the time of de Montalt and Nottidge, but later, much later. Their clothes were from the 1920s or 30s. The skirts were shorter, the styles similar to those in old movies he'd seen on TV.

His mouth felt as dry as dust. He moved the beam of light along. The uniform of this one looked oddly familiar. A trickle of sweat ran down his back as he recognized where he had seen it before. In the photograph, Moira Bradigan had shown him. Taken in the late fifties. Were the tales true then, and this was where those missing people over the years had ended up? If so, this might be the nurse who disappeared, the one whose father's accusations resulted in the asylum being closed down.

He let out a shaky breath. Was this the work of one man, or members of the supposedly defunct club? God only knew. He steeled himself to examine the face but, with its vacant eye sockets and crushed chin, it was unrecognizable. The head was tilted unnaturally to one side. He looked closer. Where the bodice had been torn away from the poor woman, as well as the expected chasm, he could see a deep mark around her neck as though she'd been strangled. Or hung.

He clutched the flashlight and shone it on the previous figure. It too had the tilt and same marking. So far these were the only females he'd noticed with this anomaly.

As he moved farther away from the entrance, beyond the reach of the other lantern and candles, he relied solely on his torch and a lamp that barely flickered. His steps now resembled a crab-like sideways shuffle as he felt there was less danger of treading on something he'd rather not.

On his next slide along the floor, his foot connected with something. Something that moved and clattered. He directed the torch's unsteady beam downward. Dozens of skeletons, sitting or lying slouched against each other. They were all naked, refused one last dignity. Some were missing limbs, others were charred in places. Alex recoiled as a couple of rats scurried over the bones.

His barely-controlled panic threatened to erupt. All these macabre faces staring at him in eerie silence. The glow from the anteroom looked more inviting than ever. He glanced at his watch. He'd been down here all of five minutes. The longest five minutes of his life. He retraced his steps, his torch continuing its jerky surveillance to ensure nothing was about to sneak up on him. He swung the light round and it caught the back of the weird sculpture in the center of the room, the monstrosity with its barbed tail. Curious to see the front of it, Alex shuffled toward the middle of the chamber.

As he got closer, he put out his hand to touch the figure. His nervous laughter echoed round the crypt. Of course, it was a statue, he knew it all along. Made from nothing but wood. He knocked on it for good measure. Wait until he told Paul and Gary about this. They were never going to believe it. He wondered about taking a memento. Bad idea. He didn't want to touch anything else in this God-awful place.

Keeping his flashlight shining on the gigantic figure, he edged round it. An immense erect phallus came into view. Typical. But he could now see the statue was more than just this monster. It was part of a larger tableau. In front of the priapic beast was an altar, on top of that a recumbent form. God, he hoped it too was made of wood. As he pointed the beam of light, he caught the glint of something metallic. His heart pounded. Keeping his distance, he reluctantly stepped forward to face the scene side on.

He shone the torch on the bare arm of the body, on its silver and turquoise bracelet.

Oh, Christ. He knew it well. He stopped, trying to hold down the wave of nausea. Claire's Christmas present. One of the pieces that Marianne had kept and, to his discomfort, continued to wear.

He swallowed and resisted the urge to retch. He moved closer, unable to accept what he was seeing. It couldn't be Marianne. Grimacing, he shakily directed the beam of light onto the head. It looked like Marianne's face but, as with the other bodies, it was as though everything had been sucked out of her and a wizened carcass left in her place. The hairs at the back of his neck stood on end as, frozen to the spot, his eyes swept over her mummified remains. At the ligature marks around the neck. At the opening where her heart had been cut out, to the initials, JN carved at the top of her chest.

That fucking bastard!

Alex's panic, already close to the surface, spilled over. The torch slid from his hand. He staggered toward the anteroom, dropping the lamp by its twin at the entrance. He took the steps two, three at a time, but his legs were like rubber. He slipped, jarring his knee on the stone. His eyes brimmed. He struggled up to ground level. As he emerged into the chapel, distraught and sweating, it seemed different. No longer a Christian sanctuary, but a corrupt and unholy place once more. Just as it had been in the beginning.

He limped as fast as he could out of the door, grateful to be free from the confines of its malignant atmosphere. When he reached the grass, he slumped onto the nearest bench. He closed his eyes, leaned back, and sucked in air. In, out, in, out. His breath ragged at first became more even. His mind followed no such path, flitting wildly from one unbelievable explanation to the next. Moira Bradigan had certainly lived up to her word.

Raising himself upright, he reached into his back pocket for his wallet. He opened it and took out a card. One he'd been given when the police were looking to him to provide an explanation for Claire's death and they'd reluctantly had to let him go. As he stared at the number, a thought flashed into his consciousness. He groaned. It must have been Nottidge who gave Claire syphilis but that was lunacy and to think such a thing was leading him down a dangerous path. His rage ignited a desire to somehow make the man pay. He was aware he was standing at the edge of a precipice, his future dependent on the decision he made. There was only one option. He owed it to Claire. And Marianne.

And to Moira Bradigan.

She was now in her grave. For her, it was the end of the story. Beyond further questioning. He wasn't, though, and, as he tapped in the number for Chief Inspector Pugh, Alex wondered how the hell he was going to explain all this.

And what he would do about Nathan de Vere, once known as Johnson Nottidge.

Epilogue

The woman joined the queue serviced by a male immigration official. She'd already caught his eye as she sauntered across the concourse. Lucky break for her. The man had 'dupe' written all over him.

After a tiresome wait, she was next in line. While he dealt with the elderly couple at his window, she reached into her bag and rummaged around: purse, brush, mobile phone, solicitor's letter confirming she'd inherited, amongst other things, Moira's apartment at Belle Vue and the two other properties it had been necessary to acquire for the plan to work. Her fingers kept moving until they felt smooth calfskin. She pulled out the passport holder and held it ready in her hand.

The old-timers shuffled off to the next staging post and the man turned toward her. As his gaze met hers, she licked her lips…slowly. She moved forward, pleased to note he wore an expression like all his Christmases had come at once. Perspiration ran down his face. With this air conditioning?

He grinned, cleared his throat, and asked for her passport and papers. She placed the holder in front of him. After a few long seconds, he glanced down, took out the document and flipped through the pages.

"A new one. Is this your first visit to the US?"

"You could say that." She paused, then gave him a look guaranteed to send his brain south, "I like to try new things. Don't you?"

He nodded, pulled out her immigration forms, and checked through them. His finger paused over the name of where she was staying. One of the best five-star hotels in the city. He looked up at her with hunger in his eyes.

She could imagine what he was thinking. Dream on, big boy.

He cleared his throat again. "What's the purpose of your visit, Miss Gradwell?"

"Call me, Marilyn." And what a relief to no longer be grumpy old Moira anymore. She'd definitely stayed in that persona too long and René had proved how unwise that could be. Now, she would have the excitement of youth once more—and enjoy watching Alex do her bidding. Nottidge—Nathan de Vere as he called himself now—wouldn't know what hit him.

Her eyes moved to the name badge on his puffed-out chest.

"Randy. I like that name." Slow soft words inferring so much.

His finger rose and eased some space between his collar and thick neck.

"Thank you, miss. I like your English accent."

"Thank *you*, Randy. I'm here for pleasure. To enjoy myself. But I have a bit of business to take care of, too."

He stamped the required pages and handed the passport back.

She gave him a smile full of promise and her hand touched his. His face reddened. Watching him closely, Marilyn picked at a bit of non-existent fluff on her chest. It didn't come off so she brushed at it, gentle strokes down the curve of her breast. His eyes were riveted.

"What's the hold up? Is there a problem, Randy? Something you can't handle?"

Marilyn saw the look of humiliation and dismay on his face. Must be his boss. She looked down at the stocky woman whose uniform was fighting a losing battle to hold her in. Not only fat and ugly but, from her sniping tone, mean with it, too.

"Yes, Miss Fuentes. Just asking the set questions. Doing my job."

"And exceedingly well, too. Your supervisor must be very pleased. Thank you, Randy."

She turned and stepped closer to the woman, forcing her to move back. "Excuse me."

Marilyn swept past her.

"Have a nice day," Randy said.

Although she heard his farewell, she didn't bother to reply. The tedious charade was over, but at least it ensured more attention was paid to her than to her papers. Now she had an appointment to keep.

As she made her way through to the baggage reclaim area, she estimated Alex Palmer—her personal stooge—would have received the package by now. No doubt he'd soon be winging his way to the States, too. Angry and looking for vengeance, justice, whatever excuse he wanted to call it. Why get her hands dirty? This final battle would win the war. Winner take all. Alex Palmer was but a small price to pay.

Marilyn's eyes took in the near-empty carousel. She glanced at her diamond-encrusted watch with impatience. Surely the first-class luggage should be there by now. She tapped her foot in irritation. If the bloody chauffeur wasn't waiting for her in the arrivals hall, all hell was going to break loose.

Acknowledgements

I'd like to thank the following for all their help, support and encouragement.

To my talented agent, Italia Gandolfo of Gandolfo, Helin and Fountain Literary Management and publisher, Joe Mynhardt of Crystal Lake Publishing.

To Liana Gardner and Monique Snyman—both accomplished writers—who edited Belle Vue and helped prune and polish my text.

To the members of the Verulam Writers' Association for their valuable chapter feedback, not forgetting all the laughs at the pub.

To Jenny Barden, Professor Clare Kellilher and my daughter Kezia who reviewed much longer versions.

Any mistakes that remain are, unfortunately, my own.

About the Author

C. S. Alleyne grew up in Australia and originally trained as a hotel manager in the UK. After several postings in the Caribbean she changed tack and completed her MBA followed several years later by a PhD in Information Systems. Now based in Hertfordshire, England, she is a management consultant and also lectures at several universities.

With a lifelong love of reading, anything historical and a fascination with the supernatural and death, Cheryl's vacations usually include visits to such places as the Pere La Chaise cemetery and the catacombs in Paris, the tombs in Egypt, the Popes' crypts in the Vatican and any nice English church yard with gravestones—you get the picture!

Cheryl was inspired to write Belle Vue by her daily journey past a block of luxury apartments that had been converted from an old asylum. Like her protagonist, Alex Palmer, she started to investigate its past and learnt that one of the inmates was murdered there in the late 19th century. The victim's sister was hung for the crime. CS was also thrilled to discover the asylum's overgrown cemetery in her explorations of the area!

Belle Vue is her first novel. Jonathan Myerson (Oscar nominated, Bafta and 4 Time Emmy winner) says he is 'blown away' by Belle Vue - 'I am hugely impressed by this novel—it's ambitious and daring and amazingly imaginative'.

When she's not working, writing—or visiting cemeteries and the like—Cheryl can be found at the gym practicing her Body Jam moves…

Cheryl has a daughter and son-in-law who live nearby and a partner who, since reading Belle Vue, says he now sleeps with one eye open.

www.CSAlleyne.com

Dear reader,

It makes our day to know you reached the end of our book. Thank you so much. This is why we do what we do every single day.

Please take a moment to leave a review on Amazon, Goodreads, or anywhere else readers visit. Reviews go a long way to helping an author, and will help us to continue publishing quality books. You can also share a photo of yourself on social holding this book with the hashtag #IGotMyCLPBook!

Thank you again for taking the time to journey with Crystal Lake Publishing.

Website:
www.crystallakepub.com

Amazon:
http://amazon.com/author/crystalpublishing

Twitter:
https://twitter.com/crystallakepub

Facebook:
https://www.facebook.com/Crystallakepublishing/

Instagram:
https://www.instagram.com/crystal_lake_publishing/

Join the Crystal Lake journey by signing up for our newsletter and receive three eBooks for free: http://eepurl.com/xfuKP

Or join our interactive community of authors and readers on Patreon for exclusive content and behind the scenes access, bonus short stories, polls, interviews and, if you're interested, author support: https://www.patreon.com/CLP

Welcome to Crystal Lake Publishing—Tales from the Darkest Depths.

Since its founding in August 2012, Crystal Lake Publishing has quickly become one of the world's leading publishers of Dark Fiction and Horror books in print, eBook, and audio formats.

While we strive to present only the highest quality fiction and entertainment, we also endeavour to support authors along their writing journey. We offer our time and experience in non-fiction projects, as well as author mentoring and services, at competitive prices.

With several Bram Stoker Award wins and many other wins and nominations, Crystal Lake Publishing puts integrity, honor, and respect at the forefront of our publishing operations.

We strive for each book and outreach program we spearhead to not only entertain and touch or comment on issues that affect our readers, but also to strengthen and support the Dark Fiction field and its authors.

Not only do we find and publish authors we believe are destined for greatness, but we strive to work with men and woman who endeavour to be decent human beings who care more for others than themselves, while still being hard working, driven, and passionate artists and storytellers.

Crystal Lake Publishing is and will always be a beacon of what passion and dedication, combined with overwhelming teamwork and respect, can accomplish. We endeavour to know each and every one of our readers, while building personal relationships with our authors, reviewers, bloggers, podcasters, bookstores, and libraries.

We will be as trustworthy, forthright, and transparent as any business can be, while also keeping most of the headaches away from our authors, since it's our job to solve the problems so they can stay in a creative mind. Which of course also means paying our authors.

We do not just publish books, we present to you worlds within your world, doors within your mind, from talented authors who sacrifice so much for a moment of your time.

There are some amazing small presses out there, and through

collaboration and open forums we will continue to support other presses in the goal of helping authors and showing the world what quality small presses are capable of accomplishing. No one wins when a small press goes down, so we will always be there to support hardworking, legitimate presses and their authors. We don't see Crystal Lake as the best press out there, but we will always strive to be the best, strive to be the most interactive and grateful, and even blessed press around. No matter what happens over time, we will also take our mission very seriously while appreciating where we are and enjoying the journey.

What do we offer our authors that they can't do for themselves through self-publishing?

We are big supporters of self-publishing (especially hybrid publishing), if done with care, patience, and planning. However, not every author has the time or inclination to do market research, advertise, and set up book launch strategies. Although a lot of authors are successful in doing it all, strong small presses will always be there for the authors who just want to do what they do best: write.

What we offer is experience, industry knowledge, contacts and trust built up over years. And due to our strong brand and trusting fanbase, every Crystal Lake Publishing book comes with weight of respect. In time our fans begin to trust our judgment and will try a new author purely based on our support of said author.

With each launch we strive to fine-tune our approach, learn from our mistakes, and increase our reach. We continue to assure our authors that we're here for them and that we'll carry the weight of the launch and dealing with third parties while they focus on their strengths—be it writing, interviews, blogs, signings, etc.

We also offer several mentoring packages to authors that include knowledge and skills they can use in both traditional and self-publishing endeavours.

We look forward to launching many new careers.

This is what we believe in. What we stand for. This will be our legacy.

CPSIA information can be obtained
at www.ICGtesting.com
Printed in the USA
LVHW020627110820
662834LV00019B/2226

9 781646 693115